FIRE AND PASSION

Jenny Cheshire was born in North Yorkshire in 1963. By the age of ten she had begun to write a series of adventures for young children and during her teens, she developed this interest with a number of short stories. Having gained a top A grade A-level in English, Jenny chose a career in International Television Distribution. During this time she travelled extensively selling programmes to foreign TV stations, attending numerous Cannes Film and Television Festivals and organising programme markets in Miami.

FIRE AND PASSION was written when Jenny was expecting her first child and was leaving the television arena to concentrate on writing and motherhood. In addition to FIRE AND PASSION, she has published a series of illustrated children's books called SECRET KITCHEN TALES and now lives in Worcestershire with her husband Sam and their two children.

GW00482760

i

FIRE AND PASSION

Jenny Cheshire

Jennywren Publishing

Published by: JENNYWREN PUBLISHING, IVY COTTAGE,
BLACKWELL, WORCS. B60 1QJ.

ISBN: 0 9528323 3 X

British Library Cataloguing in Publication Data.
A catalogue record for this book is available from the British Library.

Typeset/Design by Avonset, 1 Palace Yard Mews, Bath BA1 2NH
Printed in Great Britain by Cromwell Press, Trowbridge, Wiltshire.

AUTHOR'S NOTE

This book is dedicated to a number of people without whom Bronte's story in FIRE AND PASSION could never have been told and would have remained merely a dream. It is therefore important to me to list them here.

I must include my husband Sam and my children Sebastian and Rebecca who have put up with me working for so many hours on the book. My parents David and Mary Savill and my family who have always been a tremendous support. My grandmother Lysbeth Savill for her help and encouragement. My cousin Camilla and her husband Bruce who will no doubt recognise themselves in the book. All my colleagues in International Television Distribution for their unwitting contributions! My special friends, Richard and Mos Bradley, Nick and Peta Louise Jeffery for their technical help in my hour of need. Liz Rees for her proof-reading and, of course, my good friend and tutor Robert Beaumont who also edited FIRE AND PASSION.

Lastly, I also dedicate my book to two other people who must remain anonymous. One of whom I once knew and the other, if he can ever spare the time, I would love to meet . . .

J.C.

CHAPTER ONE

It was one of those autumnal days, confused between the fading summer and the prospect of winter. The sun fought to make its presence felt amongst a battalion of grey clouds, while the chilling wind whipped up its own support, tugging at the leaves and inquisitively investigating the little group huddled in the churchyard.

Bronte clutched the collar of her coat closer to her chin and tried to focus her mind on the bespectacled vicar holding up his prayer book. Her coat, with the three large velvet buttons firmly closed, denied the world access to Bronte's tall, willowy figure. Her beret covered the majority of her cascading auburn hair which had been carelessly swept up into it. Her usually sparkling blue eyes were ravaged by the sorrow of losing a loved one and her face was red and blotchy as she lifted a handkerchief to dab her cheeks once more.

She barely heard '. . .forasmuch as it has pleased almighty God . . . earth to earth, ashes to ashes, dust to dust' and only realised just in time that they were looking upon her to cast the first sprinkle.

She could picture, all too clearly, that day last week when she had been summoned to the board room of the small television distribution company where she had worked for the past five years.

There she had been greeted by a policewoman, shifting anxiously from foot to foot as she waited to drop the bombshell. Bronte had known something had happened to Dominic, almost before she crossed the threshold.

'Mrs Richardson, perhaps you would like to sit down?'

There was already a cup of steaming tea on the bare oak table, beside the chair that was being offered to her. She looked up.

'Dominic?' she whispered, as she felt her palms mist over and her knees tremble.

'There has been an accident, on the M40. Fog. Ten car pile up. I'm so very sorry, Mrs Richardson,' was all she really heard, although there were more words of comfort floating around the room. Her first reaction was: Why doesn't she call me Bronte? 'Mrs Richardson' scared her.

Bronte took a large gulp of air, which helped to compose her. She neither cried, nor fell about hysterically. She had suffered and lost before – her mother had died when she was five. She just sat there, gazing blankly into the distance. Her acceptance was instant, she knew it had happened. She knew it was quite plausible. Dominic had set out that morning, even before she was up, to drive to Oxford to discuss the idea for his next book, which he had been mulling over for weeks, with his literary agent. The car had been serviced recently, so it couldn't have been to blame. But his route would have taken in the M40 motorway and fog had been a hazard on the roads already that month.

As she sat there, she was unaware that the policewoman's place had been taken by her boss and close friend, Alex, and that he was sitting beside her with his arm protectively around her shoulders. Meanwhile she dwelt briefly on her life with Dominic – they had been married for nearly two years.

He had recently found success with his writing and his first book had just been published. They had come round to the idea of children, now that Dominic was expecting royalties, and were hoping, month by month, for good news. Their marriage had been strong as they set out on their journey through life together.

'Bronte, are you OK? Can I get you something?' Alex's words penetrated the depths of her thoughts as a sob jarred in her throat.

As the tears were unleashed, Alex held her tight, rocking her like a mother comforting her child in a moment of grief. They sat like that for some time, not speaking, but letting her discharge what emotion she could.

Alex was wonderful. He let her cry until the tears would not come, until she finally raised her head and looked at him. He knew then how vulnerable she was feeling and he took charge of the situation with precision and speed. He took her home personally, sat with her until her girlfriend Louise arrived, held her hand when she went to identify the body, and in the absence of Dominic's parents (who lived in Argentina) helped her with the funeral arrangements.

Bronte's thoughts jolted back to the present and the sudden coming to terms with what could only be a period of lonely solitude. Her partner and best friend cruelly seized from her, she knew she had to face the world alone once more, and already her self-protective shell had snapped tightly around her. In itself, it brought a kind of secret comfort to an otherwise utterly miserable situation.

'Bronte darling, will you be alright? Why don't you come up to Yorkshire and stay with us for a while? Your father and I would be happy to take care of you, just until you get back on your feet. What do you say, will you come?' Bronte's step-mother stood there in her calf-length fur coat. She towered over Bronte's father, symbolising the domination she had over him, as he shuffled awkwardly and carefully examined the folds of his black umbrella.

'Actually, Clare, I need to be here with Dominic. I can't face people and places right now. I need to be in our flat, surrounded by our things. I'm really OK. I have my work and I'll pull through. Thanks for coming today.'

Her father looked up: 'If you're sure. I mean, you know there's always a home for you if you need it. I'm sorry we can't take you back to Fulham now, we have to catch the flight up north . . . business . . .' he tailed off, avoiding her eyes and poking at the leaves with his umbrella.

'Bye dad, bye Clare. I'll be in touch.'

Bronte had never been close to her father and had never really felt any warmth at the house in Yorkshire since her mother died. Her father had been kind enough, but somewhat bewildered by the loss of his wife at such a young age, and even more confused by the prospect of his dependent, five-year-old daughter. His well thought-out solution to the problem had been to re-marry. Clare had been a friendly but loveless mother to Bronte. She had performed her duty as required but lacked the little comforts, the cuddles, the games, the genuine love that Bronte could remember, even at the age of five, from her own mother.

The house in Yorkshire was decorated to perfection. Designer this adorned the walls, while designer that had more than taken care of the soft furnishings. Bronte, however, had never been materialistic and her memories of school holidays held very few moments of real affection for her.

Bronte turned her attentions to the group of people dispersing from the graveside. A couple of aunts huddled away together, shaking their heads at such an unjust tragedy. Dominic and Bronte's good friends, Louise and James, who had remained at a distance behind the group, hung around to offer any support that was needed. Louise, weighed down by the baby who threatened to be born at any moment, came across to Bronte.

'What are you going to do now? Do you want to come home with us? It's no problem, we've got nothing on tonight.'

'No thanks, Lou. I feel guilty that I haven't organised to have everyone back, but the flat's a tip and I can't get my head round food right now. Anyway, Dad and Clare have had to go and the others don't seem to be expecting it, or do you think they do?'

'Heavens no! It's not the time for entertaining and certainly no-one expects it.'

'OK.' She took a deep breath. 'Look, I think I need to be on my own, just today. It's funny but I still see him around the flat, I feel him there. It's like he's watching over me, taking care of me. I don't feel completely alone yet, but I guess that'll hit me at some point. I'm going to have to go through his things tomorrow, I suppose Oxfam ...' She shuddered at the thought of pulling his clothes from the drawers, clothes that would evoke memories of every occasion he had worn them. Clothes that would remind her of both good times and bad times, but mainly just of Dominic.

James gave her a hug: 'You'll pull through, old girl. Come over tomorrow night. Louise and I need all the social we can get before the baby's born.'

Bronte caught his green eyes and the flash of his smile, just about managing one back.

'I'll see you then. I must go and talk to the vicar, I think he's waiting to see me. I'll be round tomorrow night.'

Bronte made her way over to where the vicar stood, talking in depth to Alex and his wife, Helene.

'Bronte, my child.' He lifted her chin and looked kindly into her eyes. 'You must take comfort from the fact that Dominic is now at peace with this life, but at the same time, he remains with us all. He's here in the air that you breathe, in the ground that you walk on and in the trees that you see. He is beside you, in front of you and behind you, and you must not forget it.' His words brought fresh tears to her eyes, but with them, a calming sense of relief.

'Thank you vicar, for your words and support.'

'My child, you must also go in peace and pray for Dominic, as I shall pray for you. Call me anytime, here at the vicarage. I shall be there if you need me.'

She raised her eyelids in gratitude and the vicar, sensing she needed her own space, backed quietly away, bidding farewell to Alex and Helene.

Alex put his arm around her and led her gently from the churchyard. He brought out a silk handkerchief, something he had done for her several times lately.

'What are your plans? Home? Want some company?' Helene stood discreetly behind them.

She shook her head: 'No thanks, Alex. Just home alone.'

'You know however much time you need, it's no problem. We'll cover, I'll even get on the word processor myself!'

She smiled. 'I don't think the machine would cope! No, if you don't mind, I need to sort out the flat and Dominic's things tomorrow. But Thursday I'll be back. I have to concentrate on normality or I'll get buried in this. Thanks for everything, Alex, I couldn't have got through it without you.'

'You're really alright to drive now? Do get a taxi if you'd prefer. I think the company could stretch to that.'

'I'll be fine. The car's all I've got left now. I'll see you on Thursday. Bye Helene.'

She gave a little wave and turned towards her car, her friendly, faithful car which had never let her down and had always been there for her. She knew she could pick up the pieces. She had never been afraid of her own company, she

5

was a survivor and she would fight on, secure in her belief of an afterlife and that Dominic would be there, so long as she needed him. But it was going to be hard. Thank goodness for work – she would willingly and consciously allow it to envelop her time, as it had had a tendency to do in the past without her consent. There would be no Dominic clocking her back from the office, grumbling if she was late and if his dinner wasn't on the table by seven thirty. Perhaps she would even miss that, or perhaps not. Perhaps her destiny held surprises, things beyond her wildest dreams, good things, bad things. She had to cling on to the belief in good things. She had to reach out and grab at life, which had so unkindly tried to throw her off its merry-go-round.

As she drove home down the Fulham Road, she shrank again, her inner strength once more zapped and she teetered on the edge of fresh tears. Maybe there was some part of Dominic inside her, growing and forming daily. She was three days late. But she had none of the symptoms of pregnancy which Louise had often discussed at length. What would she do if she were pregnant? What sort of world was it for a widowed mother of a tiny baby? But abortion was not a consideration, and if it came to it, she knew which road she would take.

She parked the car with difficulty. There were twice the number of cars in London for the street spaces available and the daily routine of circling the immediate area of the flat was a well-rehearsed performance. Shunting back and forth, the car was finally lodged in a space and she could return to the flat.

Bronte kicked her shoes into a corner of the hall, at the same time tugging at her beret which sent a mass of wavy, coppery-coloured hair sliding down the back of her coat. She pushed the hair that had fallen over her face behind her ears as she shed her coat. Standing there, almost like a child in her simple black dress, holding her hair back at both sides, she wondered what to do next. She neither cared to see anyone, nor wished to step out of the security of her flat again that day.

'Oh Dominic, did you really have to go and leave me?' she sighed. 'What am I going to do? Who am I going to organise now that you're not around? I'm only twenty-five,

6

and yet so much has happened in the last week that I feel old. Old and tired.'

Her words drifted up to the ceiling and mingled with the particles of dust which danced around the light bulb. But there were no answers forthcoming, at least not then.

CHAPTER TWO

Bronte had tossed and turned all night. Her sleep had come in waves, only to be disturbed by the reality of her life and the worry of her future. She had finally managed to close her mind for a few hours deep sleep, and when she awoke it was morning. In some ways she was relieved to get up. She found the days friendly but the nights quite frightening. Her already vivid imagination was sparked by the curtain of dusk and it carried on working right through until the day preoccupied her. It had been the same every night since the accident.

That day she had to clear out the flat. It was no good putting it off any longer. It depressed her to see so many reminders of Dominic. He lurked in every corner, in the wardrobe, in the drawers, in the cupboard where his golf clubs and tennis racquet lay discarded. She had to be strong, and by removing his day-to-day belongings, she would psychologically start out on her solo journey again.

She poured herself an orange juice and, with that in one hand and a piece of honey toast in the other, settled down on the sofa, tucking her long slender legs underneath her. She knew it could only take one day. She would not draw it out beyond that and besides, she was needed at work. Apart from anything else, she *wanted* to be there.

The 'phone broke the silence, as she had once again succumbed to memories.

'Hello.'

'Bronte? Bronte, it's Alex. Just checking on one of my most important members of staff. Wanted to make sure you're still thinking of me! You OK today?'

Alex and Bronte had hit it off from the word go. Alex was old enough to be her father, but instead had fast become one of her most trusted and respected friends. There had never been any question of a relationship between the two

8

and she was grateful for just having him in her life.

'Hi Alex! I'm always thinking of you! Seriously, I feel a bit like I'm on an emotional tightrope. One minute I'm on top and the next I slip, only to recover again. I guess it's probably to be expected.'

'Now you wouldn't be sitting doing nothing and feeling depressed, by any chance, would you?'

'How did you guess?' He knew her better than most. After all, they shared the same sense of humour.

'Well, a little bird told me to ring because I've got this great idea. You're going to do whatever you have to do this morning and I'm coming round at lunchtime on my white charger, or perhaps the next best thing, in my car, and we're going out for lunch!'

'But Alex, my company leaves a lot to be desired . . .'

'Sorry, boss's orders. I'll be round at twelve thirty. Any preference as to where we go, or shall I use my initiative?'

'Initiative sounds good, I'm lacking in that at the moment.'

'See you at twelve thirty then?' He had not allowed her time to think or to dream up an excuse.

'Yes Sir! And Alex, thanks.'

'You can thank me when you see me.' He hung up.

It dawned on her, as she contemplated her cold toast, that she was very fortunate to have such an understanding boss. That she was also lucky to have a job which she enjoyed, which gave her the chance to travel the world and which brought with it the kind of friends of which Alex was only one example. In short, being involved in the theatrical world made her part of an industry, unique in its sense of fun and opportunity.

As she shed her dressing gown and looked at herself in the mirror, she faced up to the realisation that there was to be no baby with Dominic. She had woken with the familiar stomach cramps which decisively put the lid on any advances in that direction. She couldn't help but feel divided. In her heart she knew that her way ahead would be so much harder had she been pregnant, and yet, she longed to cherish that final part of Dominic forever. It was not to be. There was no point dwelling on it.

The face staring back at her from the mirror reflected her time of the month. A couple of pimples threatened under the surface of an otherwise blemish-free skin and her hair, which always had a mind of its own, hung lifelessly around her shoulders. She stepped into the shower and stood statuesque under the jet of warm water. It felt good, better than anything else that day, as she closed her eyes and let the water stream over her head, run down the curves of her body and fall onto the tiles. She washed away her pain as she soaped herself. She attacked it head on, as she massaged her hair, and when she had finished, she punched and kicked at it, as she rubbed herself vigorously with the towel.

She put on a pair of leggings and an outsized diamond sweater and hoped to goodness that Alex wasn't going to take her anywhere too smart. Still, she could change if she had to. She padded around in bare feet, searching the utility cupboard for suitcases and weekend bags. They would probably be the best way to transport Dominic's clothes to Oxfam.

Bronte was determined not to dwell on the clothes item by item. She couldn't bear to keep any of them, despite the fact that his sweaters could have come in handy for her. She managed to jam all his garments into a couple of cases and was glad to remove them from the bedroom. When she came back into the room, the hole in the wardrobe looked naked and needed covering fast. She spread her own clothes neatly into the newly-found space.

Dominic's pine bedside cupboard was harder. It was in there that he had kept his most personal and private momentoes. It had been a no-go area for Bronte until then and she hesitated, crouching before the door of the little cupboard. Gradually, she pulled it towards her, dreading what she might find which would further remind her that Dominic was gone.

It was no easier than she had expected. Dominic had been a sentimentalist! To have been able to write a romantic novel with the skill and aptitude of his last book, it was only to be expected. He had kept every card from birthdays, Christmas and Valentine's Day that she had ever sent to him. Not only that, he had kept all her letters and cards sent when she had been travelling abroad on business. He had photographs of her, going right back to one taken when she couldn't have been more than two, in the bath. One by one, Bronte drew out precious memories for them both – old theatre tickets, the receipt from dinner the night he had proposed, airline tickets from their honeymoon, photos taken at his stag night. She knew it was a part of her life that she had to bury in that coffin with Dominic. The sooner she could face up to that, the easier it would be for her. She stuffed the tote bag full, pulling his research books from the shelves, his family photograph albums – it all had to go.

She paused by his precious word processor in the spare room. That room had seen the birth and blossom of his novel. The word processor had shared his ideas like no-one else and Bronte could not bring herself to turn it from her life. She would take it to the office and use it. After all, Alex would be glad of another machine as they were always short.

His golf clubs and tennis racquet would have to wait. She had to find a good home for those and that would take a little working out.

She piled the bags and cases in the hall. Maybe if she asked, Alex would be a darling and help her with them that afternoon. It was not really something she felt like doing on her own.

Outside, the rain was seeping down, not pouring and not spitting, but enough to make her decide to wear boots. The time was nearing twelve twenty, she should get ready as Alex would be there soon.

Bronte had very natural looks which did not need enhancing with caked-on makeup. She always managed to get away with minimal help in achieving the kind of beauty which left men staring after her as she wandered down the street, the kind that most girls pay and diet for, but still never achieve. From her hair, which was always a talking point whenever she met new people, to her skin, to her shapely body and the slim legs which seemed to go on for ever, Bronte was an extremely attractive girl.

With a braid loosely gathering her hair into some sort of order at the back, and gold earrings the size of sovereigns at

11

her ears, she was ready to give Alex a hug when she greeted him at the door.

'Feeling that much better, uh?' he asked her.

'Yeah, and relieved that it's just me and mine here now.'

'How did you get on this morning?'

'I know what I've done is probably one of the hardest things I'll ever have to do, but all the time I was doing it I felt Dominic was there, supervising and approving. It's as if he was telling me that the things I was coming across he no longer had any use for and that they would not be the way to remember him. Anyway, I'm droning on and you've come to drag me away from all this.'

'Only if you're willing to be dragged. Mind you, you'd really be missing out if you weren't.'

They locked the door and stepped out into the road where Alex had parked his sports car. Alex oozed style. From his car, to his appearance, to his joie de vivre! That day he wore a dark suit and a red bow tie with white spots. His sunglasses were ever-ready on the ledge inside the car – perhaps it would stop raining after all.

Bronte read the new licence plate on his car: 'ATC 10.'

'A bit flash aren't we?' she remarked.

'As a matter of fact, I've been looking out for my initials for ages. Found them the other weekend in the paper.'

'Very debonair, goes with the image.' She pulled his leg.

'Image?'

'Never mind. And where is my knight in shining car, who has come to save me from my lofty tower, going to take me for lunch, may I ask?' she quipped.

'No, you may not. Wait and see.'

She didn't have to wait long, as they drove up the Fulham Road towards Knightsbridge and turned into Hollywood Road. He parked the car on a meter, which by lucky chance was just being vacated by a couple who had come out of the Hollywood pub. Ever the gentleman, he opened Bronte's door and ushered her out, escorting her towards the Wine Gallery.

'I thought you'd prefer busy and casual to quiet and formal? Will this do?'

'Of course.'

They were shown to a table on the first floor of the wine bar, just near to the rear patio garden. Once they had taken their seats and chosen from the menu, Alex asked her: 'Well now, what's the plan? Are you going to stick around or do I have to throw myself from that window?'

'You know me better than that. Of course I'll be sticking around, for the time being anyway. Where else would I go?'

'I thought you might have an idea waiting in the wings, ready to spring. And there's Yorkshire.'

'No, I need this job right now. I need to have a direction in which to focus when I wake up each morning. Each day and even each hour that passes, I'm getting more positive about the future I have to face without Dominic. After the accident last week, I was almost ready to join him, any way I could. But that's not the answer and certainly not what he would have wanted for me. Yorkshire's not the answer either. If I ever really needed them, Dad and Clare would be there. Even though the flat's rented and I could go away tomorrow, I'm better off where I am.'

'Brave words. I admire you, really I do, Bronte. Not many girls could have come through this so quickly. OK, so now we've established that you're around for the next month at least and you're back on the team, I didn't bring you here with the intention of dwelling on recent events, unless you wanted to. So let's look ahead. We're fast approaching the MIPCOM festival down in Cannes, it's what . . .' he looked at his watch, 'only three or four weeks away. You're still on for that?'

He watched her, as she picked at her deep fried camembert.

'Try and keep me away! There are buyers from the two new stations in Jamaica and Trinidad, the ones I was telling you about, coming over for the first time and quite a few of the African stations have also confirmed they'll be there.'

'That's my girl! The four of us will go down as usual, and between us, we can cover the buyers we need to see. I'm hoping to explore some co-production possibilities through our finance partners. We could really do with some strong new product to flog.'

Bronte took another sip of wine and Alex resumed: 'What are you going to be pushing at MIPCOM? I guess with the

13

new season starting on the American Networks now, you should get some renewal orders as well as some new commitments?'

'Yes, three series that we have the rights to sell in the Caribbean have been renewed, two on NBC and one on ABC. Then there's a new drama which has a thirteen episode commitment from CBS, but as there are a few similar legal series around already, we may have to wait and see how well it does in America before it sells for us.'

Bronte had the bit firmly back between her teeth, as she and Alex discussed sales tactics for the up-coming television programme market. It felt good to be immersed again and to shut out the empty side of her life for a while.

The conversation turned to industry gossip. Every business boasts of inside stories and none more so than International Television Distribution! There seemed to be a certain prestige attached to working on films or in television. A mystical excitement surrounded the idea of film sets, of meeting the stars (which in distribution, one scarcely ever did but the idea was there) of travelling, often First Class. Gossip flourished freely, particularly at the markets where people were trapped in the same town together for up to a week. There were lots of spare evenings, all of which needed to be filled with exciting people.

Alex told her: 'I had a drink with Kevin Patterson the other day and he told me that Boston Communications are cutting back the sales team. Not a great time to be out of a job and certainly not at sales exec level. It's only recently that Trisha Cross joined them as Head of Sales. I bet she's miffed!'

'Is Kevin still seeing Alison Moss from ACB Distribution? I bet his wife doesn't know what goes on at the markets,' Bronte enquired.

'How did you know about that? I thought it was really hush-hush. Kevin would be livid if he knew people were talking about it.'

'I can't remember who told me now. I think it was someone from ACB at MIP TV last April.'

The conversation continued through the main course. The Wine Gallery had filled up, without Bronte really noticing because she was facing the tranquil garden outside. But when she stopped to listen, there was a distinctive hubbub of talking, interspersed with the chink of cutlery. Alex raised the subject of the new receptionist at work. He always valued Bronte's opinion as she was an uncanny judge of character and usually had people and their worth, weighed up with remarkable speed and accuracy.

'Amanda's not really working out. What do you think?'

'She's a pleasant enough girl but her telephone manner, or lack of it, is a problem, I agree. Do you give her much typing?'

'Donna has given her some copy-typing. But it comes back full of mistakes, so much so that Donna ends up doing it herself anyway. She's never got the hang of the switchboard and seems to cut off about one call in three that she puts on hold.' Donna was Alex's secretary and also a friend of Bronte's.

'It's a shame, but when she's in the front line for the company, you can't afford to put people off. How's Helene's painting coming on?'

'She's been hard at it for months now. She's trying to put together enough work to merit an exhibition locally.'

'I saw a couple of pictures she brought to the office. I'd say she should do well – are you bringing her to Cannes?'

'Yes, she likes to give the shops in the Rue D'Antibes the once or twice over – usually ends up costing me a fortune!'

'So, you'll have to be a good boy then? No staying out 'til all hours.' Bronte teased him because she knew how he relished his nights out with the boys.

'I'm always a good boy. Well, most of the time anyway.'

Coffee was served and Bronte took hers strong and black as usual. She felt better than she had for a week. It was the most nutritious meal she had kept down since the accident and it had perked her up. The bill followed soon after and she plucked up the courage to ask him: 'Alex, I need you to hold my hand again.'

'Just say the word.'

'Will you come with me to distribute Dominic's things this afternoon? I'm rapidly becoming Miss Bravery here, but I've got a little way to go.'

'You know I'll hold your hand any time you need me to. Come on, let's go.'

The rain had surrendered to patchy sunshine and the wet leaves sparkled on the trees. A rainbow struggled to make it to the other side and gradually petered out. Oxfam were a suitably pleased recipient of the clothes and it felt good to Bronte that, in some small way, she was doing right by someone else. It was harder to let go of the two tote bags at the tip and as she left them behind, she also gave up of a part of her which had belonged to Dominic and would never again be found. It was as if a candle had burnt down to the wick and had snuffed peacefully out in a single puff of smoke.

As Alex drove her back to the flat, she gazed through the tinted windows of the car, with a once-more heavy heart and dampening eyes. Alex knew that she did not want to hear him say anything. Instead he rested his hand gently on hers, which she knew was a token of his affection and support, with no strings attached.

Later that evening, Bronte stood on the doorstep of James and Louise's house in Putney, clutching a bottle of red wine in one hand and her car keys in the other.

The doorbell shrilled into the night sky and James ushered her inside. Louise had impeccable taste and fortunately for her, the money to satisfy it. The house was filled with antique pine – not cluttered but tastefully arranged. Although small, it was warm and cosy and not a speck of dust was allowed the privilege of a home.

Louise waddled out of the kitchen, bringing with her all sorts of tantalising smells. James, meanwhile, took Bronte's coat and Louise gave her a big warm hug.

'You're skin and bone, darling. I bet you haven't been eating, I guess I can understand why. Come into the kitchen and take a pew, I'm just grating some cheese for the soup.'

James asked her: 'How'd it go today? Bet it wasn't easy, but it was a good thing to get done.'

'Actually, I went on a long ride down memory lane and once I'd come to the end, it really felt like the right thing to do, to close the door on most of it. I don't feel I threw anything important away, more locked it up for safekeeping somewhere.'

'Drink?' asked James, holding up a bottle of wine.

'Please, whatever's open. How's your junior boxing champion doing in there, Lou?'

'He's gone several bouts today, that's for sure! This last bit's the worst. I've been really lucky up to now, as you know, but I just feel knackered all the time and my legs really ache.'

'Listen to her, you'd think she was an old woman,' James dared.

'Male chauvinist pig!' exclaimed Louise. 'This is your doing too, you know,' and she gave him a friendly peck on the cheek.

It was hard for Bronte to sit there in the lap of domestic bliss, when her own had been so shattered. But she had to remember that she needed friends more than ever and it would be all too easy to crawl away into a hole and feel sorry for herself. She knew that by getting out and returning to normal as quickly as possible, she would be able to shift Dominic's memory from the place where it currently hurt her, to a place where she felt more comfortable.

She couldn't stop herself from reflecting on the carefree times the four of them had spent together. Louise was an old school friend and they had been through much, side by side. First loves and first heartaches. Courtings, weddings, holidays – they had even planned to have babies at the same time, only Louise had managed it and she had not.

They talked about mutual friends, her work, James's new sailing course, even plans to go away all together the next summer. They left alone times spent with Dominic and any other subject which might have encouraged the pain to sweep across Bronte's face once more.

Louise was a wonderful cook and produced a special meal for them. Bronte had a small appetite at the best of times, but she managed to do justice to Louise's efforts.

'What are you going to do about the flat?' asked Louise over dinner. 'Are you going to stay there? You could always come here if you prefer. We've got space, even with the baby.'

'Thanks Lou, but I want to stay on at the flat for now. I can afford it, just, because we got a very good deal initially. I plan to stay in London for now and maybe look for something in the States next year, although it would be hard to leave Alex after he has been so good to me over the last five years.'

'Would you really want to work in America?' James questioned.

'Either there or somewhere else abroad. I've had the travel bug ever since I started in this business and maybe it would be good for me to get out there and explore a bit.'

Bronte was the only one of her close girlfriends who really had a career. Most had married even younger than her and had decided to conserve their energies for motherhood, or some part-time work to keep boredom at bay.

It had never been a point of discussion for Bronte. It was simple – on two counts. She had a brain which required stretching and they needed the money while Dominic was struggling for recognition as an author. There had never been any doubt about her working full time, until the book was published a few months before. For some reason, that seemed to have made Dominic broody and perhaps even secretly, Bronte too. However, there was no question of that now.

After supper, they collapsed into squeaky arm chairs in the sitting room. James glued himself to the television, leaving the girls to chat.

'What about names for the baby, Lou?' Bronte tried to show an interest.

'James likes William for a boy, or Oliver. I prefer Oliver, but we can't seem to agree on girls. Stephanie is a possibility, but I hate the shortening of that name – Steph, ugh! By the way, did you hear that Caroline's pregnant again? She'll really have her hands full with two children under two. I want to wait at least a couple of years after this one.'

Bronte idled over a couple of fashion magazines while Louise talked. 'Have you seen Sarah lately? I wonder how the wedding plans are coming on?'

'I had lunch with her in town about ten days ago. She's got her dress organised now. She's found a design she likes

18

and a local dressmaker to copy it,' replied Bronte.

'She will need to lose some weight before the wedding. Mind you, I can't talk. I've put on nearly three stone, which is much more than I should have.' The conversation crept back to babies.

'I mustn't keep you two up any more,' said Bronte a while later. 'It was a lovely idea to come over tonight. The evenings are the hardest right now, the days seem to take care of themselves.'

She unfolded her legs and took her hand out of her hair which she had been twisting into knots and loops. James went to find her coat, while Louise puffed up the cushions where they had been sitting, just as if they had never been flattened.

Part of her was glad to go, as she kissed James and Louise fondly on both cheeks. She felt a little alien in their world. Something was brewing inside her, a feeling of rebellion, the desire to run until there was nowhere left to go. Perhaps she should ask around at MIPCOM to see if there were any jobs going in New York or Los Angeles. Perhaps a change was what was required. A new challenge in her life. It was certainly food for thought as she weaved through the traffic, back across Wandsworth Bridge.

CHAPTER THREE

The day she had been waiting for had dawned. The October sun streamed through her open window, fighting with the curtains for supreme power as it passed by. It was the day she would fly down to the French Riviera! MIPCOM started the next day and she had arranged to meet the others at Heathrow to catch the flight for Nice.

The last few weeks had dragged. Since Dominic's accident she had become accustomed to returning each evening to a dark, unwelcoming flat. She had got used to shopping for one, in fact food shopping and cooking were much easier now she no longer had to buy meat. Dominic had always insisted on his meat and two veg, while Bronte had thrown together a vegetable or fish dish for herself.

But no amount of convenience made up for the loneliness in her bedroom or the void in her heart. Her childhood teddy bear was little substitute for the warmth and comfort that sharing her bed with Dominic had always meant to her. She felt starved of love, physical love, not sex necessarily, but physical affection.

Work had become busier by the day. The deadline to ship audition cassettes and publicity leaflets had come, amid a flurry of panic in the office. There had been availability sheets to prepare, meetings to arrange in Cannes and instructions to be left behind with the others, should any particular problems arise while she was away.

She had tried to tackle her packing the night before. Cannes was always unpredictable. The weather in October, for a start, could either teem down at a hundred miles an hour, sending one scuttling from hotel to restaurant, to the Palais des Festivals, or beat down, producing hot, red faces and freckles where applicable. Since she was little, freckles had always been the summer nightmare for Bronte. It

20

wasn't until she met Dominic, who adored her however she looked, that she began to realise that perhaps they did enhance the character of her face after all.

For the television markets she always made an effort to look business-like during the day. It was important to command respect and to create an air of elegant efficiency, something she had always managed quite successfully. Not that there was a uniform. Just wandering down the exhibition corridors observing people provided amusement and entertainment. Executives paraded in suits, while bimbo secretaries competed with the stands next door for the shortest skirts and the highest heels. Then came the 'trendies' who worked mostly in the music business and had the need to stand out from the crowd. Most achieved it without too much difficulty.

The evenings could be complicated. There were agents' dinners, meals with buyers, casual evenings with friends and sometimes they were dragged out to bop the night away at Studio Circus. One suitcase was never really enough to cater for all eventualities, but Bronte hoped she could mix and match to suit the occasions.

She jumped into the shower, without which her day could not begin. The taxi was booked for eight o'clock and she was due at Heathrow by eight thirty. If the M4 was crawling, she'd be late, but with any luck the commuters who felt the daily need to examine the tarmac at a walking pace, would all be going the other way. After the shower, she rubbed at her hair with the towel before throwing it all upside-down and sentencing it to five minutes fly-away time with the hairdryer.

Damn, she cursed, as she tried to force her bulging washbag into a hole in the suitcase which was half the size of the bag. Surrendering, she chucked it into her hand luggage and turned her attentions to the clothes she had chosen to travel in.

A pair of faded jeans did perfect justice to her long legs and gave her a 'great little ass', as Dominic had always called it. She did battle with the polo neck of her jumper – it always seemed to shrink round the neck when she washed it and left room for either her or her hair, but certainly not both

21

together without an almighty struggle. Her favourite battered leather flying jacket lay on the hall chair, so she'd be sure to remember it. She could never understand people who dressed up to fly. More often than not, you were trapped in a small seat with barely any room to expand, be it outwards, frontwards or backwards and just as the coffee had been served, the predictable pocket of air turbulence would send it leaping from the small plastic cup to a much more exciting adventure in your lap! No, it was comfort before style. There was plenty of time for style once you were there.

The doorbell startled her as she was fixing her twisted gold earrings in place. They had been a present from Dominic.

'Coming,' she yelled, as she snatched up her watch and threw it round her wrist.

'Taxi for Heathrow?' she asked, opening the door.

'Yeah. You wanna hand, love?' came the cockney accent from under the tilted cap.

'I've got a case over there.' She pointed back into the hall. 'Give me a minute, I just need to lock the windows and round up a couple more things.'

He stepped in behind her, allowing the odour of stale cigarettes to seep from his clothes and into her flat.

'I'll wait in the cab, love. Jeez – how long you goin' for?' He was glad to find the wheels on her case. Wouldn't do his back any good, any good at all, to heave that one around. Why did women always pack as if they were never coming back?

It wasn't long before she closed the door, clutching her briefcase and her flight bag. She was grateful for the partition in the taxi, at least it managed to contain most of the cigarette smell.

As she sat there, chasing a couple of stray hairs that had wiggled down the front of her jumper, she felt she was rising to the challenge that life had thrust upon her. She had coped. At the age of twenty-five, she was a widow and yet she had not crumbled into tiny pieces, to be scattered like leaves on the breeze. She had cried streams but certainly not oceans. With the support that had overwhelmed her, she had struck out and defied all that intended her harm. She had survived as she knew she could and there she was, on her way to France to mingle once more with the jet-set and hopefully even find a little fun, something to laugh at, to really laugh so that she cried from joy and not loneliness. It had been a while since she had done that. Her thoughts were intruded upon:

'Where you off then?'

'Cannes. Well, from Heathrow to Nice and then on to Cannes.'

' 'oliday?'

'No, work actually.'

'What line of work you in then?'

'Television.'

'What, you an actress or summat? I thought your face was familiar, like.'

She smiled to herself. How many times had taxi drivers asked her that? Whenever she travelled in the Caribbean or in Africa and asked to be taken to the local television station, most presumed that she was appearing on air or promoting a show. She had been flattered by their assumptions, and even more so by the ones who asked her if she'd come to model because, rightly or wrongly, she'd never considered her looks particularly striking. Indeed she would have changed several things about herself, given the chance. But then who wouldn't?

'No, sorry to disappoint you. We sell television programmes – the finished shows. It's not quite as glamorous as it sounds.'

'Don't know, Cannes and such like, sounds pretty grand to me.'

Once engaged in conversation with a taxi driver intent on worming out your life history, it was always hard to stem the flow. But she was lucky that the traffic was remarkably light and Heathrow loomed before he became too much to handle. Bronte felt a little uncharitable, because for a taxi driver the only variety in the job must come from the punters. She shuddered as she tried to think of something worse than driving all day in the snarl of London's traffic.

'Which airline you goin', love?' he asked as they headed towards the imposing WELCOME TO HEATHROW sign.

'Sunshine Airways, it's a charter airline. I think they go from Terminal 2.'

'Yeah. OK, no problem.'

They encountered a jam through the tunnel but soon drew up at the departure area. She paid the fare, which seemed enormous! Good job it was on expenses. She declined the offer of help from a pimple-faced porter who charged a fixed fee to carry a case from the pavement to the check-in desk. There were plenty of trolleys parked to the side and one of those would do just as well.

Her airline was situated at one end of the check in area, typically at the far end from where Bronte had come in. It was just her luck to have selected the trolley with the obstinate left wheel which refused to turn, instead dragging itself sideways down the concourse with Bronte pushing for all she was worth behind it.

She knew before she got there that she'd find a queue – and so she did. It snaked haphazardly back from the check-in counters. There were only three for the Nice flight, and of those, it was hard to figure out who was at the back of which, amongst the piles of cases, lines of trolleys and groups of enthusiastic travellers.

Bronte had arranged to meet Donna and Jane from the office there so they could hopefully get seats together on the flight. Alex and Helene were already in France, in the hope of soaking up some sunshine before the market began. She could just about make out Donna standing in the furthest line from her and made her way over, politely at first and then when that did not seem to disperse anyone, a bit more firmly.

'Bronte, over here,' called Donna. 'Any sign of Jane? I thought you might have shared a taxi?'

'No, she decided to drive down and so we agreed to make our own way here. Can't see her yet. She's always a last minute traveller. She's probably in some horrendous panic on the motorway.'

Donna and Bronte had been friends for some years. Donna was Alex's right arm, without whom he wandered around the office like a lost child. He relied on her to organise, not only his business life, but much of his home life as well. Donna excelled at her job and was also responsible for selling to various territories around the world.

Bronte looked around her. There was the usual gaggle of industry people on the flight. Some stood in pairs, straddling suitcases, carrying coats, vanity bags, briefcases and even tennis racquets. Alex was a keen player and would no doubt have her on the court before the end of the week. Bronte recognised a few faces – there was the ACB contingent – she couldn't disguise a quick glance at Alison Moss, about whom there had been the gossip. She waved to John Redpath with whom she dealt at ACB, when he caught her looking at him.

The trendy set from Sounds Inc stood near to her, supporting the leather industry with their usual aplomb. The company had approached her once with the idea of her doing something for them in the Caribbean and Africa. But with their hour-long concerts starring way-out, and as far as she, let alone the buyers, was concerned, unheard-of bands, nothing had ever come to fruition.

Few, if any, of her television colleagues had seen Bronte and only one or two had talked to her on the 'phone since Dominic's accident. This was partly because she had kept busy and partly because most of them were rather backward at coming forward on the subject. It was understandable because death was a pretty tough nut to swallow. She became conscious of what she felt were people talking about her, doubtlessly sympathising, but it weighed on her and made her feel isolated. It gave her the sudden urge to shout out loud: 'Yes, my husband has recently been killed, but I'm still here and I'm getting on with my life.' Fortunately, Donna became aware of the situation.

'Let's just ask for three seats together, if we can. Jane is sure to find out if we've checked in and see that we've reserved her a place.'

'Yes, OK. Why can she never manage to turn up on time? I don't know how she ever catches a plane!'

'I'm not sure she does half the time. It amazes me too.'

Their turn came and they hauled their cases on to the weighing machine, managing to get away with no excess baggage charges.

Armed with tickets and boarding passes, they found the escalator up to the first floor and looked for the departure gate.

'I need some batteries for my Walkman and I wouldn't mind something to read,' said Donna as they passed their hand luggage onto the X-ray machine.

Bronte always seemed to trigger the alarm when she walked under the metal sensor. It happened whenever she flew. Either jewellery or hair clips or something usually set it off and she heard the familiar beep as she stepped through.

'This way please, madam.' She was taken aside and a woman, only recognizable as female by the calf length, stiff navy skirt and pounding bosom, seemed to enjoy whisking her hand up and down Bronte's thin frame. A shudder ran down her spine as her belt buckle, which turned out to be the offending item, was given a thorough examination. Once given the all clear, she gathered up her bags and caught up with Donna at passport control.

'Alex wants us to get some duty free booze for the stand. A bottle of whisky and a bottle of gin should do it. We can get the mixers down there, but spirits are really loaded in Cannes,' said Donna.

'Good idea. I wouldn't mind some perfume. I'm getting really bored with mine.'

On their way to duty free, they were stopped in their tracks by a voice which boomed across from the cafeteria.

'Bronte, hi there! Look, wait a minute.'

The owner of the voice was a chaotic but attractive character who worked for an American sports company with whom she dealt. She always maintained that he charmed for America and whenever the opportunity arose, they would have lunch or even dinner.

'Rumour has it there's a lady in distress over here.' He rushed up and swept her into his arms, taking care not to singe her with the cigarette which he still held between his fingers.

She smiled: 'Mike, it's good to see you too!'

'Poor babe! You've had it rough. My 'Caribbean queen' obviously needs a little attention.'

Bronte had almost forgotten about Donna, who knew of Mike by reputation only.

'Hey Mike, do you know Donna Wilson? She's a friend from the company.'

'Good to meet you, Donna. A friend of Bronte's is a friend of mine.'

'You do say all the right things, Mike,' teased Bronte.

'Are you on the ten o'clock flight too?'

'Yes we are,' replied Bronte. 'Whereabouts are you sitting?'

'Probably in the hold! I hear it's full to the brim. No, seriously somewhere near the back. Some of us have to keep the fag companies in business, you know.'

'Point taken. Are the others coming down too, or are you going solo this time?' asked Bronte.

'Sheree and Julian are already down there. I hope they've got the stand sorted by the time I get down. I had to fly over via New York and it gets me in a day later. Say, how about dinner tonight? Both of you, if you're free?'

'Mike, I'd love to, really, but Alex insists on all of us eating together on the first night. He likes to drill us on our sales technique.'

'No problem, how about the hotel bar afterwards? You guys are in the Martinez, right? It's a popular watering hole but I'll find you.'

'Great. Look, we've got to run, duty free beckons and they've already called the flight.'

'Sure, I'd better go rescue my coffee anyhow. See you soon . . . and Bronte,' he put a hand on her arm, 'it's really good to see you again. I've missed you.'

'Missed my sales more like! Well, I'm back at the helm now.'

Donna and Bronte hurried into the duty free.

'He's gorgeous!' said Donna. 'How have you kept your hands off him? I mean, I had heard about him, but I wasn't prepared for that.'

'It's been more a question of keeping his hands off me!' Bronte laughed. 'But that's not entirely fair, he's always been a gentleman. I've never been bowled over by blond men – not my type, but I guess he's alright really. Now look, we'd better get a move on. Can you manage the booze if I run and get some perfume? I'll get your batteries at the same time.'

'OK, see you back here in five?'

Bronte followed the scent of perfume, which wafted up and hung in the air like a balloon released from a willing hand. She spent a few moments spraying this and that on to her palm, her wrist and into the air, until she really couldn't tell which smell was which. She plumped for a classic one. Dominic had always liked its sweet floral aroma, and it in turn reminded her of him. She needed the occasional reminders of him around her. It made him feel less distant.

Donna was already waiting for her, holding a bag of goodies. They barely had time to whisk into the news stand and snatch up a couple of magazines before they heard the final call for their flight. All that time, Jane had remained a mystery to them. There was no sign of her at all.

The departure lounge bulged at the seams. There wasn't a seat to be had and the walls were also lined with people waiting for the boarding announcement. They were heading towards the exit that would lead them to the 'plane, when they heard a frantic 'Donna, Bronte' escape from the sea of faces. It was Jane! Red in the face, her shoulder length hair falling this way and that, she had obviously only just made it.

'What happened to you?' asked Donna.

'I overslept. Can't understand it. The alarm went off, but I just slept through it.'

'I bet you were up packing until all hours.' Bronte knew her well.

'Not as bad as usual. I've left the ironing to do when we get there.'

'Did they give you the seat next to us, we did try and save it for you?' asked Donna.

'Yes, they did. Thanks for doing that.'

They were interrupted by an announcement.

'Sunshine Airways would like to welcome its passengers on flight SA 452 to Nice. We will be boarding by seat row numbers and would ask any parents with young children or persons requiring special assistance to please proceed to the gate at this time. Our First Class passengers may board at their leisure.'

How many times had Bronte heard that at airports? She could repeat it parrot fashion. On an African or Caribbean sales trip, she would need to fly up to fifteen times in three weeks! Fortunately she had no fear of flying. On the contrary, she found it exciting and exhilarating.

'We would now like to board those passengers seated in rows twenty through thirty six only, please.'

They had been allocated no-smoking seats in row twenty three and so they collected up their belongings. As Bronte walked down the corridor to the 'plane, she found herself level in the queue with Jackie Owen from Starlight Ltd. They were acquaintances because Jackie also handled areas of the world covered by Bronte. She was a short girl, with an untidy mop of dark curly hair.

'Bronte, how are you? I . . . I . . . I'm sorry to hear . . . I mean, I saw Judith from Central the other day, who told me about . . .' She couldn't get the words out.

Bronte could cope with the Mikes and needed the Alexes of this world, but the Jackies who bumbled their words, hedging round the subject but never actually mentioning it, made her lose her nerve and she felt anger both at the unfairness of losing Dominic and the ignorance that Jackie showed in handling her.

'He was called Dominic, Jackie. He died about five weeks ago now, in a car accident.' There, she had said it. She had come clean and admitted it and it wasn't as painful as she had been dreading.

Behind Jackie was her boss, Charlie, who threw Bronte a sympathetic look and immediately diverted Jackie's attention. Bronte was grateful.

They each accepted a newspaper from a stewardess. As they tried to get down the aisle, the progress was slow as people wrestled with overhead lockers, blocking the gangway in the process. When Bronte reached their row, she stepped over to the window seat. She always preferred to sit by the window, as that way she could quite happily lose herself outside or lean against it for a doze if she felt like it.

As she balanced on one knee at her seat while she rummaged in her bag for a tape, Bronte caught Mike's eye several rows behind and she smiled as he winked and then grinned at her. She noticed that he was trapped by a most unfortunate, hugely-fat female. He beckoned questioningly at Bronte, silently suggesting she might like to swap places with his co-passenger. But she shook her head and acted as if she too was trapped in her seat.

The departure was only delayed by a few minutes and as they taxied down the runway, Bronte sat back in her seat and settled her headphones comfortably on her ears. Beside her, Donna was scanning the financial pages of The Times and beyond her, Jane was engrossed in the social pages of a society magazine. Bronte decided to listen to Chris De Burgh. His music and in particular his lyrics, held evocative messages for her, which she had come to find comforting since Dominic's death. Music had always figured strongly in her life and she was never far from a radio or a stereo machine of some kind. She had always found it a kind of escapism, both for happy and sad times.

As the 'plane roared back down the runway like something possessed and finally stretched its wings, lifted its feet and soared into the sky, the words from the song The Last Time I Cried filled her head. She turned up the volume and sang for all she was worth, but only for herself to hear.

The song was powerful, no, majestic, as the 'plane climbed higher and higher. The clouds rushed in and out again, parting their curtains and making way for the penetration. The sky seemed hostile as it grasped the 'plane and shook it, causing the fuselage to shudder. The tiny patchwork fields and roads far below were scarcely visible through the cluster of clouds.

It felt good to be lost for a brief time in a world of music and wild weather. Bronte felt strong as she shifted sideways, tucking her legs up under her. She was ready for whatever was destined her way. The final few bars of the song faded out leaving silence at the end of the track.

'What are you listening to, Bronte?' Donna turned to her as Bronte pulled out her tape to turn it over.

'Chris de Burgh.'

'I've got a couple of his CDs at home. I nearly forgot about tapes when I dashed out this morning and only managed to grab a couple.'

'Help yourself if you like, I never travel without a selection,' offered Bronte.

'Thanks, maybe once we've had something to eat. Do you want to look at my paper?'

Bronte, who always preferred the tabloids because of their lighter reading and gossipy content, declined the offer and pulled out her own magazine. She flicked through the pages and noted that they were heading out over the Channel.

Bronte travelled abroad on business on average about five times a year. Two of those trips were to Cannes. She was therefore no stranger to the journey and yet that one seemed special, she could sense it in her bones. It had come at a time in her life when she most needed distraction, preferably overseas. She knew that, although there would be hard work, there would be fun too, if she could allow herself to look. For a week she would not be forced to witness anyone else's domestic harmony or feel the ghosts that sometimes wandered the flat when she was there alone.

Deep in concentration, she had not noticed the food trolley weave up the aisle and arrive beside their row. Her pre-packed tray of preserved rubber was passed across, as she undid her table from the seatback in front of her. What she guessed was intended as the starter appeared to be shrivelled varieties of lettuce accompanied by an oozing sachet of salad dressing. The main course, which consisted of slices of salami, ham and cold beef, looked as if it had been put out to dry in the sun and the lone gherkin arranged decoratively on top did little to spark an appetite. Bronte managed to put together a cheese bap of sorts using her bread, a rather unwilling piece of cheddar and a few fragments from the salad bowl. The spring water, still firmly sealed, was voted the best thing on the tray.

Donna and Jane fared little better than her.

'This is revolting,' said Donna, as she curled out her tongue in pursuit of a rebellious drop of salad dressing.

'I agree. Actually, I'm not too hungry or I'd be more bothered,' replied Bronte.

'Have you been eating properly?' asked Donna. 'You've taken off weight again.'

'I eat when I'm hungry, which isn't that often at the moment. It's not the same when you're cooking for yourself.

When I cooked for Dominic, I used to go the whole hog with a meal. Now frankly, it's an effort.'

'I wish I had your willpower. I just seem to be hungry most of the time.'

'Yes, but you do lots of exercise to burn it off. Besides, you don't have a problem, you're right for your height.'

At that point, Jane interrupted them: 'I've just been through the hatch, match and despatch columns and guess who's getting married?'

'Go on.' They were intrigued.

'Jeremy Duncan!'

'What, your ex?' asked Donna.

'Yes, the creep! And he said I was getting too serious. I'm livid!'

'But would you have wanted to marry him?' interjected Bronte.

'I thought it was on the cards at one time, but I always suspected he was rather keen on Ashley. I can't wait to ignore him at the next drinks party!'

'Gossiping, girls?' Mike leaned over the three of them.

'What are you doing?' grinned Bronte.

'Going walkies. That woman on my left is just too much. And what's worse, she doesn't appear to have heard of deodorant,' he added in a hoarse whisper.

'Oh no, how horrible,' giggled Bronte.

'Seeing as you, darling, did not want to change places with her, I'm stuck.'

'Come on! She'd never have fitted into my seat.'

'She hardly fits into her own.'

'Jane, have you met Mike Foret from USA Sports? I apologise for the fact that he's leaning all over you, but as you've gathered he's in need of a change of scenery!'

'Hey, give me a break! The Duchess back there might hear and I don't want her to think that I'm not enjoying her company.'

'Pleased to meet you, Mike,' laughed Jane, who was rather prone to blushing when introduced to amazing-looking men.

Mike, noticing Jane's plight, made it worse by picking up her hand, planting a great smacking kiss on it and saying to Bronte:

'Keep on introducing me to these beautiful friends of yours, Bron.'

'Look, you're blocking the aisle,' was her reply. And he was indeed hindering the progress of the trolley.

'See you in Nice, girls.'

'Bye.'

Jane looked across with stars in her eyes: 'Is he always like that? Are there any sales I can do for him in the Far East or Australasia?'

'I'm sure there's a lot you can do for him, if you give him the chance,' said Donna, not unsarcastically, because she too had her eye on Bronte's friend.

'Believe it or not, he's madly in love with his girlfriend in Los Angeles,' Bronte disappointed them.

'They all say that, but when do they ever *produce* the girlfriends?' asked Donna.

'Actually, I've met her. They were in London last year and we went to lunch. Predictably, she's very attractive, a model I think. Anyway, he's good for a laugh when we meet and he always insists on picking up the tab.'

'That must keep Alex happy anyway,' said Jane.

The subject was temporarily forgotten as steaming coffee was once again being offered to them.

Bronte had hardly finished reading the fashion pages when it was announced that they would shortly be landing at Côte d'Azur Airport, Nice, and would everyone return to their seats and fasten their seat belts ready for landing. The journey had passed quickly and safely, despite the occasional turbulence and it was only then, as they skimmed down through the clouds, that the outline of France's Riviera coastline became discernible. The nearer they approached Nice, the clearer the weather became. For some reason the cloud mass hung almost angrily inland but allowed the virgin blue sky to cover the sea.

The aircraft circled a couple of times, waiting for ground clearance to land its precious cargo, before swooping down over the runway and charging once more, like the cavalry to battle. A smooth landing. Everyone was relieved.

The 'plane disgorged its passengers from both the forward and the rear doors. That reduced considerably the hanging around, waiting for other passengers to gather their belongings, put on their coats, check their hair and general appearance and even more importantly, fish around in their pockets for the all-important sunglasses, without which their entrance to the glamour of the South of France would not be complete. They walked precariously down the narrow portable stairs and wandered across the tarmac to the waiting buses. From there, they were driven towards the terminal building, all clutching rails, balls which bobbed down from the ceiling, or each other, as the enthusiastic driver did his best to break the all-speed record and, at the same time, ensure his passengers got to know the others around them with as much intimacy as possible!

The queue for passport inspection began at the entrance to the building, but soon melted because most people held EEC passports and therefore the scrutiny was minimal. Bronte stood a little ahead of her companions, seemingly unaware of the desirous looks she was attracting from the majority of the male population in the room. Donna and Jane chatted together, each one hoping secretly that Mike would come over again, but it was not to be because he was engaged in deep conversation, further up the line with an older man.

Bronte turned to Donna: 'Have you remembered the documents for the car rental?'

'Yes, I've got them right here with my passport. Have you two got your driving licences with you?'

Jane put her hand to her mouth: 'Damn and blast! I put it out last night and I know I've left it on the kitchen table. Never mind, if you both have yours, it won't really matter.'

They reached the passport desk and passed through quickly without incident. A little further on they were faced by a barrage of drivers, all holding up name signs in order to meet various delegations to take to their hotels in Cannes. Alex had always advised the girls to hire a car for the short drive from Nice to Cannes, because by the time they had taken taxis and then again in the evenings and finally back to the airport at the end of the week, the hire charge was pretty much the same cost and it was so much more convenient.

Jane's case must have been 'last on, first off' because it was one of the first pieces of baggage to wobble onto the carousel. Bronte thought she had gone overboard with her packing, but she had seen nothing until she helped Jane (who was pretty small in stature) hump her case onto the waiting trolley. 'What have you got in there, Jane?' gasped Bronte.

'A really hunky man!' she laughed.

'At least two, I would have said.'

The other cases followed and after a short wait at the rental desk they were soon loading their possessions, with some difficuly, into the little hire car. Donna jumped into the driving seat and Jane, who often felt carsick, got in beside her. Bronte wedged herself into the tiny space left in the back and drew down her sunglasses from the top of her head, bracing herself for the ride to Cannes.

As they drove out of the airport compound and joined the autoroute, she mused at the insincerity of people – in life generally, but she had been reminded of it more specifically at the airport. There she had met a number of industry people all heading for the same place as her, with whom she was familiar and in some cases even did business with, and yet both parties had failed to acknowledge each other.

She was probably as much to blame, particularly then when encounters with people she had not seen since the accident led to awkward questions and general discomfort. But the irony which struck her, and not for the first time, was that when she bumped into the same people in the exhibition hall over the next few days, they would undoubtedly greet each other as long lost friends, discuss how business was faring and grumble about the weather or their hotel. It rekindled her natural feelings of apprehension towards people and the shallow way in which they often behaved, however much a friend they liked to be considered.

Through the pure blue sky overhead, the sun shone down on her face as Bronte stripped off her jacket and rolled up the sleeves of her jumper. By wriggling forwards, she managed to pull a scrunchie from the back pocket of her jeans which she wound loosely round her hair in an effort to cool down a little. It was wonderful to feel the warm air brush her face, as she sat back gazing out of the window.

'I hear that Channel Four are bringing Dudley Moore down to promote their classical music series, Bronte. Do you think you'll get the chance to meet him?' asked Jane, turning briefly round to look at Bronte.

'I doubt it. There's a cocktail party at the Carlton Hotel on Wednesday, but with the hundreds of other people there, he's hardly likely to come my way.'

'You never know.'

'You got a lot fixed up for the week then, Bronte?' asked Donna, as she steered past a dawdling truck.

'A fair few meetings. Most lunches and dinners seem to be booked up too. The majority are agents' dinners where I always seem to get landed beside the agents for Turkey or Greece, who leer wildly all night and hardly speak a word of English. Not exactly my scene, but you have to go along with it.'

'I've got a rather heavy evening ahead with some Eastern European buyers tomorrow night,' sighed Jane. 'Any chance of you two being free to help lighten the load?'

'Sorry, Jane. I'm on a Western TV agents' do at the Cap d'Antibes tomorrow night. I'll hardly know a soul, but at least it's out of Cannes and it's the most amazing place.'

'I went there once,' said Jane. 'It was a Metromedia dinner, wasn't it? I can remember they had the most scrummy food and the view is fantastic.'

'That's right,' replied Donna. 'I was there too. All the big stars stay there for the Cannes film festival. I bet it'll cost Western TV an arm and a leg to take you lot there. Jane, I'll help out tomorrow if you like, I'm sure I'll need the same from you before the week's out. Where are you taking them?'

'I haven't decided. I'll ask our receptionist, Alexandra, to book something tomorrow.'

Bronte removed her glasses and rubbed an irritated eye: 'What's the plan tonight?'

Donna, who could be relied on to organise them all with ultimate efficiency, replied: 'Alex wants us to meet in the Majestic Hotel bar around seven for cocktails and then I think he had in mind for us to go to La Salle de France.'

'I loathe that place,' groaned Bronte. 'It's hopeless for anyone who doesn't eat meat and I always feel nauseous after I've been there.'

'I know the food's not brilliant but Alex likes the fact that it's small and has a very French atmosphere,' said Donna.

They fell silent for a while as they headed down the long, straight road which led into Cannes from the autoroute. The traffic began to build up the nearer they got to the centre of town. Some drivers were unnecessarily aggressive and impatient and the air was full of the sound of wailing horns and French expletives.

'Did you see that?' exclaimed Donna, as she slammed on the brakes, sending Bronte's knees jarring into the back of Jane's seat. 'What an awful bit of driving! He's going to have an accident.'

An open-top jeep in the hands of an unshaven blond Frenchman came out of a side road and proceeded right across the road, in the path of both the incoming and outgoing traffic, creating several instant enemies as he went.

'I'm glad I'm not driving, he's got a nerve,' responded Jane, once she had regained her composure.

Bronte was extremely grateful when they finally pulled into the Croisette, which ran the length of the beach and passed directly in front of the major hotels. She was even more pleased to sweep onto the forecourt of the Martinez and come to a stop, enabling her to unfold herself and stretch her legs. They were greeted by two porters whom she recognised from previous visits and who also recognised them, Bronte in particular. It was refreshing, after a day which seemed to have begun a long time before, to have someone to valet park the car and take charge of their luggage with a smile.

'This way, madam.' They were ushered to the reception area.

Already propped up at the desk and awaiting their turn to register were a few of the blank acquaintances from the airport. While they too stood at the reception desk, Donna turned her attentions to Ben Brown, a six-foot-four, pale-skinned individual who had worked for a brief spell at their

37

company but whose skills and charm had since been pinched by someone else.

Bronte was keen to establish that her room was not at the rear of the hotel, which overlooked the railway line, notorious for causing insomnia in the early hours. She was politely assured that it was not.

The Martinez was vast. It was one of the five-star hotels in town and was much sought after as a place to stay for the festival. The reception area was blooming with brightly-coloured flower arrangements and bustling with the comings and goings of guests checking in and out. The swimming pool outside was swarming with white-robed bathers, keenly working off a few pounds before the onslaught of another full French meal or lounging in the afternoon sun, cultivating a tan for display in their evening attire.

There was no time for sunbathing when you worked for Alex. He expected them to be on the go almost twenty four hours a day, but made sure they were generously rewarded for their efforts. There would just be time to unpack and settle into their rooms, before they had to go down to the Palais to register and find their entrance badges. Donna had also arranged to meet up with Alexandra so that they could inspect their stand.

Bronte, armed with her room key, turned to the others: 'When do you want to meet? I'm going to have to walk up the Rue D'Antibes on the way to the Palais and go to that boulangerie, the one that sells the walnut bread. I'm starved after that rubbish we had on the 'plane.'

'Fine,' responded Jane. 'I need some cards to send home. Actually, I don't know why I bother because I always buy them and end up posting them when we get back to England.' She suddenly remembered that perhaps Bronte wouldn't want to be reminded of the cards she always used to send to Dominic whenever she was away travelling, and changed the subject.

'Half an hour, down here? Is that enough time?'

'See you at three thirty.'

Bronte headed for the lift, beckoning as she went to the bellboy who already had her case scientifically balanced on top of other luggage on his cart. The doors opened and she sank thankfully inside, grateful to have a little time to herself.

The journey had been somewhat of an ordeal. The trouble was that she kept swinging like an emotional pendulum from strength to weakness. Most of the time she could cope. In fact all of the time she could cope, but just sometimes her heart would weigh her down.

The bellboy helped her into her room which, much to her relief, was a very comfortable one, with light, airy walls and a high ceiling. It was almost the size of her entire flat! The twin beds were dwarfed by the magnitude of the room. The bathroom, with its separate shower room and loo was bigger than her living room in Fulham. Mirrors flashed on the front of the sliding wardrobe doors in the corridor leading to the bedroom, and again in the bedroom itself. She tipped the boy, who seemed awed by her beauty and reluctant to go, as he lingered over the demonstration of the television, the mini bar and the telephone system.

Taking a mineral water from the fridge, Bronte gulped it down and set about the task of unloading her suitcase, which burst open gratefully when she undid the catches.

Around three forty-five, Bronte was strolling beside Jane and Donna down the Rue D'Antibes in search of the long-awaited boulangerie.

'I'm sure it was on this side of the street,' puzzled Bronte, looking up at the shop signs overhead.

'Wasn't it nearer towards Gray Street and the Gray D'Albion Hotel?' replied Donna.

'Possibly, let's carry on. How are your rooms?'

'Mine's small. I've had so many different styles of room at that hotel since I've been coming to Cannes that it's hard to believe they're all in the same place!' moaned Jane.

'But you're only in the room to change and sleep, so does it really matter?' asked Donna.

'I guess not, as long as I can't hear the trains in the morning.'

'Well I've got the bar under me so we can compare notes on how much beauty sleep we manage.'

'Donna, Bronte ...!' hailed from the other side of the street.

They looked over and saw Alex, laden down with carrier bags, escorting an immaculately-dressed Helene, on what seemed to be a mammoth shopping expedition. He crossed the road dramatically – most things Alex did had an air of the theatrical about them – ignoring the indignant car driver who almost ran him over.

He put the bags down and kissed each of the girls fondly on the cheek.

'How are my lovely ladies, then? Flight on time? Journey OK?'

'Fine so far,' laughed Donna as she looked at Alex who was quite obviously in one of his most extravagant moods.

'We're off to the Palais and to meet up with Alexandra. Have you been to the stand yet? How are they getting on?'

'I did wander in there but got waylaid by a whole host of people and never made it to the stand. We're still on for dinner then? Seven o'clock at the Majestic for drinks first?'

'We'll be there,' said Donna. 'Casual?'

'Come as your are. I'm not changing.'

But then, in his expensive cream trousers, double breasted blazer and bow tie, he really had no need to. Bronte, who had been quiet up to that moment, glanced to where Helene remained on the other side of the street, looking anxiously towards Alex.

'Alex, duty calls.' Bronte pointed to Helene, now with her back to them, taking in another shop window.

'Yes I know, I must go. You all right?' He looked at her with concern and she gave him a reassuring nod.

They knew when the boulangerie was close. All they had to do was follow the tantalising smell of warm, freshly baked bread and they found the shop. Bronte discovered her walnut bread which Jane decided to share as it was quite a sizeable loaf, while Donna chose a sticky chocolate croissant, which simply disintegrated in her mouth! It was the sustenance they needed to see them through to dinner, some hours later.

They found the registration desk inside the Palais and were given their badges and festival guide books, which really amounted to a who's who of the television industry. Once they had pinned on their badges, they were allowed to go down to the lower ground floor housing the main exhibition area, which they found to be a hive of activity.

It was the norm to commission a company to build your stand and the men who worked on them carried on right through the night, adding the finishing touches right down to the plastic flowers which adorned most of the stands. At nine o'clock the next morning, the flood-gates would open and the hundreds of people gathered outside would scuttle down the stairs and dash to their stands in case they missed that all-important buyer.

Having walked along the main aisle and then branched down one of the side runs, they came to the area which had been allotted to their company. To her horror and dismay, Donna found that their stand was still a mass of planks and boards and had taken very little shape at all. There was obviously no point in trying to unpack their audition cassettes or arrange their publicity displays for quite some time.

'I'll murder that Ian Christie when I get my hands on him!' raged Donna. 'I specifically asked him to have the stand ready for us to unpack our crates this afternoon. Trouble is, they take on too many other companies and then stretch themselves to the limit. I'm going to look for him. Will you wait here for Alexandra?'

Jane and Bronte, exchanging glances, had little choice. They settled themselves down on one of the crates and started to flick through the guide to see who was going to be there that year.

The Majestic bar heaved. It positively panted and choked with television executives all vying for attention. The hotel housed the big-wigs of the industry, the company chairmen and presidents, and as a result the bar was notoriously filled with eager bods, hoping to be noticed and to get in where it mattered. It was in there that they saw the paths to promotion and success. Bronte had no time for most of them. She was not overly ambitious and certainly had strict limits as to how far she was prepared to go for her own success, unlike several other females she could name. As she sipped her white wine and listened to Alex outlining a new deal he hoped to pull off with the BBC, she glanced around at the throng of faces, some of whom she recognised but most she did not.

The day had started to take its toll a little. She felt drained, partly due to the lack of food but also due to the strain of the little empty place that had become embedded in her heart. It was hard to compete with the raised voices and she had no wish to, hoping furiously that they would go on to the restaurant soon, where at least it would be more peaceful.

Alex must have sensed her sober mood, because he turned to them and said: 'Drink up, dinner calls. That shopping's really given me an appetite.'

'Where are we going, Alex?' asked Helene, as she crossed her legs neatly, revealing a glimpse of her black suspender for a second.

'La Salle de France, I don't think you've been there. You'll like it. It has a real taste of France and they do a magnificent pot au feu! Hello, Dave.' His attention was caught by a heavily-bearded man whom Bronte recognised as the head of the ITV purchasing committee, a very important figure to be in with, particularly if you had designs on selling a package of programmes to the ITV network.

Not a moment too soon, they stepped out of the back of the hotel into one of the little winding streets which would lead them to the restaurant. Bronte was glad of the exercise and the warm air, as she walked a little ahead of the group.

Alex, once more sensitive to her state of mind, caught up with her stride and linked his arm loosely through hers.

'Tired?' he asked her.

'A little.'

'We won't be late. Helene likes to have me all tucked up by eleven, so don't worry. What are the plans tomorrow? Are you lunching?'

'Yes, I have arranged to see one of the new buyers from Trinidad, if he manages to turn up, that is. And it's the Western TV agents' do in Antibes tomorrow night.'

'Busy day, huh?'

'I guess, but I prefer it that way. We're here to turn the bucks or so you tell us.'

'That's my girl! Look, we're nearly there.'

He turned to wait for the rest of the party, before holding the door of the restaurant for his 'ladies'. Inside, the room was tiny. There could only have been about five or six tables at the very most, all crammed close together. The decor was representative of all that was French. Onions hung from the ceiling, pictures on the walls depicted Parisian scenes and garlic came wafting convincingly from the kitchen area. They were shown to the round table in the corner which Alex had specifically requested. The menu was such that they did not order food apart from the main meat course. The dishes just arrived. And kept on arriving! It was an amazing feast and the only person who did not feel bloated by the end was Bronte, who had merely picked at the courses.

The conversation ranged from industry gossip, to political events back home and talk of the up-coming elections.

Finally they settled on serious sales strategy and anticipated targets for the week ahead. Alex dominated the conversation, but everyone seemed content to listen to what he had to say.

Bronte ordered a large black coffee which usually helped to settle the nausea that, psychologically if nothing else, always hit her in that restaurant. She declined the sickly chocolates which were offered with the coffee, because she had never really had a sweet tooth and found that chocolate ruined the taste of the coffee anyway.

After a pregnant pause in the conversation, Alex asked: 'So, are you lot gracing the Martinez bar tonight then?'

'Looks like it,' replied Donna, who was game for maximum social activity.

'I promised to meet Mike Foret there for a drink. But I'm beginning to wish I hadn't, because bed sounds like a far more attractive prospect,' said Bronte.

Jane butted in: 'I don't know, I'll meet him for you if you're having a problem staying up.'

'Thanks, Jane. I'd better make the effort for a quick drink. He is, after all, quite an important producer for us.'

They parted ways at the door of La Salle de France, Alex and Helene wandering back arm in arm to the Majestic, while the others managed to navigate their way through the streets to the Martinez.

One of the main advantages of staying in that hotel was that if you did become ensnared in the bar as most people seemed to, there was always an escape route upstairs rather than having to rely on being accompanied home by the person you had gone with originally, whom you had probably lost sight of as you walked through the door. That night was no exception. The bar was so full that the overflow spilled out onto the swimming pool terrace as well as into the lobby area. Bronte took one look and thought, yuk, do I really have to? As it turned out, the choice wasn't hers because hardly had she stepped through the revolving doors than she was whisked back out again and onto the terrace by an enthusiastic Mike!

'Babe, come this way, it's murder in there. We've got a table out here. It's a little chilly but you can have my jacket if you like,' he offered with a twinkle in his eye.

'I'm alright for the moment. Why's it so packed? Is it really just first night social?'

'No, one of the Australian soap stars is in there – you can't move for heaving breasts! He's been brought down at vast expense to promote his series. Looks as though he's having the time of his life, surrounded by dazzling women!'

'He's probably on holiday down here and one press conference in the Palais will cover his whole trip. I can't imagine what he's doing in here, though.'

'It's all publicity, darling. The man thrives on it, or so I'm told. Look, come and meet some friends of mine – say, while we're on the subject, what happened to yours?'

'You abducted me so fast from the lobby that they're probably still standing there open-mouthed, convinced that we're having some illicit affair!'

'What, us? You on for that, then?' he chuckled wickedly.

'Don't be ridiculous, you know I don't fall for blond men.'

'Well, if that's my biggest problem then I'm doing OK, wouldn't you say? I suppose it was worth a try.'

Mike led her to a table where two men and a woman sat deep in conversation.

'Hey guys, what's the debate about? You must meet a

44

really good friend of mine, Bronte Richardson. She does a great job for us in Africa and the Caribbean.'

Pleasantries exchanged, Mike whipped up a couple of extra chairs from nowhere and searched around for a waiter. As usual, there were far too few waiters to keep pace with the thirst of so many people, but eventually he managed to make contact with one and summoned him over to their table.

'What'll it be, Bron?' he asked her.

'Gin and tonic I think, thanks.'

'Gin for the lady and do me a scotch on the rocks. How about you guys?' he asked around the rest of the table. Two shook their heads, while the third ordered another beer.

'So how's it really been, Bron? People taking care of you properly?'

'It's tough, Mike. To be a widow at twenty-five was not exacty what I had envisaged for myself. But it's happened and I'm facing it, and yes, I've had plenty of support.'

'Damn it, Bron, it must've been a hell of a shock. How d'you find out?'

'The police came to tell me at work. Alex was wonderful and took charge of me because, looking back, I needed it.'

'I bet you did. And you coped with the funeral and everything, all by yourself?'

'I'm a big girl now, Mike.' She smiled into his eyes. 'Life goes on. This trip should do me some good. The flat's bearable, but it was our home together and it's hard to shake out those memories.'

'I know I lark around, but you know me better than some and if anything ever happened to Carey, I know I wouldn't surface the way you have.'

'You would, you know. You find strength you never knew you had and it takes over. Can't explain it any better than that, but I hope you never have to find out. How is Carey by the way? Ever thought of bringing her down here, or would it cramp your style?'

'She's up to her eyes in modelling contracts right now. I'm not sure she'd want to come here. She'd really like the shopping and the beach bit, but she'd want me around for more time than I'd be able to spare. You know how wrapped up in these festivals we get.'

'Yes. I never asked Dominic to come down, probably for much the same reasons. That, and the fact that he probably couldn't have afforded it.'

'You want to look after yourself, Bron. There's a lot of guys out there who'll have their eyes on you, now that you'll be considered 'available'. Most of them are bastards, so be careful.'

'You sound like someone's father! Perhaps *you* ought to keep an eye on me,' she flirted harmlessly.

'Just give me the chance!'

Bronte felt better and for the first time in ages, really comfortable in someone else's company. She liked the caring side of Mike, which was normally well disguised. It added another dimension to his already likeable character. She felt safe with him because they had long ago reached an understanding, beyond which their relationship did not go.

She didn't linger there too long. One drink was enough to relax her, and some time later, she bade goodnight to Mike and his colleagues before retiring gratefully upstairs to bed. It had been a long day. The week ahead would loom longer and she needed some sleep to face all that the next few days would hurl at her.

It took her no time at all to shed her clothes and pull her night-shirt over her head. As she sat cross-legged before her pillows, she considered what to write in her diary and wondered what the next day would bring for her.

CHAPTER FOUR

'Bonjour, room service.'

The voice became more impatient and the rap on the door louder, as Bronte gradually came to. She fumbled for the clock trying to make out why there was someone at her door in the middle of the night. She managed to focus on the time by screwing up her eyes and was horrified to see that it was already eight o'clock! The curtains in her room were so thick and heavy that they forbade any morning light to enter the room, giving the impression that it was still dark outside.

'Coming!' she yelled, leaping out of bed and grabbing her bath robe.

She undid the door chain and turned the handle, rubbing the sleep from her eyes and doing her best to keep the folds of her robe from revealing all.

'Bonjour madam. Le petit déjeuner?'

A fresh-faced garçon greeted her at the door. He balanced her breakfast tray, complete with red carnation, on the palm of his right hand which was raised above his head. He breezed past her and she ducked lest she upset the tray as he went. Bronte stood bemused as the whirlwind swept around her room, touching his forehead and giving her a little bow, as he smiled: 'Bonne journée, Madam' on the way out.

She went over to the window and flung open the vast curtains, allowing the sunlight to stream into the room. Once she had figured out how to open the doors to the tiny balcony, she stepped outside and drank in the heady scent of the sea air. She grasped the rail and leant over, looking down on the bustling street below. Cannes was awake and alive and already people were out, going about their daily business. If she were to make the Palais by nine, regrettably she had to get a move on.

Bronte shook a coffee sachet, forcing the granules to one end and ripped it open at the other, tipping the contents into her breakfast cup. They had provided her with a jug of piping hot water which she poured over the coffee. Taking a sip and snatching the pointed end of a crumbly, warm croissant, she went in search of something to wear.

She had made up her mind to hit them with all she had that first day and pulled out her new suit from the wardrobe. Its stylish cut gave her an air of sophistication, as she checked herself in the mirror. It had been her only extravagance in the past six weeks and she felt she deserved it

She felt good, confident and ready to face the world. Collecting up her handbag and briefcase, she went down the passage to the lift. On her way out she picked up a copy of one of the daily trade magazines.

The Palais was only a ten minute stroll down the Croisette and as the sun was out and there was plenty to look at on the way, Bronte was only too happy to walk. She hadn't gone more than a couple of hundred metres, when she heard a wolf whistle and then a voice she recognised behind her: 'Take a look at that! Nice suit.'

She turned round to see Mike, who had just come out of the Carlton and was also heading for the Palais, walking up behind her. She was tall but he had a good few inches on her and looked equally impressive in a check suit and dark glasses.

'Oh shut up, everyone's looking!' Bronte was embarrassed.

'And so they should, it's worth looking at! Mind if I accompany you to the Palais?'

'You don't look too bad yourself.' She made an exaggerated point of taking off her sunglasses and looking him up and down. 'Dressing for anyone in particular are we?' she teased him back.

'Not in particular, just my usual good sense of style. Expecting the unexpected and all that. What's on the agenda this morning, then?'

'Only a couple of fixed meetings. I really need to buzz round and track down my buyers who have a habit of being elusive on the first day. I must also arrange some screenings with the producers I didn't manage to get in touch with before I left. How about you?'

'There's a lot going on for us. We've got the new tennis schedule – you need to take a look at that by the way, you might get some interest from your countries – there's the basketball, golf, volleyball and various other things. I guess we're lucky, most of the sports broadcasters seem to know what they want to use and come to us for it.'

Bronte looked down at her watch.

'It must be five after nine by now, isn't it?' asked Mike. 'Hopefully the rush'll be over and we can go in there with some sort of dignity.'

Sure enough, when they reached the Palais, the crowd had gained entry a few minutes earlier and they were able to walk in the door at their own pace, giving the security guards a chance to inspect their badges as they went.

'We're up here this time, on the sunny first,' said Mike as he pointed towards the stairs. 'Come and have a drink when you can't stand it down there any more.'

'See you later, Mike. Oh, and you can take your shades off now.' She couldn't resist it.

'Never know who you're going to run into, might need to hide,' he whispered in her ear, and with one hand on her shoulder, he pecked her on the cheek and was gone, swallowed up by a throng of Japanese buyers who crowded onto the escalator.

Bronte carefully negotiated the stairs and passed through further security checks before coming out onto the main exhibition floor. The transformation from the previous day was startling! Carpet had been laid, flowers added, reception desks made available to each stand – most of which were manned by over made-up girls, anxious to fill all the spaces in the appointment diaries, as they had been directed to do. When they were approached by anyone who even remotely looked like a buyer, that person received a silky smile, which one knew was all part of an 'isn't our stand busy?' act.

Bronte had seen it all before, many times. Some companies went to vast expense to decorate their stands with varying degrees of elaboration, while others preferred to stick to big company logo signs and posters of the programmes they were hoping to sell at that particular festival. She was just admiring Paramount's creation (who had a reputation for producing the most imaginative stand) when she spied out of the corner of her eye, Cecil Chong, the buyer from the new station in Trinidad whom she was supposed to meet for lunch.

'Cecil,' she called after him. 'Are we still on for lunch?'

He stopped in his tracks and turned round to find Bronte towering over him: 'Bronte, how nice to see you! Yes, lunch is fine. What time did we say?'

He searched in his bag for a diary.

'How about twelve thirty? Shall we meet at our stand and I will have my notes and brochures with me? I thought I'd book something with tables outside, is that OK with you?'

'Yes. Right now is storms and hurricanes threatened in Trinidad. It is better here in France. I see you later.'

'Righto, Cecil. Our stand is number 201.'

With the new station opening there was opportunity for selling volume hours and that would certainly make the lunch worth it, or so she hoped.

'Morning all!' Bronte arrived at their stand. Jane was already engrossed in a meeting in one of the two screening rooms, while Donna was filling plastic pockets with publicity.

'Would you like some café, Bronte?' asked Alexandra, a local girl of about nineteen whom they hired to help out at the festivals. She was extremely polite and helpful and her command of the English language was excellent.

'No thanks, Alexandra. I had some in my room just a little while ago.'

'Can I have a few of your business cards to give out if anyone comes to the stand asking for you?' Alexandra went on, 'and I need you to fill out this page that I have made out for your appointments, so I know when you are free.' She pointed to a sheet of paper.

'OK, give me a chance and I'll find some cards.' Bronte took the paper and sitting down in the corner of the stand, took a handful of cards from her wallet. She handed them and the completed sheet back to Alexandra.

'Don't make any appointments for me if you can help it. I would prefer you to take a message and I'll get back to them to arrange a meeting.'

Experience had taught her that she could so easily get landed in lengthy sessions with small-time producers who wanted her to market their half hour, brainchild documentary which they had been slaving over for years, expecting her to make them a fortune in the process! It was hard to be rude, especially for Bronte, and what they failed to realise was that a one-off programme earned her so little commission that it really wasn't even worth discussing.

There was no mistaking Alex as he breezed towards the stand, sporting the customary bow tie and a Panama hat! They were all used to his little idiosyncrasies which complemented his appealing character.

'Hello, Alexandra. It's nice to have you with us again. I hope you'll enjoy your week . . . and yes, before your ask, I have my cards at the ready. Here you are.'

Alexandra replied with a rosy smile: 'Thank you. I too, am happy to be working with you all. Can I fetch you some café?'

'That would be most welcome, thank you.'

Alex turned to where Bronte was and went to occupy the seat next to her.

'I've got a proposition for you! I've booked a court up at the Montfleury hotel for tennis this evening and I'm looking for a partner. I ran into a couple of buyers from Germany at breakfast this morning and promised them a game. Will you help me out?'

'I have to be at the Carlton for the Western TV bus by seven thirty. What time is the court?'

'Five thirty. I can pick you up from your hotel and you'd be back for six forty-five. Look, I need a good net player because I've heard the opposition's pretty hot stuff.'

'You don't waste any time do you?' she laughed. 'I knew I'd be dragged on to the court at some point, but I thought you'd give me longer than one day.'

'It's good for you. All this French food – you might put on weight otherwise,' he teased, knowing that it was in fact highly unlikely that Bronte would put on any more weight for quite some time.

'Chance'd be a fine thing! And I'll be shattered for this evening.'

'I'll slip my mate at Western the nod and tell him to go easy on you.'

'You are impossible! Look, I can't sit here all morning, I've got people to find in this place. If I don't bump into you before, what time do you want me ready?'

'Five fifteen OK?'

'I'll see you then. Oh, and try and make sure the Germans have a hearty lunch. It sounds as if we're going to need some advantage.'

'That's why I asked you to play.'

Donna interrupted them, just as Bronte was gathering up her things: 'What's the conference about? Anything I need to know?'

'Alex is already trying to get me into a tennis skirt,' replied Bronte.

'Oh, and is he succeeding?'

'Looks like it.' She turned her back on where Alex had put his nose into a trade magazine. 'Your turn next. Once is enough for me.'

The exhibition occupied all four floors of the Palais. Traditionally the most important floor was the lower ground, but in recent years, some of the larger companies who needed to expand their displays had taken space on the upper floors. Some companies had managed to snap up the most eagerly sought-after areas which took in large hospitality balconies, overlooking the harbour. On a fine day it was worth every excuse to arrange a meeting on one of those balconies, soaking in the Mediterranean sunshine and breathing the fresh sea air.

Bronte left the stand to set off down the bulging corridors, in search of various clients whom she hoped to track down. Time sped by during the morning, so much so that she was half way through her third cup of coffee that day, talking to a producer on the Entertainment Today stand, when she glanced down at her watch and noticed to her horror that it was already twenty five to one!

'Listen Greg,' she interrupted the description of a long, drawn-out documentary on the jungle forests of South America, 'I've got to dash. I have a lunch, five minutes ago! Send me the brochure on that programme once it's completed and I'll do some estimate sales figures for you.'

She politely excused herself from his clutches and hurried back in the direction of her own stand.

Fortunately, Cecil had also been held up, as often tended to happen when meetings were booked back to back every half hour, and he had not arrived at their stand when she got there, flushed and out of breath.

'Alexandra, I'm dashing to the loo. If Cecil Chong comes while I'm gone, tell him I'll be back in a second and perhaps offer him a drink will you? Thanks, you're an angel.'

The ladies' rooms were not far, but she had a little wait as there was a great deal of powdering of noses, touching up of lips and combing of hair going on, not to mention the fact that all the loos were occupied. When she finally made it back, looking more relaxed and composed, Cecil was waiting for her.

Alexandra had recommended a French bistro which had tables set out on the pavement and was situated only a couple of minutes walk away. As they emerged from the Palais, they were blinded by the brilliant sunlight which glared down from a cloudless sky. Bronte had her sunglasses to hand and Cecil, well-used to the sun, didn't seem to mind.

Lunch passed amicably enough. Bronte had met Cecil that spring on her annual island-hopping visit and so she had already had the chance to weigh him up and decide on the best approach to sell to him. He hoped that the new station would be up and running before Christmas and so was actively looking to close some deals, which suited Bronte. Much of their lunch was spent discussing the type of material he was looking for and, every so often, Bronte would rummage in her briefcase for a leaflet, offering a programme which might be appropriate for his needs.

The food came and went. Bronte was satisfied with the outcome of the meeting, as she scoured down her hand-written list of programmes ordered. She would process those on her return to the office and, in time, contracts would be issued. Alex would be pleased as she had managed to sell more than two hundred hours of programming in just two hours. She felt more able to justify skiving off early for the tennis with that under her belt.

When she returned from lunch, Alexandra handed her a couple of messages from people who had stopped by to see her. One she was mildly irritated to have missed, as he was a most unreliable buyer who only ever surfaced at his own request, the rest of the time he was never to be found. The other showed all the signs of Mr Small-Time Producer, whom she really wanted to avoid like the plague!

The afternoon was not without its further frustrations. Her four o'clock appointment failed to show up at all. But perhaps he had never made it to Cannes, as he was from one of the tiny African stations who were notoriously unpredictable. By four thirty she was tired of waiting for him and decided to slip away discreetly, back to the hotel to change for tennis. She whispered to Alexandra what her intentions were, leaving instructions for her to report to any interested parties that Bronte was tied up in a very important screening and could not possibly be disturbed for the rest of the day.

It was only at the last minute that she had remembered to stuff in her tennis skirt and trainers and when she reached her room at the hotel, warm from the walk, she took them together with a T-shirt and socks from the drawer in her wardrobe. As she slipped on the skirt, she was glad she had managed to retain some of her summer tan, and once she had put her socks on too, her legs looked respectably bronzed. She hoped Alex would be able to hire a racquet for her, otherwise she'd have a problem playing.

On her way down, she prayed Alex would be on time because the idea of hanging around dressed like that did not appeal. She need not have worried because he was there at the door waiting for her, quite at home behind the wheel of a red convertible which he had hired for the week.

'Hop in.' He leaned across and opened the door. 'We're meeting Hans and Olga up there because they're staying at the Montfleury. How did day one go? Donna mentioned that you managed to charm Mr Chong over lunch.'

'I'm not so sure he was charmed, but he certainly took a good range of products from us. Around two hundred hours, I worked it out to be. It was a good thing I got in there on the first day, because his budget'll be exhausted by tomorrow if he carries on like that.'

54

'Well done! You've earned the tennis, now all you've got to do is play like a champion and thrash them to bits.'

'What if Olga plays like Steffi Graf? And whatshisname like Boris Becker – then we'll be in trouble.'

'I've heard they're good, but they can't be that good. Anyway, if it helps to flog the package of movies I have in mind for them, it'll be worthwhile.'

They left the car in the hotel car park and wandered across the road to the tennis centre. The club comprised a number of courts, all maintained to the highest quality with floodlights provided for evening play.

Hans and Olga were already knocking up on court when Bronte and Alex joined them. Introductions over, they parted to assemble in their respective halves to begin the process of assessing the opposition. Bronte had been an impressive player at school. She had an athletic build and could move about the court with lightning speed. Lack of practice had resulted in her game going a little rusty, but she still had plenty of power behind her shots and her serve/volley style soon began to give her opponents something to think about.

Alex was a steady baseline player. He rarely hit the ball out of court, but then again, was not renowned for hitting the winning shot. The Germans were quite clearly fiercely competitive players and, although extremely pleasant, gave little time to conversation. The serious spirit in which the game was played made Bronte a little nervous and in the first couple of games, she managed to hit a few returns into the net and, in her opening service game, produced two double faults.

The score in the first set was four-two to the Germans, when Bronte and Alex accelerated through the gears and decided to show them a thing or two. It all began when Olga threw the ball up to serve and did a complete over-reach, sending it spinning into the foot of the net. Her second serve was considerably weaker and brought Bronte forward, near to the half way line, making her mind up in a flash to return a well-disguised drop shot which fell cheekily just over the net. With a gigantic effort, Hans scrambled it back, lobbing it high over Bronte's head where it met the face of Alex's racquet for the return pass. That time, Olga, who had moved forward a little, angled her racquet for maximum spin and aimed low and hard in the direction of where Bronte hovered, bending in anticipation. She had it taped, even before it left Olga's racquet. She knew exactly which way it would travel and she was waiting for it, hyped up for the kill. Putting her full weight behind it, she slammed a powerful volley back cross-court right to Olga's feet where she was unable to do much more than a feeble flip of her racquet as it flew past her, landing on the baseline!

'Shot, Bronte!' cried Alex with a big smile of encouragement.

'Yes, vell played indeed,' muttered Hans.

It was the boost she needed. It paved the way for her service game which followed. She powered her first serves over the net, resulting in two clean aces, one of which was against Hans. Bronte managed to dart this way and that, retrieving impossible balls and turning them into winners, to the point that Alex felt he ought to keep out of her way and that she could do quite nicely without him. She felt like a woman possessed. Something was driving her from within, something out of her control and she was merely the object of its direction. It felt satisfying to slam her frustrations and emotions into that small white ball and once they had swept the first set six-four from under the feet of the Germans, there was no stopping her. Her confidence soared and she and Alex won the second set by six games to one!

They had reserved the court for just an hour and by the time the second set was over, it was already six-twenty. Not really time enough for a third, and besides, the match was already decided. Unexpectedly, the Germans turned out to be gallant losers, as Alex had begun to worry that after such a thrashing they would never consider buying his movies. However, as they shook hands at the net, they suggested that although they had to leave to prepare themselves for a cocktail party, Alex and Bronte should continue on the court for the last ten minutes and what time would Alex like them to come round to his stand for a meeting tomorrow? All was not lost after all, and Alex was much relieved because a German sale would certainly be a welcome boost to their annual turnover.

'A Steffi Graf in the making then?' he teased her, once the German pair were well out of sight and they were left knocking up for a few moments.

'Hardly. Just a lucky streak – that, and the strong desire to commit murder for some reason!' She smiled back at him.

'I guess that's understandable. But I'm glad you chose the tennis balls! I'm going to be really stiff tomorrow after all that running around. I haven't played for a month or two.'

'You're going to be stiff! What about me? I was the one doing the running around, not you. I'm also going to be looking my most attractive tonight with a bright red face and blisters on my hands.' She looked down at the skin on her thumb which was bubbling suspiciously and felt generally sore.

'It'll at least keep the lecherous foreign agents that you're always complaining about off you.' He reached for a lob she had deliberately thrown up to make him stretch himself.

'I wouldn't mind someone to talk to, if you don't mind. I only know a couple of people at Western. It's going to be one of those evenings when you walk into a room, knowing no-one, and have to latch yourself onto the first face that notices you and then spend the rest of the time looking down at your shoes, wishing to goodness you had polished them before you came out!'

'Don't you just love the television business!' he grinned.

'It's alright for you. You know everyone and those you don't know, you charm your way in with. It doesn't come that easily to me,' she defended herself.

'Hang on a minute . . .' He shot her a look before hitting a well-angled return from Bronte, straight into the top of the net. 'I'm not that bad.'

After checking his watch, he continued: 'Come on, Cinderella. If I'm going to have you back for quarter to seven, we need to get going. Grab the balls on your side and I'll get the one we sent over the netting.' He disappeared through a gate at the side of the court.

Once they were back in the car, they sped swiftly through the narrow streets, crossed the main dual-carriageway and headed further down towards the Croisette. He dropped her off outside the hotel, where a number of people returning from cocktail parties, late meetings or even just from their stands, streamed in through the swing doors and across the lobby to the lifts. Bronte felt conspicuous in her sporting gear and hoped that no-one important would see her and come to the conclusion that she had been skiving. She was in luck. No-one appeared to recognise her as she bowed her head, avoiding all eye contact and hurried up to her room.

There was not much time before she had to meet the assembled Western TV bus party at the Carlton. It would be embarrassing to miss the bus because there was bound to be a seating plan at dinner and her absence would surely be noticed. She wouldn't have really minded missing the evening that much, but she was curious to visit the Cap d'Antibes and she also tried to convince herself that it was bound to turn out better than she expected. At that time, she could have had no idea whatsoever just how the evening, which was about to change her life forever would unfold. She threw her skirt and shirt into a laundry bag, pausing only for a moment in front of the mirror to look at herself. She really should try to eat a little more. Her stomach was concave and she was certain that her breasts had shrunk. It was hard to keep weight on when she didn't feel hungry, and when she did, a mere few mouthfuls were sufficient. The shower felt as good as usual. It was the most relaxing and satisfying part of her daily routine. She closed her eyes and raised her head to the ceiling as the torrent of water rushed over her face and fell in rivulets down her smooth, brown body. She opened her eyes again and reached for the flannel, beginning to rub the soap up and down. As she rinsed the conditioner from her hair, she was tempted to stay there a few moments longer, but knew that she would already have to rush and reluctantly raised her arm to turn off the water supply.

Bronte wanted to appear chic and elegant that evening because in some way, what she wore often had the effect of boosting her confidence. She therefore decided on a black jacket with gold buttons and a short suede skirt.

It was seven fifteen, just time to gather her hair back into the velvet bow she had worn in the daytime and brush her wrists and neck with her new fragrance. Her clutch bag was barely big enough to take her hair brush as well as her lipstick and powder, but she managed to cram it shut on her way down the corridor.

It was a balmy evening and out on the street couples strolled romantically, either on their way to dinner or just for the sake of it. Once more feeling out of place because she was comparatively smartly dressed and was also un-accompanied, Bronte followed the cracks in the pavement with her eyes as she walked down the few blocks to the Carlton. She was in such a world of her own that she failed to notice Jane come pounding towards her from the opposite direction.

'You look dressed to kill! That jacket's fabulous. Is it new?'

Bronte stopped in her tracks.

'Oh, Jane you startled me. Um . . . the jacket – no, it's not that new.'

'Enjoy your evening, look forward to hearing all about it tomorrow. I heard that Jordan Innes, the Hollywood movie star, is staying there at the moment – hope you catch a glimpse!'

'Extremely unlikely, but I'll keep a look out. Enjoy your Eastern Europeans.'

'Cheers. I'm sure it'll be a bundle of laughs! See you.'

By then it was exactly seven thirty and Bronte stepped up the pace for the last hundred metres before she turned into the semi-circle driveway in front of the Carlton.

The Carlton was one of Cannes' most famous landmarks. Both its exterior and interior had been used as the backdrop to countless films and it became particularly prestigious during the annual Cannes film festivals each May. The terrace bar was humming with the sound of voices, as people downed their pre-dinner champagne. Once inside the impressive marble lobby, Bronte couldn't mistake her party because an obvious group was forming beside a magnificent indoor plant arrangement. She also noticed a couple of familiar Western TV faces amongst the gaggle. Her reservations simmered below the surface as she joined the party, not recognising anyone well enough to approach them directly. A round-faced Chinese woman of about forty smiled broadly and introduced herself as Shoji Shimoa. She wore a brightly coloured silk dress almost to her ankles which Bronte began by admiring.

'Ah, you must be Bronte Richardson? I'm Cheryl Dane from the PR department at Western. We're glad you could make it. You must know a few faces?'

'One or two, thanks. You're a relatively new producer for us, so I've only dealt with a couple of people so far.'

Cheryl had little time for Bronte's reply, as she moved on to welcome two further guests who had just arrived.

'I think that's everyone now.' Cheryl consulted her clip board. 'Could you all make your way to the bus which is waiting outside, please?' She smiled sweetly – too sweetly.

Bronte and Shoji, who were still standing beside one another, followed the rest of the group to the bus. Bronte counted between forty and fifty people as they queued up to step aboard. She felt more uncomfortable by the minute, but realised that it was an important PR exercise for her to go. Shoji had some difficulty lifting her tight silk dress high enough to make the step up but somehow managed by twisting her leg sideways. Bronte followed her down the bus about half way and for want of anywhere better to sit, slotted herself in beside Shoji. Glancing down the aisle as they pulled away from the Carlton, Bronte noticed that nearly every seat was occupied and she settled herself back, taking in the burble of conversation and the scenery which flashed by outside.

The journey lasted around thirty minutes during which she exchanged a few meaningless words with Shoji, mostly on the saleability of the Western TV programmes in their respective areas. The bus driver took them on the scenic route, giving all on board a rich view of France's famous coastline. As they negotiated the narrow winding roads, they could see the evening lights twinkling and dancing on the motionless treacle waters of the Mediterranean. On the streets, cafés spilled out onto the pavements as passers-by and locals alike supped their drinks to the sound of swaying French music, undisturbed by the intrusion of such an ugly bus on their harmonious tranquillity.

Inside the bus the voices died away one by one, as the passengers attempted to capture some of the external atmosphere and those with weaker stomachs prayed for an early deliverance from the feeling of nausea that the twists and turns imposed on them. They arrived in Antibes and drove up the road which circled round and round, leading to the famous hotel. It was a difficult manoeuvre turning the bus into the gateway and it necessitated several shunts back and forth before they finally drew to a halt at the top of the drive. There was a general feeling of relief amongst all concerned, to have actually arrived and be able to put two feet down on solid ground again.

As they wandered across the tarmac in the general direction of the hotel entrance, Bronte felt a hand on her shoulder and turned to find herself face to face with Brian Alvin, with whom she had corresponded at Western TV in recent months.

'Bronte, I didn't see you before. How are you? I was really sorry to hear about your husband.'

'Thanks, Brian. I'm OK. Being down here in Cannes and keeping busy is a good tonic. How are things with you?'

'Frantic, to tell you the truth. My girlfriend's coming down at the weekend and we're taking a few days much-needed holiday after all this is over.'

Bronte dwelled only momentarily on how she would be feeling at that moment, if she had Dominic to look forward to at the weekend. Dangerous road – she steered her mind away and scrambled back to the present.

'Have you met Sally, who's in charge of Scandinavia and some of our European business?'

Brian introduced her to a tall thin girl with a pale complexion and long dark hair, before he was accosted himself by an over-enthusiastic Italian couple.

Bronte turned to Sally: 'Hi, I'm Bronte Richardson. We handle Africa and the Caribbean for you. Have you been here before?' Bronte didn't really care but felt she should make the effort.

'No. I've only been with Western for eighteen months and they didn't come here last year. It's an amazing place! Simply dripping with movie stars during the film festival, so I'm told.'

Bronte, who didn't go in for star-gazing, was unimpressed as she held the door for Sally to pass through. They found themselves in a large clinical corridor which led to a reception room. It was an imposing room with elegant double doors into the dining room on one wall and at the opposite end, through a matching set of doors, one could see the bar area. Immediately ahead of them was a huge window, spanning the entire length of the room. Beyond that she could make out a terrace, gradually giving way to gentle sloping rocks and finally to the sea, which lapped cautiously at the heel of the rocks.

Sally had latched herself firmly on to Bronte for some unknown reason and, as they went to the window to admire the view, she just caught sight of Shoji sidling over, accompanied by a diminutive Indian gentleman who was not much taller than Shoji herself. Stiff-looking waiters served them with a welcome glass of Bucks fizz, while a couple of little waitresses buzzed in and out with delicately-prepared canapés.

'I say,' exclaimed Sally, in a voice which was just beginning to grate on Bronte's nerves, 'do you think this door opens?'

She tried turning the handle of the balcony door which instantly opened outwards, allowing them to go and sample the view for themselves. It would pass a little more time and besides, now that she had come all the way there, she might as well be able to tell people what it was like. They ambled out and wandered the length of the terrace towards the area in front of the bar windows. In the fast fading light, they managed to make out a path which wound down to a natural seawater rock pool with a diving board at one end. What a place to spend a holiday! It exuded relaxation and Bronte could drink in the scent of suntan lotion, mixed with dreamy champagne cocktails. She shivered; it was much too romantic for her present state of mind. She couldn't get carried away.

Sally's voice broke through the subtle roll of the sea: 'Look, I've got my camera here. I must have some photos! Would you all mind standing over there, sideways on to the sea so, hopefully, I can get some of the view as well as the hotel? Oh, thanks.'

Bronte, Shoji and her Indian companion obliged. Bronte couldn't help smiling at the incongruous-looking group, as she posed for Sally's camera. Sally was one of those infuriating people who had the most sophisticated camera possible and seemed to take hours to set and focus it for each picture. As she waited, her beauty standing out from the crowd like a jewel in a cluster of glass, Bronte glanced towards the bar window, just for a second.

That second was locked in time forever. She was drawn as if by magnets to those huge dark eyes, where she wallowed and drowned for a moment. Gradually the lips parted and grew steadily into the warmest, sexiest, cheekiest smile she had ever seen! The parting shot was a bronzed hand which rose up, and fingers which brushed through that dark ruffled hair, before his attentions were diverted to the blonde sitting in the chair with her back to the window. There was no doubting those looks. One of America's hottest movie stars, Jordan Innes, was even more attractive in the flesh than she had ever thought possible on screen!

She had heard through the grapevine that he was holidaying in the South of France and it was rumoured he would be giving a press conference during the festival. She had never, in a million years, expected to set eyes on him and was more surprised still by the effect which that brief moment of recognition had had on her. So startled was she at her reaction that she had blotted out every word which Sally had just thrown in her direction.

'Bronte? I said, would you mind awfully taking one with me in? I've set the focus so all you need do is point and press, as they say!' She chuckled in a most annoying fashion.

'What? Oh sorry, I was drifting. Yes, of course I'll do that. Give me the camera.' She stepped forward, struggling to drag herself to the present, unaware that from where he sat, Jordan, similarly transfixed, kept her under careful but concealed surveillance out of the corner of his eye.

'There you lot are!' Brian's voice called from the other end of the terrace. 'We're about to go into dinner – I thought you would like to know. I say, this is a fantastic view from here. I should think you'll have some great photos, Sal. Been here before, Bronte?'

Bronte, who had just about mastered the complications of Sally's camera, pressed the button to capture her waiting subjects, before responding to Brian.

'No, as a matter of fact, I haven't. Bet you wouldn't mind spending your holiday next week here.'

'A little out of my price range, I fear. Still, it's something to talk about back home. How are your drinks doing? Are you ready for top-ups yet?'

The little party retraced their steps back to the door, oblivious to the magnetic waves which had darted back and forth, waves which were abruptly shut outside to race on the warm sea breeze. Bronte glanced down the room to the bar as Brian led the way into dinner, but there was no sign of Jordan. Perhaps he was sitting out of sight? Or perhaps he had left? Or perhaps he was never there at all? But something had set her heart beating at a long-forgotten pace and it certainly wasn't the little Indian at her side, who suddenly blew his nose noisily into a blue and white striped handkerchief.

The dining room was equally spacious, with an L-shaped trestle table off to the right and more long glass windows to the left. Just inside the door was an elaborately-drawn seating plan, nailed to a board which was balanced precariously on a small easel. They gathered round, searching for their names and table numbers to establish where they would be condemned to sit for the next couple of hours. Bronte located herself on table four and as predicted, it turned out that she had been put beside Western's Spanish agent and the husband of their Latin American agent, whose English was even more patchy than that of the Spaniard. Brian was at least at their table and she hoped to goodness that she would be near enough to be included in his conversation.

Matters worsened when she arrived at the table to find Brian on the opposite side of the circular shape, and in front of each place, the starter which consisted of a rich-looking liver pâté glared up at her. The Latino graciously pulled the chair out for her and made sure she was settled, before sitting down next to her and enveloping her in a nauseating cloud of cheap aftershave.

It became clear that apart from the Spanish agent, who obviously had something going with the Greek female agent on his left, none of the rest of the table were acquainted with each other. Wine and mineral water were politely distributed, as were figure of eight bread rolls on which to scoop the high-smelling pâté. After much stopping and starting and embarrassed smiles, Bronte managed to establish that the Latino and his wife came from Mexico. She immediately regretted bringing up the recent earthquake, because she was then subjected to a drawn out, graphic description of how their house had been destroyed and the story of their own lucky escape, as she chased a piece of cucumber round her plate. He seemed to have verbal diarrhoea which was impossible to cure. At least he required very little prompting and it was one step better than sitting in stony silence.

The Spaniard still had his eyes glued down the Greek's cleavage and had completely failed to acknowledge Bronte's existence, when the waiter approached their table, beckoning them to help themselves to the main course from the buffet.

'Sorry you seem to be having a bit of a hard time with the guys on either side of you,' Brian apologised as they stood together in the queue, 'but it's impossibly difficult to talk much across that table.'

'I know, it's OK. Etel's husband is very nice. It's just that he doesn't seem to draw breath and I only manage to understand about one word in six that comes out of his mouth!' she giggled.

'Etel's not much better. And as for Jose, all he seems to be interested in is how quickly he can get Voula into bed!'

'Oh, so you noticed too. We'd better keep our voices down, the love birds are right behind us.' Bronte hushed to a whisper.

'They wouldn't notice if the earth opened up and they fell in.'

'I'm not so sure. Anyway, I've got to go back and sit next to him.'

'Yes, I'd forgotten. Poor you.' He handed her a white china plate when they reached the buffet.

A splendid array of hot and cold food dazzled them – ranging from lobster to steak, to king prawns and to individual poussins, all magnificently adorned with intricate decorations. The salads and vegetables competed side by side, each dish as appetising as the one before. There was a big temptation to try everything, to pile your plate far higher than you could possibly manage to eat. Bronte however, helped herself to a few moderate portions and waited for Brian, who seemed determined to cover any trace of white china on his plate.

'Is that all you're having? I noticed you didn't eat the pâté. You'll fade away.' Brian was genuinely concerned.

'I don't have meat and just at the moment, I'm not a great eater.'

'Yes of course, sorry. Anyhow, the lobster looks pretty good. Hope you fare a little better with your dinner companions this time.'

He left her at her place with a knowing grin. She gave him an equally knowing smile and picked up her napkin before returning to her seat. The Spaniard remained oblivious of her and the Latino rattled on as before. They did at least achieve some conversation which included other people at the table, but that did little to relieve the monotony which dragged on through the sweet course and into the coffee.

There was the usual round of speeches to endure after dinner. The first was from the Managing Director of Western Television who managed to spend nine minutes welcoming them to the Cap d'Antibes! Next came the Director of International Sales who enthused about the figures achieved in the last twelve months and hoped those would long continue. Finally, the Financial Director stood up and delivered a long speech on the escalating costs of programme production and the way ahead for the future. Everyone in the room, including the speakers themselves, was glad when the formalities were over and people were then free to move about and chat to other tables. Bronte had the desperate urge to escape for a few minutes – the loo, outside – anywhere where she could take a deep breath and just be herself, alone. Jordan Innes crept uncannily back into her thoughts.

She excused herself from her table, on which only six people were left and weaved past the other tables towards the exit. She knew she wouldn't be missed for a few moments as she searched for the ladies' room. As one might have expected, the powder room was lavish and comfortable. There were easy chairs, magazines and ample supplies of hand lotion, hair spray and expensive-smelling soaps. Shoji had beaten her to it and was combing her hair when Bronte opened the door.

'Ah . . . Bronte. How was your meal? Good . . . yes?' she enquired.

'Yes, fine thanks. I didn't have a very easy table though.'

'No? That's a shame. I was lucky and met some very interesting new people.'

'Excuse me, Shoji, I'm just popping in here.'

She dived into a cubicle. Deliberately taking her time, she emerged to find the room empty. She checked her face in the gilt edged mirror, pawing at the skin on her cheeks to look for threatening lumps. Once she had touched up her lipstick, she left the room cautiously lest anyone should see that she did not intend re-joining the party right away. Instead she stole across the reception room and hurried through the terrace door, like a thief in the night. Turning right and away from the bar area, she headed down a prettily-paved path on to the level below. There she found a manicured garden and in the centre, a large water fountain which was lit by subtle underwater bulbs. There was a low, flat stone rim just wide enough to perch on and she decided to rest for a while with her back to the hotel, facing out to sea.

The water had a little more life to it than before and every once in a while, it charged at the rocks, only to retreat just as quickly before re-gathering its strength. Directly ahead, the moon shone silently down creating a golden shaft of light which shimmered and danced as the sea constantly changed its mood. The air was warm and strong and folded around her like a kind of protection, as it breathed on and toyed with the wisps of hair which fell around her face.

The hairs on the back of her neck stood up and she froze when she heard footsteps coming down the path in her direction. She sat rigid, not daring to turn round and willing them to leave her alone. No-one knew she was there and she was certain that she would not be missed from the party. A polite cough behind her.

'Uhm . . . excuse me, mind if I join you?'

The voice was like liquid chocolate and the American drawl unmistakable. She stood up, startled, and all at once became awkward.

'I'm really sorry if I frightened you. I'll go if you like?'

'N. . . no problem,' she managed to stammer. 'Please, be my guest. It's just that I wasn't expecting anyone and I was miles away.'

As he passed in front of her, the lights from the water fountain shone into his deep, mystical eyes and highlighted that smile which had haunted her for the last two hours. He wore a pair of black jeans with a white sweatshirt and the overall effect in the moonlight was electric.

Where was her self control? She had to get a grip of herself because about the only three things she did know about Jordan Innes, apart from some of the films in which he had starred, were that he was thirty years old, married to a Swedish model and was the father of a beautiful little girl.

He sat down beside her and leaning forward with his elbows on his knees, turned to look into Bronte's face:

'Allow me to introduce myself, I'm Jordan.'

That was an understatement! He certainly required no introduction as far as Bronte was concerned. For some reason, which she tried to figure out long afterwards, she was glad that he had only said 'Jordan', and not 'Jordan Innes', in a sort of, 'don't you know who I am?' way.

'. . . and I'm Bronte.'

'OK, so you're English. I thought so.'

CHAPTER FIVE

'It's quite a night out there.' He rested his chin on his palms and gazed out over the water.

'It's a lot more peaceful out here than it is in there.' She inclined her head in the direction of the dining room.

'I saw you earlier up there. What were you doing with that strange crowd of people? Were they friends of yours?'

'No, no, Heaven forbid!' she laughed and then again overcome by nerves, began to twist one of the corkscrews at the side of her face.

'So you're here on vacation then? Or are you part of that group?'

'Vacation – I wish! No, the dinner is being hosted by Western Television for their sales agents.'

'Of which you're one?'

'You could say. Our company represents their programmes, mostly in third world countries like Africa and the Caribbean.'

'That sounds pretty neat. So you do that yourself?'

'Yes, for my sins,' she grinned, forgetting for a moment that there she was, all by herself in the gardens of one of the French Riviera's most acclaimed hotels, talking to a film star whom many girls would have given their right arms to meet.

'Does that mean travelling a lot? Do you get to see those places?'

'I go to each television station once a year. It's not really all it's cracked up to be. Most of my time is spent in 'planes, hotels and taxis, it's not like having a holiday.'

'I can imagine. I guess you get to meet all sorts of interesting people on your trips though?'

'Sometimes.' She refrained from adding that she had never met anyone like him and probably never would again.

69

'So, tell me Bronte, how'd you like Bermuda? I take it you sell there too?'

'Yes, we do. It's a small market for us but I love to visit because it's more civilised. I've been there about three times now. I've never found it hot at the time of year I've been, but sometimes it's a relief to escape from the humidity.'

'We have a little place there. We use it as our retreat. There's times when you need the sanctuary of a small island and I really love the great British feel about Bermuda. All those colonial buildings and bizarre shorts they wear!'

'Whereabouts is your house?' She felt that was a safe and non-leading question.

'It's just a small beach house, but it's pretty much on its own. We don't manage to get down there enough but when we do, it's a wonderful place to be. So you must be here for that television thing over in Cannes?'

'Yup. Just for the week.'

'You like it down here?' His conversation was relaxed and put her more and more at ease, as she began to come out of the awe-struck, tongue-tied state he had put her in initially.

'It's a great place for a festival. I've been here a few times now, but it's always pretty much the same each time I come. One of the days, it'd be nice to make it down here on holiday.'

'You live in London? I've got to be in London soon.'

'Yes. I've got a flat in Fulham. At least it's not mine, we . . . I rent it.'

'How long have you been in this business?'

'About five years now. I work for a great little company and we're all like part of a family.'

'Sounds good. You like what you do?' He leant back, propping himself on his arms and stretching his legs out before him.

'It's a living. I've never really sat and analysed it that closely.'

'That's not unlike me. I act. I direct. It's a living. But I find escapism in what I do. Life's tough a lot of the time and playing the part of somebody else, living in another person's shoes if you like, switches you away from your own life. It kind of puts your life on hold while you take up someone else's.'

'Are you working down here?' Another safe question.

'Partly. Actually, I'll be in Cannes tomorrow. My agent's fixed a press conference.'

She asked: 'Have you been in the Palais before?' and immediately regretted it, because what film star had not attended at least one of the festivals there?

'Yes, I was down at this year's movie festival in May, but briefly. I think we only made it for one night that time.'

She sneaked the odd glance in his direction. His long muscular legs were flung casually out, while she had kept hers firmly crossed and tucked underneath her. His profile was as perfect as his face full on, with a well angled jaw bone leading to stylishly cropped hair, combed back at the sides but left ruffled on top. He had dark eyebrows, a deep forehead and a cute-shaped nose.

'So what brings you out here, all by yourself when you should be living it up at that party?'

'That's a really uninteresting story.'

'Try me.' He smiled warmly down on her.

'You don't want to hear about it, believe me.'

'It'd make a change from people hearing about me. I'm a good listener.'

'OK ... I came tonight, not because I really wanted to, but more because I had to – out of duty. In other words, I felt I would be conspicuous by my absence if I didn't. Frankly I hardly know anyone, not that that's any real problem, but I have just spent two hours being completely ignored by a Spaniard on one side and listening to the pidgin-English ramblings of a Mexican on the other!'

'You've got my sympathy. No wonder you opted for out here. All I can say is that the Spaniard needs his eyes testing and the Mexican was pretty lucky to have you to himself for two hours!'

She was embarrassed. She hadn't anticipated his flattery, but when it came it was somehow natural. He didn't appear to be implying anything – after all, he was there with his wife who Bronte later realised had been the blonde with him in the bar.

'I bet your boyfriend wouldn't have approved of your dinner companions. Or are you married?'

She took a deep breath. She mustn't bore him with the story of Dominic, he surely wouldn't be interested. There was absolutely no reason for a man of his position to care about her problems. But how to answer that one?

'I was.'

'Divorced?'

As she turned away from him, he saw the pained expression on her face and suddenly and quite unexpectedly, he had the overwhelming desire to reach out and touch her – nothing sexual, just a fellow soul in trouble.

'No. Look, it's still hard to talk about, but my husband was killed in a road accident.'

'It was recent wasn't it?' he asked her softly.

'Yes,' she swallowed hard. She must not cry, on any account. She forced herself to turn back and look at him and what she saw, melted her heart. His hand was outstretched towards her on the stone rim, not touching her but extended like a bond. His face bore a message of understanding – not patronising, but genuine support as his eyes drove far, far into hers and bore on into her soul.

'I lost my parents in a 'plane crash when I was small. I guess it's not like losing a partner, but at the time it devastated my world. I've got an idea of what you're going through.'

'It's not easy. Sometimes I can talk about it and other times I can't. Some people I see come right out with it, which in many ways is better to cope with, but others seem to be avoiding me because they don't know what to say.'

'Are you managing OK back home? You have family and such?'

'I've got good friends but I'm not too strong on family ties. My mother died when I was five and my father married again soon afterwards. They live in the north of England now.'

'Will you carry on with your job?'

'I have to. I need an income and right now, it's seeing me through the worst. This trip's helping. Cannes is never something I shared with Dominic, so there are no haunting memories.'

'That's something. Have you thought about uprooting and taking off some place?'

72

'Like where?'

'Anywhere. The States perhaps?'

'The thought had crossed my mind, but it'd have to be something pretty tempting to get me to go. It comes down to a conflict of securities. I have that in my job and would need something concrete to go to.'

'What about the TV industry? You must have some contacts there?'

'It might be worth asking around, but I'd feel bad about leaving my boss because he's been really wonderful, especially since the accident.'

'Sounds like a hell of a guy and if he is, I'm sure he'd want you to be happy and get on with your life.'

'Thinking of it like that, you're probably right.'

'You don't own your apartment so there's no problem there. You should think seriously about it. You have to rebuild your life after something tragic like that.'

'Yes, 'Dad'!' she smiled at him.

He laughed and shook his head.

'God, am I lecturing that badly? I've got no grounds to organise anyone else's life until I've got my own house in order.'

She began to feel as if she had known him for a thousand years instead of nearly an hour. His company felt so easy and natural. She felt she had met him before. They had been friends, family, even lovers – not there but in another time. They rode the same wave. They understood each other without words and yet he was a complete stranger. A man adored by millions but known by few. She was privileged enough to enjoy his exclusive time for just a short spell, time that was probably worth thousands of dollars.

'So what brings you out here now?' The questions need not be so safe.

'Chelsea's gone to bed, she's had too much sun today. It was early and . . .' he paused, 'the only trouble with this place is that it's too quiet for me. We come here to wind down and relax for a couple of days, but once you've done that, there's really not much else to do. I've got a lot on at the moment and if I go to bed early, I only lie awake. That answer your question?'

'Yes, I think it does.' Bronte couldn't help daring to wonder for a second, whether he had seen her come out and followed her. Later she discovered that the suite in which he and Chelsea were staying did not overlook that side of the hotel and he could not possibly have seen her.

She glanced down at her watch.

'Oh help, I'd forgotten the time. I must go. I really hope I haven't missed the bus back.' She stood up and listened. She had been oblivious to the silence from the dining room. The sound of voices had long been replaced by the murmur of the sea. Jordan got up too, standing a couple of inches taller than her.

'I hope your coach hasn't turned into a pumpkin, Cinderella.'

She chuckled, still hovering between the need to run and the desire to stay and talk some more.

'What's funny?' He melted her once more with his smile.

'Oh, sorry. Nothing, it's just that that's the second time I've been called Cinderella today.'

'Careful, or it'll stick. Well, Bronte . . . I don't even know your last name, I guess this is goodbye.'

'Richardson . . . and I suppose you're right.'

Both seemed reluctant to part.

'Thanks for the company, it's been really great meeting you. You should think seriously about fleeing the nest. You deserve good things in your life.'

His words penetrated her soul but she did not object to the intrusion.

'I'm glad I met you too. My girlfriends'll be really jealous!'

He took a step towards her and ever so gently, resting one hand lightly on her shoulder, brushed her cheek with his lips.

'Take care of your life, it's precious,' and he was gone, without so much as a backward glance, along a different path which she presumed led to the bedrooms and suites.

She turned on her heels and fled back towards the upper level and the familiar terrace where it had really all begun. She flung open the door and rushed inside, only to find to her horror that there was no-one to be seen and all the tables in the dining room had been cleared. Checking her watch, she realised that it was twelve fifteen and it began to dawn on her that the bus was long gone and had left without a thought for her. Perhaps that was a little unfair. She had wandered off of her own free will, after all and, as it was dark, they had probably not noticed that one person was missing.

What was she to do? Walking was out of the question, it was much too far. She could hardly go to the reception desk and ask for Jordan Innes' suite number! It wasn't his fault she had been left behind and besides, his wife would probably have something to say about their little meeting, innocent though it undoubtedly had been.

There was nothing else for it but to see if the hotel would order her a taxi. Luckily, the receptionist spoke perfect English because she was so fazed by the whole evening, that although her French was not all that bad, she found she couldn't string two words together!

She only had to wait about fifteen minutes before she saw a set of headlights come up the drive. She was immediately worried that she wouldn't have enough to pay the taxi fare back to Cannes, but was relieved to establish when she stepped inside that it would only cost four hundred francs which would be more than covered by the five hundred franc note she had slipped into her purse that evening – just in case.

As she sank into the warm leather upholstery, some unknown force drew her attention back towards the hotel. As she glanced up she saw a face at a third-floor window. The black and white silhouette gave her the distinct impression that it was Jordan. She was probably wrong, but if not . . .

CHAPTER SIX

Bronte had finally pulled the covers around her shoulders at one fifteen that night. She was glad she had been able to avoid the hotel bar because she desperately needed to be alone in her room with her thoughts. After all, it wasn't every day she met someone like Jordan Innes and she wanted to relive and savour their short time together and to imprint firmly on her mind the image of how he had appeared to her. She needed to remember his clothes, his face and that unforgettable smile, because, although she was unlikely ever to see him again, she would always remember that evening.

Sleep was understandably distant. She lay there, examining the dark, not really wanting to shut her eyes in case she awoke and found it had all been a dream. Perhaps it had. Perhaps she had drunk too much somewhere along the line and had created in her head a wonderful man who could maybe fill the gap in her heart left by Dominic. But that wasn't entirely true, because no-one would ever be able to take Dominic's place. They would have to find a new avenue of their own, when the time was right.

She must have dropped off eventually because she woke to the sound of the alarm, which rudely shattered her dreams. It had been important to remember to set the alarm before getting into bed, because that morning she had a breakfast meeting at the Carlton and she must not be late. Jordan's memory, with a strange sense of him being a friend and ally, was still etched on her mind as she clocked herself in and out of the shower in record time. It was a weird feeling. There was an undeniable physical attraction, but there was a moral barrier too – either Dominic or his wife, she couldn't tell. Delving deeper into the recesses of her mind as she put an outfit together for the day ahead, she began to wonder whether what she really felt was gratitude towards him for stirring up certain emotions within her – for the first time since they had been numbed that day back in the office in London. He had made her realise that just maybe she was entitled to a life again and perhaps it was right to bury Dominic peacefully in the back of her mind?

It was already quarter to eight and she was on the go again. She gathered up the papers needed for her meeting and dashed out of the door, letting her hair fly around any way it chose.

She was in such a hurry that she didn't see Donna emerge from the other lift until they were nearly through the swing doors leading to the Croisette.

'Bronte, what's the rush? Where are you off to?'

'Oh, hi Donna. I'm supposed to be at a Screentel breakfast meeting at the Carlton in a few minutes.'

'I'm heading down to the Majestic for breakfast with Alex. He wants to go over a few things and no doubt have me running around for most of the day. I'll walk as far as the Carlton with you.'

'How did you and Jane get on last night? I did think of you,' Bronte asked.

'Pretty grim really. It was jolly hard trying to make yourself understood and once you got over the 'whereabouts do you come from?' and 'what's the weather like there now?' conversation, there really wasn't too much to talk about. What was your evening like?'

'Oh, much as expected.' Jordan was her secret for the time being, until she was ready to share the experience, or until she had really sorted it out for herself. 'I had a really difficult table place next to some Spanish agent who didn't say a word to me all night and a Mexican who was friendly enough, but a bit tedious.'

'I bet you got some amazing food though, didn't you? I remember when we went there it was absolutely delicious!'

'I wasn't all that hungry but the lobster was definitely worth writing home about.'

'And what about the hotel? Did you have a chance to snoop around at all?'

'Not much. A few of us went out on to the terrace overlooking the sea before dinner, but apart from that, we only really saw what we were meant to see.'

'Any sign of famous faces?' Donna was fishing.

'Sorry to disappoint you, but none that I recognised.' She prayed that lie wouldn't have its repercussions. 'Was Jane OK last night? Despite the company, was she pleased with the way dinner went?'

'She was certainly glad they all turned up – granted they were late, but at least they were there. I don't know whether it was the strong liqueurs they kept serving at dinner, or whether she had too much when we went for a drink afterwards, but she was all over everyone in the bar!'

'Really? That's most unlike Jane. Did they mind?' Bronte was intrigued.

'On the contrary. As you would expect, everyone was having a whale of a time – they couldn't get enough of her!'

'Poor old Jane. I bet she'll be in for some teasing today.'

'I only hope she's OK now and not too hungover. I did escort her to her room and she assured me she'd be fine. I must say, it was all really rather amusing though. Oh, and your friend Mike was in there asking after you – I think that may have been what started Jane off. Dutch courage and all that. Why didn't you come and join us?'

'I sneaked in around one-ish. I did contemplate the bar . . .' (again she crossed her fingers and hoped for the best) 'but it looked so crowded and smoky and I knew I had to be up for the meeting this morning. Besides, Mike might think I'm after him if I keep showing up where he is!'

'More like he's after you, judging by the night before last.'

Bronte detected a note of sarcasm, but knowing that Donna had a heart of gold and a habit of speaking her mind, she ignored it.

'I hear you thrashed the Germans last night on the tennis court?'

'We got it together in the end. It's ages since I last played and I really screwed up to begin with.'

'That's not what Alex said when we ran into him in the street last night. He was full of it. In fact he was so keen on the whole game that he insisted I play with him tonight and find another couple!'

Bronte was relieved not to have to play again that day.

They crossed the side street before the Carlton, mindful of the excitable French drivers who systematically ignored all road signs, zebra crossings and, in particular, pedestrians, and ploughed ahead.

'You coming to the Palais after this?' asked Donna, as they slowed their pace, level with the hotel.

'Yes, I've got a nine-thirty appointment. Oh, and that reminds me – if you get into the bunker before I do, would you be a darling and make sure Alexandra has reserved me a screening room? It'd be really embarrassing if I had nowhere to meet the Ethiopians, having made such a fuss about wanting to show all this fabulous new programming to them.'

'I'll try and remember. You'd better hurry, you'll be late. See you later.'

'Bye – tell Alex I hope he's not too stiff!'

'You can tell him yourself, later,' Donna twinkled.

Unsure of her destination once inside the marble enclosure, Bronte asked the bell captain where the Screentel meeting was being held. The charming man, who was obviously just as charmed by Bronte, came out from behind his desk and led her part of the way towards the room reserved for the meeting. She followed her nose and his directions down a plushly-decorated corridor and turned right half way along, into an extensive room with elaborate velvet drapes, gathered at each side by thick cord and gold fringed tassels. A long oak table was laid for breakfast, with glasses of fresh orange juice beside baskets of warm croissants and pastries. Pots of coffee were set down at intervals with little jugs of frothy milk at each side.

Already half of the places were occupied and as there was no obvious seating plan, Bronte opted for the chair nearest to her and slid into it, setting her briefcase down neatly at her feet. She smiled in recognition of a small, grey-haired man at the head of the table, whom she recognised as the President of the company. Beside him, she noticed Melissa Firth who was Bronte's day-to-day contact.

A red-veined, overweight and slightly sweaty New Zealander introduced himself as Bob Rosden and offered to pour some coffee into her cup.

'Thanks. No, just black, thank you.' She refused the frothy milk.

'So where are you from, Bronte?' He was already stuffing his mouth full of Danish pastries.

'We're based in London, but operate pretty much all over.' She went into the barest essential details of her particular responsibilities and was a little relieved when a lady sat down on the other side of Bob, thus diverting his attention temporarily. It gave her the opportunity to sip her coffee while taking a look around to see who else had been roped into the meeting.

She couldn't hide a knowing smile when she recognised the Spanish agent from the night before, sitting on the other side of the table with his arm resting quite suggestively on the chair of the same Greek lady who had held him spellbound the previous evening! She, for her part, wore an even more plunging neckline than the one she had chosen for the Western TV dinner and Bronte (as well as the rest of the room, if they cared to) couldn't help but notice a heaving bosom which spilled forth every so often. It was a fairly revolting sight from a woman well into middle age and Bronte wondered why, when they had probably spent all night romping it up together, they couldn't save the petting for the bedroom where, in their case, it most definitely belonged.

Unnoticed by most people in the room, probably because he was so small, the President had got to his feet. As this did not seem to stem the hum of conversation, he picked up his cereal spoon and banged it loudly on the table several times.

'I would like to thank you all for coming here this morning and to welcome you to our agents' breakfast meeting.'

There was a polite titter.

Although they were an inescapable part of the job, Bronte did find the agents' gatherings somewhat monotonous, particularly when they began at such an anti-social hour. She stifled a yawn.

'I would like to begin by drawing your attention to the three brochures in front of you.' He picked up his own copies and held them aloft. 'We are very excited about the potential for these new shows and I would ask you to please study the details while I give you some further information.'

He then proceeded to rattle off the synopsis, production expectations, sales estimations and other particulars which Bronte found hard to take in just then. She picked up her pencil and absent-mindedly flicked open her spiral notepad and began to doodle. Her mind wandered dangerously from the present, only to be snapped sharply back to the meeting when she realised that the President had sat down and the ruddy-faced New Zealander beside her had taken the floor. She had no idea how long she had been away or what she had missed, but hoped that it was nothing too vital.

'Thank you, Bob.' The President was speaking again. 'And next, Bronte, could you give us a résumé of the current sales potential in Africa and the Caribbean?'

Bronte hated being put on the spot and she was certain he had noticed her not listening and had deliberately decided to pick on her next. It was fortunate that she had planned for the meeting in the run-up to the festival before they left London and she had come prepared with notes of current offerings in her territories. Had she not, she most certainly would have made a complete and utter nonsense of her reply. As it was, while she fished in her folder for the appropriate details, she composed herself admirably and got to her feet.

She beamed down the room. It was a trick she had learnt previously and it always helped to steady her nerves and win votes on to her side.

'Right now, we are very encouraged by the news of up to three new television stations starting up in Trinidad and another in Jamaica. This will undoubtedly have the effect of introducing competition into the market place, resulting in increased programme appetite and internal price wars, which can only be positive for television distributors . . .' She did her best to give the impression that it was spontaneous and kept her notes as concealed as possible. She managed to carry on for nearly five minutes, at the same time impressing those around her with her business acumen and detailed knowledge of her territories.

'That was most enlightening.' The President spoke once more. Then the dreaded bit, where he would fire out questions and she would really have to concentrate.

'. . . and do you believe cable television will be active in all your markets in the near future?'

That one at least, was answerable.

'If sufficient choice is not presented to the viewer on each island in the form of several TV channels, there is an inevitable opening for cable enterprise.'

'How can this choice be implemented and is that being done?' Before he gave her the chance to answer, he threw a comment out to the others in the room: 'We, like all other production companies, are most concerned about the piracy which seems to be rife on a number of these cable channels worldwide. I would be glad to hear other opinions on this subject in a moment. Sorry, Bronte . . .' He gave the smile of one in authority.

'I think half the battle will be won if the television stations themselves become more aware of this problem before independent cable has the chance to get off the ground. They need to counteract it by providing alternative viewing now. They need to utilise existing facilities and open new channels or subscription services. The problem here in the smaller countries is the funding for this kind of expansion.'

He seemed momentarily satisfied on that point and posed one last question to her: 'Our three new shows – what sort of potential could we expect from your markets?'

He had noticed her not paying attention! What a mean trick, he had done that on purpose and now she was really stuck because she had no idea what the programmes were about, or if they were even suitable for her stations! Her cheeks began to hot up. She mustn't pause too long because that would emphasise her panic.

Come on, Bronte, bullshit for all you're worth, she thought to herself.

'To make a proper assessment, I really need to see some viewing cassettes and talk to one or two buyers.' She heard a couple of agreements from people around her and was relieved. 'Do you have screening material available yet?' There, throw the ball back into his court.

'We'll send you some. Melissa, please make a note.'

Phew! Her turn was over. She took her seat once more and gulped some orange juice down to revive her. Each person in the room was asked to take the spotlight for the same scrutiny, even Melissa, who issued pleas for more organised administrative co-operation in some camps. Finally, the President drew the session to a close at nine fifteen, with more words of thanks and appreciation for the marvellous job they were all doing, spreading the Screentel name across the world.

Bronte couldn't escape fast enough. If she wasn't there when the Ethiopians pitched up, it was just like them to take off, never to be seen again. As she had already set an appointment with Melissa for later in the week, there was no need to linger.

The sun smiled down again that morning. Really, they were very lucky with the weather because it had been known to rain every day at some of the previous festivals. The pavement was heaving as she battled towards the Palais, giving up the fight when she came across a roped-off section in front of a demolished building. She retired to the other side of the road.

As she neared the side entrance of the Palais, she noticed a small crowd assembling. They were obviously awaiting some celebrity, because there were a number of reporters with cameras at the ready. As she tried to reach the doors, she was stopped about a hundred metres short by a couple of French gendarmes, who were making room for an extended black limousine to creep forward onto the tarmac beside the Palais.

Drawing level with where Bronte was standing behind a gendarme who had both his arms outstretched, as if trying to prevent a crush (which was rather unlikely, because although there were a few interested parties, most people seemed happy enough to continue about their business) she had a split second view of the person in the back seat.

Her heart skipped a beat, for there, large as life in a black leather jacket, sat Jordan! For the second time in just over twelve hours, it was as if the earth stood still as their eyes met and held for what was the merest second, but felt like an eternity. Mutual recognition flickered briefly in both expressions and then was gone. He was swept towards the waiting flash bulbs and poker-faced photographers who shoved forward, each determined to be in the front line for the best picture. She slipped away to screen to her Ethiopians. But there was no mistaking that familiar smile and haunting eyes and she knew that he had seen her too.

Having no idea whatsoever of how she made it across that final stretch to the door of the Palais, she found herself searching in her bag for her identity pass, before bowing her head and rushing headlong down the stairs, lost in thought.

CHAPTER SEVEN

It was all she could do to keep her mind focused on the small screen in front of her. She sat in silence, apart from the noise of the television, in the tiny screening room with two strapping Ethiopian gentlemen. Her buyers had arrived at her stand early. Wonders would never cease, she thought, as she approached the seats which they had been allocated by Alexandra. There was no time for dreams – it was strictly business in that room and she had to conduct it in her usual efficient manner, giving no hint of the turmoil which was erupting inside her.

She could tell from the shuffling of papers that they had seen enough of the wildlife documentary and realised that she needed to hot up the tempo to hold their attention.

'Next, we have a brand-new mini series, which is a dramatisation of a best-selling novel. It played recently on the BBC over two weeks, in an eight to ten evening slot and the ratings were extremely good for both episodes. Do you think this type of programme would work well for you? It should be good commercially.'

There was a nod and a grunt from the one nearest to her and she decided to put it on anyway. It was one of the best new things she had to offer and if they didn't like it, well that was just tough. They didn't know what they were missing.

As it turned out, they did decide to buy the programme after an involved conference, during which Bronte excused herself to go and fetch refreshments and give herself a little breather.

There was not much communication during the rest of their meeting but, having visited their station a couple of times, Bronte wasn't too surprised. After an hour and a quarter of screening, they presented her with a list of programmes in which they were interested and then asked her to send them audition cassettes for each title! She swallowed hard and remained polite.

'Certainly, we can arrange to despatch those immediately,' hoping to goodness that the producers to whom the cassettes belonged, wouldn't mind. 'Now, the little matter of your outstanding account with us . . .'

They promised to do their best to settle all their debts within the next two months. If that really happened (and Bronte knew it wouldn't and that they were probably just playing for time until they could escape from her room) it would be a first. She wasn't sorry when they stood up, thanked her for her time and took their leave, muttering something about being late for a ten thirty meeting.

Alexandra looked up from her post at the reception desk.

'I think there is something wrong with the air conditioning today. All the stands, they are hot. Would you like another drink?'

'I'm sure she would and so would I!' Mike swept onto the stand in a haze of aftershave. 'And how are my favourite ladies today? I missed you last night – don't tell me you crept off early?'

'I thought you were supposed to be really busy down here?' Bronte couldn't help laughing.

'I am – but now and again, there's the odd cancellation and so here I am to check on your welfare.'

'I'm touched. What do you want to drink?'

'Nothing too healthy. Regular coffee'll do – plenty of sugar.'

'Thanks, Alexandra. Mineral water, please.'

'Your room free?' he motioned towards the screening room.

'Yes, at the moment. Why?'

'I've got a sailing programme I want to get you to see.'

'OK, let's take a look.'

She took the VHS cassette from his hand and went to put it into the machine. 'Do take a seat.'

He had already done so.

'You need some air con in here.'

'I know. I've just had a meeting with two guys from Ethiopia and one of them was a heavy smoker.'

'I'll say! Anyhow, so where were you last night then?'

'I thought we'd come in here to look at your programme?'

'That, and a chat and a momentary escape from our stand. The President's flown in today and he's driving us all mad. So, last night . . .?'

'My, we are concerned! I told you yesterday or the day before, I was going to Antibes on a Western TV agents' dinner.'

'That's right, and what about the bar afterwards?'

She giggled: 'I've heard all about that from Donna this morning. You are naughty! What on earth did you do to Jane?'

He raised his hands in all innocence: 'I didn't force those scotches on her, she ordered them all by herself. The fact that I was also on them doesn't come into it.'

'She didn't try and keep up with you, did she?'

'I really wasn't counting.'

'She must have a major crush on you.'

'People have been known to suffer from that, you know.'

'Oh, stop it! If she's in there tonight, don't you dare go leading her on.'

'Me? I'm a happily-married man, or as good as. You know me, harmless to a fault.'

'I know that, but she probably doesn't.'

'Anyway, I'm off on a little trip out of town tonight, so I'll more than likely give the bar a miss . . . unless I thought that you might be there, of course.'

Alexandra leaned in with the coffee and water.

'I'm not going to tell you either way, you can keep guessing. Now, what's this programme about that has been on for nearly ten minutes?'

'It's a new series we're thinking about taking on. It highlights the different major sailing races in the year. It goes into the history, the crews and techniques etc, that sort of thing. Think it'd sell in your places? We need to have some idea of the returns before we put up any guarantees.'

'How long is it and is there anything of local interest for us?'

'Thirteen half hours. I haven't seen them all but I think there's one set around Antigua and the Virgin Islands.'

'Might be worth a try. Better for the Caribbean than Africa, being islands and into sailing. Have you got any literature?'

'Yes, here you go. Come back to me with a few estimates, will you?'

'I'll bring it up at my screenings this week.'

'Right, business over. What else is in your diary?'

'Lunch with buyers from Zimbabwe.'

'Sounds wonderful.'

'You should join us. It'd be good for you to meet some of our buyers.'

'Very sorry, but I'm lunching with guys from the Beeb sports department. Otherwise, you know I'd love to.'

'Of course.'

He checked his watch.

'I'd best get going. Shame we can't crash on the beach, it's a real pearler of a day out there. Still, never mind we're all in the same boat. I'm out of here but look, let's run into each other later?'

He got up and took the cassette back from her, shoving it into his bulging briefcase.

'See you later, girls. Thanks for the coffee.'

He was gone.

The stand was comparatively quiet. Alex was just visible in the far meeting room with the Germans from last night and Donna and Jane were nowhere to be seen.

'Oh, Bronte, I have a message for you.' Alexandra bent down and took an envelope from a shelf marked 'Bronte'. 'A lady came by and left you this.'

Bronte took it from her hand and frowning, turned it over a couple of times. It was just marked 'Mrs Bronte Richardson – personal'. There was no company name or stand number and no other clue to be found on the outside. Instinct told her to open it in private so she thanked Alexandra and retreated back into the screening room, closing the door behind her.

The message was written in black ink on Cap d'Antibes notepaper. Her fingers shook as she read the words to herself:

BRONTE:
I HOPE THIS REACHES YOU, BECAUSE I REALLY DON'T KNOW HOW I'M GOING TO GET IT TO YOU.

I'VE SPENT A LOT OF TIME THINKING ABOUT WHAT YOU SAID LAST NIGHT AND I'VE GOT A PROPOSAL FOR YOU. I'VE TALKED IT OVER WITH CHELSEA AND WE NEED TO SPEAK AGAIN. CAN YOU MEET ME AFTER LUNCH, AROUND 3PM AT THE CARLTON HOTEL TERRACE?

He had signed the letter simply, 'Jordan'. She found it hard to believe it was real. But there it was, in black and white. Why her? He must meet hundreds of girls all the time. Why take an interest in her? And what 'proposal' could he possibly have in mind, that he had shared with his wife? She couldn't act to save her life, so he was wasting his time if that was the idea. Besides, they hadn't really talked about films at all last night. *He's been thinking about what I said* – she tried to recall in her mind just what they had talked about. But how had the letter reached the stand? Alexandra had said a woman brought it.

'Alexandra, can you come here a sec?' She popped her head out of the screening room and beckoned.

'What is it? Is something wrong? Not bad news?' Donna had filled Alexandra in on the details of Dominic's accident and she was worried lest Bronte had yet more troubles.

'No, I don't think so. When did this arrive?'

'About half an hour ago, just after I got back with the café for your friend.'

'And can you remember who brought it?'

'I think it was a lady from the MIP organisation. Yes, I remember she was French because she asked me where I lived in Cannes. Are you alright? You look very pale.'

'Yes I'm fine, thanks. It's just a meeting that I wasn't expecting, that's all.'

'Well, if you're sure, I must go and see to that gentleman who's just come on to the stand.'

'Sure, and thanks, Alexandra.'

How on earth would she wade through lunch with the two Zimbabweans with that hanging over her? The suspense was already killing her! She checked her diary to see what she had on at three – whatever it was, it had to be cancelled. That was one meeting she would make on time! He must have brought the letter with him from Antibes and for that matter, had it on his person when she saw him in the car. Then he must have given it to someone to deliver. No wonder he wasn't sure if she would get it, he didn't even know the name of her company, let alone her stand number and it was only at the end of the conversation last night that he had asked her surname.

Fortunately, Bronte had a heavy schedule with meetings at some of her producers' stands. Otherwise she would have gone out of her mind with the wondering and waiting. Alexandra had booked a beach restaurant for her and, as she knew it would, the meal dragged slowly by. Every minute seemed like an hour and on several occasions her mind went completely blank and she couldn't think of a thing to say. It was a blessing that the restaurant had a buffet menu, which at least meant getting up and down a couple of times. It turned out that the Zimbabweans had come to window shop rather than buy, and normally she would have been disappointed not to have taken any orders, but that day she really didn't care. They had to dash off before two thirty for further screenings, leaving Bronte alone at the table, waiting to pay the bill.

Another half hour! She couldn't possibly go into the Palais – what if she got diverted by some unexpected buyer or producer and missed Jordan altogether? No, if needs be she would pretend she had to go the chemist for some vital necessity and would kill time looking at the shops in the Rue d'Antibes. She had already forewarned Alexandra not to expect her until at least four, saying she had arranged to meet a producer at his suite in the Carlton to screen some new shows. A little white lie wouldn't hurt.

The shops had just re-opened after the mid-day siesta and as she wandered up the street, she browsed in windows admiring the chic couture of French fashion. Most of the garments were totally unaffordable, but that only mildly detracted from their interest.

Every few minutes, she sneaked a look at her watch. Two thirty-five. Two forty-one. Two forty-seven. She didn't want to be late, nor did she want to sit on her own for too long before he showed up – that was, if he showed up at all. There had to be some doubt. It had never really occurred to her – did film stars wander freely in a place like Cannes? Would it be feasible for them to meet on the terrace, without him being mobbed? She presumed it must be or he wouldn't have suggested it.

On the other hand, maybe it was all a huge joke at her expense. She shuddered and told herself that if it was, then at least no-one else knew about it and she had got over far worse than humiliation lately.

Two fifty-three. Time to head for the hotel. She knew she wasn't far away and therefore didn't hurry her pace excessively. She took a deep breath as she mounted the steps in front of the Carlton, veering to the right in the direction of the terrace. It was quiet. The majority of tables were deserted, just a few were occupied, mostly by coffee drinkers. Of course, there was no sign of Jordan. Two fifty-eight. Where should she sit? She didn't want to miss him by sitting out of sight, but she also had an idea that he would not want to sit in full view of all passers-by. She opted for a small table, nearer to the hotel than the road and pulled out a chair. The garçon barely gave her time to put down her bag before he was there, cleaning her table and ready to take her order. Should she order something? Was she staying? Would he turn up?

She thought to herself, crumbs Bronte, you've really done it this time! You've allowed yourself to be reduced to a nervous wreck by a film star, who happened to be bored last night and here you are not knowing whether to order a stiff gin or a coffee!

'Café noir, s'il vous plait.'

Another deep breath and a chance to look around discreetly to see if there was anyone else she recognised in the near vicinity. It was crazy! She felt like a criminal. Her fingers, which had a mind of their own, kept finding twists of hair and twiddling them, while she tried to concentrate on sitting back and looking relaxed. Three eight and no sign. How long should she wait? Her coffee arrived and the garçon tucked the bill under a glass ashtray.

'Merci,' she smiled at him.

'Gee, I'm really sorry I'm late!' Jordan arrived all at once, alone and took up the other seat at the table. 'I would have been early but Chelsea wanted me to go pick up something for Phoebe, that's my daughter.' His smile revealed white flashing teeth. 'You been here long?'

'Not really. Just long enough to order coffee.'

'Good idea.' He raised his arm and summoned the garçon. 'Waiter, can you bring me a coffee, please? Regular, white with no sugar. Thanks.' Turning to Bronte, he exclaimed: 'Say, you look great! You should keep your hair down like that, it's really pretty.'

She blushed: 'Thanks.'

'It was strange seeing you this morning. I wanted to reach right out and hand you that note, but I didn't get the chance. I thought I was going to have a problem tracking you down. After I had this great idea, I knew I had to find you to see what you thought. Fortunately, they have a book or something with everyone's name listed under their company and someone seemed to know exactly where to find you.'

A couple who had recently (and probably deliberately) sat down at a table nearby, were gazing intently in Jordan's direction. He was oblivious. Bronte decided he must be used to that sort of attention and lowered her gaze into the bottom of her dark coffee, as he began to speak again.

'Look, I'll come right out with this and hope you won't think I'm being too presumptuous. You can always tell me, right?'

She nodded and smiled. Just then, he could be as presumptuous as he liked!

'I'm looking for someone to work with me and help, basically to take care of arrangements in my life, both business and to a certain extent, personal as well. Someone who is prepared to travel with us, who can book flights, arrange accommodation, hire nannies, type, be presentable at meetings and put up with constant changes. We've had a girl from New York with us for a couple of years, but she's got herself pregnant and wants to quit the travelling.'

Bronte's eyes widened in astonishment, but she carried on listening.

'When I met you last night and you told me about the awful time you've had lately, I got to thinking. You've travelled, you'd go down really well with people I have to deal with and I know we'd get along. Cancerians are my kind of people.'

'But how . . .?' He didn't let her finish.

'How'd I know about the birth sign? Intuition.' He touched his temple. 'Look, frankly we're in a bit of a jam. I've got a big project coming up soon and I'm not going to be able to do everything without help. Chelsea and Phoebe'll be with me which means nannies, renting an apartment and more than usual to worry about. I'm going to be pretty busy and it'd be good to know that someone with your kind of efficiency was in charge.'

'But you hardly know me! There must be hundreds of people you know, much more qualified for this. There's probably agencies with trained staff for that kind of work. Why me?'

'You came along at the right time and besides, I think you kind of need it yourself, if you really admit it.'

That took the wind out of her sails.

'Where would we be going? And how soon?'

'We have to fly back to New York tomorrow. Then we're due to arrive in London in a couple of weeks where I have to meet some financiers. The next stop is Hong Kong for a few days and then on to Sydney, where we'll need to stay for two or three months.'

'I still can't believe you want me. What would I do about my job? What about my boss? I can't just walk out after five years.'

'If you really want this, talk to him. Tell him you need a break. Tell him you've had a fantastic offer, if you like. Tell him anything and make him understand that you need your life back for a while. You've worked hard for him – give him the example of that dinner you suffered last night – you said he's a great guy and if he really is, he'll want what's best for you.'

'And there's my flat . . .'

'You said the apartment was rented. Can't you find someone to take it over?'

'I suppose I could. I think we only need to give two weeks notice.'

'Perfect, so what do you say?'

She laughed. She really didn't know what to say. All she could think of was how he had the cutest habit of shaking his head and smiling into his lap, before re-fixing his eyes on hers, all of which she found hard to resist.

'If it's a question of money . . . we'd look after you well and of course, 'plane fares and hotels would be covered.'

He reached out and covered her hand with his. She froze, as the contact sent her stomach to butterflies.

'You owe yourself a good time. You're a great girl with everything going for you and when I told you last night that your life is precious, I meant it. I know you'll like Phoebe, she's a fantastic kid.' He didn't mention Chelsea.

The garçon approached their table once more and hovered until he was noticed.

'More coffee?' Jordan asked her.

'No, thanks.'

He reached into the back pocket of his jeans and produced a two hundred franc note to cover both his and Bronte's bills, which he handed to the garçon. 'Keep the change.'

'Thank you, sir.'

'Do you really think I'd be any good at this?'

'You'd have a good teacher. I'd be right there with you, showing you the ropes until you got the hang of what's required.'

'I must confess that a hot summer in Australia, rather than a cold and miserable winter in London, does have its appeal. What exactly will you be doing there?'

'It's mostly confidential at this stage, but if you're going to take me up you'll find out soon enough. There's plans for a new movie based in Australia, mostly in Sydney if it all works out. I would be acting as well as directing it, with Greg Hill, who is a great new Australian actor, as co-star – but all that's being worked out at the moment. The script's coming along and we're talking to backers. The producer's already down in Sydney and once I've had the talks in London and Hong Kong, I'll be joining him so we can firm things up with Greg and get shooting underway. There, I've told you far more than I should have done so you'd better not back out on me now.'

'Are you saying I haven't got a choice?' she asked softly, and terribly innocently.

'That's about the size of it. My last pitch, I promise – give it a try for six months and if you can't stand the sight of me in the mornings – then fine. Put the whole thing down to experience and call up your boss and see if he'll have you back. Is there really anything to lose?'

She strongly doubted that she would ever feel that about him in the mornings and hell, he was right, she really didn't have anything to lose. Her flat meant little to her now anyway and she'd probably be better out of it. Her friends would always be there. Alex might be a problem, but she thought she could win him over and the salary sounded like another incentive. Probably a lot more than she was on now. She might even save most of it for a deposit on a flat later on.

'Can I call you tomorrow? I've got to sort a few things out first.'

'Only if you promise to say yes.'

Her head and her heart were both in agreement and as she looked up briefly, at the clear blue sky towards which the gnarled branches of an old tree at the side of the terrace reached out, she saw a solitary bird perched on a flimsy twig, singing his heart out to her. It seemed to be telling her to take a chance, to flee the nest Jordan had mentioned last night. It was the right decision. She needed her freedom. Was it really the little bird or was Dominic up there, telling her what was best for her?

The terrace had filled up over the last half hour, not exactly by coincidence and more than a few curious stares were being aimed in their direction. Jordan was very recognisable, but who was the attractive girl with the long wavy, auburn hair? Was a scandal about to break?

'Sadly, I can't stay and persuade you any more, Bronte. I've got to fly back to Antibes to make some calls. Please think seriously on all I've said – we really need you.'

'I promise to get back to you tomorrow.'

'Here's my direct number at the hotel. We'll be leaving around nine for the airport, so you'd better call before that.'

'I have to be in the Palais by then, so I'll ring before I leave my room. Jordan ...' That time it was she who touched his arm, without thinking – it just seemed a very natural thing to do. 'I still don't really know why you're offering me all this, but I guess you have your reasons and I just wanted to tell you that I'm sorry I didn't jump up and down straight away, but you've got to know that I'm very grateful to be given such an opportunity. It's the chance of a lifetime and I can't believe I'm telling you I'll call you tomorrow. I should be signing on the dotted line now.'

'Bronte,' he burrowed deep into her eyes again, 'if you had 'jumped up and down' as you put it, I would probably have told you that I was joking. That I was being a real bastard and would you please forgive me, because I'd have known then, that you were accepting it for all the reasons that wouldn't be right for you. The fact that you've been level headed and realistic about it, because after all it is a considerable gamble for you in some ways, only convinces me more that you're right for it. I know now, as I was almost sure I knew after last night, that I have made the right decision and now it's up to you. Enough of the serious talk, I'm lecturing you again and I certainly didn't intend to.'

The same smile into his lap, but also into her eyes. He got up and folded his chair away under the table, while she remained where she was, looking up at him.

'So, I'll expect your call in the morning?'

'I'll ring, Jordan, I promise.'

He gave her a last secret smile, which said that really, he wanted to kiss her as he had the previous night. But already tongues around them were wagging. The smile was enough for her. Anything else would have been far too confusing.

CHAPTER EIGHT

'Alex, it's Bronte. Have you just got back from tennis?'

Bronte had dialled the Majestic Hotel and asked for Alex's room. Her afternoon had passed in a whirl of deception. Already her interest was flagging, as she pictured the opportunities that lay ahead of her should she accept Jordan's offer, which she had more or less made her mind up to do. She had always been impulsive and acting on impulse made her feel good. It didn't always turn out right, but when you were wilful by nature and had your heart set on something, it was worth the gamble.

'Missed you on the court, Bronte. We got hammered by those friends of Donna's from the BBC, not like our little victory last night. Your day go OK, I've only seen you from a distance?'

'Alex, I need to talk to you about today.' She couldn't give anything away on the 'phone. It had to be face to face, let him think she was having a problem with her work.

'Fine. What are you up to for dinner?'

'I'm free but Alex, I really need to talk to you on your own.'

'I'm intrigued! Anything I should worry about?'

'What about Helene?' She steered around his question.

'Hang on, I'll check with her.'

He put his hand over the receiver to muffle his voice and Bronte waited, perched on the side of the bed in her bath robe, with her wet hair wound round in a towel on top of her head.

'Helene's going to have room service. She's had a lot of sun today and she's quite happy to put her feet up for the evening. Where do you fancy taking me?'

'Any preferences?'

'Not really. How about pizza? We could go down to that place in the old port.'

'Great. I'll come down to the Majestic. What time?'

'Give me time to jump in the shower. Say, eight thirty?'

'Alex, can you make sure it's just us two?'

'You sound very secretive. I hope it's good news. I'll see you later and you can fill me in.'

'Bye.'

She put the receiver down very slowly. The first part was done and now she must go through with the rest. She had told Jane and Donna she was staying in to catch something on the movie channel and get an early night. Praying they wouldn't try her room or decide to go to the same pizza restaurant, she went over to the wardrobe and hung up the clothes she had worn all day, which lay marooned on a nearby chair.

She regretted that her relationship with her father wasn't closer. It would have been nice to think she could have called him and discussed the major career move that she was contemplating. But he would simply have listened to her, if he had had the time that was, and told her to do what she thought best.

No, Alex was about the only person she could talk it over with before calling Jordan in the morning and she only hoped that he would be able to advise her from an impartial point of view, which after all, was asking a great deal.

'You look suitably casual.' Alex wandered up to her in the lobby of the Majestic and gave her a kiss on both cheeks. 'Are we walking or driving? Do I need the car up from the car park?'

'I think we can manage to walk, don't you? It'll only take about ten minutes.'

'Whatever you say, but don't forget I've had an hour running around the tennis court tonight.'

'So you must be fit!'

'Hardly, I feel exhausted.' He linked his arm through Bronte's. 'So will we get rich on your sales today?'

'Much more likely to on yours, if the Germans came up with the goods. Did they?'

'The screening went very well. They seem interested in at least five of the titles which would be fantastic! They want me to send cassettes and then I'll probably fly over to Germany next month to firm up the deal. Last night go OK for you?'

'Um, yes . . .'

'You sound hesitant. Meet any interesting people?'

'That's what I wanted to talk to you about over dinner.'

'You're not in love are you?'

'Alex! After everything that's happened recently? I don't consider myself to be 'on the market' right now.'

'You'd better watch out, because other people might not see it like that. An attractive girl like you. . .' His eyes danced.

'That wouldn't be fair to Dominic's memory. Seriously, I'm just not interested, I'm still numb in that direction.' Genuinely, she felt that way.

'So, who'd you meet that's so secret as to require me to be dragged out for a private pizza?'

'Hold on and I'll tell you.'

Within a few moments, they arrived at the restaurant. The smell of melting mozzarella, garlic and herbs wafted seductively through the door and out on to the street. The place was already a hive of activity with most tables taken. Near to the open oven, waiters were tossing dough mixture in long-handled pizza pans.

'Une table pour deux?'

Alex's accent was an insult to the French! But the moustached waiter realised what he meant and picking up two vast menus, led the way to a table at the back of the restaurant. Hurry! Hurry! Hurry! There was nothing quiet or peaceful about that place. Bronte was glad, she needed the atmosphere to help her with her story.

They ordered a carafe of house red and, after a brief consultation with the menu, selected their pizzas. Bronte remembered from a time she had been there before, that the waiters always wrote the order down on the paper table cloth and then tore it out at the end of the meal, handing it to you as the bill.

'You can't keep me in suspense any more. Out with it, before I force it from you.'

It was only fair that she tell him now.

'Well, this is probably going to sound like a really good story to you and believe me, it still does to me too, but I swear that every word I am about to tell you is true. I did meet someone last night but romance hasn't got anything to do with it.' That was ninety nine per cent true.

'Who then? Do I know this person?'

'By name, but I doubt you know him personally.'

'Go on . . .'

'Jordan Innes!'

'What, *the* Jordan Innes? The actor?' He nearly choked on his wine.

'Yes, it was totally by chance and certainly nothing I planned. In fact, none of what I am about to tell you was planned in any way. It just happened.'

She proceeded to relate everything to him, from the reason she had gone outside in the first place, to the chance meeting, the missed bus home, seeing Jordan again that morning, the note and finally the exchange at the Carlton. She left no details out, as that would not have been right. After all, she was asking for his advice, his support and his blessing to leave his company, if that really was the right thing to do.

After his initial surprise, Alex's expression did not betray his thoughts. He did not interrupt her, instead let her spill all her words out until there was nothing left to add.

'. . . and then he got up to go. I guess his car was waiting or something. I'm really not sure how he got back to Antibes.' Bronte came to a grinding halt and looked up at Alex for the first time since she had begun.

Alex painstakingly reached out for his wine glass and took a deep draught before setting it down again, just as carefully.

'I don't see a problem, Bronte. It's a fairly obvious decision.'

'It is? What do you mean?' She had been prepared for anger, for irritation, even for fatherly correction if it came, but nothing had prepared her for blind acceptance.

'I mean, you must go. Bronte, you have worked for me for five years. During that time I could never fault your work. You have had a marvellous innings and I knew one day, that you'd up-sticks. I thought a baby would do it, but since Dominic died I have really been waiting for this. Obviously, if you had chosen to stay, I would have counted my blessings but did you honestly think I'd stand in the way of something like this? I'm too fond of you for that.'

'But do you really think I'd be doing the right thing? Am I crazy to throw up my career for this?'

'How many people get offered the chance to travel with a movie star, to get involved to the extent you would have to in the film world? I would have thought it's beyond most girls' wildest dreams. And, as for crazy, frankly, you'd be crazy to turn it down.'

'Yes, but is it sensible? Would 'my father approve'?' She lifted her eyes.

'Your father doesn't come into this, but that's another subject. All my life I've acted impulsively. You have too, if you think about it. Perhaps that's why we get along so well. Think of your life, like it or not, you're a widow and you're only twenty five. You rent your flat and you've been doing the same thing now for five years. This is the break of a lifetime! You'll meet lots of people, travel and who knows who you might fall in love with on the way. You should see it as a new beginning.'

'But I don't even know Jordan. What if he's taking me for a ride?'

'Then you get off. You're old enough and capable enough to get on the first 'plane home. It's hardly likely to be physically dangerous for you if he's taking his wife and child too, he's not going to risk their lives is he?'

'I suppose not. Alex, you're amazing me! This is a complete reversal of roles from what I expected. I thought you would be the one pointing out all the negative aspects and I would be the one arguing them down.'

'What did you actually want me to say? Did you want me to tell you to forget it and to stay in London? How much would that have affected your own intentions? Be truthful.'

'OK. I wanted to hear you say that I should go. That it is the right move for me and that the company will survive without me.'

'Isn't that exactly what I've done? I guess I knew what you wanted, but I needed to hear you say it. As it happens,

I stand by everything I have said and I really do mean it. As for the company surviving without you, of course it won't!'

'Oh, Alex.'

'We'll go out of business.'

'No you won't. Anyone can do what I do with a bit of teaching.'

'Precisely. They can do it, but they won't do it half as well. I'm teasing, take no notice. We will, of course, miss you and me more than most, but you'd better stay in touch or there'll be trouble.'

'What have I done to deserve a boss like you?'

'You've just been your own self, Bronte. Seriously, if things don't work out for you I'm sure we could squeeze you back in as tea girl!'

'That's unnecessarily decent of you,' and she meant it sincerely.

'So, how soon does he want you to start?'

'When I call him tomorrow, I'll ask. I have a feeling he meant that I should be ready to go to Hong Kong when they arrive in London in a couple of weeks time.'

'A couple of weeks? Wow, that's very soon! He doesn't hang around does he?'

'Well, to be fair, he couldn't have known he'd meet me last night and I imagine that a movie takes a lot of planning ahead. It's probably been in the pipeline for ages.'

'Yes, I realise that. Still, if it's only two weeks, it's only two weeks. You'll have to pass your work over pretty fast.'

'Dare I ask if you have an idea about that? Will you look for someone new?'

'If I did, this would be the place to talk to people.' He thought for a moment. 'No, I think for the time being I'll get Jane and Donna to take on part of it each, just until I have a reshuffle and decide what to do.'

'Alex, I'm so sorry to be doing this to you. I told you before, I didn't plan it and if anyone had told me yesterday morning that I'd be quitting on you in two weeks, I'd have thought they were losing their marbles.'

'Anything can happen in life. We might have gone bust and then I'd be turning you all out. Allow me wisdom with my years.'

'Don't be ridiculous, you're not old. But I can't help feeling I'm letting you down.' She noticed his expression and raised both hands in defeat. 'I know, I know, I'll shut up.'

'Now that's decided, next subject please. How's the pizza?'

Bronte tossed this way and that between the linen sheets. She was restless, as her mind hurtled on like a racehorse over the final furlong. So much about the day had been unbelievable. Why had Jordan come into her life? Had she really told Alex she was leaving work? Even more surprising, had he really insisted that she go? Was she mad to accept? Was it disloyal to Dominic? But how long should she remain loyal to a dead person when she was only twenty five? Perhaps she should talk to Alex again and try to negotiate a six month sabbatical – 'getting over Dominic time' – and then return to life as normal? But was that being fair to Alex? No. Yet again she found sleep impossible. It was fast becoming a habit. She finally succumbed to a fitful state of rest, as she continued to deliberate the decision which she had to confirm in a few hours time.

'Can I speak to Jordan Innes, please?'

She had already dialled the number twice and hung up before it started to ring at the other end. Each time she had left her bedside and gone into the bathroom with the excuse of a mission in mind, which in truth was just a delaying tactic, enabling her to gather the nerve to talk to him.

A woman's voice had answered: 'Hang on a moment will you? Darling, it's for you. Some female, I didn't ask the name.'

A few seconds, each of them seeming like an hour, ticked by on the clock beside her bed, until she heard the receiver being lifted.

'Hi! Is that you, Bronte?' The chocolate seeped down the 'phone. It was the first time she had heard his voice without seeing his face.

'Yes, it is.'

'How are you this morning?'

'I'm OK, thanks.' She felt tongue-tied and needed prompting.

'So, what's the decision? Are you coming with us?'

'If you're really sure you want me and you think I can do everything you need, then . . .' deep breath, ' yes, I'll come!'

'You will? That's great news and a real weight off my mind.'

'And off mine, now I've told you.' She laughed nervously.

'Did you speak to your boss?'

'Yes, I did. I threw his world into turmoil last night over dinner.'

'My name won't be too popular then! What did he say?'

'You were close to the mark when you said he'd be happy for me. I honestly think he is. He was very positive about it and he really wants to meet you.'

'I knew he wouldn't try to stop you. So, you can start in a couple of weeks? You'd better have a rough outline of our schedule. Hold on and I'll check some dates.' He put the 'phone down while he went to find the details.

'Hello, Bronte? OK, we need to arrive in London on the sixth of November because I have a meeting arranged for the seventh. I'll get Helen to organise the flights to London and book the Dorchester – she's with us until we leave for England. Can you start on the sixth? We'll probably need to get together that evening to make plans.'

'I'll put it down.'

'I'll give you call from New York once you're back in London and I can fax you more details, but we'll need to be on a flight to Hong Kong by the evening of the seventh. Just a few days in Hong Kong'll do it and then I promised Art (who Bronte later discovered was the producer of the movie) that I'd be in Sydney by the fourteenth.'

Bronte found it hard to take it all in. It was like a television play which left the viewer trying to figure out who was who and what relationship they were to each other.

He went on: 'There's the hotel in Hong Kong. Then we'll need a place in Sydney for a few months. We can talk about it again next week. Oh, and we're going to need to find a nanny in Australia, as Chelsea'll be doing some of her own work down there.' (Bronte remembered reading somewhere that, as well as modelling, Chelsea dabbled in freelance feature writing).

'I hope you don't expect me to recite all that!'

He laughed and she could visualise his expression.

'Start now! No, I'm joking. Look, I'm very pleased you've said yes and I know it's going to be fun. Not all the time I'm sure, but I know you won't regret it. I've got to run to the airport now. Give me your numbers in London and I'll call you.'

She read out her work and home numbers.

'And fax? Can I fax you at work?'

'Yes, Alex won't mind and the others will know soon enough.'

'Take good care and we'll see you in a couple of weeks.'

'Will do. Oh, is there a number I can reach you on, if I need to ask something?'

'Sure. I'll give you one in New York.' She wrote down the number of his penthouse apartment, overlooking New York's famous Central Park.

She had done it! There was no turning back, not that she really wanted to. Whatever lay in store for her with the Innes family, she would go along with. It probably wouldn't all be roses, but it had to be exciting at times, as well as fun, and she desperately needed some new fun in her life. At that moment, if she could have jumped six or so months into the future, she would never have believed that it was her life and not some Hollywood movie she was witnessing. But right there and then, she had no notion of just what was to unfold in such a relatively short space of time.

Four more days of Cannes had passed before she found herself once more in the back of the hired car on her way to Côte d'Azur Airport. Those days had brought the usual round of meetings, screenings, frustrations with buyers and a certain amount of social activity in between. The evenings had consisted of more than a few drinks, most of which seemed to include Mike and at least one formal dinner, which, when he had asked her to help him out with some important Italian buyers from RAI, Bronte had been unable to refuse Alex. On the last night, Alex had taken his gang out to Mougins, which was a charming little old town, right up in the hills overlooking Cannes. He had sought out a friendly, family-run bistro which served the French style fish soup with garlic croutons and parmesan cheese that everyone raved about. It had been an amusing night, with all present tired but on generally good form, and the atmosphere of the quaint old French houses, cobbled streets and pretty gardens contributed to the success of the evening.

There had been no word from Jordan since she had accepted his offer. She had not expected to hear, since they had arranged that he would contact her back in London the following week. Bronte had done her best to keep busy for the remainder of the week and in doing so, time passed more quickly than she had imagined it would. Alex had taken her aside to find out what Jordan had said to her on the 'phone and was genuinely happy that she had not changed her mind. They had agreed that Bronte should break the news herself to Jane and Donna, at a time she deemed appropriate, providing of course, one arose. They would be doing the bulk of Bronte's work.

No opportunity presented itself while they were in Cannes. They were either in a group of other people or they met in the corridors of the hotel or of the Palais, neither place being suitable for Bronte's story, nor the inevitable questions that were bound to follow such an announcement. There was nothing else for it, but to bring the subject up in the car on the way to the airport, as the journey would last half an hour at least and that would be plenty of time to share her news with her colleagues. For some reason she found hard to put her finger on, she couldn't find the words to start to tell them. She wasn't a hundred per cent convinced that they wouldn't think her totally mad and she also feared an element of jealousy, which often made decent people turn nasty. She waited until they had just left the outskirts of Cannes before launching into it.

'I've got something I need to tell you both.' She took a deep breath.

'You sound awfully serious, Bronte. Has something happened?' Jane turned round and Donna looked at her through the driver's rear view mirror. Both immediately had their own ideas of what news Bronte was about to impart.

Jane was sure Bronte was going to tell them she was pregnant, after all she had been off her food for a bit. Meanwhile Donna had had her suspicions about Mike's attentiveness towards Bronte all week but unfortunately, she had totally failed to understand the affectionate but entirely platonic friendship that Bronte had with Mike, now into its third year or so.

'Yes, something's happened all right, but not in the way you would think. I've been offered another job. Not really even to do with television, but I've decided to take it.'

'That's pretty sudden isn't it? Have you told Alex?' asked Donna.

'Sudden's the understatement of the year!' Bronte laughed nervously, not sure why she was still so on edge in the company of two friends. 'I promise you both that I neither looked for this nor even agreed to it straight away when it happened, but I've thought long and hard and yes, Alex and I have talked it out at length and I know now, that I can't turn it down.'

'So when are you going, Bronte?' Jane asked her.

'Probably in just under two weeks. I have to start on the sixth of November.'

'I bet Alex didn't like that one too much, did he?' Donna, again.

'Actually, Alex couldn't have been sweeter about it all. He was the one who really convinced me I should go.'

Donna was silent.

'So, come on, don't keep us in suspense any more, I can't bear it! Who are you going to work for? Will you stay in London?' Jane needed to know.

'Not initially. From what I can gather, I will be travelling around a lot of the time and I won't really be based anywhere in particular for very long.'

'Oh, stop being so horribly secretive and tell us the rest.' Donna was becoming impatient.

'I'm not being secretive deliberately and of course, I'll tell you everything. Just hold on and I'll start from the beginning, which is only five days, or should I say nights, ago. It all started the night I went to Antibes for dinner with Western TV. . .'

They listened to her story in silence, Jane twisting round with wide eyes every so often and Donna glancing up in her mirror. She told them all about the meeting in Antibes, right up to the 'phone call the day Jordan had left for New York.

'Well, Bronte Richardson, you certainly do fall on your feet!' exclaimed Donna expressionlessly.

'Bronte, I'm really happy for you. You've had very rotten luck lately and it's about time something nice happened to you. How do you feel about it all?' Jane was always generous.

'To tell you the truth, I'm really excited one moment and rather apprehensive the next. It's a step into the unknown. I could have a great time but then again, it might all turn out to be too good to be true.'

'What's Jordan Innes really like? I've seen all his movies.' Jane was bubbling over like a forgotten pan of milk.

'He's not at all what I expected. He doesn't come across as arrogant or self-centred. In fact, and I know this is going to sound corny, but he's a really normal sort of guy, not affected at all.'

'Is he as dishy as he looks on the screen?' Jane was in total awe.

'He's certainly good-looking, if that's what you mean.'

'I always think he oozes sex appeal whenever I see him in a movie. What about his clothes, what was he wearing?'

'I've only seen him twice and both times he looked pretty casual. You know, jeans and a jacket?'

'Did you meet his wife? She's supposed to be gorgeous.' Donna was not in quite so much awe.

'No, I didn't. She was with him at the hotel, but I only saw her head from the back.'

'She's a Swedish model, I believe, and did you say they had children?'

'A little girl, Phoebe. Jordan talks very fondly about her.'

'So tell me again, where you're going in two weeks time?' Jane wanted all the details right so she could relay them to her friends.

'Hong Kong and then Australia, that's about all I know. He's supposed to be faxing me more details next week.'

'I've always wanted to go to Australia. You are lucky, Bronte!' said Jane.

'Hong Kong's not up to much. It's a concrete jungle with a permanent smell of Chinese food everywhere. It's not a place I would take my child.'

'I don't think we'll be there for more than a few days, so I suppose it won't matter. I expect Jordan's been already and must know what it's like.'

Donna directed her attention to finding the right turn for the airport complex and did not respond for a moment. However, as they drove towards the hire car drop off, she asked another question.

'What is Alex going to do with the Caribbean and Africa after you leave? Has he got anyone in mind?'

That was an awkward one because Bronte knew that they both were busy enough already and would probably not welcome extra work.

'I think you'd better let him talk that one through with you. I believe he has some ideas, but I wouldn't want to tell you the wrong thing.'

The subject was left, with Jane envious and fantasising about the prospects of Bronte working for such a famous star, and Donna envious and irritated by the fact that Bronte seemed to get more attention than she did. She also seemed temporarily to forget all that Bronte had been through in the last few weeks.

They had left Cannes later than intended and consequently arrived at the airport with only twenty minutes to spare. As the flight was full and most of the passengers had already checked in, there was no chance of getting a row for them all to sit together. The best they could manage was two seats together and the third on the aisle, three rows behind. Bronte took the single aisle seat and really was quite glad to do so, because it would give her an opportunity to drift off into a reverie of thought over the events of the past week.

The flight went smoothly. They had equally disgusting food on the way back, but at least it was towards evening and they had eaten well at lunch time.

Once they had piled their luggage onto three trolleys at Heathrow, they negotiated the Customs green area without being stopped. Jane offered Bronte a lift home as it was on the way for her, while Donna, who had cheered up considerably during the flight, went off in search of a taxi. The stars were out in force, as the nights had already begun to draw in early, preparing the way for winter. The moon was clearly visible against a backcloth of rich velvet sky. Rush hour was over, which meant they had a fairly clear run into west London.

'Bronte, when you said Alex had something in mind for Africa and the Caribbean, you meant Donna or me, or both of us, didn't you?'

'Yes, only I didn't want to say anything in front of Donna because I think she'll take a dim view of extra work and I know Alex can get round her better than I can.'

'I didn't think he'd want to rush into replacing you. Can I ask you something? If he mentions it to you again and it looks as though we might get the choice, can you put in a word for me for the Caribbean? I really don't fancy the idea of travelling round Africa on my own.'

'Of course I will. It may not even come to that. It may just be a case of following up on the administration until Alex finds somebody else to do the travelling. So don't worry too much until he talks to you. I'm just sorry that it will mean more work for a while.'

'In your shoes, I'd have done just the same thing. There are moments when you should think of yourself. You can't live your life according to others all the time.'

'You've been a brick over this, Jane. I'm not so sure Donna approves, though.'

'She'll get over it. I think she's had a bit of a thing for Mike this week and she's probably peeved that it didn't come to anything.'

'It's such a shame because it never would with him. He plays around but his girlfriend's got an amazingly strong hold over him. I'd be really surprised if he ever strayed.'

'Do we take this turn?' Jane had only been to Bronte's place a couple of times.

'Yes, that's right. There's a short cut I can show you which misses the lights. Go down here to the bottom and turn left.'

They drew up outside the flat and Jane got out to help Bronte in with her luggage. It took her a little time to find the flat keys but when she finally did and fitted them to the lock, the door just seemed to fall open – there was no need to turn the key.

Inside, the flat had been ransacked! The door had obviously been forced and hung on its wobbly hinges in a wounded fashion. Chairs had been turned over, papers distributed, crockery smashed, drawers pulled out and not put back. In the bedroom, clothes lay strewn across the floor and dripped over the edges of drawers. The precious bedside cupboards had been emptied and pictures were skewed on the walls.

'Oh my God!' Bronte put her hand to her mouth as she surveyed the awful mess in her flat. 'What the hell's gone on here?'

'Bronte, I'm so sorry. What a ghastly thing to come back to. We'd better call the police.'

The receiver lay a little way from the base unit, but it was still attached and they managed to get a dialling tone after a bit of prodding and poking.

'Is that the police? My flat's been burgled. I've been away and just come back to find the place completely wrecked.'

'We'll send a car over right away. What's the address?' He wrote it down, '. . . and the name?. . . Mrs Richardson, if you could manage not to touch anything until we get round, there might be some finger prints we can pick up.'

'Of course.' She hung up and looked around.

'Can you tell what's missing?' Jane asked.

'Well from here, the TV, the video and the stereo are gone. We had a few bits of silver which were all wedding presents over on those shelves . . .' She pointed towards a set of ornamental pine shelves. 'I bet they've taken those.'

Jane went to have a look, careful not to tread on anything that might be considered evidence.

'Yup, there's no sign.'

'My jewellery,' gasped Bronte, 'I bet that's gone.'

She dashed through to the bedroom. Sure enough, her green leather jewellery box had been forced open and the lid broken off. The few pieces of jewellery of any value that she possessed, like the diamond and sapphire heart-shaped

111

brooch which had belonged to her mother, her pearl earrings, a couple of gold chains and worst of all, her diamond engagement ring which she hadn't wanted to take to Cannes, had all been stolen. All that was left were a set of sparkly but worthless beads and some cheap clip earrings.

'The bastards! They've taken my engagement ring!' An unwelcome tear escaped from tightly controlled eyes and trickled down her face, landing with a tiny splash on her jacket.

'Oh Bronte, I'm so terribly sorry.' Jane put her arms around her and gave her a hug. 'God, this is so unfair! How could they?'

'Our wedding photo . . .' Bronte bent down and picked up a picture of Dominic and her taken on their wedding day. It was torn where someone had tried to force it out of the silver frame in which it had stood for the last two years. Needless to say, the frame was gone too. She straightened the photo and tried her best to make it whole again, propping it up against an upturned vase on the shelf.

The bell sounded and as the door was still hanging open, by the time she reached the hall, two policemen were already inside.

'Mrs Richardson?'

'Yes.'

'I understand you've been away? Could we go through a few details?'

They followed her into the living room and proceeded to ask her a number of questions about how long she'd been away, who else had keys to the flat and had she noticed anything suspicious before she left?

'. . . and she's recently widowed, Officer!' Jane was outraged by the whole incident.

'We'll need you to give us an idea of what is missing, Mrs Richardson and then leave the rest to us. There really isn't much more you can do tonight. Do you have someone you can stay with?'

'She can stay with me.' Jane was glad to do something to help.

'Good. Then if we can just go round and take a note of the missing items, we won't need to keep you further now.'

112

Bronte did her best to describe the things they had taken, even Dominic's golf clubs. They had gone through the place with a fine-tooth comb.

Jane couldn't have been more sympathetic. She took Bronte home, forced a bowl of soup and hot buttered toast down her and then made up a cosy bed in the spare room.

As they sat sprawled over cushions in Jane's living room, Bronte tried to rationalise the situation.

'You know, Jane, perhaps this awful mess is all part of some big plan to convince me it's right to take Jordan's job. Perhaps it's some kind of message to tell me that the days of happy marriage with Dominic are well and truly over and the flat should be left behind too.'

'Bronte, you're tired and understandably emotional.'

'You're right, Jane, but you know, I've always been a fatalist and I can't help thinking that now there's nothing left but the memories. My ring has gone, the wedding presents, Dom's golf clubs – even the wedding photo was ripped in half. Perhaps it's a sign from Dominic himself.'

'I find that hard to believe. I think I'm more of a realist. I see your flat destroyed and your possessions stolen or damaged – facts – but I find messages and signs from beyond the grave a bit spooky.'

'I'm being realistic too, Jane. I'm trying to justify the fact that my cosy life of the past two years has been shattered into tiny pieces and the only opening now for me, seems to be this thing with Jordan Innes.'

'I'm sure you're right about the future. I felt that before we found the flat, but I question whether the flat being burgled is a sign of anything. I think you're reading too much into it.'

'I don't know, let me explain. I'm standing, no, staring at this massive crossroads in my life. I can safely go with security and stay here with you all and probably in time, build my life up to something like it used to be. Or I can fling myself into the unknown. I made my choice in Cannes, partly with Alex's help, but now I feel that some force out there is trying to confirm to me that I am doing the right thing. It's something along the lines of being cruel to be

113

kind. The weird thing about all this is that, after the initial shock, I don't even mind too much about the burglary. OK, it's a real hassle and I wouldn't have chosen to have my possessions rifled through, but I almost don't care. It's like a 'fait accompli' – something done, finished with – a driving home of the truth, if you like.'

'I really admire your strength, Bronte. If everything that has hurled itself at you over the last couple of months had come my way, I'm sure I would have had a nervous breakdown by now! Instead, you are so philosophical about life. How on earth do you manage it?'

'I guess it's my self-protective nature. It's also probably got something to do with having to fend for myself from a very early age. After my mother died, I really didn't get too much attention and most of my learning process was done by trial and error. Do you think I'm being callous, Jane?'

'I really don't see how anyone could accuse you of that! I think you are being extremely brave and you certainly don't deserve criticism.'

'Thanks for the support and for everything else, Jane. If I had to go through this with anyone, I'm glad it was you. I don't know where I'd have gone tonight if you hadn't been there.'

'I hope you would have called me. Look, come on, you'd better get some sleep. No doubt there's going to be a fair bit to do tomorrow and for the next couple of weeks too. Will you be OK in the spare room?'

'I'll be fine. You're a darling. Thanks again for being there.'

She leant forward and gave Jane a hug.

'If you want to stay tomorrow, or even until you go, it's no problem. I'm not planning to have anyone else here. I would kick you out for Mike, though!' She grinned sheepishly.

'Sorry, but he's on his way to L.A. right now. He doesn't know what he's missing!' She threw back her straying hair and laughed. 'That's a great offer. Can I let you know, once I've seen the flat in the daylight? If I can get it sorted out, I will probably stay there so I can be on hand to get my things packed up.'

'Sure you wouldn't be spooked?'

'I hope not. Besides, they've taken what little I had of value, so there's really not much point in them coming back for round two.'

'Well, if you're sure you've got everything you need, I'll say good night. Shall I wake you in the morning?'

'No need, I'll be awake early. Sleep tight.'

Bronte let herself into the bathroom and leant across the basin to take in all that stared back at her from the mirror. Her skin looked pale, she could do with that Australian sunshine to draw out her freckles and bronze over that gaunt, lean look which haunted her face when she examined it closely. She pulled down her cheeks and checked out her eyes – what a lot they had witnessed of late. She felt the urge to scrub herself, to brush her teeth vigorously and to exorcise the evil that had been done to her, to be cleansed, ready to face the future.

But Jane would be waiting for the bathroom, she mustn't be long.

CHAPTER NINE

The next morning Bronte returned to the flat, refusing Jane's offer of a lift because she knew it would only delay Jane from getting to the office, where the post-Cannes pile-up of work would be waiting. It would be waiting for Bronte too, but she couldn't possibly leave the flat in the state it was. She knew Jane would do all the necessary explaining and that in all likelihood, she wouldn't make it in at all that day.

Once she got there, she found that the door no longer teetered so sadly, but had been set firmly back on its hinges. Inside, a young constable seemed to be making some notes in the living room.

'I hope you haven't been here all night?' She broke the ice.

'You must be Mrs Richardson?' The constable blushed all the way up to his temples, faced with all five feet ten of Bronte in her short black skirt.

'That's right.' She felt strong and ready to fight. The stuffing was firmly back in place.

'Actually, I haven't been here all night.' He coughed with embarrassment.

'I came round to tell you that they managed to finger print the place last night and it is OK for you to put things straight again. Can I be of help?'

'I'm sure you can. How long have you got? This is going to take a while.' She didn't intend to confuse him further, but certainly succeeded in doing so.

'Where would you like to start?'

'In the bedroom.'

He glanced at her nervously.

She continued: 'At least I will, if you wouldn't mind picking up a few things in here.'

'Right. Is there a Hoover around?'

She walked past him towards the bedroom.

'There used to be one in the cupboard in the hall. I don't suppose it was worth nicking, so it's probably still there.'

Bronte had made up her mind in the depths of the night that the best way to cope was to remain detached and to pretend it was someone else's flat, someone else's possessions and to just get on with the job in hand. She could then concentrate over the following few days on winding up her work and preparing for her imminent departure. She felt a little guilty for her business-like approach towards the constable, but her guard was up and anything less was dangerous. She didn't want too much sympathy because that would lead her down the slippery slope to self-pity and she was determined not to go that road.

Once she had folded her clothes back into their drawers, re-hung others in the wardrobe, collected up the scattered memorabilia from the floor and tried to put her jewellery box back together, the bedroom began to look like its old self. When she went to fetch the Hoover from the living room, she was pleasantly surprised to see that the constable had already done a fairly thorough job in putting that room right too. Perhaps matters weren't so bad. The things that had gone were material possessions and, as long as she managed to close the lid on the sentimental emotions attached to some of them, she would be OK.

The 'phone shrilled out from the living room.

'Coming,' she yelled, setting the Hoover down by her bed. 'Hello? Oh, Alex, it's you.'

'I let you out of my sight for a few hours and look what happens! What ever'll you do when you're on the other side of the world?'

'I can't imagine! You'd better come with me,' she chuckled down the 'phone.

'Seriously, Bronte, are you all right? I mean, what a nightmare! I couldn't believe it when Jane told me.'

'I'm fine, thanks, Alex. Just sorting out the mess here. I don't think I'll be in today if that's OK?'

'My dear girl, I wasn't expecting you and what's more, would probably send you away if you did appear.'

'I'll remember not to then.'

'You need some help round there? You know I'm not that good on the domestic front, but if it's moral support you need, I'm your man.'

'You're sweet, Alex, but don't worry. There's a policeman here doing a great job and between us, we'll have the place back to normal.'

'Do you need somewhere to stay? What about friends? You know I'll get you a hotel room if you like.'

'No, honestly Alex, Jane's already offered her spare room but I'd prefer to stay here so I can get myself organised. I've got a fair bit to do if I'm going away for a while and it'd be easier to be here. Thanks anyway.'

'Well, the offer's there if you change your mind. If you're sure there's nothing I can do for you, I'll let you go.'

'I'll call if I need you – and thanks for ringing.'

'Make sure you do. Bye for now.'

Later that day, when she had managed to make the flat look more or less like it had before she went to Cannes, she reflected on the fact that as her home had become more impersonal, it would be far easier to leave it behind. Memories were portable and would be packed in her suitcase along with her immediate belongings, but there would have been long deliberations over some of the other items, but as they had been taken from her, there would no longer be the need to find homes for them.

Back in the office the next day, Alex took the decision that there was no time to waste in telling Bronte's clients that she would be leaving the company shortly. That way, any immediate problems would surface before she left and could be attended to with expertise. Everyone was to be told that for the meantime matters would be in the capable hands of Jane and Donna (whom Alex had somehow managed to charm from reluctance to positive willingness) which would be a straight-forward handover, because most people Bronte dealt with had come across either Jane or Donna at the television markets.

A couple of days later, when Bronte was firmly engrossed in some programme availability sheets, Amanda's voice bellowed from the switchboard: 'Bronte? Bronte, it's your Dad.'

'Thank you, Amanda. Hello Dad.' Bronte was curious to find out why her father should be calling her at work. They rarely spoke and hardly ever in office hours, as he was usually far too busy.

'Bronte? How are you? We've been worried.'

'Dad, I'm OK. Really. I've been busy with Cannes and work and I'm sorry I haven't got around to calling you. How's Clare?'

'She's very well. We were only saying the other day that it would be nice if you had the time to come up and visit.'

She was touched by her father's concern. Rather late in the day, granted, but she was determined to accept it in the spirit in which it appeared to be meant.

'I've got some news to tell you. I've been offered a new job which'll mean my travelling away for a while.'

'That sounds exciting. Are you going soon?'

''Fraid so Dad, so it looks like Yorkshire'll be a problem. It's a shame because I would like to have seen you before I went.'

They were both making an effort and appeared to be giving each other the benefit of any age-old doubts. Bronte strained to remember the last time her father had rung to invite her to stay. Usually she called him, really just to keep in touch or suggest she visit for a night at the most.

'What's the job, Bronte? Is it in television?'

'Partly.' She proceeded to give him an abridged account of her time in Cannes.

'Are you sure this is a good idea? You don't even know the man!'

'I've been taking care of myself for twenty years . . .' The dig slipped out of its own accord, but it wasn't wasted on him. 'This is just what I need now that I'm on my own again. Please be happy for me.'

Suddenly her father's blessing became very important to her.

'Will you keep your flat on?'

'No. I want to try and save while I'm away so I've already given notice to the estate agents.'

'Bronte, I hope this works for you. I know I haven't always done right by you, but I've never stopped caring and I want you to know that Clare and I are here if you need us.'

His words stimulated a flow of emotion. He had never been a man to air his feelings and this was about as close as they had come as father and daughter, without the interference of a third party.

She took a deep breath: 'That's a real comfort to know. I promise I'll stay in touch and I'll write. When I get back, perhaps I could come up for a few days, if Clare wouldn't mind?'

'Mind! She'd love it. She's really fond of you, Bronte. I do hope you enjoy yourself. You looked so miserable that day at the funeral – I'm sure it's time for things to go right for you again.'

'Bye Dad. Love to you and Clare.'

'Take care of yourself, now.'

'Don't worry.'

Over the next few days, the time galloped past. The days at work bulged with queries and problems, as gradually word spread that she would be leaving shortly. The evenings were taken up with contacting her closest friends and trying to squeeze in time to see them all before she went. What few spare moments she managed to find were spent working out what she would take away with her and what she would put into storage, which had very kindly been offered by Alex at his home.

There had been no word from Jordan all that week and she was hesitant about contacting him. It was to her great relief that a fax came through marked for her attention, just one week before the sixth of November when he was due to arrive in England.

Amanda, who had become completely star struck by the prospect of Bronte working for her pin-up actor and secretly prayed that she would have the chance to meet him too, rushed into Bronte's office one morning, crashing the door back on its hinges as she came in, brandishing a couple of sheets of fax paper.

'Bronte! There's a fax here for you from Jordan Innes!'

She was breathless and her eyes sparkled like a million diamonds.

'Thanks. Just put it down there will you?' Bronte indicated towards the top of an already wobbling pile of papers. She was determined not to betray the fact that her heart was pounding almost as fast as Amanda's. Sure that Amanda would have read every word on the fax before handing it over, she was not going to further her pleasure by showing any excitement or discussing the matter in any way.

Amanda, obviously disappointed by the reaction, put the fax down as requested and hovered, stabbing the carpet with the toe of her shoe.

'Thank you, Amanda.' There was no mistaking the 'please get out' tone of Bronte's voice and she realised that there was nothing else for it but to leave. Once the door was firmly closed and Bronte was sure Amanda wouldn't find some excuse to re-enter, she reached over and snatched up the fax.

Bronte:

Sorry I have not been in touch before but things have gone a little crazy round here. Don't worry, everything is getting sorted and we will be over next week as planned.

We arrive on Wednesday, the sixth on the Concorde flight from New York which gets into Heathrow at 15:45. Can you arrange a car to meet us – use London City Limo Service – ask for Harry.

The suite is booked at the Dorchester – can you get round that evening so we can make contact?

I will need you to make some bookings for the rest of the trip:

1) Overnight flight to Hong Kong on the seventh – we will need Harry again for the car to Heathrow.
2) A two-bedroom suite at the Mandarin Hotel in Hong Kong – and a room for yourself, of course.
3) Flights to Sydney from Hong Kong – four days in Hong Kong will be enough – so try and get something on the twelfth.
4) We need a place in Sydney – in the Mosman area, if possible – call Rita at Australasia Travel in Regent

Street – she has done this kind of thing for us before. Five or six bedrooms – something discreet, with a pool.
5) Ask Rita if she can get you on to a nanny agency in Sydney. We will need someone as soon as possible after we arrive.

Helen has got me fixed up with meetings in Hong Kong, so there is nothing to do there. Feel free to call Helen on the above number for any advice – she is used to these kinds of itineraries.

I will call you today or tomorrow. That's about it for now. Hope all is OK with you.

JORDAN

He had signed his name in stylish script. What was she letting herself in for? She was intrigued by the lifestyle and couldn't wait to speak to Harry and Rita to find out more about how Jordan Innes' life was organised. Her other work temporarily pushed aside, she began to make notes on all that she had to do. Jordan was not going to regret hiring her and she felt certain she would have no regrets either. She would already have some arrangements made by the time he called her.

Harry was eager to oblige one of his most famous clients and promised to have the limo at Heathrow as requested. There was space on the overnight flight to Hong Kong on the seventh. Bronte had never thought until she put the 'phone down, whether she was supposed to book everything in Jordan's real name, but came to the conclusion that he would have told her if she was to use a different name. He seemed to have thought of everything else.

Hong Kong – The Mandarin Oriental Hotel! She had heard that it was supposed to be one of the grandest and oldest hotels in Hong Kong. She couldn't wait to see what was available and fortunately, the local travel agent came up with the telephone number for her. The reservation department couldn't have been more helpful. It turned out that Jordan was a well-known client, who usually booked the Alexandra suite, which boasted an excellent view and had the required second bedroom. They were more than happy to take the booking and did not require any further confirmation. What it was to be famous!

Australia. That was going to be more tricky. How would she know that the house which Rita might find would be suitable for Jordan's requirements, particularly when she was somewhat uncertain of those requirements herself? What she needed was someone already in Sydney who could go round and check out any prospective house. That way, there wouldn't be any embarrassing mistakes. What's more, she knew exactly who to ask, someone who would probably be able to assist on the nanny front too.

Bronte had two cousins on her mother's side who lived in Sydney. They were about her age and both were married. She had met them a couple of times in England when they had travelled over and since then they had kept in touch – mostly via Christmas cards. However, she did know that the younger one ran her own travel agency and would be sure to know all the contacts for renting houses. She would dig out her number when she got home and give her a call first thing in the morning, as that would be evening time in Australia.

If the rest of her job with Jordan was going to be as straight-forward, there would be little to worry about. Now she had to return to the papers on her desk which were certainly not diminishing.

Later that afternoon Amanda had popped out to the post office and, at such times, it was a scramble between whoever was around to answer the 'phones. Bronte took her turn with the others and grabbed it a couple of times. The first call was for Alex, but the second asked for her by name in an unfamiliar, female American voice: 'Bronte Richardson, please?'

She was usually reluctant to admit to who she was when she answered the switchboard, just in case it was some pestering person whom she seriously needed to avoid. But that voice intrigued her and so she replied: 'Speaking. . .'

'Bronte, it's Helen Delaney here. I work with Jordan.'

Bronte's heart jumped several paces forward and she instinctively tensed her fingers.

'Helen, hello. I was going to call you later.'

'Well, Jordan's right here and he wants to talk with you but first, did you get the fax I sent through?'

'Yes, thanks. I'm glad you wrote all that down – it's much easier to work from. Actually, I've already done some homework on the reservations.'

'Great. It's mostly self-explanatory but let me know if I can help.'

'Can you give me a credit card number I can use? The airline need it for the flights to Hong Kong.'

'Sure. Hold on.' There was a pause, before she returned with a string of numbers corresponding to a gold card.

'If that's all I can do for now, here's Jordan – and good luck! I know you'll have a great time and he'll look after you.'

'Thanks, Helen, and I hope all goes well with the baby.'

Americans were so friendly. It was hard to imagine a similar conversation with an unknown English person.

'Bronte?' The chocolate was at work again. 'How have you been?'

'I'm fine, thanks. I got your fax today.'

'I wanted to call and see you hadn't decided to do a runner when you saw the fax!'

'No chance! Everything's set for me to leave next week, so if you change your mind, I've got a problem.'

'Don't worry, we won't. Does everything look OK on the fax?'

Bronte allowed her mind to imagine, just for a second, Jordan on the other end of the 'phone, probably looking as stylishly casual as he had on the two occasions they had met in Cannes, running his bronzed fingers through that dark hair as he spoke to her. Jolted back to the present, she realised she had paused in her reply.

'Yes, no worries. I've already spoken to Harry who's taking care of the car. The flights are booked and I just need to confirm the credit card. The Mandarin Oriental seem to know you and say there's no problem with the suite you usually have. I'm still working on the Australia end but I've had an idea which I'm going to check out in the morning. A cousin of mine lives in Sydney and runs a travel company. I thought I would give her a call and see what she can find – that way, she could take a look at the place before we get there.'

'My, Miss Efficiency! Where have you been all my life? Great – we only suggested Rita because she's done this for us before, but go ahead, the cousin idea sounds good. So when do you finish at work?'

'I told my boss I would work until Tuesday. I reckon I'll need Wednesday to pack. When do you want me round that day?'

'Come by around seven and we can maybe grab something to eat. You can also meet Chelsea. She'll want to go shopping on Thursday, so you can liaise with her to arrange a sitter for Phoebe. I've got a meeting in the morning, but I won't need you at that.'

'Do you want me to call and tell you about the house in Sydney?'

'Yes – talk to Helen if I'm not around and she'll fill me in. I've got to go – someone on the other line. See you next week.'

'Bye.'

The 'phone went down abruptly, but it didn't really matter as they had discussed all that was necessary.

Phew! She let out a sigh and clutched the corners of her desk. A rather distracting day so far!

'Chris? Chris is that you? It's an amazingly clear line! It's your long-lost cousin from England, Bronte.'

The morning had dawned hazy and chill, with the sun trying to force its way through the unyielding blanket of cloud. Outside, the milkman clanked down the street, delivering one bottle here and two there. Bronte shivered as she pulled her dressing gown over her legs. She balanced the 'phone between her shoulder and her neck, with a pen in one hand and a pad in the other. Jordan's fax from the previous day lay close by. The strong Sydney accent came back down the 'phone line.

'Bronte! Wonderful to hear from you. How goes it?'

'OK, thanks. How's Mark?' (Chris' husband of ten months).

'He's doing great. We've been really busy lately. Everyone seems to want to travel this Christmas.'

'What about Angela and Murray?' (Angela was Bronte's other cousin).

'They're up in Perth right now, with Murray's parents. Say Bronte, we were all so sad to hear about Dominic.'

'Thanks. It was a bad time but I'm getting over it. Thanks, too, for the flowers you sent, I'm sorry I never got around to writing.'

'We didn't expect you to. I'm just glad they got there.'

'Chris, I need to ask you a favour.'

'Sure, anything.'

Bronte gave Chris a brief outline of what was required and why.

'Wow, Bronte, that's fantastic! You say you just bumped into him in France?'

'Something like that, yes.'

'What a great opportunity! What's he going to be doing over here?'

'He's working on a new film. I don't know much more than that yet,' and what she did know, she wasn't supposed to say.

'I'm so pleased you'll be here too. It's about time you came Down Under! You must try and come over for Christmas. We're all going up to Angela and Murray's beach house at Avalon.'

'I will try, but it'll depend on what my work involves then.'

'I still can't believe you're actually working for the great Jordan Innes, and that you're coming to Australia with him!'

'Don't get any ideas, Chris. He's got his wife and daughter with him too, remember.' She laughed.

'Sure, but even so! Anyway, about the house . . . should be no problem. I'll ask around. Mosman you say?'

'That's what Jordan wants.'

'Good idea. It's an up-market suburb and we should be able to find something private. This is a good time to rent because quite a few people go away for the long summer holidays and can be away for three to four months. Are there any other specifications, other than five to six bedrooms and a pool?'

'None that I know of. I'll let you be the judge. Would you mind looking the place over, if you do manage to find something? I really don't want to screw up on my first assignment.'

'No problem. Anything for Jordan Innes!'

'Oh yes, and before I forget, he wants a nanny to start from the time we get there. Any chance you can come up with an idea for that too?'

'I'll look into it. There must be some reputable agencies around. Leave it to me and I'll get onto this right away. How long will you be on that number for?'

'At least half an hour. I've only just got up and am about to shower.'

'Right. Give me the number again and I'll call you as soon as I can. What about your work number?'

Bronte reeled off both her numbers.

'This is terribly kind of you, Chris. You sure you don't mind, only I thought it would be far better to talk to you in Sydney, than go through one of the agencies over here?'

'Look, I'm delighted to help and even more happy that you'll be over in two weeks.'

'Well, if you're sure, then I'm very grateful. I'll talk to you later then?'

'I'll call you. Bye.'

It had been really good talking to Chris again. Bronte had forgotten just how friendly her Australian cousins were and she began to feel pleased that at least she would know them when she got to Sydney, and wouldn't arrive in a city of total strangers. If things didn't work out with Jordan, she could always stay on if she liked Australia. There was, after all, very little to rush back to England for.

She had barely stepped out of the shower and was still drying herself, when the 'phone sounded from the living room. If that was Chris, she had done a very fast job! She dashed through and snatched up the receiver, lest it stop ringing.

'Hello.'

'You sound breathless. Have I got you out of the shower?'

Relief! It was Chris.

'No, I just didn't want you to think I'd gone out. That was really quick, have you found something already?'

'Your Jordan Innes has the luck of the Gods! Or you do. Actually, I have. How does this sound? I spoke to Mark after putting the 'phone down to you and by coincidence, his uncle has a fabulous house on Raglan Street, which is close to Mosman Junction. It has a great view of the harbour and its own drive, with quite a lot of mature bushes which should ensure privacy. There's a pool in the garden and a couple of garages – I guess you'll be renting cars?'

'I hadn't thought of that, but yes, I suppose we will. How come it's available?'

'I was just coming to that. Mark's uncle and aunt also have a place in Florida and they usually divide their time between the Sydney house and the one in Florida. Oh, to be retired and rich! Anyway, they do occasionally let family or friends use the houses if they are not there. Mark has just spoken to his uncle and apparently, they leave for Florida this weekend and had not planned to have anyone in the house. When he heard about Jordan, I think he must have liked the idea of having a celebrity, because he immediately said that would be fine. Mark did also say that you'd be there, so indirectly, it's family too.'

'That's incredible! It all sounds too easy. Have you seen inside the house?'

'We were there for Uncle Mack's seventieth earlier this year. From memory, it's very tastefully done. It's spacious and there's a lovely conservatory leading onto a huge sun deck. I don't think you'd have any problems with it.'

'Sounds wonderful. What about the rent? And deposits?'

'I'll check with Mark. There'll probably be a small deposit against any breakages and I'm not sure what the rent is. Do you have a budget?'

'No. Jordan's given me a free hand. Judging from what I know of his lifestyle, I think there are certain standards to meet, if you know what I mean. I've got a credit card number to use for guarantees.'

'That's fine. I don't expect the rent'll be extortionate, but I guess Jordan Innes isn't short.'

'How long could we have the place for?'

'Certainly until April. Uncle Mack and Aunty Flo find the Sydney summers too hot, so they tend to go away for quite a while. Would that be long enough?'

'I presume it would. He did say for three months.'

'I'm sure if you needed to leave before April, there'd be no problem with that either. So, do you want me to confirm all this?'

'I guess so. I will call Jordan today, but go ahead for now. Could you fax me the rent charges, so I can let him know when I ring?'

'Yes. What's the fax number?' She wrote it down. 'I haven't done anything about the nanny yet, but I'll work on that today and give you a call. If I find someone, do you want me to meet her first?'

'Would you mind awfully? I would feel happier.'

'It would be quite fun. I've never had to think about nannies before, so I guess I'll have to dream up some questions. Any ideas?'

'It's not actually my forte either! As long as she's completely trustworthy, has good references and could manage to be totally discreet about who she's working for, I'm sure that would be OK.'

'You can always fire her when you get here if she's no good. Anyhow, let me get on to this now. I tell you what, I'll try to get over there and take some pictures of the house today, so I can send them to you.'

'I really owe you one for all this, Chris. I could have made a real mess up without your help.'

'No problem. I'm glad you called. Speak to you later then.'

'Yes, and thanks a million again.'

CHAPTER TEN

Wednesday November the 6th arrived incredibly quickly. Only the previous week she had been planning and making arrangements. Now they were taking shape. She was secure in the knowledge that all the flights were confirmed, the hotel in Hong Kong would be expecting them and best of all, that Jordan was absolutely delighted with the description of the house she had come up with in Sydney! The photographs, which had arrived from Chris only the day before (she had even managed to get a snap shot of the nanny she had engaged for them) were safely tucked into her bag, ready to take with her to see Jordan that evening. She had also called up the Dorchester to arrange for a baby-sitter to be on standby, so that Chelsea need not worry about her shopping. Every little detail had been churned over in her mind. The flat had been cleared of her belongings, all except for the case she would take with her. Alex had appeared on Saturday and had driven her, together with the boxes for storage, up to his house in the country.

She had lent her treasured car to Louise, who, now that she had had the baby, was very grateful to be able to get out and about when James was using their car for work. She was due to hand the keys of the flat over to the estate agents the next morning and was really looking forward to doing so.

Tuesday had been a very emotional and sad day for all at the office. Bronte was popular and it was if a member of the family was leaving home. Most of the girls spent the day with misty eyes and free-flowing mascara, which they made no attempt to conceal. Alex had suggested a formal lunch, but Bronte had opted for a much more casual gathering in the local pub, over sandwiches and a glass of wine. They had clubbed together and bought her the most fabulous watch with a metallic and gold strap and a sharp white face. Bronte suspected that Alex was mostly responsible for that, but she thanked them all equally, with a little extra hug for him.

As she rolled over in bed, dragging the duvet with her, she reached out to a adjust the tuning of the radio station. She was so organised that there was not too much she had to do that morning – really just a matter of packing her case, wiping over the kitchen, which she had deliberately left until the last moment, and perhaps a little shopping; she would go up to Oxford Street and see if she could find a couple of new things to take away. The trouble was that the shops were hardly likely to be full of summer clothes in early November! Still it would pass the time, which she suspected would definitely require passing that day.

After she had gulped down a bowl of muesli, she debated as to whether she should call Harry to check on the car for the airport. She decided against it, because Harry was obviously known to Jordan and would hardly forget to collect such a famous customer! The Dorchester had the suite reserved, she had checked on that when she called about the baby-sitter. So really there was very little she could do until her rendezvous later that day.

As Louise already had Bronte's car, it came down to a choice between bus, tube or taxi to get up to Park Lane that evening. She had allowed herself plenty of time, being determined not to arrive any more flustered than was necessary. The bus would take forever. Taxis were too expensive – perhaps she would treat herself to one on the way home. That left the tube which was a pretty lousy option, but would at least guarantee her arrival at a given time. She would get the District Line to Earls Court where she could pick up the Piccadilly Line to Hyde Park Corner. From there, the Dorchester was a mere five minutes walk.

She had taken a second shower that day, to scrub away the filth and grime that hunted out all possible victims in London, particularly in the central part of town. Smelling of gentle herbal shower gel, she put on a skimpy black leather skirt. Being fashion conscious but barely having the budget to satisfy herself, she took quite a bit of time and effort over her appearance.

The problem that night was that she really did not know what to expect. All Jordan had said was that she should come to the hotel to make contact. Whether that meant dinner at the hotel or elsewhere, with or without his wife, or anyone else for that matter, she had no idea. Therefore all she could do was hope she was suitably attired for any possibility. She twisted a pair of gold spirals into her ears and tried to encourage her hair to fall away from her face rather than right into it, as she didn't want to fix it up too severely.

Shopping had met with marginal success during the day. She had managed to pick up a pair of cycling shorts and a couple of plain cotton jumpers, all of which would be useful in Australia. Once she had jammed those into her bulging suitcase, there wasn't room for much else. Hopefully, the last-minute things would fit.

It was a warm evening for the time of year, as she stepped out into the street. The air was still filled with the sound of fireworks and the smell of gunpowder. Obviously, some people had delayed their Guy Fawkes celebrations by a day and parties were just getting underway.

The tube was no more appealing than usual. At least they didn't allow smoking in the carriages and so those who had previously objected were no longer condemned to arrive at their destination smelling like a stale ashtray. The District Line did, at least, stay mostly above ground, so it was possible to open the windows and breathe whatever air could manage to get in. But the Piccadilly Line was far deeper and altogether more unpleasant. Still, it was the quickest way to move around London as the roads had become increasingly blocked with traffic.

As Bronte trotted up the steps at Hyde Park Corner, the sky far above her shimmered its rich velvet cloak in the warm winter breeze. The cars, buses and lorries thundered round Hyde Park Corner, no-one anxious to give way and lose a precious second, which of course resulted in indignant car horns from time to time. But Bronte was unaware of all that was going on around her. Each step she took up Park Lane steered her nearer to her future and a journey through unfamiliar territory. It was still not too late to run – but run she wouldn't, because she was being driven by some sixth sense which kept her going. Bronte went through a moment's panic when she realised she had not called the hotel, or even Harry, to find out if Jordan and his family had arrived safely. But on the other hand, the hotel would probably not have given out that sort of information over the 'phone for security reasons, and Harry, who had her number, would surely have let her know if there was a problem.

Bronte had not been inside the Dorchester before and she was most impressed by the grandeur around her. Now that she had arrived at the hotel, she wasn't really sure what she should do next. It had not occurred to her to arrange a specific meeting place. There was no sign of Jordan in reception, but then he would hardly sit around for all to see. There was nothing for it but to ask at the desk.

The receptionist was temporarily preoccupied with an Italian guest, who seemed to be having great difficulty making himself understood and so she patiently waited her turn.

'I am sorry to keep you, madam. Can I help?'

'I hope so. I have arranged to meet a Mr Innes here. Mr Jordan Innes . . .'

The receptionist looked blankly at her, but then maybe he was trained to do so.

'Mr Innes and his family were due to arrive from New York today and should have checked in a few hours ago?'

The blank expression did not alter.

'They did arrive, didn't they?' She began to feel jittery.

'Madam, I am afraid we have very tight security. May I ask, are you a friend of Mr Innes?'

'Look, I work for him. Please tell me if he is here.' She had no intention of being rude, nor of entering into an argument, but she was getting worried.

'Mr Innes did check in today. But I am afraid I cannot disclose his room.'

Relief, at least he had arrived! There had to be a way of making the man understand her dilemma.

'Can I ring him then? I was supposed to meet him here at seven and I don't want him to think I'm not coming.'

'I am sorry but that is out of the question. All his calls are screened by the operator and only she can dial Mr Innes' suite.'

It was exasperating and, she desperately hoped, not a taste of things to come.

'Well, can you ask her to please call through for me, and give him the message that I am here in reception?'

'That would be best. Your name, Madam?'

'Bronte Richardson.'

'If you wait here, Miss Richardson, I will try the operator for you.'

'Thank you, and it's 'Mrs'.'

He turned to a house 'phone behind him and made a muffled call. He needn't have been so secretive because by that time, Bronte was neither interested nor really cared, as long as she managed to contact Jordan.

Several hushed whispers later, he turned to Bronte: 'Mr Innes would like a word.'

He stretched the 'phone across to the desk and passed her the receiver, which she accepted with a look of triumph on her face.

'Jordan?'

'Bronte. Hi! You just arrived?'

'Yes.'

'I'm coming down. Can you hold on there for a few minutes?'

'No problem.'

'Won't be long.'

'I'll wait.'

She handed the receiver back once she heard the click at the other end. She had had enough of the receptionist, so she turned round and marched off to wait for Jordan nearer the lifts, unaware of the general gaze of admiration that was focused on her back.

She thumbed through a couple of magazines, thrown casually on the table beside the squeaky white leather sofa, and was just beginning to wonder whether Jordan was really coming at all, when suddenly he burst through the doors of the lift, hardly waiting for them to open.

She had just managed to take in the vision in black, when

he rushed up, gave her a peck on the cheek and ushered her towards the door.

'I'm glad to see you too!' she managed to get out and the doorman touched his forehead as they hurried past him. Jordan looked at her and smiled, but still didn't say anything, or let go of her arm, until they were well into Park Lane.

'I'm sorry about that. I've had about all the hassle I can stomach today and I didn't need any autograph hunters in the hotel.'

'It's OK. I don't mind. I've actually had enough of that reception myself.'

'Did you have a problem getting me?'

'Problem? It was like trying to contact the Queen! You're really well protected there, you know.' She giggled as the breeze caught her hair.

'Sure, and I'm sorry about that too. I should have left your name downstairs, but Chelsea's gone to bed and Phoebe's been playing up and I forgot about it.'

'Is Phoebe all right now?'

'Yes. The hotel have sent up a sitter and she's reading to her. It's a shame Chelsea isn't up to coming, because I wanted you two to meet, but she's been working hard lately and she just flaked out when we got here.'

'It doesn't matter because I'll see her tomorrow anyway.'

'About tomorrow, we probably won't need you until we go to the airport. What time's the car due?'

'It should be there at three o'clock.'

'What about you?'

'Oh, I can get a taxi to the airport and meet you there.'

'Don't do that. Get Harry to collect you first and then come on for us.'

'But I live on the way out to the airport!'

'Doesn't matter. Call Harry in the morning.'

'If you insist.' She raised her eyes from the pavement and locked with his for a second.

'I do.'

'Can I enquire where we're going?' So far, they had headed back down Park Lane, retracing her steps to the underground station.

'Sure. I thought we'd go eat. I'm starved and I know the Hard Rock Café is just down here.'

'I haven't been there for ages.' She glanced at her watch. 'We should be all right now. If you get there any later, there's usually a massive queue.'

'I guess we should be sampling good old English cuisine and not American burgers.'

'I don't actually eat burgers.'

'Are you vegetarian?'

'Mostly. I do eat fish, but not meat.'

'Chelsea is too.'

They wandered past the window of the restaurant which was already buzzing with activity. Jordan had set quite a pace, which was ruffling his hair. Bronte's hair, meanwhile, was happily bouncing around any which way it chose!

The waiter recognised Jordan and hastened them to a small table near the back of the restaurant, which was partly shaded by leafy green houseplants.

The waiter held the chair for Bronte and then made a great fuss of unfolding their napkins before resting them on their knees. He produced two menus from nowhere and thrust them in front of Jordan and Bronte.

'Welcome! We have some specials tonight, if you would care to see the board over there. Can I get you something to drink while you are deciding?'

Jordan, who looked preoccupied and was obviously making a fast recovery from his trying day, glanced at Bronte.

'Wine?'

'Yes, please.'

'White or red?'

'I'd prefer white, but if you drink red, go ahead and order red.'

He spent a brief time choosing a white wine, during which Bronte managed to select a salad from the menu. Looking gingerly around her, she found herself feeling more and more unsure of the looks aimed in her direction, of which Jordan seemed blissfully unaware. She should try and ignore them too and in time, she would probably get used to it.

'So, tell me, what's been going on in your life since I last saw you at that hotel in Cannes?'

She looked up and then back down slowly, still avoiding his eyes.

'Where should I start? It's been very hectic trying to wind up at work and at the flat too, but I think I've covered everything and anything I've forgotten, well that's just too bad. Oh, and there was the burglary too.'

'Burglary?'

'Yes, when I got back from Cannes, the flat had been broken into and was a real mess.'

'How awful. Did they take much?' He frowned with concern.

'The usual things you would expect – the TV, video, stereo and jewellery. The worst was my engagement ring.'

'You're kidding! I'm so sorry to hear about that. Can you get insurance compensation?'

'Yes. I've put a claim in, but it doesn't repay the sentimental loss.'

'I guess not.' He changed the subject. 'And what was the reaction to your giving up your job?'

'From friends or family?'

'Both.'

He had a way of making her feel there was no-one else in the room. That it was just the two of them and that what she was talking about was of genuine interest to him. He never once diverted his attention from their table and kept his glance fixed on either his place setting, his glass or on Bronte. For her part, she found her eyes travelling up the walls, across the ceiling and down the other side, and only daring momentarily to look at his face. When she did look at him, she could make out what he must have been like in his teens. There were all the trimmings of manhood with the stubble beginning to show, but the skin was bronzed and soft, the eyes were deep and mystical and the smile was cheeky but, at the same time, spoke a thousand words. She had to get back to his question – what was it again?

'I'm sure some of my friends think I'm making it all up.' She sneaked a look in his direction and they met half way. 'The rest are fiercely jealous and dying to meet you sometime. The girls at work were good about it and took on my responsibilities without too many grumbles. We had a farewell get-together and they all bought me a watch.'

She lifted her arm and turned back her sleeve so he could see the latest addition to her now depleted jewellery collection.

He reached out and held her arm, drawing it nearer to his face so he could examine the watch more closely. His grasp was gentle but firm and she tried to let herself go limp, praying he wouldn't feel her pulse, which was thundering out of control.

'That's really pretty. Nice to keep. What about your family?'

She had always found it hard to talk about her family and this was no exception.

'Well, I told you my mother died when I was younger and I'm not all that close to my Dad. But amazingly, he did call me the other day and for the first time really since I can remember, he did seem to take an interest in me. I must try and get up to see him sometime.'

'Do you ever wonder what it would have been like to have had a really close family? I mean a Mom and a Dad and brothers and sisters too?'

'When I was a child, after my mother died, I can remember longing for my Dad to take me into his arms and hug me, or spend time playing with me or just take me out somewhere. But he was always so busy and I really think he believed that by marrying my step-mother, someone else would take care of me and the pressure would be off him.'

'I can hardly remember my parents. I know we lived way out of town and I can see the trees and the grass stretching to the horizon, but all that changed when they died. I guess they never got around to providing me with brothers or sisters.' His serious tone lightened.

'Where did you go after that?'

They were interrupted by their main course, which was set noisily down in front of them. They chose various dressings and were once again left to talk, and eat.

'Where was I? Yes, after they died . . .' He picked up his cutlery and began sawing his burger. 'I was shunted from grandparents to aunts and uncles, really anyone who could have me for a while. I was sent away to school and the holidays were spent in different places.'

He took a mouthful of food and chewed deliberately, while she picked at her salad.

'It sounds all very miserable but actually, it wasn't. I did OK and I'm not complaining. I suppose a stable home would have had a steadying influence, but I stayed on the rails – well most of the time!' Another bite.

'So when did the acting start?'

He swallowed. 'I've always been a show off.'

She looked up in surprise.

'Come on, I admit it. I have.' He watched her reaction. 'I knew from early on that I would never be able to work nine to five behind a desk. I had an interest in sport, but never shone enough at anything to make it worth pursuing, so I just followed my nose. I studied drama for a while and it sounds unoriginal, but it was a lucky break that saw me into my first film.'

'Which was that?'

'Don't even ask!' He shook his head into his lap, just the way she remembered. 'It was some God-awful movie about a pool player. I don't even want to admit to it. It was released in the States and taken off so fast that I think hardly anyone even realised it had shown.'

'Didn't that dishearten you?'

'Sure, for a while. But unbelievably, someone must have seen it, because I got a couple of scripts as a result of that, and things went from there. My break came with Red Light.'

'That's probably the first time I saw you. How long ago was that?'

'Around six years now, but it doesn't seem that long.'

'How many films have you made since then?'

'Oh, quite a few.' He grinned, as he continued to tuck into his ever-decreasing plate of food which made hers look almost untouched.

'Don't you ever want a change? I mean, how do you decide what's coming next?'

'Sure I need changes. But those come with each movie. No one movie is like the previous one, because you're all the time working with different actors, directors etc. Locations are usually fairly unique and besides, I guess I'm lucky in that I call the shots now. I have a team of people who spend their time reading the scripts that come in – I just don't have the time – and I can afford to be selective. Just do the work that appeals for whatever reason. You see, directing too is a new field for me – that's why I'm getting such a buzz over the movie in Australia. All the threads are coming together now – after months of planning – and it's just a question of tying them up.'

'How about the travelling? Don't you feel the need to put down roots?'

She carefully arranged her food at the side of the plate and drew her knife and fork together, trying to attract as little attention as possible to her manoeuvre.

'Roots? And just what are those, Mrs Richardson? Seriously, the gypsy in me thrives on travel. I'm a wanderer, Bronte, always have been, and I can't really imagine what it would take to tie me down for long. I'm not sure it's so great for Chelsea and Phoebe, but it's my career and they have to understand that.' He had become more serious, like someone on the brink of unburdening himself upon another, but must have thought better of it because he changed the subject.

'You're not hungry?' His plate was spotless.

'Since you ask . . . nerves, if I really admit it.'

He neither smiled nor frowned, but bore deep into her soul with sincerity and support. He beckoned to the waiter to clear the table.

Jordan reached over and topped up her already half-full wine glass, setting the bottle carefully back down, deep in concentration. He glanced at her and subconsciously admired her curvaceous outline as she sat, oblivious to his scrutiny, examining the sweet menu. The waiter shattered his train of thought.

'Would you like some dessert, Mr Innes?'

'Bronte?' His manners had been faultless so far.

'I couldn't, Jordan. There's no room.'

'How about coffee then?'

'Yes, thanks. Black for me, please.'

'Just two black coffees then.' The waiter headed for the kitchen.

'Bronte, look at me. You're pensive. A dollar for them . . .'

'Sorry? A dollar?' She looked up in surprise. 'Oh, I know what you mean! We say, 'a penny for your thoughts' over here.'

'Well, I haven't got a penny, so will a dollar do?'

She smiled: 'They're worth a darn sight more than that!'

'Name your price, Mrs Richardson.'

'If you don't call me Mrs Richardson, I might.'

'Sorry.'

Something had happened, ever so briefly, which neither of them understood at the time. But both were aware of it. Jordan had shaken it off first, perhaps being the one who was able to grasp more of what was happening. He knew he had to approach safer ground.

'OK, so we're all set for tomorrow?'

'I think so. I really hope I've remembered everything. I'm sure I'll get the hang of this more, as I go along.'

'Don't worry. You're not trying to pass an exam. So far, you've more than taken care of it all. The rest'll fall into place as we go.'

'I nearly forgot to show you these.' She reached down to her bag and drew out the photos that Chris had sent her.

'What are they?'

'Pictures of the house in Sydney. My cousin sent them over. Here, that's the house with the drive in front. This must be the garden at the back with the pool, and I suppose this is the view of the harbour.'

He took them from her one at a time, examining each closely before turning to the next.

'It all looks impressive. Well done, and well found.'

'I have my cousin to thank for that.'

'I guess we'll owe her a drink or something when we get down there. Now, if you don't mind, I'd better make a move and check that all's well back at the ranch. Phoebe'll be hell tomorrow if she's not had enough sleep.'

Bronte was very ready to go too. She needed some air . . . and some time to herself to think. To try and work out just what was going on in her head. Jordan pulled out a wad of notes and settled the bill, leaving a generous tip for the waiter. As Jordan stood back to allow Bronte to pass in front of him, several pairs of eyes looked up in surprised recognition and some degree of amusement. Once outside, Bronte shivered and glanced up at the sky which twinkled back cheerfully at her, offering no help at all. Making nothing of it, he threw his arm around her shoulders offering her some protection from the now piercing night air, and said: 'Come on, let's get you a cab. There must be some in Park Lane.'

'Oh look, it's OK, really. I can easily jump on the tube.' She was overcome with confusion, both by her emotions which had been playing tricks on her most of the evening, and also by the physical contact offered by Jordan, however casually applied.

'Rubbish! It's not safe down there and I'm counting on you for this trip.'

'Millions of people use the tube all the time and nothing happens,' she protested weakly.

'Yes, but isn't it nicer to take a cab?'

She couldn't deny it and had been intending to travel home that way anyhow.

'OK, you win. Look, there's one over there.'

She ran to the edge of the pavement and thrust out her arm wildly.

'Taxi, Taxi!'

Luckily, the driver was cruising for business and was only too glad to stop for her, especially when he recognised her companion.

Jordan leaned in through the open window, gave the driver a ten pound note and then opened the door for Bronte, who with one foot still on the pavement and the other in the taxi, turned to face him.

'Thank you for dinner, Jordan. I'm glad we had the chance to meet before the trip. I feel a bit more confident about the whole thing now.'

'I'm glad to hear it.' That million-dollar smile. She turned to step inside. 'And Bronte . . .' She glanced over her shoulder. '. . . it's good to see you again. You're great company and I know we'll all get along fine.'

She sank heavily into the seat as he closed the door, raised his hand and turned to walk back up Park Lane.

Her first instinct was to reach in her bag for her vanity

mirror to check that something dreadful hadn't happened to her face – like her lipstick smudging, her eyeliner descending down her cheek or even worse, blobbing in the corner of her eyes. The driver pulled out and ambled into the traffic which was heading down Park Lane and as he did so, she caught the reflection of the street behind her in the mirror, just in time to see Jordan turn his head in the direction of her fast-disappearing taxi.

CHAPTER ELEVEN

Bronte heard the horn outside. Rushing to the window, she waved furiously at the driver of the large, sleek, black limousine whom she sincerely hoped was Harry. From where she stood, it appeared as if the bonnet was parked outside her front door and the boot finished somewhere in the next street! What money could buy! It would definitely be a first for her.

She cast a final look around her empty flat which no longer resembled the love nest she had shared with Dominic. The little reminders of their time together were packed away in trunks and boxes for future repatriation or disposal. Instead, what stared her in the face were the stark realities of bare walls, rented furniture and hollow cupboards. It was no longer a place to conduct her widowhood. Time to move on with speed and fortitude.

With a sigh, she whispered: 'Goodbye Dom. If you can hear me up there, I hope you can understand why I'm doing this and that you can find it in your heart to send me on my way with your blessing. Even though I'm leaving our home, I'm not leaving you. I think of you always and I will always love you in a very special way, no matter what happens to me from now on. Think of this as closing a chapter, and here I go, starting a new one on my own. Goodbye, my darling . . .'

She grabbed a hanky from her bag and wiped away the tears that ran freely down each cheek, hoping to goodness that her mascara hadn't gone with them, and that her face wasn't too streaked. She must try not to be quite so sentimental, but sometimes it was hard and it was only two months since Dominic had died.

'Goodbye, flat. I hope you get some decent people in next . . .' But of course there was no answer, just a large empty space ready to be rented out to someone else.

Dressed in cream leggings which clung to her long legs, revealing their shape to perfection, flat boots and her denim jacket, she slammed the self-locking door and struggled with her case towards the car. Harry leapt out of the limo to help.

'Hey, put it down! You can't lift that. Here, let me do it.'

'Thanks, Harry. It is Harry, isn't it?'

'Yes, that's right. It's good to finally meet you after talking so much on the 'phone.' He touched his chauffeur's cap in polite recognition.

After he had put her case to one side of the gaping black hole which was the boot, he turned to open the passenger door for her.

'You like to ride up here with me?'

'Harry, I've never been in one of these before. I wouldn't know what to do back there!' She looked at the extended back seat – complete with telephone, CD stereo system, cocktail cabinet and television and that was just what she could see from where she sat! Who knew what other gadgets nestled in the drawers under the seat and in the side cupboards.

'It's probably best for the family to sit back there, as there'll be three of them,' he told her.

The car's engine was so quiet that Bronte could hardly tell it was running. Once they had set off, the sensation of motion was very smooth, making Bronte suspect that if she were to travel far in the back, she would more than likely be sick! She was much better up front with plenty of fresh air. Fortunately, Harry didn't seem to mind her fiddling with the window switch.

'So, this is a new venture for you, is it?' Harry began.

'That's right. I've given up everything to travel the world and work for the Innes family. Actually, that's not strictly true, circumstances have played their part in my decision.'

'I can think of worse people to work for. Jordan Innes is a charming man. Always polite and treats one right. Known him long have you?' There was a flicker of suspicion in his voice, which Bronte wasn't quite sure how to interpret. Either way, she decided to set him straight from the start.

'Actually, no. I've only met him two or three times. The first, only a couple of weeks ago, in Cannes. To be perfectly honest, I was amazed when he offered me this job, seeing as we hardly know each other. Anyhow, it's a long story but for better or worse, I've accepted. I haven't actually met his wife yet. What's she like?'

'Swedish. You know the type, blonde, petite and devilishly attractive. But I don't know that she's all there. She's a distant type, not particularly forthcoming.'

'Maybe she's shy?'

'No, I don't think it's that.' It had taken them no time at all to reach Knightsbridge, which was unusual for the time of day. 'She's obviously an intelligent sort, elegant and classy too. She's not exactly rude but I wouldn't call her friendly either. No, distant is about the best I can do for you.'

'I'm intrigued! I hope we're going to get on. I must say, I'm worried about what she must have said when Jordan asked a virtual stranger to accompany his family half way round the world.'

'I think you've got grounds to worry too. Someone as pretty as you.'

She blushed. Chelsea's reaction to her going with them had started to concern her, particularly when she hadn't shown up for dinner the previous night. Still, it was too late to back out. She'd just have to face whatever came her way.

'Jordan said she's been working hard lately.'

'She did look washed out when I picked them up yesterday. Sat back there and hardly said a word. Used to be a model by all accounts, but I understand she does some sort of writing these days. Not that I've ever read anything she's written, mind. Now take the kid – I've forgotten her name . . .'

'Phoebe?'

'That's it. Knew it was something out of the ordinary – if it comes to that, what sort of names are Jordan and Chelsea? Anyway, where was I? Oh yes, the kid – she's a cutie. Got the best of both her parents' looks – blonde curls and a tanned skin. Only about two, I'd say, but never stops chattering. It's plain for all to see that he adores her. Plays with her in the car and points out all sorts of things through the window. A real bond there – much more than either he or the kid seem to have with the mother. Anyhow, who am I to say?'

Who indeed, Bronte thought to herself as they rounded Hyde Park Corner and progressed up Park Lane. But he certainly did seem to have enough to say. What a relief that they were nearly there.

Harry swept into the forecourt of the hotel with pomp and ceremony, as the doorman rushed up to greet him.

'Come for Mr Innes, have we, Harry?'

'That's right, Guv.'

'Give me a moment and I'll go and let them know at the desk.'

'Righto, Guv.' Harry pulled out a spotless white duster from his pocket and began to polish away imaginary specks from the bonnet.

Meanwhile, not sure if she should stay in the car or go into the hotel to greet Jordan, Bronte hovered by the passenger door looking nervously around her. A couple of Japanese tourists, who had cameras slung round their necks with lenses the size of the Eiffel tower, looked on with interest to see who was about to come out of the hotel and step into that fabulous car. They didn't have to wait long, because the Innes family emerged after a few minutes.

Jordan came out through the main door, carrying the most adorable little girl Bronte had ever seen. She was dressed to match her dad, with miniature jeans, a diminutive black leather jacket and bright red trainers. Her hair bounced along happily, as the little ducktail curls sprang all around her cheerful, smiling face. A few paces behind, with no suggestion of a smile, a small attractive woman appeared, wearing an expensive fur coat, which flowed all the way down to her lower calves, revealing only a tiny bit of her black suede trousers and narrow lace-up ankle boots. One hand clutched the fur tightly to her chest, while the other carried an exquisite tapestry and leather vanity bag. Her blonde hair was swept up and pinned at the sides, but the fringe had been backcombed and allowed to sit precisely around her forehead.

Bronte was immediately apprehensive when she set eyes on Chelsea and stepped aside to allow her to get into the back of the car. Jordan, on the other hand, seemed pleased to see Bronte and anxious for her to meet his family. So while the head porter loaded the boot of the car, supervised by the vigilant Harry, Jordan made the necessary introductions.

'Hi there, Bronte. Right on time – well done. I'd like you to meet a very special girl in my life.' He gave Phoebe a squeeze, as she still straddled his hips. 'Phoebe, this is the lady who's coming with us and she'll be keeping an eye on you, so you'd better be a good girl! Say 'hi' to Bronte.'

'Hello Bwonte.' She couldn't quite get the 'r'. 'Are we going in the car now, Daddy?' Her accent was clearly American.

'Yes, honey, you go in there with mommy.' He leaned through the door and passed Phoebe to Chelsea, who was already settled in the back seat.

'Chelsea, this is Bronte.' There wasn't much more he could say, because Chelsea was in the car and Bronte wasn't, and he was standing between the two, blocking most of the view they had of each other.

'How do you do, Bronte? It's good to have you along.' Chelsea was stiff and formal.

'Hello, Chelsea. I'm really looking forward to coming,' and she hoped she was.

The luggage was stowed. A small crowd had gathered, partly drawn by curiosity to see what all the fuss was about and then realising, they stayed to have a good stare at Jordan. It was time to leave. Bronte climbed up beside Harry while Jordan joined the others in the back. There was a smoked glass partition which soundproofed the rear of the car from the front, and as this was fully closed, Bronte had no choice but to tune into Harry's ramblings all the way to Heathrow, terminal four.

The traffic had begun to clutter the streets as the evening rush hour approached and so it took them nearly fifty minutes before they turned off the motorway towards Heathrow. Travelling with the Innes family, everything seemed to just happen. When they drew up at the curb outside arrivals, two smartly-dressed porters were already opening the car doors, helping the passengers out and unloading the cases.

There was a child's buggy amongst the luggage, but Phoebe seemed to prefer Daddy. So with her in his arms, Chelsea by his side and Bronte in tow, Jordan said goodbye to Harry and made his way across the concourse in search of First Class check in.

'You got the tickets, Bronte?'

'Yes. Here you are.' She had been clutching them firmly since they left the hotel.

Still very unused to the attention that was focused on Jordan wherever he went, Bronte tried not to look back when she noticed undisguised stares aimed in their direction.

'You mind holding her?' Jordan passed Phoebe to Bronte while he sorted out the passports and tickets.

Phoebe very quickly latched on to a new game that proved to be enormous fun! Bronte's stubborn ringlets which fringed her face, were just the thing for inquisitive little fingers.

'Don't pull Bronte's hair, Phoeb. You want me to take her?' Those were only the second words that Chelsea had directed at Bronte.

'I don't mind. She's really sweet.'

'She has her moments, but you wait until she's had a fourteen hour flight.' The tension eased a little.

Jordan was nearly done.

'Here are your boarding passes, Mr Innes. These are your invitations to the First Class lounge. Have a very pleasant flight.' The perfectly-painted lips framed a glossy smile.

'Right, let's go. Come here, tiger!' Jordan put both his hands under Phoebe's arms, innocently brushing the sides of Bronte's breasts as he did so. Something unnoticed by him, but certainly not by her.

As they queued to put their hand luggage through the X-ray system, a pair of autograph hunters, who couldn't believe their luck when they realised who was standing in front of them, rushed up to Jordan waving their boarding passes and a couple of biros. Jordan, who still held Phoebe, seemed adept at signing his name while balancing his daughter on one hip and treating the two teenagers to his most public smile at the same time.

Once through passport control, Chelsea wanted to go straight to the lounge. Jordan, seeing Bronte's confusion over what she should do next – shop? disappear? run home? – turned to her.

'You coming to duty free?' Chelsea was already wandering towards the first class lounge, trailing a reluctant Phoebe, who quite clearly wanted to stay with Daddy.

'Why not?'

Out of the blue, Jordan said: 'Give Chelsea time. She's stressed out at the moment. She needs a rest.'

For some reason, Bronte felt awkward discussing his wife with him and was at a loss for words. The day was saved by the magazine stand which loomed up ahead of them.

'British Airways wishes to announce the departure of its flight BA 482 to Hong Kong. Would all First Class and Club World passengers please board the aircraft now through gate twenty one. Thank you.'

The announcement shrieked over the tannoy, making Bronte almost jump out of her boots! She threw down the last drops of coffee, before gathering up her bag and heading for the gate. Jordan had left her in duty free to go and find the others. There was no sign of them at the gate, nor on the 'plane as she boarded through the foremost door, just at the back of First Class. They would probably be last to get on to avoid unnecessary attention.

A very camp, bejewelled steward, with greased-back hair which had been sliced off just below ear level, took Bronte's hand luggage and led her past the galley to the first row of Business Class. She was pleased to find her request for a bulkhead window seat had been complied with.

'I'll just put this up here for you, dear, alright? Please feel free to take it down again once we're airborne, but we have to keep these emergency exits clear for take off, alright?' He could have done with a more prominent Adam's apple and a macho voice.

Most of the rows of seats in her immediate cabin area had already been filled. All around, people were settling into their seats, fiddling with the recline-seat and lift-leg-rest buttons, or extracting inflight entertainment from their bags. From where she sat, she was unable to see when Jordan and Chelsea boarded the 'plane, which in fact, was only moments after her. They were shown to two sleeper seats in the front row of First Class. In recent years, Jordan and

Chelsea had flown trans-Atlantic so frequently, as indeed had Phoebe, that they thought no more of it than they did of getting out of bed each morning. It was a way of life and the inside of an aeroplane was almost like a second home.

The 'plane was a little late taking off. Being an overnight flight, the fourteen hours flying time would pass quickly and by the time they had been served a meal or two and shown the customary films, they would be there. The time difference between the UK and Hong Kong meant they would not reach their hotel until early evening, the next day.

Bronte was amazed and secretly pleased that the only vacant seat in the cabin was right next to her, which enabled her to put her belongings alongside and stretch out. She was never left alone for very long; drinks were served, hot white face-cloths were distributed, a cosmetic wash bag and navy blue slippers were provided, all compliments of the airline.

After dinner Bronte reclined the seat as far as it would go, brought out the leg-rest and curled herself up to read the inflight magazine. She noticed that one of the possible films to be screened during the flight was a big hit from last year, starring none other than Jordan Innes! What a coincidence. She really hoped they'd choose it so she could study him a little more closely. It would be the first of his films she had seen since they met, and she was just wondering whether anyone else around her knew he was on the 'plane, when two things happened to divert her attention.

There was an announcement that duty free was available for sale and Jordan put his head through the curtain just in front of her, and still carrying Phoebe, slipped quickly into the seat beside her.

'How goes it? Comfortable, Mrs Richardson?'

'Will you stop calling me Mrs Richardson!' She gave him a playful swipe across the arm. 'It makes me feel like an old maid.'

'Which, I might add, you most certainly are not!' And nor did she look it.

'Have you eaten?' She changed the subject.

'Have we eaten, Phoebe?'

Phoebe, distracted momentarily from the doll she was busy undressing on his lap, looked up at him adoringly and grinned.

'I think you could say we have, yes. Madam here managed to get more food on her clothes than into her tummy, so we're already on outfit number two.'

'It's not easy though, is it Phoebe, when the 'plane decides to move around just when you're about to eat?' Bronte tweaked the child's ear and Jordan was touched to see how natural Bronte was with his daughter. Phoebe too, seemed to have taken an instant liking to her new friend because she offered the doll to Bronte saying: 'Clothes on, please.'

'You're honoured, Mrs R . . . I know, I know . . . I promise I won't say it again.' He lifted his hands in defence of her raised arm. 'Anyway, not many people are given the privilege of dressing Mary Rose, are they Phoeb?'

Phoebe was once more engrossed in locating the previously discarded garments and was fastening them back onto her treasured dolly.

'So, you're OK back here?'

'I'm fine, really. Fed and watered and about to watch you performing on the screen!'

'I know, it's embarrassing. They've got it up front as well. Chelsea's gone to sleep at the prospect.' Bronte couldn't help thinking that was perhaps a little unsupportive? 'I can't believe they're showing it so long after it was released.'

'But you're such a star, Mr Innes!' she teased.

'Don't you start! I think we'd better have a pact on the 'Mr' and 'Mrs'.'

Bronte was suddenly overcome with worry that she was becoming too familiar and flirtatious. Still, it was easy to be that way with him because he seemed such a fun person, hardly ever serious (not that she had seen yet, anyhow) and she couldn't deny that he was incredibly attractive. Enough! Alarm bells rang in her head. She was there to work and he was there on business with his wife. Work she had better do.

'How about me looking after Phoebe for a bit, give you two a break?'

'What d'you say to that, Phoeb? You want to stay here for now with Bronte, while mommy gets some sleep?'

Phoebe was such an easy-going child that she didn't seem to care where she stayed, as long as she wasn't to be parted from Mary Rose.

'If you're sure, that'd be great. I'll grab some sleep myself and rescue you a bit later on. What's the time?' He glanced down at his watch, drawing Bronte's eyes unwittingly to his well-manicured hands. 'A quarter off nine. Just come through with her if she plays up. But she'll probably sleep once they dim the lights for the movie. Say, how did you manage to get a spare seat beside you anyway? The rest of the 'plane looks completely full. Did you turf some poor, unsuspecting guy out?'

'Actually, yes. I made the most terrifying faces – like these . . .' She pulled the sides of her mouth with her little fingers, drew down her eyes with her index fingers and stuck out her tongue – at which Phoebe set off into peals of laughter, 'and he just ran away!'

Jordan looked at her with even bigger eyes than usual and giggled.

'I can't say I blame him. See you later.' He got up and made a hasty exit in the direction of First Class.

Oops, Bronte, there you go again. Getting carried away, she worried to herself. But despite feelings of regret, she felt happier and more positive than she had in ages. Jordan seemed to bring out the best in her and better still, she was beginning to feel more and more distracted from past troubles in his company.

He hadn't been far wrong in his predictions for Phoebe. Once the lights were turned down and the movie began to roll, Phoebe clambered over the armrest and snuggled into the pillows which Bronte had set in her lap. She clutched Mary Rose tightly, all the way to sleep.

Bronte couldn't help looking down at the angelic face, rosebud lips and freckled nose. For a moment, Bronte stepped out of herself as if in a dream, to gaze down on the scene in which she cradled the small daughter of a famous film star on her way to the other side of the world.

*   *   *

'Ladies and Gentlemen, we have commenced our descent into Kai Tak airport, Hong Kong . . .'

Bronte could scarcely believe they were about to arrive. The flight had passed effortlessly and she had had one further visit from Jordan to collect a playful Phoebe for her next meal. It had been fun minding Phoebe, who seemed easy to amuse.

Just before they landed, Bronte checked her face and stabbed at her hair with a long pronged comb to try and shape it back into some kind of order. They had already come down quite far, before the 'plane broke through the clouds to reveal a concrete horizon, the like of which Bronte had never seen in her life! Skyscrapers, tens of storeys high, loomed from every available piece of ground space. As they neared the runway, she wondered how they missed hitting the rooftops of Kowloon amid which their dramatic landing was about to take place.

Not normally a nervous flyer, Bronte held her breath and leaned over with her face pressed against the window, as the pilot swivelled the plane to accommodate his approach. Time had not permitted her to read up about Hong Kong prior to her departure, and she now regretted that, for it might have helped to prepare her for all that she was seeing. Bearing in mind that his task was considerable, the pilot made an excellent landing before braking hard to avoid any mishap at the end of the runway. It took some moments to taxi to the terminal building, during which Bronte was transfixed by all she could see around her.

First Class passengers were allowed to disembark first, but Bronte soon caught up with the others who were making their way to immigration. Jordan held tightly to the toddler's hand and to Chelsea's on the other side. She was carrying her fur coat, enabling Bronte to see her tiny slim figure from behind for the first time.

The major hotels in Hong Kong operated their own limousine services for VIP guests and Bronte had been assured that a car would be there to meet them. She had requested they use her name, rather than Jordan's, to try to deflect attention from the star's arrival. Nonetheless, she stood nervously, craning to see if there was a board with her name printed on, while a porter piled their luggage onto his cart. They hadn't let her down. As they passed through the baggage inspection area, she noticed a spotlessly turned-out Chinese chauffeur, standing almost to attention, bearing a plaque with 'MS RICHARDSON and Party' emblazoned on the front.

When they stepped into the limousine, only the second Bronte had ever been in, she felt unsure whether to sit with Jordan and Chelsea or to ride up front, as she had with Harry. However, the chauffeur didn't seem to make any distinction between his passengers and, indeed, probably didn't know who Jordan was anyway, as he ushered her into the back. Bronte felt a little uncomfortable with that arrangement and to make matters worse, a now-tired Phoebe insisted on sitting on 'Bwonte's' knee rather than anyone else's.

Fortunately Jordan must have sensed the difficulties, because he soon began the 'know where you are, guide to Hong Kong', with Chelsea contributing happily too – both had obviously been there several times before. That made it much easier for Bronte, who was genuinely interested in the hustle and bustle going on around them.

The journey from Kowloon through the tunnel to Hong Kong island took far longer than the distance covered would have suggested, because the rush hour traffic was bumper to bumper all the way. They went through Wanchai to the heart of Central, the city's commercial and banking district. The hotel itself towered over the waters of Victoria Harbour which were filled with ferries, junks and upper class yachts, as well as the humblest of houseboats.

As they walked into the main entrance, with Jordan striding ahead as if he did that sort of thing every day (which actually wasn't too far from the truth) Bronte was struck by the black Italian marble lobby and the impressive gold carvings.

Bronte was floating on the crest of a wave. She had travelled in her time, mostly to the Caribbean, Africa and the States, granted, but this was something completely different. She was unable to take any of it in her stride, unlike Jordan and Chelsea who seemed so accustomed to this lifestyle.

'You guys wait here. I'll go check in and get the room keys. No, Phoebe, stay there.' A miserable-looking Phoebe pulled a face, as if about to burst into tears.

'Darling, she's tired. Hurry up so we can get her to bed.' Chelsea looked tired herself.

The reception staff jumped to attention when Jordan approached and hardly had he time to complete the necessary forms, than he was back and they were ready to go upstairs.

'Come on, honey, it's bed for you.' He swept Phoebe up in his strong arm and took Chelsea's vanity bag in the other. 'Bronte, here's your room details. Get the guy over there to show you up. Take your time to sort yourself out, you must be pretty exhausted. I'll call you later.'

Bronte followed his direction as he disappeared into the lift. Her room was every bit as luxurious as she had thought it might be. The bed was big enough to sleep an army, the marble bathroom was like something out of a royal palace and all the little extras that you might expect were ready and waiting. The room even had a substantial balcony over-looking the harbour.

The bell boy who brought her luggage up spent several moments showing her how the various room gadgets worked. After he had gone, she flopped down on the bed, threw her arms back over her head and tried to imagine what a suite in that hotel would look like, if hers was a standard room! She thought of Jordan, who was probably unpacking or seeing to Phoebe – something at which he seemed more proficient than Chelsea. As she lay there, she could hardly believe that she was actually being paid to live in that luxury, and if that was how work could be, she couldn't imagine what she had been doing for the past five years.

After a little while, the 'phone went: 'Hello?'

'Bronte? You unpacked yet?' Jordan's voice.

'I've just finished.'

'Room OK?'

'OK? Jordan, it's a palace in here!'

'Glad to hear it.' She felt him smile. 'Look, Chelsea and I have just been asked to go eat at the Hong Kong Club tonight. We can't really refuse because the guy's a producer friend of mine. Can you organise a sitter for Phoebe? It's a little after seven now and we'll have to go in around thirty minutes.'

'Do you want me to sit for her?'

'No. You make sure you eat and get some sleep. You'll be on duty tomorrow, don't worry. Just get someone up to the Alexandra suite – the concierge or housekeeping should be able to fix that. I'll call you tomorrow.'

'If you're sure. Have a good evening.'

'Thanks. You too.' He seemed to be in a hurry to get off the 'phone.

Housekeeping was only too pleased to supply an amah for Phoebe and assured Bronte all would be taken care of. That really left her very little to do, other than order a light snack from room service, put her feet up and try to digest all that had happened in the past twenty four hours.

CHAPTER TWELVE

Sleep had been annoyingly elusive for what seemed like hours. She had lain awake with her mind rambling over the peaks and troughs of the last two months. When she did manage to drift off, she awoke only a short time later with a start. Not sure what had disturbed her, nor really fully aware of where she was, she shot out of bed and stumbled towards the chink of light which peeped through the heavy fabric curtains.

Bronte tugged them aside and slid open her balcony door, enabling her to step out and feel the warm night air, tainted with the odour of Chinese cooking and salt water spray from the sea. Below her, the water hummed with activity. Some of the junks sloshed to and fro, as passing vessels stirred the murky waters. The lights from Kowloon frolicked in the moonlight, as the rippling water did not permit any one pattern for more than a fleeting second.

It felt good to watch that wide expanse between the shores of Hong Kong Central and Kowloon. It symbolised an open space for her – there was no suggestion of claustrophobia, of the buildings closing in on her, which was all too easy to experience amongst the high-rise streets and crowds of Hong Kong. She needed spaces, both physically and psychologically.

She shivered as the sea breeze tugged at the folds of her night-shirt, causing her smooth skin to roughen to goosepimples and her nipples to become hard. She swept her hair from her face and slipped back into the room, closing the door all but an inch. At that precise moment she would have been surprised to know that several floors above her, Jordan too was taking a little night air on his balcony, his mind so preoccupied that sleep had become impossible.

Often insomnia leads to the deepest of sleeps and the weirdest of dreams. Jetlag probably contributed somewhere too. Bronte was firmly wrapped up in a tale of her childhood, when she became aware of a nagging disturbance, drawing her to the surface. She reached for the receiver: 'Yeah?' Barely able to focus.

'Sorry, Bronte. I must have woken you.' Jordan sounded bright and breezy.

'What . . . what time is it?' she managed.

'Nearly eight thirty.'

She came to with a start: 'Eight thirty? Wow! I'm sorry.' She never normally slept that long.

'Don't be. It was a long day yesterday. Anyway, I've got to shoot by nine thirty and I need to touch base with you first. How does breakfast sound?'

'Good. Give me ten minutes and I'll be there.' Even for her that was ambitious, but she was embarrassed about oversleeping and thought she had better sharpen up her initial impressions.

'Come to the suite and I'll get something up here. What's your order, madam?' She didn't need to try too hard to picture those melting eyes.

'Whatever you're having is fine.'

'Juice, fruit, croissant and coffee sound OK?'

'Sounds very healthy! Won't be long.'

She rushed to the window and threw back the curtains and the nets. Outside, the sky was crystal clear. There was barely time to race into the shower, hurl on some clothes (which she hoped didn't look too creased) try to introduce a degree of control to her tangled locks and brush her face with the merest hint of makeup, before she realised she was already five minutes late! She charged down the corridor, remembering at the last minute to bring a pad and her room key, darted around the maid's cart which had been purposely left like a speed bump in the middle of the hallway and thrust herself at the lift button. Once in the lift, she glanced at the mirror and realised that she was looking her most natural but vowed to remember to book an alarm call in future!

'Coming.' Bronte heard Jordan respond to her knock, which had actually been far more timid than she had meant, but her nerves got the better of her at the last moment.

'Hi! Come in. Breakfast has just arrived.'

She stepped cautiously over the threshold, trying not to stare too obviously, but unable to resist the draw of the plush interior which hit her straight in the face. The room was filled with the most exquisitely delicate mahogany furniture complete with oriental carvings, ornate fabrics and attention to colourful Chinese detail in every corner.

From where she was standing she could see that the suite consisted of a living room with a dining room table, and one room leading off at either end, which she assumed were the two bedrooms. Both the doors were closed and there was no sign of either Chelsea or Phoebe. Her expression must have questioned that because Jordan promptly said. 'Phoeb was up really early. I guess her time clock's out. Anyhow, Chelsea's put her down for a rest. Here, come grab some coffee before it goes cold.'

The table was laid for three people. At each place was a glass of freshly-squeezed orange and a dish of precisely sliced mango, decorated with jagged strips of kiwi fruit. As Jordan passed her a steaming cup of coffee, she noticed that he wore an expensively-tailored suit.

Bronte took up the seat he indicated for her and sipped her orange juice, which tasted like nectar.

'Plan of action for the day. I've got a meeting at ten with the co-financiers of the picture. There's several guys I have to see there so it'll take me through lunch. Can you get this tape typed? It's partly correspondence I didn't have time to get out before we left New York and also, some ideas I want to get down in print.' He passed her a dictaphone tape. 'They'll tell you about secretarial services downstairs. Oh, and check for faxes – Helen might have sent some through. She's keeping an eye on a few things back home. Use hotel paper for the letters.'

'No problem.' She was glad to be made to feel she was there to do a job and even more glad to divert her attention from those eyes of his. 'What about Phoebe today?'

'Chelsea's going out this morning. She'll go to the tailor's and probably get you to book a hair appointment or something. Can you get a sitter for Phoeb? Liaise with Chelsea.'

'I don't mind taking care of Phoebe, if you like? I'll do

this for you first,' she still clutched his tape, 'and then we can go exploring together.'

'If you're sure? I'm not paying you to baby-sit.'

'I know.' She looked up. 'I'll put a call in to Chris in Australia and check on things there too.'

'Good idea. When is it we leave? The twelfth?'

'Yes. It's a morning flight.'

Jordan bent down and semi-disappeared from view, much to Bronte's surprise. Surprise which was only temporary, because he came back up with a basket of deliciously warm croissants, which he had taken out of the warming oven, cleverly disguised under the table. He offered the basket to her, and just at that moment, the door at one end of the room opened and Chelsea emerged, wearing a long white robe and a turban-shaped towel round her head.

'Good morning.' Bronte felt uneasy as Chelsea approached the table where Bronte was breakfasting with her husband.

'Oh, morning. Sleep OK?' Chelsea was distracted.

'It got better as the night went on, thanks.' She laughed nervously.

Instead of sitting in the obviously vacant chair between Jordan and Bronte, Chelsea stood by the side of the table and poured herself a cup of coffee, ignoring the juice, the fruit and the croissants.

'I was just running over with Bronte what we need to do today.' Jordan was the first to speak.

'Right.' That was all she said.

'Tell Bronte if you want her to get you into the salon downstairs. She's offered to take care of Phoebe for a bit.'

Chelsea raised her eyebrows in momentary surprise, before reaching for the sugar.

'You know you don't have to. She's well-accustomed to having people sit for her.'

'It's no problem. Really, I'd like to.'

Jordan went on: 'Bronte, we've been asked to a barbecue this afternoon by a lawyer friend of mine who lives up on the Peak. I want you to meet some of my business associates whom you may have to deal with and it'll give you a chance to sample some local culture.'

'Darling, do we really have to go? If it's the guy I think

161

you mean, he's so boring.' Chelsea turned to Bronte. 'Honestly, all this man can talk about is movies and when we were here last year, we spent hours in the damn cinema he has under his house. Can you imagine?'

Bronte wasn't sure how she should respond, so she said nothing. Jordan replied instead: 'He's not that bad and his wife is charming. Besides, we're probably going to need some favours over the next couple of months. The least we can do is accept his hospitality, which last time was incredibly lavish.'

'So what time have you arranged this for?' demanded Chelsea – by that time, Bronte was looking for the nearest hole in the floor.

'We're invited for four, but we won't have to stay too long.'

'Shall I book a hotel car?' Bronte wanted to emphasise to Chelsea that she was there as an employee.

'There's actually one at our disposal downstairs. It comes with the suite,' Jordan told her, as if it was nothing out of the ordinary. 'I'll mention it when I go out this morning.'

Bronte spent her first day in Hong Kong running errands for Jordan and entertaining his daughter. By lunch time, she had seen to the necessary arrangements – all the while, Phoebe had played quite happily with the few toys they had brought or trotted contentedly after Bronte as she rushed up and down from the hotel typing-pool.

Bronte decided to venture out, and armed with a guide book and Phoebe's buggy, she set off in the direction of the shops. Having the responsibility of Phoebe's welfare and safety firmly on her mind, she steered towards the more fashionable thoroughfares and kept away from the street markets which were tucked away in side alleyways. As she only meant to window shop she was quite content to gaze into the most expensive establishments, but did hope in the back of her mind that she would have a chance to check out the street markets, before they left Hong Kong.

Lunch was spent in a hamburger restaurant. Phoebe must have been a regular customer of that chain, because the minute she spotted the sign she cried: 'I'm hungry, Bwonte. Can we have some fries?'

Bronte had not been given any instructions as to Phoebe's diet, nor what she should do about lunch, so she decided there was no harm in giving her what she seemed to want. It would probably be safer than trying some unknown Chinese dish.

They had great fun with fries and strawberry milk shakes, which Phoebe managed to smear all over her face, her playsuit and even her buggy, at which Bronte couldn't help laughing.

'What are we going to do with you, eh?' she asked, as she dabbed at the sticky mess with a handful of serviettes. 'Your mum will have my guts for garters if I take you back like this. Come here and let me clean you up.'

Phoebe just grinned by way of reply. She was a happy little girl, considering she must have been carted from pillar to post for most of her life. Perhaps that's why she seemed so carefree. Her life was one long adventure and every moment was unpredictable.

Bronte had lost track of time after that and only just managed to get back to the hotel and be ready by half past three, which was when she was supposed to meet Jordan and Chelsea in the lobby to go to the barbecue.

'Thanks for the typing, Bronte. They did a good job.' Jordan greeted her and seemed pleased with her morning's efforts. Relief.

As they headed out through the doors, with Chelsea on Jordan's arm and Bronte following a little way behind, a group of American tourists – detectable a mile away in their shorts, sneakers, flat caps and large cameras – paused to admire one of the most famous hotels in the world and noticed who had just passed them.

'Gee, Wilma. Take a look! Ain't that whatshisname?'

'Where, Joe?'

'Walking out there, with that blonde on his arm. You know, the one from all the movies?'

The rest of the party were by now straining their necks to try and identify the source of the excitement.

'Say, it's Jordan Innes! Don't you just love the way he walks? I would just give the world for a night with him!'

The Texan accent flowed from the mouth of a woman who must have been all of sixty.

'Honestly, Annie, you do talk so.'

Bronte didn't try to hide a smile, as she reluctantly followed Jordan out of earshot.

'And what did you get up to with our little monster today?'

Bronte was sitting opposite Jordan and Chelsea, in an even longer car than the one which had collected them from the airport. She hadn't thought they could make anything more obscenely large.

'We had a great time. She ran around helping me until lunchtime and then we went for a roam around the shops.'

'Did you get to eat?'

'I don't think I'd better tell you where we went.'

'It can't have been that bad. She didn't look any the worse for it when I saw her.'

'OK, I'm ashamed to admit that we went to a burger bar.'

'What's wrong with that? We go to those all the time back home.' Jordan looked amused.

'I wasn't sure you'd approve. We didn't exactly set any records with our healthy eating.'

'She gets that from her father.' Chelsea patted Jordan's knee and he glanced at her for a second.

'Don't tell me . . . fries and a strawberry milk shake?'

'How'd you know that?'

'She has it every time we go and usually manages to get tomato sauce or milk shake everywhere but her mouth.'

'Darling, don't forget she's only two.' Chelsea put her hand to the back of her head to check that her French plait, which had been painstakingly woven by the hairdresser, was still holding in place. She then turned to the scenery outside, which Bronte too found breathtaking.

They were winding up and up, round and round, higher and higher, leaving most of the city dotted beneath them. However, some of the high-rise apartments did seem to climb with them. The roads were never straight for more than a few metres. The conversation in the car had waned, each was lost in their own private thoughts which would have made very interesting listening to the others, had they been forced to speak them aloud. Bronte tried not to look at Jordan, who still had Chelsea's hand resting casually on his right leg.

Bronte's stomach was just beginning to churn from a combination of travelling backwards in the car and twisting round the roads which led up to the Peak, when the driver slid back the partition and asked in his most practised English (which was still barely understandable) what the exact address was. Jordan thought it better to show him, so he leant forward and passed through a piece of paper on which he had written the address that morning. For a split second, as he put one hand on the seat beside her to steady himself, Bronte could feel his breath on the side of her cheek. She could sense the electricity from his body warmth, which sent shock waves to the very core of her soul. Then he was gone, returning to his seat, leaving Bronte praying that he had not been aware of the momentary confusion that the contact had thrown her into.

The Peak was the mountainous area of Hong Kong, which played host to some fabulous houses and apartment buildings, catering mostly for the rich and successful. The more luxurious dwellings nestled in the hillside, screened by evergreens, but still competing for the most spectacular view of the island. It wasn't long before they turned into a driveway and stopped briefly at the gate which was manned by a fierce-looking guard, who seemed more than a little reluctant to open it for them. They proceeded down a drive and drew up beside an elaborately carved front door, and opposite a garage which played host to a Phantom Rolls Royce, two Porsches and a Ferrari!

On their arrival a manservant rushed from a side door and helped them out of the car, much to Bronte's amusement. It really was another world. A second later, the main door was flung open and a Chinese gentleman, grinning from ear to ear, welcomed them to his home. The first thing they were asked to do, even before introductions, was to remove their shoes and place them on a rack just inside the door. Bronte was totally unprepared for this, but was glad that her hold-up stockings were clean on only an hour before. She was lucky that she never needed to rely on her shoes for height, whereas Chelsea seemed tiny in stocking feet.

They were led down a long corridor into a vast living room, of which one whole side was taken up with windows looking out over the valley and the huge array of buildings far below.

'They have one of the best views on the island from this house,' Jordan whispered in her ear.

There were a number of other people already assembled in the room, both Hong Kong locals and also some English people. It seemed that Jordan was the only American. Then began the round of introductions. Bronte lost Jordan and Chelsea, who were led away to another corner of the room by their host. His wife, however, who smiled even more broadly than her husband and didn't seem inclined to reduce the smile even when she spoke, took Bronte under her wing and steered her over to a small mixed group of young and older people.

'So you work for Jordan Innes?' Bronte was immediately accosted by a pock-faced English boy in his late teens, who had 'I went to public school' written all over his face.

'Yes, I do.'

'I say, what a frightfully interesting job. How did you manage to get it?'

'Really by chance and being in the right place at the right time,' she replied, wishing he wouldn't keep leering down her cleavage which was only just noticeable under her silk blouse.

'Yes, but what do you actually do?'

'Well, it's still very early days, but basically he's about to work in Australia for a while and he's employed me as his personal assistant.'

She was jolly well going to do up another button right in front of him in a minute!

'Wow! So, what's he really like then?'

They were interrupted by a maid bearing a tray of hors d'oeuvres, followed by a waiter who thrust a glass of champagne into her hand.

'He's an utterly charming and definitely non-pretentious person.' Shame the boy she was talking to wasn't.

'Has he tried it on with you?'

'I beg your pardon? He happens to be a happily married man,' – that was the image he portrayed anyway, 'and I'm

166

recently widowed!' She shut him up and, with that, crossed the room towards the window to admire the view.

On her way she encountered a whole suckling pig, decoratively displayed for all to see, prior to being barbecued. Part of her was repulsed by the lifelike animal, skinned and sprawled on the dish like a trophy, and the rest of her was amazed because she had never seen anything quite like it at the barbecues she had been to in England, where sausages and drumsticks were the norm.

Jordan noticed her standing alone, staring out of the window and excused himself from Mr Chang, the banker, who was currently boring the pants off him.

'You look flustered.'

'It's warm in here.'

'You sure that's all?'

Bronte was not about to tell him that even drinks parties back home with good friends were never really her cup of tea, let alone ones like this, where she hardly knew anyone. She simply nodded and said: 'Have you seen that pig over there?' She was referring to the dinner and not the person she had just been talking to.

'He's really something, isn't he? I'm sure they're going to have masses over.' He giggled. 'Come, meet a friend of mine who worked with me on Red Light.'

As Bronte politely refused a slice of garlic bread, she noticed that there was no sign of Chelsea in the room. Perhaps she had gone downstairs, where, judging by the smells wafting up, they had lit the barbecue.

Jordan's friend, Julian, turned out to be an interesting Englishman of about forty five, who had settled in Hong Kong a few years previously, because as he put it, 'the Far East is where it all happens now. Everyone wants to shoot over here.' He went on to tell Bronte how he worked freelance and was responsible for researching suitable film locations, setting up local facilities and generally getting the show on the road, in preparation for crew and cast to start shooting.

There was still no sign of Chelsea upstairs.

'So, tell me, Bronte, how did you land yourself in the media business?'

Julian's head was tilted to one side, as he propped himself against the window ledge, concentrating all his weight on one leg.

'Actually, I've been working in television for some time and it's only recently that I've made the switch . . .' She then launched into a shortened version of how she actually came to be working for Jordan, a version she was now perfecting, because the question seemed to be on the lips of everyone she met.

Julian listened intently to every word. Unbeknown to her, like most men she met for the first time, Julian was transfixed by her looks, her style and her manner. He digested all that she was saying, but paid just as close attention to Bronte herself. He secretly wondered just how long Jordan was going to be able to keep his hands off her, because any hot-blooded male would have a problem. But then Jordan was already married to a stunningly-attractive woman. He would have to remember to try and get down to Sydney if he could. It might be worth pursuing.

A gong sounded downstairs, signifying that the feast was prepared and would everyone make their way down. The room immediately at the bottom of the stairs was very similarly laid out to the one they had just vacated. The window became a set of floor-to-ceiling doors, but apart from that, everything was much the same, particularly when it came to size. The room was huge.

Outside on the patio, four barbecue grills were being manned by a flurry of little maids, each anxious to watch that the food was not allowed to overcook. The dishes ranged from lobster to lamb cutlets, to chicken halves, to fillet steaks – and that was all in addition to the suckling pig, which took pride of place on the lawn.

Bronte had never seen so much food in one place and all that to feed only about thirty people. As she went down the stairs, with Julian in hot pursuit, she noticed that Chelsea was deep in conversation with two English women on one of the sofas. She must have gone down there almost as soon as they had walked into the house.

Their host led the way outside onto the lawn, where several tables had been set with the finest silver cutlery and crystal goblets. One whole table was devoted to wooden bowls containing every possible type of salad. Carnivores and vegetarians alike were not meant to leave hungry.

'My dear, here's a plate – please do help yourself.' Their host was a balding man, who could have been anything from thirty to fifty, but essentially, he was a most generous person who showed all the signs of self-made wealth – in obviously large quantities – as he wandered around shoeless.

Bronte put her plate forward for lobster only and then proceeded to serve herself from the salad bowls, before selecting the furthest table from the house and sitting down. Predictably, Julian ended up beside her, with Jordan, who seemed to have been latched on to by two glamorous women, each old enough to be his mother, opposite. Jordan's charm oozed and it was lapped up on both sides. Julian broke her train of thought.

'Expensive taste in food or just not a meat eater?' He was eyeing up her lobster.

Bronte pondered: 'A bit of both, I suppose.' She studied his heaped plateful of meat, with side salads on an extra dish and laughed.

'Do you always eat that much?'

'Only at barbecues. Seriously, I live on my own and I'm not the greatest of cooks, although you're about the first person I've ever admitted that to. I figure, why not take advantage when I'm asked out? Would you like some of this wine?' He reached for the bottle of red set in the middle of the table, briefly read the label and offered it to Bronte: 'I certainly recommend you take advantage of this, it's a particularly fine vintage.'

'Thanks.' She pushed her glass forward to where he was about to pour.

'Old Charlie's two hobbies are wine and movies. When you come here, you are guaranteed to enjoy a first-class glass of wine and watch just about any film you care to name. Are you into watching movies?'

'Now and again. When I have time, which hasn't been that often lately. Why, is it compulsory here?' She giggled.

She really was delicious and so natural – he shouldn't let his mind wander: 'Might be. Depends how many guests ask

169

to see one. With your boss here today,' he nodded in the direction of Jordan, who had his head inclined towards the ample bosom of the woman on his right, as he listened to her high-pitched twittering, much to the obvious disgust of the scowling woman on his left, 'the mood of the party's bound to be films at some stage.' He drank his wine, savouring the full-bodied flavour.

'Whereabouts in England are you from?' He tried a different tack.

'My father and step-mother live in Yorkshire. But, to be honest, I don't really consider anywhere to be home.'

'That's a shame. No roots. The eternal gypsy! Sounds very romantic.'

Bronte couldn't help but think of what Jordan had said about his gypsy spirit earlier that week.

'Hardly romantic. More like a bit lost.'

'Ah yes, but think of the freedom. The opportunities to spread your wings. The lack of responsibilities. Where is your sense of adventure?'

'Not as well developed as yours, by the sounds of it!' She laughed again.

To Julian, it was infectious, carefree laughter, betraying nothing of her recent troubles (which she had taken care not to elaborate on, because pity was hard to handle from strangers).

'You're right, of course. I've been a bachelor, allowed to wander for too long. Time I got my act together. I say, you're not in the market for marriage are you?' He teased and she took it as a tease.

'Not just now, if you don't mind. Try me again this time next year.'

'Just checking. Same time, same place?'

'If we're both invited that is, and of course, allowing for the fact that either of us might have fallen hopelessly in love with someone else by then.' She reciprocated the flirtation – there didn't seem to be any harm in it. Out of the corner of her eye she had noticed, more than once, Jordan's eyes travelling in her direction.

Much to her surprise and embarrassment, Julian leapt off his chair and went down on bended knee.

'Madam, I shall save myself for you!'

Jordan, whose attention had been attracted by that little scene, shouted across the table: 'Jules, give her a break! She's only been in Hong Kong for twenty four hours. Where are your manners, man? Get her a dessert.'

'He's absolutely right. What would you like?' Julian stepped up quickly and brushed down his trousers, while Bronte couldn't help feeling flattered by the way Jordan had come to her defence, even though the situation was never heading out of control.

'Anything fruity. No cream, though.'

'Something fruity for the lady, coming up!' He cleared her plate and took it inside.

During the pudding course everyone – apart from Bronte – moved tables and mingled with fellow guests. She lost sight of Jordan and Chelsea. To her horror, the jerk from earlier ended up at her table, although thankfully, not next to her. A quiet Chinese lady, who turned out to be the wife of a prominent banker, asked if she might sit beside Bronte and once they got chatting, Bronte was pleased to learn from a local person, where she should shop, what was worth buying, and what other points of notable interest she should try and take in during her brief stay in Hong Kong.

After some half an hour, they were interrupted by a young man who had previously been introduced as the eldest of Charlie's three sons.

'Dad's about to show The Abyss and wonders if you two ladies would care to join us?'

Mrs Chang, which was as much of her name as Bronte knew, replied: 'No, thank you Alfi, but I'm sure my companion here would like to.' She brushed Bronte's arm gently.

Driven mostly by curiosity to see just what a cinema in a private home looked like, and also to ensure that there wasn't anything she should have been doing for Jordan and Chelsea, she stood up, thanked Mrs Chang for all her advice and followed Alfi inside. The party was well dispersed by that stage. The tables were less than half occupied and some people stood around inside, sipping cups of China tea with both hands. Chelsea was still elusive and Jordan seemed to have vanished too. She hoped they hadn't left without

171

telling her. Still, if they had, there must have been a reason and she was very capable of ordering a taxi back to the hotel.

Alfi led the way down another flight of stairs and through an open door at the bottom. The cinema was every bit as large as the rooms upstairs and at a quick guess, Bronte estimated seating (in leather arm chairs) for at least twenty five people. The side walls were stacked with shelves, just like the local library back in Fulham. Only they were not lined with books, but with disc cases, each meticulously labelled according to title, subject, stars and duration. She wondered how many of Jordan's films were stored in there.

The screen filled the facing wall and the transmission equipment was sunken into the ceiling, being operable by remote control from below. Bronte stood in the doorway of the dimly lit room with eyes wide open.

'Pretty neat set-up here, Bronte.' Jordan, who had been sitting in the back row chatting to Julian, had noticed her come in.

'You startled me!' Her hand flew to her chest and she took a seat in the next row from the back. 'This is quite amazing! Does he use it often?'

'Oh, all the time.' Julian answered. 'He comes home from work every day and puts on a film. Great way to relax! Apparently, when the kids come back from England for the school holidays, they comatose themselves in here for up to forty eight hours, only coming out for calls of nature and to collect the next meal.'

'The quality of sound and picture is something else in here,' Jordan continued. 'He's got everything on laser disc.'

Bronte was speechless, as she took in all around her and she was still looking about in awe, when Charlie came in a few moments later to start the show. About half the seats were taken. The 'jerk' was unmistakable in the front row and Alfi beside him. Perhaps they had been at 'the' public school together?

The movie was suspense-filled from the beginning, which caused Bronte to put off her nagging need to go to the loo for as long as possible. It did, however, reach a point where, if she hadn't got up and gone, the result would have been an accident right there in the middle of the cinema, which wouldn't have done her reputation or the leather seats any good at all! As she stood up and excused herself past the couple next to her, she was surprised to glance into the row behind and see Jordan's seat empty. She wondered when he had gone, because she hadn't been aware of any movement behind her. But then she had been gripped by the action on the screen.

Once on the level where they had eaten, she accosted a maid and asked where she could find a bathroom.

'Ladies' room, on first floor.'

She managed to find the stairs and made her way up to the bathroom. As the door was ajar, she never thought for one moment that anyone would be inside and walked straight ahead.

The scene that hit her right between the eyes was so unexpected, that she took a step back in shock. There, on the thick cream pile carpet, lay Chelsea, apparently lifeless, with Jordan kneeling beside her.

'My God, what's happened to her?' Bronte put her hand to her mouth.

Jordan looked round for a second: 'I'm glad it's you. Shut the door will you – I don't want anyone else coming in on this.'

'Is she breathing? Is she going to be OK?' Bronte rushed to the other side of Chelsea and crouched down for a closer look.

'Yes, it's not as bad as it looks. She's thrown up – only just made it here by the looks of it and she's choked on her vomit. I think she must have just passed out before I got here.'

'Thank goodness you did.'

At that moment, Chelsea coughed up the vomit that had lodged in her wind pipe and Jordan reached into his pocket for a handkerchief to clean her mouth. Turning her on her side to help her breathe, he said to Bronte: 'Say, would you mind helping me cleaning up a bit? I really want to play this down.'

'Of course I will. But are you sure she's going to be all right? Shouldn't we call a doctor or get her to a hospital or something?' She looked around for a cloth that she could use to wipe the lavatory seat, where Chelsea's aim had not been too good.

'Trust me. She'll be all right. I'll get her back to the hotel.' He stood up and went to the window which he opened wide to let some fresh air into the room. He then searched for a hand towel, which he soaked with cool water and began to wipe Chelsea's stained face, which to Bronte, looked a sinister ashen colour. All the while, Chelsea's breathing was becoming steadier and deeper, but her body still seemed limp and her eyes remained closed.

Bronte managed to restore the bathroom to its former state and a bit of detergent, mixed with a spray of scented freshener, helped to dilute the smell of vomit. The fresh air did the rest. Between them, they fixed Chelsea's hair back into position and straightened her clothes, by which time all traces of the drama which had taken place only moments before began to fade into memory. Bronte felt desperate for Jordan, as he knelt on the floor with Chelsea propped up against his stomach, and her heart went out to him as he stroked the cheek of his sickly wife with one hand, while supporting her tiny frame with the other. His now crumpled suit betrayed his superstar image and his hair, instead of lying in its usual controlled layers, fell forward as he bent over Chelsea.

'Look, Bronte, thanks for all this. I'm sorry you had to walk in on that scene but thanks again for helping.'

'Jordan, anyone would have done the same.'

'Yeah. Anyway, I'm going to take her downstairs and get the car to drive us back. I'll find Charles but I don't want to run into too many people, so could you do me a favour and not mention this to anyone? If anybody asks, just tell them Chelsea felt unwell and we've gone, will you?'

'No problem. I'll get a cab down when the movie's over.'

'I'd appreciate that because I don't want us all to make an exit – it's not worth the hassle. But get Julian to drop you back. He comes down that way.'

'Don't worry about me, just take care of her.' She rose slowly from his side and as he reached out his hand and touched her forearm, she swam for a moment in those dark pools where his eyes should have been, feeling totally heady.

174

'Thanks, Bronte.' He really meant it and she knew it. 'I'll call you later.'

On her way back down the stairs, Bronte took a deep breath and glanced at her watch to see what the time was – only eight o'clock, but it felt more like after midnight. She had been terrified to see Chelsea looking so deathly, but on reflection, it was almost as if Jordan had done it all before. He had been far calmer than she could ever have been and seemed to know just what to do. It wasn't until later that night that she found out the truth.

Needless to say, her concentration wavered constantly from the screen from then on. The film, which had held her attention at the beginning, seemed meaningless and she couldn't wait for it to end. A further hour had clocked up before the end titles rolled up the screen, much to Bronte's relief.

'Did you enjoy that then, old girl?' Julian put his hand on her shoulder, making her jump.

'What?' She was miles away. 'Oh, yes – really impressive. Look, I'm not in the habit of asking strange men for lifts, but Jordan's taken Chelsea back to the Mandarin because she wasn't feeling well and he said you might be able to drop me down there on your way home?'

'I thought something was up when he didn't come back in here. Of course I can take you. Do you want to go now?' He was suddenly serious.

'Would you mind? Only I may be able to do something to help.'

'Come on, let's go.' He grabbed his jacket from the seat next to him and escorted her out of the cinema.

Charlie was just saying goodbye to the Changs when Julian and Bronte came to look for their shoes.

'Not leaving already, my friends? I was just about to come down and take requests for the next movie.'

'This one's jetlagged, Charlie,' Julian put his arm protectively around Bronte's shoulders, 'and I've got to put a couple of hours in at my desk for a meeting tomorrow.'

'I understand. I would like to thank you for coming and to say that it has been our pleasure to entertain you today.'

There followed a certain amount of kowtowing and pleasantries before they managed to escape into the night. Bronte had been grateful for the way Julian had taken charge of her. It was reassuring to have him by her side, just at that moment of need.

'What happened when you went out of the film?' Julian asked her, once they were through the gate and back on the road to town.

Just how good a friend of Jordan's was he and how much should she say? She didn't want to lie to him, but equally, she was not about to impart the whole truth of that scene in the bathroom, which she could still picture only too vividly.

'I bumped into Jordan, who told me Chelsea had passed out upstairs and that he was taking her home.' She wasn't exactly lying, merely bending the facts a little.

'That figures. It isn't the first time this has happened, you know.'

'What do you mean?' Bronte turned to look at his profile.

'Jordan having to take Chelsea away from parties.'

'Why?' She didn't understand.

'Jordan's a good mate of mine and we've worked together several times now, but I don't know exactly what it is with her. Since you are working for them, you are bound to find out sooner or later, but I just think you should know that this has happened before.'

Why did her own intuition seem to tell her that same thing? He changed the subject.

'What's happening tomorrow, then? Got any time to sightsee? Need a guide?'

Bronte paced her room anxiously. Her handbag lay discarded on the bed, along with her room key. Should she call the suite? Or go up there? What if it was worse than it looked? What if Chelsea had been rushed to hospital after all, or, Heaven forbid, had died on the way home?

Oh why have I been blessed with such a vivid imagination? she thought frantically to herself. I'll go mad in a minute if I don't do something. Perhaps she ought to just try and get some sleep. But Jordan had said he'd call her 'later'. Did that mean later that night, or later being the next morning? She'd never be able to sleep if he'd meant the latter.

She had just reduced her clothing to her bath robe, when she heard someone at the door. She hadn't ordered room service, nor called for housekeeping. 'Damn,' she said out loud. She really didn't want to see anyone just at that moment and so, dragging the chain across the door, she called out: 'Who is it?'

'It's me, Jordan. Can I see you?'

She flung the door open and it was all she could do to refrain from throwing her arms round his neck in sheer relief that it was him and not some unwanted intruder.

'Come in.' She stood aside. The faint scent of his aftershave wafted round her as she closed the door.

'Mind if I grab a scotch? I could really use one right now.'

'Please, help yourself. The minibar's just here.'

She opened the fridge door and searched in the cupboard for a glass.

'Want one?' He looked up, still crouched by the fridge.

'Yes, OK. Can you put some ice in mine?'

Watching him pour the drinks, she suddenly became self-conscious of the fact that she only had a dressing gown on and no make up at all, but he seemed not to notice as he opened her balcony door.

'Jordan, do you want to talk about it?'

He stood with his back to her leaning against the railings, with one hand in his trouser pocket and his drink in the other.

He took a deep breath and letting it out gradually through puffed cheeks, he turned to face her silhouette outlined in the doorway. He still didn't say anything as he went inside, passing without touching her.

'You don't have to. I only thought it might help.' Had she put her foot in it?

'You're right, Bronte. You deserve that and I probably do need to talk to someone. I've bottled this thing for far too long in the hope it would go away.'

'Jordan, what exactly was wrong with Chelsea tonight?' she asked him quietly, as he sat down beside her on the bed.

Throwing back the contents of his glass, he said: 'Chelsea suffers from anorexia nervosa. You've probably gathered that I don't normally talk about this, and so I need your word that it isn't going to go any further.'

'Like you said to me earlier, trust me.'

'You know? I really think I can.' There appeared the faintest trace of the first smile she had seen that evening, and it was a relief. 'I found most of this out after we were married. She suffered badly with it in her teens, but then she went to some clinics in Sweden and it got better. She was a different person when we met, Bronte, and she was OK until she fell pregnant. I need another drink.' He reached for the fridge. 'Phoebe wasn't planned and even before I knew Chelsea was pregnant, it was clear things weren't right. It was as if her mind had flipped. She wouldn't eat, as if that would make the baby go away and stop her from putting on weight. To cut a long story short, Phoebe is a miracle considering the state her mother was in during pregnancy. Chelsea has never been the same since Phoeb was born.'

'Jordan, I'm so sorry.'

'Sometimes I look at her, Bronte, and I really feel I'm losing her. It's like she's drifting away before my eyes and there's nothing I can do to haul her back. Of course, it's not that bad all the time, but it's a strain to constantly watch her eat and make sure she keeps it down.'

'Hence the sickness tonight, right?'

'Exactly. She's been better lately. I really thought she had done with bringing it back, which is partly why I made her come on this trip so I could keep an eye on her and see if I could get her back to normal.'

'I understand.'

'But now I'm afraid it's happening all over again and what's more, I'm scared it will affect Phoebe too.'

'But she's such a happy child and it's obvious that she adores you.'

'I know, but that's just it, there's no real bond with her mommy and that's bad for a kid her age.'

'So what are you going to do now?'

'What can I do? She was out cold when I found her and I'm pretty sure she won't remember much, if any of this, tomorrow. Thank God we didn't have Phoebe with us today, because I never want her to see her mommy like that.'

'Of course not. Is there anything I can do?'

He leant across and put a hand on her leg for a second. It was not a pass, that was far from his mind. More a friend in trouble reaching out for comfort. She didn't comment and tried her best not to stiffen noticeably.

'This is a hell of a thing to put on you. You hardly know us and now you're in at the deep end of our problems. If you can stick it, just having you around will help. It will be a stabling influence for Phoeb and who knows where it's all going to end, but what's important is that it doesn't get into the press. I don't care for my sake, but it might just send Chelsea over the edge, while she's in a fragile mental state.'

'Jordan, I'm not going to run out on you now. I'm here because in some ways, I'm already running and maybe I need to have a bit more to care about.'

'Jeez, with all this I keep forgetting what you've been through too. I'm sorry. Are you sure you're not lonely or homesick or something?'

'Not in any way that matters. It gets easier the more time passes and keeping busy helps.'

'Yeah, but I bet when you let me talk you into all this, you never envisaged such emotional involvement. You've got to believe, I never thought you'd have to see any of this. I had really hoped it was all behind us.'

'Has it been this bad before?'

'Worse. Parties seem to be the hardest for her, particularly when there's so much food on offer. It's as if she can't cope.'

'Well, we'll just have to avoid the parties for a while. Either that, or keep a close eye on her.'

'What did we do to deserve you?' Again he smiled.

'Oh, I don't know. It works both ways, remember.'

'Thanks for hearing me out. It's good to have you on my side, especially for Phoebe's sake.'

'Don't keep thanking me or I'll call you Mr Innes again! A listening ear's all part of the service.'

He stood up and gathered his jacket from where he had flung it on the bed. She suddenly felt fidgety and needed to get up too, so she took the two empty glasses into the bathroom and began to swill them round with cold water.

'Get some rest, Bronte. It's been a long day.'

'You too. Business as usual in the morning?'

'Everything just as normal. I'm sure it's the best way to handle this. I know Chelsea'd be mortified to think you were there this evening, so no mention of it, eh?'

'Of course.'

He swung the jacket over his left shoulder and opened the door.

'Breakfast tomorrow? I need to run a few things by you and there's a couple of people you could try and see – but more of that tomorrow. Sweet dreams.'

'Thanks. I'll try not to oversleep again.'

She closed the door behind him and leant against it for a moment, listening to his footsteps disappearing down the corridor.

CHAPTER THIRTEEN

The cyclone which had wreaked havoc over much of the Darwin area for the past two days had a major effect on the air as far down as Sydney. The fasten seat-belt sign had been illuminated for much of the flight, as they ducked and dived through the pockets of turbulence. Even the crew had been asked to take their seats at one point, near to the eye of the storm, but as they continued on the journey to Sydney a normal service was resumed.

With only half an hour left of the eight-hour flight from Hong Kong, Bronte pondered briefly over the past couple of days. The day after the barbecue, she had joined both Jordan and Chelsea for breakfast in their suite. Either Chelsea could not remember what had happened the previous evening, or was putting it behind her, because she appeared to be in better spirits than Bronte had seen all week. She ate just about as much as they did, talked about taking Phoebe to the Zoological and Botanical Gardens that morning and seemed particularly affectionate towards her husband. Jordan, for his part, appeared visibly relieved at his wife's apparent recovery and, for a moment, Bronte seriously wondered if it had all been a bad dream.

She had accompanied Jordan to a couple of meetings that day and had been very interested to be given a 'behind the scenes' tour of some of what was involved in getting a movie off the ground. Julian (who had been on the 'phone at least three times that day) joined them for a quiet dinner in the suite, after which the conversation turned to very in-movie talk and Bronte had followed Chelsea's example and gone back to her room for an early night.

Their last day in Hong Kong had been divided between shopping (Bronte had managed to snatch a quick hour to herself at Stanley Market) a little sightseeing, and to round off the evening, a business dinner at the Chang's home.

Less than a week into her new job, Bronte was by no means discouraged. In fact she had learnt more about the movie business in four days of being with Jordan Innes than she had in her life up to that point. She was, however, looking forward to seeing Australia and to settling into the house, which would inevitably be more inviting than a hotel room, luxurious though that had undeniably been.

'That was quite a flight! You get food served in your half?' They were once more waiting for their luggage to emerge on the carousel.

'Breakfast went down OK but it petered out after that. Did Phoebe mind the bumps?'

Phoebe was, at that moment, sitting against her father's chest with her head on his shoulder. As Jordan had just noticed some of their baggage and was pointing it out to the porter, Chelsea, wearing dark glasses replied: 'She's a seasoned traveller, this one. She slept most of the way. Didn't seem to notice it.'

'There was a baby near to where I was sitting who screamed for about two hours solidly. I think she was frightened, poor thing.'

'I couldn't have stood that. You should have come through to us. There was hardly anyone in First.'

'I turned up my Walkman.'

'I don't know how you can listen to those things. They really irritate my ears. It's bad enough watching a film on a plane.' She took off her jacket as the humidity, already soaring for November, had filtered into the arrival hall.

Chris had arranged to have them collected from the airport and again, the name on the card was Richardson, rather than Innes. Although judging by the people gathering all round them, Jordan had already been recognised. As they left the customs area, cameras flashed in all directions and there was even a reporter from the local television station to record the arrival of the famous American film star. How news of his arrival had leaked out, Bronte wasn't sure, but at the same time, hoped Jordan didn't think she or her cousin had been indiscreet. But looking at him, still carrying Phoebe and looking every bit the family man, he was smiling broadly for the cameras and didn't seem to be worrying about blame.

'Is it always like that when you arrive places?' asked Bronte, after they had forced their way through the autograph hunters and budding amateur (as well as professional) photographers, to the car which was waiting just outside the door.

'Depends on where I go and for what reason. It's probably got out here that we're making the movie. The Aussies are very proud of Greg and local patriotism will be riding high on the strength of us doing this thing together in Sydney.'

'Aren't you concerned about security?' She was beginning to wonder if the house Chris had found for them would be suitable after all.

'We have minders for when we think we need them, but they are incredibly intrusive,' Chelsea replied for him.

'One hopes they're all fans. But you're right, several people I know do get hate mail and threats. It's a risk you take. You can't protect yourself all the time,' added Jordan.

There was a lot she would need to find out, but it made interesting learning. The journey from the airport was slow. Again, they had hit the evening rush hour but fortunately, their driver was adept at short cuts and managed to avoid the worst of it.

The route he chose took in spectacular views of Sydney's famous Opera House, with its tall white sails reaching up in a tribute to its own glory, while all around the harbour waters glistened as the ferries darted to and from Circular Quay, carting flustered commuters away from their hectic city day.

Mosman Junction was positively provincial compared to the frantic traffic lanes over the harbour bridge. There Bronte experienced her first taste of relaxed Aussie life, as she peered out of the window and saw bronzed barefooted surfers with bleached blond hair, strolling up from the direction of the sea, and casual shoppers browsing in windows in no apparent hurry to move on.

They reached the top of Raglan Street within the hour and crawled slowly down the steep hill, stopping before a set of impressive white iron gates. No sooner had the car stopped outside, than a tall, slim girl in her late twenties, with short cropped dark hair, came rushing out of the house.

'Welcome!' mouthed Chris, as she beckoned the chauffeur into the drive.

Bronte jumped out of the car and was swiftly locked in a warm embrace with her cousin, who seemed remarkably unchanged from the last time Bronte had seen her in England.

'Welcome to Sydney! How was the flight? The car there OK? I hope the traffic wasn't too bad coming across town.' A torrent of Australian twang!

Bronte, with her arm resting on Chris' shoulders, led her to where the others had just surfaced from the depths of the car.

'Chris, come and meet Jordan and Chelsea, and this little one is Phoebe.'

Phoebe had rushed over to Bronte and wrapped her podgy little arms around Bronte's knees.

'Bwonte . . . thirsty.' She looked up adoringly and Chris smiled, already enchanted by the handsome family.

'I guess you'll all be ready for a drink. It's been so hot lately. Far earlier in the season than normal. Come inside and I'll show your round. There's cool beers in the fridge.'

Chris led the way across the steaming tarmac to where the house, cool by comparison, with long windows and creamy white walls, stood waiting to make their acquaintance.

'It sure is great to see you again, Bronte! You haven't changed a bit. Maybe even skinnier but otherwise the same. Angela's dying to see you too, and to get you up to their beach. Oh, mind the step . . .' she turned to where Jordan was helping a tottering Phoebe up the three steepish steps to the front door. 'Come and meet Beccy and Charlene.'

Chris then whispered hastily to Bronte, 'I hope they'll be OK. They both had great references from the agency and Beccy's done several catering courses.'

Chris led them into a large hallway, with polished wooden floorboards, covered here and there by pastel rugs.

'Ah, Charlene. Here's your charge. Her name is Phoebe and this is Mr and Mrs Innes.'

Charlene looked about Bronte's age.

'I'm glad to meet you, Mr Innes. Mrs Innes. . .'

'Look, please it's Jordan and my wife is Chelsea. We don't need the formalities.' Jordan grinned at her, which instantly threw her into utter confusion and sent her down on to her knees to talk to Phoebe.

'My, that's some dollie you've got there. Can I see her?' As she smiled into the child's eyes, the groups of freckles which had been fighting for recognition on her face, joined forces.

'She's Mary Rose and she's mine! . . . but you can hold her if you like. Where's your swimming pool?'

The assembled company approved, as Charlene was allowed to take hold of Mary Rose in one hand and Phoebe's little fingers in the other.

'I tell you what, how about you and me going exploring and see if we can find the swimming pool, and possibly even some cookies? You'd like that?'

'Sure . . . but I need a drink and mommy says I can go in your swimming pool.'

'Perhaps a bit later, darling.' Chelsea, who was quite accustomed to her daughter's self-confidence, thought it as well that Charlene found out from the start, what she was in for.

'What a lovely little girl!' Chris enthused in the direction of Phoebe's parents.

'Charlene'll certainly have her hands full,' said Jordan.

'She'll cope fine. In her last job, she had six kids to take care of, so I don't think Phoebe'll pose too many problems. Come, let me show you round the house. I've completely forgotten my manners, keeping you hanging around the hall.'

Bronte had been just a little apprehensive about whether the house would be to Jordan and Chelsea's liking. But she need not have worried. The place was perfect! Not too large, but plenty of space for privacy. Not too lavish, but tastefully decorated with maximum comfort in mind and air conditioning in every room – essential for all Americans in a hot climate. The living rooms were on the upper floor, including the family-size kitchen (in which they encountered Beccy, up to her elbows in baking flour).

Downstairs was the master suite and four further bedrooms. These led off a spacious wooden corridor, the end of which opened out into a dreamy green conservatory, which housed every conceivable form of plant life nestling amongst squidgy sofas and cane tables.

'Welcome from Sydney! Welcome from Sydney!' came squawking from the corner of the room.

Bronte stumbled in surprise, almost backing into Jordan who was standing right behind her. They had lost Chelsea en-route.

'I'm sorry, Jordan, but that gave me a fright.'

She was embarrassed that she had shown such obvious confusion when Jordan had, quite naturally, reached out to steady her and prevent his toes from being stepped on – a situation that had not gone unnoticed by Chris.

'Don't take any notice of Sydney. That's Uncle Mack's parrot. He says the most outrageous things sometimes and can be highly entertaining. I hope he won't get on your nerves.'

'Is he really called Sydney?' Jordan asked.

'Yes, 'fraid so and you've just heard his party piece. Goodness knows who taught him it, but he now welcomes all newcomers to the house like that.'

'Does he ever come out of the cage?' asked Bronte nervously.

'Don't worry, Uncle Mack's gardener takes care of him. Feeding and that kind of thing. All you need do is put up with him.'

'I'm sure it'll amuse Phoeb, although I can't make any guarantees about what she'll teach him to say,' said Jordan.

'Don't worry. His vocabulary is pretty varied already. Come and see the garden.'

The large glass doors leading from the conservatory were flung wide open onto the wooden sundeck outside. There, arranged casually in groups, were the most comfortable-looking sun loungers Bronte had ever seen.

'Bye bye, see you in a minute!' boomed from the corner of the conservatory. Bronte couldn't help noticing Jordan trying not to laugh.

Beyond the sundeck stretched a striped lawn. At the end of that was a kidney-shaped swimming pool, in which Phoebe was already paddling, partially in the nude, with an ever-watchful Charlene close behind. Unfortunately, the house did not have its own sea access, as it was too far up the hill from Balmoral Beach. But in a city where houses jostled for glimpses of the harbour and indeed whose merits were often judged on their views, the house certainly had more than its share of sea outlook.

'Shall I leave you to settle in? Is there anything you need?'

'Seems great to me, Chris. Thanks for finding this place for us.' Bronte was glad to see Jordan's looks of approval.

'Can I just run over a few things with you, Bronte? And then I'll leave you in peace to unpack. Come into the conservatory. There's a fridge in there and you can grab a beer.'

Jordan headed back in the direction of his suite, while Chris showed Bronte where the fridge was hidden in a cupboard.

'He's even yummier in the flesh than he is on the screen! You've landed on your feet there, Bron,' whispered Chris, as she handed Bronte a can.

'Shh! He'll hear you.'

'Help yourself! Help yourself!' chirped Sydney happily.

'Oh, wrap up, Sydney,' said Chris.

'OK! OK! Don't nag! Don't nag!' At which Bronte giggled.

'Does he always repeat everything twice?'

'Virtually. I hope he won't drive you all crazy. It's just that it's difficult for Uncle Mack to send him anywhere else.'

'Don't worry. I think judging by Jordan's reaction, he's actually going to find it quite amusing.'

'Now, what do I need to tell you? Right. . .' and she proceeded to fill Bronte in on a few house and domestic details that she ought to know.

'. . . and the gardener is here every day, and apart from feeding Sydney, he doesn't come into the house. He used to be a security guard for one of the big stores in town, and so will no doubt be useful to keep an eye on the place in case you get curious intruders.'

'Chris, this is fantastic! You're so well organised. You haven't left anything for me to do at all.'

'Let me take care of the domestic end, and you can run around after your handsome boss. Mind you, if you ever want to swap jobs . . .'

'Don't! What about car rentals?'

'All dealt with. You wanted two, right? A sports and a station wagon?'

'Yes.'

'OK. They'll both be here first thing tomorrow. Here's my card – both office and home numbers are on there, so for goodness sake call me if you need anything. I also want to arrange to show you round a bit. You must have some time off from that slave driver of yours'?'

'Hardly a slave driver, Chris. I've felt like I'm on holiday most of the time so far. Anyhow, once we get settled in here, I'm sure there'll be chance to look around.'

'You must try and come to Avalon at Christmas. At least for Christmas day. Ange would be so disappointed if you couldn't make it.'

'I really want to, but I'll have to see what's going on here first.'

'I know. I understand. Let's just hope they follow some big happy family tradition at Christmas, and let you out of it.'

Bronte pondered on that briefly and, all at once, felt for Jordan because she sensed it was most unlikely there would be a great deal of 'happy family' atmosphere that year.

'Look, I'm going to love you and leave you if there's nothing more I can do for you now.' Chris jumped to her feet and gave Bronte an affectionate smacker on the cheek. 'Great to have you over this way at last and to think you'll be hanging around for a while. I'll be in touch tomorrow to check everything's OK. Don't bother to come up – I will see myself out.' With that she was gone.

'Bye bye, see you in a minute!' piped up Sydney, who had been nursing his head under his wing.

'Pass the mayo, darling.' Jordan reached over the table and helped his wife to some mayonnaise with her salad.

It was nearly eight thirty and they had all had the chance to unpack and were beginning to unwind somewhat. Phoebe had taken to Charlene like a duck to water and had insisted that she tuck her into bed and read her a story, rather than anyone else. In some ways it was a good thing, but Bronte felt a little sad that the child so easily transferred her affections to anyone who took time to be with her.

Beccy had done them proud with a simple but appetising meal.

Even Chelsea ate quite well after their long day of travelling, which was an encouraging and, hopefully, optimistic sign.

'It's great to be back in Sydney and have our own place. It's rare to get away from people when you're travelling. Last time I was here, we were down in the Rocks, at the Regent. Did you come then, darling?'

'I can't honestly remember,' responded Chelsea, some-what absentmindedly, as she sucked a lettuce leaf.

'Anyhow, it was a good place to stay but it was hard to move around down there. Want some more of this bread either of you?'

'No thanks. We could have done without the butter on it,' replied Chelsea. Bronte and Jordan exchanged the briefest of glances.

'I'll have some, thanks.' Bronte almost felt like having it to spite Chelsea, but was immediately ashamed of her thoughts.

Bronte had let Beccy go before supper and was only too happy to clear the table and busy herself in the kitchen, sensing an inexplicably awkward atmosphere, as the three of them had sat round the table.

However, it wasn't long before Jordan joined her, seeming temporarily to prefer her company to that of his wife – or was she letting her imagination run away with her? She had to be careful to remain impartial and not get entangled in whatever marital problems were going on around her.

'Need some help?'

'Women's work!' she retorted with a smile.

'I couldn't agree more, but I thought I'd offer, seeing as the maid's not here. What's her name again?'

'Beccy.'

'Seriously, is everything under control, with the nanny and maid etc? I'm afraid my wife's not exactly adept at running a house. She's not had too much practice.'

'Chris has been marvellous and besides, I need to earn my keep around here.'

'There'll be plenty coming up for you to do and just as importantly, we need to be able to rely on your stability.'

More and more rapidly, Bronte was beginning to realise that she was capable of providing some stability that she saw the Innes family badly needed at times, and that was a comfort to her in a world where she had doubted for a while whether she truly belonged any more.

'Come on. Let's go down to the beach. You can have your first feel of Australian sand.'

He was like a big kid, bouncing around excitedly. Bronte was only too keen to take a walk, but was worried about what Chelsea would say.

'Jordan, it's dark out there. What about Chelsea going with you?'

'She's exhausted. Travelling always takes it out of her. I think she's been so many places with me now that the novelty's worn off. Come on, it won't be dark on the beach.'

How could she rebuff his enthusiasm? Consequently, it was shortly after that that she found herself strolling down Raglan Street in the direction of Balmoral Beach, guided by a combination of the street and the moon lights, in the company of one of the most attractive but completely unattainable men she had ever encountered in her life. What's more, she felt the sort of contentment she had only ever sensed on rare occasions before, which made her fearful of the trap she imagined could lay in wait for her, if she wasn't on her guard.

A couple walked up the hill towards them and glanced back at Jordan as if they were seeing things. He appeared not to notice.

'I've got to see Art Dafon in the morning. He's producing this picture. We need to sit round the table and pool our progress so far.' He was more serious.

'Is everything going according to plan?' She was intrigued.

'The script's virtually done now. You should take a look at it once I get a final copy. Most of the script writing team are assembled here already, so it'll be easier to make alterations.'

She could hardly believe that he would involve her so much.

'Art's been casting here and in the States for the past month. Although the lead parts were decided a while ago, there's a good number of extras to be found, particularly as much of the action takes place outdoors.'

'Is it all being shot in Sydney?'

'All the location work. The studio work will be done in L.A. which will cut down the time we need to be here. Most of the scenes take place around the harbour, which is why we're going to have to take some time out to familiarise ourselves with the layout, over the next few weeks.'

'How long before you will be able to start shooting?'

'Hopefully, no more than a couple of months at the most. January with any luck.'

They had reached the sea and crossed the road to step down on to the sand. The night was warm and humidity hung around and between them.

'Is it a thriller? This movie?' She was dying to ask, but was unsure of his reaction because she knew the movie was still shrouded in secrecy.

'Kind of. The main story line running through it surrounds the kidnap of a young heiress. Then there's the good guys and the bad guys. Usual explosive stuff.' He was giving little away, even then.

'And which are you? The good guy or the bad?'

'What do you think?'

'Whatever I say'll probably be wrong.' She didn't want to commit herself.

'Then you'll have to wait until you see the script.'

She laughed a carefree laugh, which was music to his ears.

'Changing the subject,' began Jordan, 'I don't want to dictate your hours, but there are things I'll need you to do and if it's OK with you, can we take it as we go along?'

'No problem. I'll take care of the domestic end as we've already discussed, so you can leave all arrangements like that to me.'

191

'Great. You'll need access to a computer. Is the fax working in the house by the way?'

'Yes. I checked that before dinner and the computer I can arrange through Chris. I'll get on to that tomorrow.'

'Can you also put a call through to Helen and find out if there's anything she needs us for? She may like to pass over a few things to you, now that you're established with us, and she'll be having the baby soon.'

They had come to the far end of the beach and Jordan took her over to a wall, which faced out to sea. Not stopping to check whether the wall was dirty, she followed his example and jumped aboard.

'Stay there.' He wagged a finger at her.

'Why, where are you going?' But her words floated up towards the balmy night sky, to be lost forever to the sound of the sea.

She turned to see him cross the road and disappear under a huge shop awning. She was almost glad of the chance to collect her thoughts and prepare herself for the next confrontation with those heavenly eyes. She pulled her hair down from the scrunchie and kicked off her shoes which had managed to attract half the beach.

'You really should keep your hair down, you know.'

She spun round suddenly, as the familiar voice startled her.

'It drives me mad at times. Particularly when it's hot. I'll cut it off one of these days. My God! What have you got there?'

'Don't you dare cut it off,' he warned, 'and this here, is the best ice cream you will find this side of Italy!'

He passed her a dark laticed bowl (which she later realised was made of ginger biscuit) in which were delicately arranged scoops of lemon-coloured ice cream. As he sat beside her on the wall, he gave her one of two spoons which he drew from his jeans pocket.

'Here, try it. It's the finest champagne cocktail ice-cream you'll ever taste. They sell it in that shop which I discovered by chance, a couple of years ago.'

The basket was more than ample for them to share and when she had extracted a spoonful, she handed it back to him. The cool creamy taste gave way to a luxurious fizz of champagne, as she savoured her first mouthful before swallowing it down.

'Good? Eh?'

'Mmm. Very good, and well worth the walk.'

There were few people around that night and certainly no-one seemed to recognise, or if they did, bother to disturb Jordan. Bronte tried hard to imagine what it must be like to be permanently conscious of those around you, and never to be sure of guaranteeing anonymity, wherever you travelled in the world, and to live life publicly and not privately. To have to put up with constant media attention and speculation, and to accept that as a part of life, from which there was no escape.

'What's on your mind? You're miles away.' He was studying her closely.

'Oh, nothing really.' She took another dip into the ice cream basket and popped the contents into her mouth. 'I was just pondering over the sort of life you must lead with people watching your every move.'

'You get used to it.' He reached up and drew back his hair, in the way she had begun to find very sexy. 'Besides, it has its compensations at times. Think of all the starving millions. Of all those disadvantaged people. Put it into perspective, life really isn't too bad. I'm off duty now, aren't I?' He looked about him, as the Sydney night life sped by leaving the two of them well alone.

'Yes. I suppose you are.' She looked up, drawn by the force of his gaze on her, and for the longest time yet, their eyes met and held, each one reluctant to break the spell. For her, it was long enough to search deep into her soul, to imagine just what it would be like to fall hopelessly in love with that man who had burst in on her life at a time when she was so vulnerable. For him, it was long enough to examine his life, to begin to realise just what was missing, and then instinctively to shy away from what he learnt.

A car back-fired behind them. Both of them reeled from the powerful effect of momentary self-analysis. She crossed her legs and looked to where the sea was lapping gently at the sand and he took another scoop of ice cream.

CHAPTER FOURTEEN

Breakfast turned into somewhat of a moveable feast, with each person attending to their own requirements as a matter of necessity rather than desire, before leaving for their next port of call. Beccy was already proving to be worth her weight in gold, producing all the appropriate things at all the right moments. They never actually noticed her buzzing about, but were simply aware of a quiet air of efficiency breezing through the house.

Charlene, too, seemed to know what to do without instruction. She had received an enthusiastic welcome that morning from Phoebe and she appeared to know just how to strike the right chord with the rest of the family also. She was neither weak nor bossy. From what Bronte could make out, Chelsea didn't seem that bothered who was attending to her daughter, as long as the responsibility did not rest on her shoulders too often.

Bronte had encountered Jordan only briefly that morning. He seemed flustered as he flapped around the dining room, snatching a bite of toast here, a gulp of coffee there, and struggling with his tie in the mirror at the same time, not once settling anywhere for more than a second.

'I've got to run this morning, Bronte. I told Art I'd get to his place in Surry Hills around nine, as Greg's only in town for the morning and we need to go through things with him while we've got the chance to work together.' Another slurp of coffee. 'By the way, the cars turned up around seven this morning. Great choice. It'll do my reputation no end of good to be seen in that sports car with the hood down!' The first grin of the day. 'Seriously though, I presume we're all insured?'

'Chris has taken care of that.'

'I knew I needn't have asked. I'll be back later and we should get some paperwork out of the way.'

'I'll be here. There's a long fax from Helen with various instructions, so I'll wade through that. I'll also get the computer installed, so my typing's at your disposal.'

'Hang loose. See you later.' He lunged at the remaining toast, and with that, he was gone.

A couple of seconds later, Phoebe emerged at the top of the stairs.

'Daddy ... Daddy ...' but her words were drowned by the roar of the car as it snaked through the automatic gates.

Feeling a strange urge to play mummy, Bronte swept Phoebe up in her arms and with a hug, said: 'Daddy's in a hurry today, sweetheart. He'll be back later and I'm sure he'll be wanting to play with you by then.'

Two big sad eyes met hers and the teeniest tear managed to escape from one of them.

'But I wanted a ride in the new red car ...' Fortunately, Phoebe was not one of those children who whined for her own way. Her simple little request came straight from the heart – matter of fact.

'The car'll be back later, I promise. How about us getting you out of those 'jamies and you telling me what you want to wear today? How does that sound? And then if you're a good girl, we'll see if Charlene will take you down to the seaside for a paddle. You'd like that?'

It was amazing how easily toddlers could put their woes behind them and summon enthusiasm so soon afterwards. Bronte carried her downstairs.

'Will there be a sandpit?' she gurgled, by now quite looking forward to the activities planned for her morning.

'A huge, enormous one!' Bronte laughed. That was obviously what Phoebe regarded the beach as.

'Will I have a bucket?'

'You'd better ask Charlene.'

As they passed Jordan and Chelsea's room, Bronte noticed the door was tight shut and no sound emerged. For a fleeting second she wondered whether Chelsea was all right in there, but then remembered that Jordan had only just left, and would almost certainly have alerted her to anything she was supposed to keep an eye on, beyond that closed door.

'Ah, Charlene. There you are.' She was busying herself tidying Phoebe's cot and bedroom. 'Madam here is going to choose herself an outfit for today and then I promised her a trip to the beach. I hope you don't mind?' Bronte had never had to instruct a nanny before, and was not sure quite how to go about it.

'I think we can manage that, don't you Phoebe? And what's more, I know the best ice cream shop in town and it just happens to be not too far from here.'

So do I, thought Bronte to herself.

'Yeah!' Phoebe's eyes lit up even further, as she leapt down from Bronte's grasp and rushed to her wardrobe.

The air outside was already heavy and damp with the promise of more oppressive humidity for the day to come. Through the conservatory windows, Bronte could see the sun blazing down from her perch in the sky, covering all that she touched with a thermal blanket of heat, regardless of whether it was required or not. Bronte was glad she had chosen something cool to wear that day because judging by the soaring temperatures, she would positively have sweltered in anything else.

She turned on her heels and headed up towards the study, which also doubled as an office, in order to set about working on the fax from Helen.

As far as she could make out, it was Helen's way of handing over her responsibilities. The first couple of pages gave details of the arrangements for running Jordan's homes in New York, Los Angeles and Bermuda.

On subsequent sheets there was information about who to contact regarding Jordan's financial affairs, as well as his press agents and lawyers.

Finally, Helen had outlined one or two things which she recommended Bronte keep an eye on and she ended by saying that it was vital for Bronte to keep closely in contact with Jordan's agent in New York, who kept tabs on the comings and goings of his professional life. She added that Jordan would expect her to be fully-informed on all new developments, while his time was taken up with the project in Australia.

She had concluded the fax with a PS, wishing Bronte all the very best in her new employment, and saying that if she could manage to oversee all of the above, as well as retain a degree of organisation in his family life, she would be doing a fine job.

Bronte, who was used to the need for efficiency when running an office, decided there was no time like the present for her to find the nearest stationery shop and invest in files, note pads, fax paper etc – all of which would enable her to keep a smooth-running office for Jordan, however temporary it was to be.

It was late morning by the time she returned to the house, hot and thirsty after her expedition to Mosman Junction. She was greeted in the hall by Beccy who, duster in hand, was busy polishing up the already immaculate flooring.

'Hi there! You look like you could use a drink of something. How about iced coffee?'

'Oh, Beccy, you're a life saver! If it wasn't for the walk up and down the hill, it wouldn't be so bad . . . and in this heat . . .'

'You should've taken the car.'

'I didn't even think about it. Is Chelsea around?'

'She's studying or writing or something – downstairs, by the pool. I was just about to take her a drink too. Why don't you go down there and I'll bring you both something on a tray?'

'Thanks, Beccy. What a star!'

Beccy had a quiet, but appealing manner. 'By the way, if Chelsea asks, Charlene is still out with Phoebe, but said she'd be back to give her lunch here.'

'Fine. I'll pass the message on.'

First, Bronte found homes in the study for her purchases. She was glad to be getting her teeth firmly into her work at last and had to admit that she was really beginning to enjoy herself.

'Chelsea? I hope I'm not disturbing you? Beccy's brewing up some iced coffee.'

'What? Oh, right. No, come and sit down. I need an inspiration break.'

Chelsea was sitting by the pool on one of the wooden sunchairs, with papers and reference books spread across the table beside her. Her hair was swept severely up on top of her head and a multi-coloured sarong was draped loosely around her. Underneath, where the folds of the sarong parted, Bronte could see a skimpy white bikini, which enhanced the olive tan. What was just as evident, was how painfully thin Chelsea really was. Her stomach, which one would normally expect to be loose after bearing a child, was as taut as the skin stretched across a warrior's drum. Balanced on her nose were her sunglasses, through which she appeared to be studying a book on the Aboriginal culture of Australia.

Bronte pulled up the chair indicated by Chelsea and was only too ready to take the weight off her feet for a moment.

'You look bushed. Where have you been?' Chelsea seemed far more relaxed than Bronte could remember seeing before.

'I had to run up to Mosman for various bits of stationery, so I can make a start on correspondence.'

'It's good you're taking all this so seriously, Bronte. Jordan needs someone to organise him behind the scenes. He can initiate, but he needs someone to run after him to pick up the pieces. Of course, I can only do so much, what with the baby and the work I do too.' She crossed her bony knees and flexed her well-pedicured toes, as the red varnish gleamed in the sunshine.

'I was going to ask you about that. I heard you do freelance writing? It sounds fascinating. You must be able to do lots of research, just from the travelling you do?'

'I used to model, Bronte. But I found that after a while, although the money was good, it became a worthless occupation in terms of self-esteem. To be permanently at the beck and call of the photographers, to be told to eat more, to fill out here or there, to cut my hair, to grow my hair – it drove me mad after a while. It was actually on a modelling assignment in New York that I met Jordan. Once we were married, he began to realise what it was doing to me and he persuaded me to give it up. Not that it took much persuading, though.'

At that moment, Beccy interrupted them with tall glasses of refreshing cold coffee, with ice cubes bobbing on the surface.

'After that, well, I decided to develop my writing career. It was something that had always lain dormant within me, I guess from school days when I used to find a certain satisfaction in transferring my thoughts down on to paper. Now, when I have the time and when we travel, I try to concentrate on doing something on local culture or even a bit of fiction, but when it's fictional, I introduce what I can of the life I observe in whichever place I happen to be. That way, I feel I have expanded my mind and my general understanding of wherever I have visited.'

Bronte was intrigued by the new dimensions that were becoming apparent of such a complex character. The brains behind the looks and the emotional problems were evident, but she wanted to probe a little further.

'Have you written a novel? What happens to the pieces you write? Do you get them printed?'

'A novel – no. At least, not that you would call a novel. I have written a number of . . . shall we just call them, lengthy stories. But I have found up to now that I get to a point where an ending seems more appropriate than pushing the story any further and often by then, my mind has gone off at new tangents and I'm anxious to start afresh on something else. I'm actually not that bothered about seeing my writing in print, although I have had a number of things published in various magazines back home in the States. I write more to keep my brain active. To stimulate and encourage learning processes within myself, which in turn, lead to words on paper. Have you ever tried to write?'

'I can't honestly say that I have. Although perhaps I should think about recording some of the experiences I have had over the last five years in television, before they fade.'

'You absolutely should! Escapism is another great reason for writing. You can weave into other people's lives, particularly when you write fiction, things you can never have in your own. You can draw out your own hopes, dreams and aspirations and for a while, even believe that perhaps they are, or in time, will, happen to you. When real dreams end or go wrong in your life, you can escape into another life you have invented on paper and put everything straight, at least there. It helps to give you an identity from which to face the world and restore a self-respect that has perhaps started to slip from your own life.'

She drew breath and glanced to the dark waters stretching out before them. Bronte took a gulp of coffee, but found herself lost in her own thoughts, until Chelsea picked up again where she had left off.

'What you create on your page is your very own. No-one else's. No-one can lay claim to it because it evolved from the abstract in your head. It is completely private – your own world of imagination, until such time as you permit someone else to read it and then, of course, the knowledge is shared with them too, but despite that, it is never theirs to own. You really should have a go, you know. When you have the time. It would be good for you to discharge the emotions of your husband's death. I'm sure you would find it therapeutic.'

'Maybe you're right. Although I have already found that time and keeping busy have helped me enormously to get over Dominic. I really owe thanks to you and Jordan for that.'

'Life's strange, you know. It's weird how what is right for a person can come up just when it is needed, although one probably doesn't recognise that at the time. Your meeting Jordan is probably a good example. It's helped you, and we needed your help, with Helen bowing out and all that. But going back to what I was saying about identity and self-respect, I have found that these have become really important to me since I married someone so much in the public eye. There's a great pressure to keep up appearances all the time. I do realise that I'm not always the best of mothers to Phoeb. Sometimes it all becomes too much and everything just slips down a gear . . .'

Bronte still found it hard to believe that the woman who had seemed so cold and icy, and in fact, really still did, had chosen to open up and talk so frankly about herself. What had also become clear was how intense Chelsea could be, under the mask of beauty and emotion, and how highly-strung and sensitive. Nonetheless, she was interesting to talk to, with a fascinating mind that needed some delving into.

'You two seem awfully serious out here. Anything wrong?'

It was already lunch-time and Jordan was back from his morning meetings.

Bronte did not reply at first because privately she was busy wondering whether she would ever reach that depth of honesty with Chelsea again.

'No, darling. Nothing wrong. I was just bending Bronte's ear about writing. You had a good morning?'

'Very productive, actually. We finalised a number of things which included getting Greg to sign his contract on the dotted line. Art's way up with the casting now and things are looking in good shape.'

'Are you nearer to agreeing a shooting schedule?' asked Chelsea.

'The way things stand, it's looking pretty much like a January start.'

'I really hope so, because we don't want to stay here any longer than necessary.'

'Oh, I don't know. I could get used to Australia.'

'Location's one thing. Living is something totally different.'

Jordan knew when to drop a subject, which was just as well because Bronte was feeling decidedly uncomfortable for some reason.

'I need to get a feel for the main and middle harbour areas as soon as possible and Art has recommended this Captain Cook cruise thing, which takes you around for a couple of hours. It would be something to do with Phoeb and you've never seen much of the harbour here have you, darling?'

Bronte got up and collected the glasses before heading inside.

'Not today. I must get down to the State Library this afternoon. The books I have here are really inadequate for my purpose. Take Bronte with you. She hasn't been here before, remember?'

'You sure you won't come?'

'Really. I'm not in the mood for fending off your fans today, if you don't mind.'

'Even if I wear my darkest shades and disguise myself?' he teased, but it didn't lighten her reply as she appeared to have snapped right back into her shell.

'I'll see you later.'

*   *   *

By ensuring that they were early for the cruise, which left from Circular Quay, and by making their way quickly to the front of the upper deck, Jordan managed to get by virtually unnoticed – except perhaps for an over-giggly female member of the crew who could be seen to swoon visibly as he walked in front of her.

Bronte could actually relate somewhat to the swooning, because to her, Jordan wore less than no disguise and indeed looked more like himself than ever! He had shed the working suit for something more casual and the sunglasses, which were never far from his person, were firmly in position. Bronte couldn't help thinking that he looked every inch the film star and not even remotely like a tourist!

Phoebe, having been reunited with Daddy over lunch, had insisted on being carried by him ever since. She had discarded all items of clothing except for a pair of green and yellow shorts, which had 'I'm an American bum' stamped clearly on the back.

'Gee, it's hot today.' Jordan looked at Bronte who sat beside him on the front bench seat of the boat.

'I think it'll be better once we get going. There may be more of a breeze then.'

'You want a drink?'

'Drink, Daddy. Drink for Phoebe.' The child didn't miss anything.

'Look, I'll go. You stay there with Phoebe. You'll only attract attention.'

'Thanks, Bronte. Here, take these bucks.' He fished in his pocket and produced a wad of Australian dollar bills.

The cruise only took half capacity on that particular afternoon. Those who were aboard comprised a mixture of nationalities but the dominant one was Japanese, all of whom seemed fiercely competitive with one another to produce the most sophisticated camera with the longest lens. Some were setting up their tripods on deck, even before they left the dock. Their indistinguishable chatter, which sounded as if they were talking with a mouthful of marbles, resounded all round the boat but at least they were unlikely to bother Jordan for pictures or autographs.

Throughout their trip an Australian tour guide stood in the middle of the boat pointing out places of interest as they passed by. Their route took them out in front of the Opera House and showed them some of the city's most exotic, not to mention expensive, water-front homes – many with their own built-in lifts down to private boat moorings. Then they made for the two heads of the harbour – North and South, between which, despite the heat of the day, the water was a little choppy. Shortly afterwards came the famous Spit bridge and a number of the harbour beaches, including Balmoral.

Jordan had brought some notes and also a sketch map which Art had given him that morning to enable him to locate some landmarks intended for use in the film. Unfortunately, they did not go near enough to the house that had been chosen as the impressive family home of the heiress – but then that would inevitably require closer inspection than a boat cruise could allow.

Just after they had crossed in front of the heads, the same female crew member who had recognised Jordan came round selling ice creams. No doubt, she had made sure it was her job for that particular cruise.

All too coincidentally, she started her round at the front of the boat, right at the point where Jordan and Bronte were sitting admiring the view.

'It's Jordan Innes, isn't it?' She bowed low with her ice cream tray. At the same time, a rather sweaty cleavage wobbled in Jordan's direction.

'Sure . . . and you are . . .?' Jordan didn't bat an eyelid.

'Milly, Milly James. I hope you don't mind my asking, but can I have your autograph?'

'I think we can manage that one, don't you, Phoebe?' He turned to his daughter who was wedged comfortably in his lap.

'Is that your little girl?' asked Milly, ignoring Bronte completely.

'She sure is. Phoebe meet Milly,' said Jordan, as he scribbled something on his notepad and handed it past Bronte to Milly.

Bronte decided Jordan was enjoying teasing her and was even more convinced of it when she glanced at what he had written on the page: 'Keep selling the ice creams, Milly James. From Jordan Innes.' Bronte giggled to herself but Milly, who appeared to be in total raptures by that point, was delighted.

'We'd better take some of those ice creams off you, now that you have come all the way up here.' Again, he was charm itself.

Milly handed three little tubs over, winked meaningfully at Jordan, and turned to the bench behind them.

'You really meet all sorts don't you?' Bronte whispered to Jordan, covering her mouth at the same time so as to muffle her words.

He turned his face towards her, frowned, and then broke out into his private smile, meant only for her eyes.

CHAPTER FIFTEEN

Ten days just seemed to float by. There was never a dull moment or much time to wonder what to do next. Jordan was constantly on the go – appointments with bankers, lawyers, script writers, cast directors and if he wasn't wrapped up in meetings, it was location excursions or social gatherings which seemed to crop up almost daily, with all sorts of oddballs from the film world. Some of those were connected with the upcoming picture and some were not.

Chelsea seemed more and more pre-occupied with her writing and judging by some of her comments, she was pleased with the way it was progressing. She remained aloof from her family for much of the time, happy for Charlene or Bronte to run around with Phoebe, although ever since she had opened up a little to Bronte, she was noticeably friendlier. She continued to pick at her food like a sparrow, which Bronte could see was of great concern to Jordan at the meals they shared together, but the subject had not been brought up since Hong Kong.

Phoebe continued to charm everyone with her delightful little smile (a junior version of her Dad's) and extrovert character. She was always on the move and Charlene said at times that she was as exhausted each evening after spending the day with Phoebe, as she had been after all six children in her previous employment! Phoebe couldn't seem to make up her mind whether Bronte or Charlene was her favourite playmate, but she was more than happy to go along with anything either of them suggested. Charlene knew some children in the neighbourhood and introduced Phoebe to a few new Aussie friends, all the time being careful to be discreet about her father. There was no point inviting unnecessary attention to the house, which had so far remained almost entirely private.

Bronte was rushed off her feet for most of the time too. She attended some meetings with Jordan and even represented him at a couple, when he had a clash of appointments. She spent hours on the 'phone for him, both overseas as well as around Australia. Her time was also taken up answering faxes and transferring documents on to the computer. Occasionally she had to speak to the likes of Greg Hill himself – or other big names – and she tried her best to deal with them as just another client because if she imagined the face at the other end of the line, she would become totally tongue-tied and forget what it was she needed to convey.

Her work permitted her very little relaxation time and although she had managed an evening out in Kings Cross with both her cousins and their husbands, she had not had the opportunity to go to Avalon, or indeed to acquaint herself with much of Sydney at all. The domestic arrangements went like clockwork and Beccy and Charlene continued to prove their worth on a daily basis.

All in all, she felt as if she was well-settled into her job and she relished all the responsibility which Jordan happily deposited on her shoulders. She felt she belonged, almost for the first time since her world had been turned around by Dominic's death, and although little of her time could really be classed as her own, she preferred to be busy and to feel that she was contributing her part. Not to mention the vast experience she was gaining all the time in the world of movie-making. She was continually expanding her knowledge and that, in itself, brought tremendous job satisfaction.

The past ten days had not permitted any social time alone with Jordan, which somewhere inside her she knew was a good thing. She concentrated her mind on seeing their relationship as purely professional and made every effort to curb any thoughts that ventured outside those boundaries. She didn't allow herself time to wonder what he was thinking or feeling – possibly because her own thoughts and feelings were somewhat of a minefield and she decided they were best left alone for the time being.

* * *

Over breakfast one morning, the first they had managed to be together at the same time so far, Jordan looked up from some papers he was studying and said: 'I've got to make a quick trip to Los Angeles this week. A couple of things have come up and as Art's tied up here more than I am right now, and as one of us needs to get our butt over to the studio, I thought it best I go.'

'How soon?' asked Bronte.

'As soon as you can get the flights. Tomorrow would be fine. Chelsea'll come back too. I know she misses the States and she's probably ready for a trip back. Do you mind if we leave Phoebe behind here? I know we're both going to be busy and it would be much easier if she was being taken care of here.'

'That's fine by me, but will she mind?'

'I'll explain it to her and get her looking forward to the gifts we'll bring back. Besides, we won't be gone for that long. There's too much going on here.'

'What about return flights?'

'Get us open-ended tickets and we can let you know. Gee! Is that the time?' He glanced down at his watch. 'I'm out of here.'

'I'll get the flights booked first thing this morning.'

'Thanks. By the way, did I forget to tell you you're doing a great job?' He switched on the magic for a second. 'See you later.'

Why did she suddenly feel heavy inside? Was it really because he was going away for a while, or was something else dragging her spirits down that morning?

She had finally got Jordan and Chelsea packed off for the airport in a state of total panic that they would be late for the flight, because Jordan had been delayed at the waterfront house they were renting for the movie. They had taken more luggage with them than Bronte would have used in a month and as she had waved goodbye to them from the driveway, with Phoebe in her arms, she had suddenly begun to dread the next few days of peace and quiet in the house. Phoebe, too, had been subdued. Although very used to being left for periods of time in the care of nannies, she almost seemed to tune into Bronte's mood.

Bronte found that she had time on her hands to mull over all that had happened to her in the last few months. It was at times like those, that she really believed she was dreaming and that soon Dominic would sit down on the bed beside her in their little flat in Fulham with a welcoming cup of tea and tell her that if she didn't get a move on, she'd be late for work.

It was then that she would miss Dominic the most. She would miss the physical security of his touch and his embrace, and she would doubt, momentarily, whether she had indeed made the right decision to leave behind all traces of the life they had shared. But her mind would become clouded by a vision of Jordan and the two of them, Dominic and Jordan, would become fused together, to the extent that she was not sure which one she was actually missing at that moment.

Then her spell would be broken by Phoebe or by one of the two girls who worked in the house, and she would realise all at once, that dwelling on dreams was not a particularly good idea for her while her mind was so confused and she would do far better to occupy herself constructively.

It was in one of those moods that she picked up the telephone on the Friday after Jordan and Chelsea had left for Los Angeles, and dialled up her cousin Angela.

'Angela? Is that you? It's Bronte here.'

'Hi, Bronte! How are you? I've been meaning to call since we saw you the other night, but I know from Chris that you've been really busy, so I thought I'd let the dust settle. How's it all going?'

'As far as I know, everything's fine, thanks. At least I haven't been fired yet.' She laughed into the receiver.

'When are you going to come up this way, Bronte? We're dying to show you some of the beaches up here. They're so different from the harbour beaches where there's no surf. Murray can't wait to get you out on a surfboard.'

'Actually, Ange, Jordan and Chelsea have gone back to Los Angeles for a few days and that has given me a little more time to myself. I was wondering whether you two might be around tomorrow or Sunday, if I drove over?'

'Sure. We're about all weekend. Did they take the baby back with them?'

'No. She's here. They didn't want to take her back and forth for such a short trip.'

'Why don't you bring her up too? It's perfect for kids up here. We can take her to the beach for the day – stay over if you can.'

'If you're absolutely sure, I'll come up tomorrow with Phoebe but I'd better get her home again tomorrow night. It's quite a responsibility to take her away.'

'I understand. Look, I'm really excited you're coming up. The weather's just perfect right now and it's set to last for a while. Have you had much chance to sit in the sun?'

'To be honest, there has been masses to do and very little time to switch off at all.'

'Well, mind you bring some sun screen, because it's jolly hot at the moment.'

'Can you give me some directions, Ange? I've just about got used to driving the station wagon around, although it's a real tank after my little car in London.'

'No problem. You got a pen? It's really just a question of following the road out of town to the northern beaches. The most direct route'll take you through one of the national parks.'

'Hang on, I'll grab a pen and paper.'

The next morning, as the sun glared down on the car, the temperature already rising, and with Phoebe firmly strapped into her car seat in the back, Bronte set off on the journey to Avalon.

Phoebe, who had insisted on wearing her swimming costume and nothing else at all, as soon as she heard they were going to a 'sandpit' and the sea, was full of chatter for the first part of the journey. That meant, not only did Bronte have to try and navigate her way out of town in a car which was still anything but familiar to her, but she also had to give enthusiastic replies to the child's ramblings, because, after all, it was supposed to be a fun day out for both of them. Charlene had seemed grateful for a day off, her first full day since she had joined them.

One of several consolations to Bronte's hectic schedule was that she had found herself needing to spend very little of her own money. Apart from anything else, there just hadn't been time. Consequently, due to the generous salary that she was being paid by Jordan, she had already begun to build up some welcome savings. In her mind, she wanted to be prepared for all eventualities and should the 'assignment', as she liked to think of it, come to an end, which she assumed it must at some point, she would hopefully have saved up enough for a deposit on a place of her own, wherever she decided to settle next. It would more than likely be back in England, where at some time she would have to pick up the pieces of the life she had left behind. But it would be a life without Dominic by her side.

'Are you my Mommy?' came from the back of the car.

'No, Phoebe, of course I'm not your Mummy. You know exactly who your Mummy is.' But Bronte couldn't help wondering sometimes, whether Phoebe really did know who her mother was.

'Well, where is my Mommy then?' It was a totally innocent question.

'She's gone with your Daddy to America for a few days. You remember? Your Daddy told you all about it before they went. He said if you were a really good girl, and promised to go straight to sleep every night, they would bring you something nice back with them.'

'But if my Mommy's not here, will you be my Mommy for today?'

Something pulled at Bronte's heart strings.

'How about me being your big sister today? Eh? That would be much more fun, because you've never had a big sister, right?'

That seemed to go down well.

'Yeah! So that would mean, I have a friend called Mary Rose, a Mommy and a Daddy who've gone away in an aeroplane and a sister called Bwonte?' She clapped her little hands in glee.

'Sounds like a lot to me! You're a very lucky girl, Phoebe.'

But Bronte didn't manage to convince herself. Having experienced her own motherless childhood, she wouldn't wish that on anyone.

Phoebe was gradually producing a maternal instinct in Bronte, which had been barely recognisable a couple of months before. Once again, it made her sad to think of the lost opportunity of bearing Dominic's children and of the two of them having the chance to watch them grow up.

As they drove through the park, she noticed that Phoebe had dozed off in her seat, probably weary from the heat.

To the left and right gnarled trees rose up from crusty graves, while the torrid earth menaced the landscape and small wisps of red dust danced like a tribe around the stake. There were warning signs all along the road about the dangers of bush fires and wooden battens were dotted at intervals, standing erect like warriors daring anyone to put them to use. Ahead was a continuous mirage of cool flowing water streaming over the shiny tarmac. It filled her with the desire to go faster and faster, to feel that trickle of refreshing liquid, but like the mocking devil, it was always out of reach.

Bronte had never experienced a bush fire, nor had she the desire to do so. She was only too aware from news pictures she had seen, of the vast devastation that could be caused by the careless discarding of a cigarette or a piece of glass.

She was relieved to be on the coast road some time later and to have left that hot, dry area behind her. She could smell the fresh sea air and could taste the salt on her lips. Angela was right about the surf. Even in the heat, she could see the waves rising up tall and curling towards the beach. Life was evidently casual up there. Shoes were unnecessary and the general uniform seemed to be swimming shorts and vest T-shirts, with sunglasses for image. It was hard to imagine any of the people she saw on the street, working in an office five days a week, because the impression they gave was that life was there to be coasted through, at no more than the most effortless pace, and nothing much was likely to come along to speed it up.

Paying attention to the instructions she had scribbled down, Bronte managed to reach the Avalon district without taking any wrong turns and it wasn't long before she found Angela and Murray's delightful little beach house, lying peacefully beneath tall leafy green palms.

*   *   *

211

'Watch out for the waves, Phoebe. Wow, that was a big jump!'

Angela and Murray had wasted no time in taking their guests down to the beach. Angela had filled a cool box with a picnic, which included hunks of warm fresh bread which she had baked herself that morning, slabs of creamy white cheese, cold meats, corn chips, chocolate bars, peanut toffee cookies and lashings of cold lemonade and beer.

They spread their towels casually on the sand and no sooner had they donned their straw hats, than Phoebe was off, racing down to the water's edge as fast as her little legs would carry her.

'Sorry, Ange. She's never still for a second,' apologised Bronte.

'Don't worry, she's gorgeous! She'll be a real stunner when she's older, with parents like hers. Come on, let's go after her. She'll need some protective cream.'

One thing Bronte had become very aware of since she had arrived in Australia was that most of the local people covered up when in the sun, rather than exposing themselves to the harmful rays. There was much advertising of sun creams and recommendations to be sensible with sun hats.

Bronte and Angela set off down the beach after Phoebe, leaving Murray already well into the novel he had brought with him. They spent what seemed like ages jumping the waves, one on each side of Phoebe, clutching her hands. Phoebe was in her element and was clearly not in the least afraid of the water, as she demanded to go deeper and deeper, with a smile on her face that almost stretched from ear to ear.

'How about digging a sandcastle, Phoebe? I've got you a spade up there?' Angela loved children.

It wasn't long before they were reduced to hands and knees, just on the edge of the surf, digging a monster of a hole in the sand, which to Phoebe's delight filled up entirely with water, every time a large wave sloshed up the beach.

Bronte felt truly happy and was easily able to put her worldly cares on hold, as she frolicked in the sea, her long coppery hair floating on the surface. She then allowed Phoebe to bury her under spadefuls of sand. Her tangerine swimming costume was high cut and crossed seductively over her back with straps of cerise pink. Her skin was a healthy shade of brown and Angela couldn't help remarking on how fit Bronte looked.

'You ever thought of modelling, cous?'

'Sorry?' Bronte was startled by the question.

'Yes. Seriously, you've got an amazing figure and I'm certain you've got taller and thinner since I last saw you in England. I know your hair would be a photographer's dream!'

'Thanks for the compliments, but I'm not sure I agree with you.' She was a little embarrassed.

'You should keep the idea up your sleeve.'

'I wouldn't know where to start. And from what I've heard about modelling, even though the money can be good if you make it to the top that is, it's a pretty soul-destroying way of making a living.'

'Murray's got some contacts if you were ever interested.'

'Chelsea used to be a model, but she gave it up after they were married and now spends most of her time writing.'

'I've seen pictures of her in the press. Isn't she a little small?'

'I suppose she is, although she's got the most delicate features.'

'Scandinavian isn't she?' asked Angela.

'She's originally from Sweden. Although I would say she's more American than anything else.'

'How do you get on with her? From what Chris has told me, she's mostly into herself a lot of the time.'

'Being married to someone like Jordan can't be easy, with as many female fans as he has, jealous of his wife and just dying to jump into bed with him!' Bronte was taking great pains not to express opinions on her employers, even to family, just in case they were misinterpreted.

'I guess not.'

Phoebe interrupted them: 'Hungry . . . sister Bwonte.'

'I'm playing the big sister today,' said Bronte by way of explanation.

'Of course,' Angela was amused. 'I know a place, which is not very far from here, where there's lots of yummy things just waiting to be eaten! Do you think we should go find it?'

'Yes pleeese!' Phoebe was wildly enthusiastic.

'I know one little girl who will sleep well tonight,' remarked Angela to Bronte, as they made their way back to their towels.

Phoebe proceeded to tuck happily into all she was offered, as indeed did Bronte, who had just discovered she was extremely hungry too.

Murray, who had waded firmly into his book by the time they returned, had set up the beach umbrella to provide some shade while they ate. He seemed to fairly race through his food, anxious to introduce his wife's cousin to the delights of the Australian surf without delay.

'Give her a chance to have some lunch,' laughed Angela.

'Won't be long, Murray. This is what I've come all the way from England for.'

'You'll love it! Everyone gets hooked.' Murray's accent was far stronger than his wife's, and at times, Bronte really had to concentrate to make out what he was saying.

'He's down here every morning before breakfast,' Angela told Bronte. 'Mind you, for that matter, I usually go to the seawater pool over there.' She pointed to a walled area by the rocks, wired off to provide a generous Olympic-sized swimming pool, which had the added bonus of having the water refreshed every time a big wave came over the top of the wall.

'It's amazing what a difference it makes to your day, if you've had a good swim in the sea before work.'

'I can imagine. It's just something one could never think of doing in the centre of London.'

They chatted for a while, as Murray explained to Bronte the techniques for successful board surfing and Phoebe, who had become sleepy from a combination of heat, activity, and a full tummy, sat quietly under the umbrella.

'Come on then, Murray. I'd better have a go. Lead the way.'

'I'll follow you two down in a sec. I'll just sort out the picnic.' Angela began to sweep everything back into the cold box.

'See you in a minute.' Bronte got to her feet.

'Will do. Mind you don't get dumped by those waves.

They're pretty strong if you get underneath them.'

'Don't tell me any more. I'm nervous as hell as it is.'

'You'll do fine. Come on,' Murray reassured her.

By that point Phoebe was curled up in the little nest they had made for her in the sand, lined with a towel. She seemed so fast asleep that Angela thought it a shame to wake her, instead deciding to leave her sleeping and to keep an eye from the water's edge.

Bronte, who had an athletic build, took to surfing like a natural. She couldn't imagine why she had never tried it before – it turned out to be the greatest possible fun! Very quickly, she found that as long as she timed the waves right, she mostly managed to ride on the crest, nearly all the way to the beach and avoid being hurled head first into the bottom of them. Once she had taken a couple of dives early on, she made certain it didn't happen to her again.

'You're doing great, Bronte. You're really getting the hang of it,' enthused Murray, as Angela clapped wildly from the beach.

'I'm not nearly as good as you,' she replied modestly, as she watched him dart across the waves in perfect control of his body and board.

'Yes, but I've done this all my life, don't forget. You're doing very well for a Pommie!'

'Take no notice, Bronte,' laughed Angela, who had caught her husband's last words. 'I'm nothing like as good as you and it's only your first time. You're going to have to come up regularly and get some practice in.'

'I'd love to, Ange. It's a fantastic sport.'

Fantastic or not, after about half an hour of wallowing in the surf, Bronte was exhausted and decided she needed a sit down to recover from all her exertion.

'I'll catch you guys in a minute. There's a couple of my mates down there, so I'll join them for a bit,' called Murray, from a little way out.

Angela raised her arm by way of recognition and turned to help Bronte back up the beach with her surf board.

Whether it was because she was wet from head to toe and the sun had not had the chance to warm her up, or whether it was just from sheer physical exhaustion, Bronte felt cold and somewhat uneasy, even shivery, as she approached their towels. The moment they got close, she felt as if ice had begun to form down her spine, because the little nest they had made for Phoebe under the umbrella was empty and there was no sign of the child anywhere around.

'My God, Ange! Where's Phoebe?' Panic set in.

'I know she was there a second ago, because I've been keeping an eye from down there. She can't be far.'

They stood as if glued, looking this way and that to see if they could make out any little figures on their own. But the beach, which had never been that full, was dotted with groups and not small individuals. Phoebe was nowhere in sight.

'What if she's gone into the water? She can't swim on her own.'

'She can't have. She would have had to pass us and I know I would have seen her.'

'Oh Ange, what are we going to do? You hear all those stories about kidnapping of famous people's children. I should never have left her on her own. Jordan and Chelsea will kill me.'

'Look, calm down. We'll find her, I promise, and they need never know. As for kidnapping, I honestly doubt it out here and besides, no-one knows who she is anyway.'

'Yes, but what if we've been followed and someone's been watching us? They could take Jordan to the cleaners on ransom and he's not even in the country! Oh crikey, Ange.'

Angela, who was a complete optimist and a very unflappable person, realised that one of them needed to keep a rational head and took charge of the situation.

'Come on, we'll split up and we'll find her. She probably woke up a few moments ago, saw we weren't here and wandered around to find us. I'll get Murray out of the sea to help and we'll cover the beach. You go up that way and check the car park and the dunes. She really won't be far away. Stop worrying.'

'Right – but easier said than done.'

Bronte, shaking like a leaf, while her imagination ran riot over all the awful things that could have happened, grabbed a towel and vowed to herself that she would never leave Phoebe's side again. At least not while she was supposed to be in charge. Huh! 'In charge'. That was a joke. What had she been thinking of, leaving the child asleep on her own, while she indulged herself in the sea? She would never stop blaming herself if something dreadful had happened.

She dashed across the hot sand, taking no notice of what it was doing to the soles of her feet, and ran up the concrete steps to the car park. It didn't take her long to establish that there was no sign of a wandering child amongst the few station wagons and dormobiles that were parked rather haphazardly.

From there, she picked her way across the prickly grass dunes, stopping only a couple of times to wince and wrench some spiky foreign object from her foot, before continuing her frantic search.

All of a sudden she could hear voices near to where she had stopped for a moment to listen. She could clearly make out a strong female Australian accent and . . . was that the laughter of a child? Oh, please let that be Phoebe . . . she prayed silently.

She ran instantly in the direction of the sounds she had heard, over the top of one turret and down again, before she reached a partially sheltered dune in which she discovered a seemingly happy little scene. There was a woman, who looked to be in her late thirties or early forties, with a chuckling mound of flesh in her lap, which to Bronte's enormous relief was Phoebe!

Neither woman nor child had seen Bronte, who stood above them looking down on where they were sitting on an old tartan rug. They seemed to be playing a tickling game, judging by the peals of laughter coming from Phoebe.

Just as Bronte was about to burst in on the scene, a man appeared on the other side of the sand dune wearing only a pair of bathers, every bit as out of breath as Bronte was herself. She clearly heard him say 'thank God', loudly, as he dashed down to where the woman was sitting.

'Joan! What are you doing? Where did you get that child?'

The woman looked up and smiled broadly.

'Karen and I are just playing, Geoff. We're not doing any harm. Just playing together in the sunshine, aren't we, my little pumpkin?' she replied calmly, as if she hadn't a care in the world.

Bronte, still rooted to the spot, began to wonder if she had arrived on another planet by mistake. Phoebe, for her part was still as happy as ever, and showed no signs of distress at all.

'Give her to me, Joan. You know that's not Karen. Where did you find her?'

Ignoring her husband's question, she turned to Phoebe: 'Look who's here. Daddy! Come to play with us too. Isn't that exciting now?'

Phoebe, who thought he was some new dimension to the game, giggled again. However, Bronte was becoming increasingly disturbed by what she was witnessing and decided to intervene.

'What on earth's going on here? Can you please give Phoebe back to me?'

'Bwonte . . .!' squealed Phoebe in further raptures over the fact that Bronte had obviously come to join in too.

'Is this your child?' The man looked at her.

'I'm looking after her for her parents. You've no idea how worried I was when I found she was missing.'

The woman's face had changed. She looked terribly sad and confused.

'But this is Karen. She's my little girl. Why do you want her?'

'No, my love. This is not Karen. Karen died in the fire, remember? This little girl belongs to the lady. Now we must give her back so she can go and see her Mummy and Daddy. We wouldn't want her to lose them, now would we?'

'But Karen's not dead,' she protested feebly.

'Yes she is. You must start believing it. She's gone and she can't come back to us.'

Phoebe, who had begun to notice the change in atmosphere, crawled out of the woman's lap and ran to Bronte, who immediately took her up into her arms. The woman offered no resistance and, instead, looked pathetically bewildered.

'I must apologise to you for this. You see, we lost our daughter in a fire earlier this year. My wife has been in a state of shock ever since and just can't seem to accept what has happened.'

'I'm so sorry for you.' Now that she knew no harm had come to Phoebe, Bronte began to feel a little akin to the suffering that was evident before her eyes. 'I lost my husband in an accident in September, so I know what she's going through.'

'Every time she sees a baby of around Karen's age, she thinks it's Karen. I have to watch her all the time. I only hope she starts to get better soon, because it breaks my heart to see her like this.'

'I can imagine. Look, I must get back now and tell my cousin Phoebe's safe and well. Let's just forget this, because it was partly my fault for leaving her on the beach while I was in the water. I've certainly learnt my lesson.'

'I appreciate your understanding. It wouldn't help Joan any to get the police involved.'

'I hope your wife gets better,' although judging by her continuing vacant stare, Bronte thought that might take quite some time. 'Goodbye.'

'. . . and she was just sitting there? Laughing, you say?' Angela was every bit as relieved as Bronte had been to hear of Phoebe's safe return.

'She didn't seem to mind a bit.'

They were back home in Angela and Murray's garden. Bronte continued: 'The thing is, she's been used to so many different people looking after her, that I don't believe she has any fear of strangers at all. As long as they are kind and play with her or give her ice cream or something, I'm sure she'd go with anyone.'

'Are you going to tell Jordan and Chelsea about this?' asked Angela.

'I should, if only to let them know that they really ought to warn Phoebe of the dangers of going off with strange people. But I'll have to pick my moment. I don't want the sack this early on.'

'I'm really sorry this had to happen on our beach, Bronte. I hope it hasn't put you off coming up here?' Angela was worried.

'It wasn't your fault. If anything, it was mine. I should not have left her. Don't worry, I'll come back just as soon as I get some time off.'

'Thank goodness for that.'

Phoebe, who seemed none the worse for her ordeal, was happily pulling the heads off flowers and lining them up on the path. Bronte got up, deciding it was about time she went to the rescue of Angela's garden and took Phoebe back; 'Come on, you monster. Let's get you home. It'll be bed time soon and I know you're tired.'

CHAPTER SIXTEEN

Jordan and Chelsea were away for a total of six days. To Bronte it had seemed like a lifetime. Although she had been busy enough during their absence, she really missed having them around the house and ever since the incident at Avalon (which she had kept to herself) she was anxious to return the responsibility of Phoebe's welfare to her parents.

The trip had apparently gone well and even Chelsea seemed to show a new lease of life, having recharged her batteries in Los Angeles. It was only a couple of days after they got back, and one of the very rare occasions when even Chelsea made it up for breakfast, that Jordan brought up the subject of Phoebe's birthday.

'Phoeb's going to be three next week and I think we should do something about a party or at least take her somewhere. What do you think, honey?' He turned to Chelsea for support.

'Sure. Why not?' She had her nose buried in a magazine and Bronte thought she would probably have returned the same answer to whatever question he had asked.

'Only problem is, we haven't got to know too many other kids around here, so a party may not be the best idea.'

'Also,' remarked Bronte, 'if you want to continue to keep a low profile, it isn't such a good idea to have people coming here whom you don't really know.'

'I guess you're right. Pass the toast, will you?' He sank into thought.

Chelsea, who had just finished reading the article about European influences on Australian fashion, took more interest in the conversation and contributed: 'That leaves an outing then. What's there to do for kids around here?' It was a general question, aimed at no-one in particular.

'I could ask Chris, if you like? But I do know there's a large zoo close to here. Perhaps you could take her there?'

'Is that marmalade? What, with koalas and kangaroos and that kind of thing?' That was Jordan's interpretation of an Australian zoo!

'I suppose so, darling. You would expect to find those in a zoo over here.'

Bronte couldn't tell if that was meant sarcastically.

'OK. Well let's do that in the morning and then I'll have a word around and borrow a launch from someone to take us round the harbour for lunch.'

Chelsea seemed to like that idea better. Bronte had begun to wonder if Chelsea also had a problem with crowds. Perhaps it was one of the factors that contributed to her anorexia?

'That's a good idea. Let's just keep it small and go somewhere where we won't be hounded by other boats.'

'I'll ask Art and his wife. You'll like her, she's a fashion designer and they've got a couple of kids. And Bronte, you'll come? You should meet Art's wife too.' Did Chelsea's expression alter or was it Bronte's imagination? Either way, she needed to change the subject rapidly.

'How about a cake, Chelsea? I could order one locally if you like?' Bronte needed to know what Chelsea was thinking.

'Sure. Sort that out . . .' Chelsea had become vague and rather uninterested once more.

Jordan interrupted: 'Try and get something fun. We could take it on the boat and it can be a surprise for her.' She saw the child in him again. 'I'll liaise with you about the boat so you can arrange to get something on board. Can you fix up the zoo too?'

Jordan was a great one for having everything fixed up. But on that occasion, she didn't really think it was necessary.

'I'm not sure you need to book the zoo. I think you just turn up, but I'll check anyhow. Which day is this for, by the way?'

'Tuesday,' said Chelsea, in a matter-of-fact voice.

'Right.' Bronte wasn't sure what else to say.

'We must think about a present, darling. Got any ideas?'

'I'll put my mind to it. Let's go shopping.' Her expression brightened and Jordan seemed just as keen on the idea.

Tuesday came round at last. Phoebe was at the age where she knew something special was about to happen and that whatever it was, it was being arranged for her benefit. They had agreed to keep the activities as a surprise for the day but at the same time, wanted to make sure Phoebe knew it was her birthday.

There had been a mammoth shopping expedition, from which the sports car had returned jammed to the roof with packages and parcels, and both Chelsea and Jordan had emerged staggering under the weight of their purchases. As she rushed out to help them unload the car, Bronte couldn't help wondering how much of what they had bought was for their daughter and how much would hang in their own wardrobes. Still, it was their money and really none of her business. Besides, it was good to see Chelsea enjoying herself, because from what she had observed so far, it didn't happen all that often.

Phoebe was up early so as not to miss any more of her birthday than she absolutely had to and began rampaging through the house at a terrific rate. No-one had time to dress, as she summoned them all to the conservatory, where a goodly pile of presents had been assembled the night before.

Jordan emerged from his room, clad in a paisley dressing gown, and his hair sexily ruffled after a night's sleep. Chelsea, on the other hand, looked as if she had just left the beauty salon moments earlier. Bronte by comparison, felt totally unglamorous in a pair of leggings and a T-shirt which she had managed to put on with difficulty just after Phoebe had left her room for the third time that morning.

It wasn't long before Phoebe was surrounded by shreds of paper and ribbon which had been instantly dropped in favour of the goodies which she pulled out of each parcel. She clapped her little hands in delight as she discovered the various treasures which the grown-ups had prepared for her.

'Presents from Sydney! Presents from Sydney!' Sydney had just woken up to the occasion and was in full flow.

They couldn't help smiling at his outburst, which obviously encouraged him no end, because he then burst into a chorus of 'Happy Birthday', to which they were subjected at least five or six times!

Both Beccy and Charlene had made their contributions to the pile and, all in all, Phoebe did not know where to start to examine all her new possessions. So much so, that tearing up the wrapping paper even further, seemed as good a place as any.

As all that was going on, Bronte found it hard not to glance to where Jordan was perched on the arm of a chair, with his legs crossed and his dressing gown opening casually to reveal a 'V' of olive skin and a few hairs nestling around his breast bone.

Beccy and Charlene stood on the steps of the house, waving to the disappearing station wagon, which was heading in the direction of Taronga Zoo. Having made some enquiries, Bronte discovered they could leave the car on the hill leading down to the ferry wharf and pick up a cable car which would take them right up into the zoo. As Jordan had arranged for the launch to collect them from Taronga Wharf, it meant they were able to leave all their boating paraphernalia in the car, as well as Phoebe's new koala, which she had insisted on bringing with them.

As they climbed into the little bubble car, with Chelsea and Jordan sitting opposite her and Phoebe on her knee, Bronte felt totally out of place. She would far rather have met them later after an en-famille visit to the zoo. However, when she had mentioned it to Jordan earlier, he had pleaded with her to come with them, saying that he needed her enthusiasm to make it more of a party. He almost implied that he feared Chelsea might dampen the child's spirits, if she happened to be in one of her darker moods. Bronte found it impossible to argue, particularly when he bore into her with his eyes, the way he did sometimes. She was sure he could make a woman do almost anything by just looking at her a certain way. Boy, was that dangerous!

'Look, Phoeb, there's a crocodile down there. See him? By that pond. Isn't he cute?'

'Where?' Phoebe strained her little neck to follow the direction of Jordan's finger.

'There. He's just the same colour as the ground. Look at those teeth!'

The object of their attention obligingly opened and closed his jaw, in what looked like a sleepy yawn because his eyes were tight shut.

'Yuk! I don't like him, Daddy.' Phoebe was adamant.

Chelsea, meanwhile, had turned around to face the direction from which they had just come, which Bronte had to admit was a most impressive view over the harbour towards the Opera House and beyond to the high-rise apartments of down-town Sydney. She only wished she had remembered to bring her camera.

The cable ride lasted less than five minutes and when they reached the landing station, they had to be careful to scramble out quickly because the cars were linked on a constant rotational system.

Jordan stood for a moment and tried to get his bearings.

'That guy over there's got some route maps. I'll go and get one so we know where to start in this place.'

Bronte couldn't help noticing that eyes followed Jordan wherever he went. She was sure that some of them had no idea who he was, but he had a certain charisma about the way he carried himself and the way he dressed that seemed to invite attention. While they waited for him to return, Bronte became irritated by the flies and tried to waft them away with little or no success.

'Gee, this is a big place you know!' Jordan was studying the map he had just purchased. 'There's all kinds of animals here – not just Australian. Come on, guys, let's go find the 'koala tree top exhibit' – whatever that is.'

As they wandered round the various cages, each housing healthy, but sometimes sad-looking examples of their individual species, Bronte realised what a difference it made bringing a child to the zoo. She managed to look through Phoebe's eyes. The enthusiasm was infectious and she found herself darting from cage to cage, looking for the 'baby ones', or those that might be doing something other than basking in what was already becoming a very hot sun.

The wallaby area was situated near to the main entrance of the zoo and it was in that direction that they went, after examining the seals and dolphins. Someone, possibly Charlene, had told Phoebe all about kangaroos and how they carried their babies in little pouches. As soon as she saw the picture on the wire of the reserve, she let out an almighty squeal, which made several tourists who had just passed them, stop in their tracks and turn round in concern.

'Kang . . . roo, Daddy. Look over there!' She rushed up to the wire and pressed her nose through.

Jordan bent down and picked her up, setting her on his shoulders for a better view of the adorable little creatures, who were hopping about, probably in search of a little shade.

'Can I have one Daddy?' Phoebe was quite serious.

Jordan looked over to Bronte and winked unexpectedly, which immediately made her blush and turn away.

'See what Mommy says, shall we? Mommy? How about it?' Jordan seemed keen to include Chelsea.

'Don't be ridiculous, Phoebe. How on earth could we take one of those home with us? Where would we put it in the apartment in New York? Those things need bushes and trees and lots of space.'

Phoebe looked disappointed and Bronte felt for her, thinking it was not the kindest response Chelsea could have given.

'I think what Mommy means is that it would be cruel to take a kangaroo away from its Mommy and Daddy and all its friends and that we wouldn't be able to give it the kind of home it needs, if we took it back to America.'

Phoebe looked a little happier, but not altogether convinced. Bronte had a brainwave.

'Just think, Phoebe, your Koala who is waiting for you in the car would be very miserable to think you didn't want him any more, and that you preferred a kangaroo.'

That did the trick.

'Want my koala. Want to go back to the car now.' Jordan set her back down and she rushed over to Chelsea and took her hand.

'Can we get my koala now, Mommy?' she implored her mother.

'Yes, I think so, darling. We'll go and get him and then take him out for lunch on a boat.' She glanced at Jordan. 'Isn't it about time we made tracks back to pick up the boat? Besides, it's getting awfully hot to walk around here much more.'

'I'll take a look at the map and see which is the best way back.'

Chelsea, still holding Phoebe's hand, set off a few paces in front of Jordan and Bronte. She seemed anxious to get to the boat, presumably, to some sort of privacy.

'Thanks for rescuing the situation back there.' Jordan spoke quietly.

'Don't mention it. Anyway, she's a lovely little girl and I felt sorry for her. Perhaps I even remembered my own childhood for a moment. I was always being told 'no', and sometimes children just need their minds diverting to something else.'

'Did you have a really rough time when you were young?'

Bronte prayed that Chelsea wouldn't turn round and wonder what they were talking about. 'Not rough exactly. It was more a question of being left to do my own thing with very little guidance and certainly a lack of affection.'

'You and me too. Sounds like it happened to us both. Makes me determined to give Phoeb a better time than I had. A more normal childhood if that's possible, although God knows, it's hard with the crazy kind of life we lead. Anyhow, I just wanted to say thanks. I appreciated what you did.'

'You're embarrassing me, Jordan.' He immediately leant nearer to her and made matters worse.

'Why?' He removed his glasses for a moment and tried to lock her eyes, but she found it impossible to look at his face.

'I would rather not have gooseberried in on your family day.'

'I'm really glad you did. I like having you along. So does Phoebe.'

'But what about Chelsea? Does she want me 'along'?' Almost without meaning to, she had broached a subject which she had promised herself was taboo – for her mind only.

But all he would say, somewhat ambiguously but deadly seriously, was: 'We needed you, Bronte.' His voice was so soft and warm that it would have melted any frosty heart.

*   *   *

227

Fortunately, the boat was waiting for them when they reached the wharf. Also waiting, but for the ferry, were a large group of American tourists, who had presumably 'done' the zoo and were on their way to 'do' the Opera House. Once one of them recognised Jordan word spread like wildfire and fifty pairs of eyes fixed themselves on him. Again, seemingly accustomed to the attention, Jordan simply waved in their direction and shepherded his family on to the motor launch, with quiet instructions to the skipper to get the hell out of there as fast as possible. All the time he maintained his public smile for the benefit of the audience.

'Phew! Am I glad the boat was here.' Chelsea sank into the nearest comfortable chair.

'The worst thing is having to sign your name fifty times. I would have started to write Jack Spratt or something, if I'd been asked to do that.' He rarely seemed ruffled. 'Oh, Art, good to see you. Sorry about the hasty departure. Monique, glad you came along.' The charm was on maximum volume, as he brushed the well made-up cheeks of the woman who had just approached him.

'Come and meet the family. Darling, this is Art's wife, Monique. Monique, my wife, Chelsea, and this little terror is the birthday girl.'

In all, Jordan had assembled about twelve for lunch. They were made up of a combination of film people, a couple who turned out to be old friends of Jordan and Chelsea, and the rest Bronte had met during the past few weeks of working with Jordan on the movie. The other two children on board were both Dafons – a little boy of about Phoebe's age and a girl who appeared a bit older. It wasn't long before they latched onto Phoebe and began exploring the boat together under the careful supervision of the Dafon nanny.

The cloudless blue sky, which had remained unchanged almost since they had arrived in Australia, offered no shade from the heat of the mid-day sun. It was for that reason, that the food had been laid out on the rear deck, beneath an erected canopy.

No expense had been spared for the lavish buffet. Bronte still felt a little uneasy about tagging along with the Innes family and decided to put as much distance between herself and Jordan as was possible on a seventy two-foot boat. She had gathered that the launch belonged to one of the companies who were financing the movie and that it was mainly used for entertaining or impressing wealthy clients who came into town. Presumably, Jordan qualified.

As she weaved her way to the bow of the boat in search of a quiet place to sit and eat, and also to indulge in a little sunbathing if possible, she found herself admiring the sweet-smelling varnished woodwork, the spotlessly clean decks and the gleaming, white leather cabin interior. She shuddered to think what a boat like that would cost, but then thought that if she mentioned it to Jordan, he would probably announce to her that he had one just like it in Bermuda!

When she reached the front, she found Monique Dafon by herself, already applying the sun oil.

'Hi there! Come and sit down. It's a great boat, isn't it?'

'Yes. It must be lovely to have something like this to use when the weather's so hot.' She arranged herself near to Monique.

'You're English, aren't you?'

Ten out of ten for observation. 'Yes, I am.'

'So tell me, what brings you out to sunny Sydney? What's your connection with the Innes'?'

How to explain that one?

'I met Jordan a couple of months back in France and he was looking for a personal assistant to travel with them.' She began to tuck into her lunch.

'Such a wonderful person, Jordan. Art's worked with him on a number of projects now and he's always charm itself, don't you think?'

'I don't really know him that well yet.' Be evasive, Bronte.

'Strange, I've never met his wife before, though.' She produced a long diamond-chip nail file and started with her thumbs. 'Pretty little thing . . . and what a delightful child. Quite a handful, I imagine. Similar age to our Charlie.'

Bronte couldn't help wondering why some women bothered to have children, if they simply palmed them off with nannies from the word go. Presumably, the offspring gave them a chance to indulge in the egotistical satisfaction of producing carbon copies of themselves.

'Put your swimmers on. You should get some of this sun on your body. My, but you have got a fantastic figure there. Do you diet and exercise a lot?'

'Actually, neither. I must be hyperactive or something. I usually find it hard to put on weight.' There – rub it in!

'Wow, but aren't you lucky! I work relentlessly on mine . . . and I'll still never get down to your size.'

Yes, and you are a good deal older, thought Bronte to herself. She was just about to remove her T-shirt when the next awkward question came flying out: 'What does your husband think of all this travel away from home? I see you're married.' She was referring to Bronte's wedding ring.

'Yes. I am . . .' Just at that moment, Jordan came to her rescue, without even realising it.

'There you are!' He appeared from below deck, stripped to the waist. 'Phoebe's about to cut her cake and she wants you to come too.'

She turned to Monique: 'Can't miss this one. I had it made locally in Mosman. It's shaped like a kangaroo!'

'How perfectly sweet. Jordan, darling, tell her to make a wish for me, will you?'

Jordan either failed to hear or deliberately ignored that one, as he stood back to allow Bronte past him. Out of earshot, she turned to him and said: 'Thanks on my side that time. You came just at the right moment. She was veering on to the subject of Dominic . . .'

'God, how awful for you. She's harmless enough, but brainless.'

'I suppose she wasn't to know. Where's the cake? I haven't seen it yet.' She made up her mind that distance between her and Jordan was actually not what she wanted at all, particularly when she studied that tanned back, as he led her downstairs.

'In the lower cabin. The caterers thought it would have less chance of melting down there.'

Phoebe was thrilled with her cake and Bronte had to admit that it had turned out even better than she could have hoped.

It was about eighteen inches in length and all of the most intricate features of the kangaroo's face, body and tiny paws had been painstakingly reproduced in the icing. There was even a little baby peeping out from the pouch. Everyone who had assembled for the grand cutting agreed it was a work of art and, indeed, a shame to cut into it at all! But since it was made from a combination of sponge and vanilla ice cream, if they didn't dive in, it would quickly smudge anyway. Fortunately, the crew had a camera and managed to capture the expressions of sheer delight on Phoebe's face, as she blew out the three pink candles.

After that, rather than everyone getting themselves sticky and covered in melting ice cream, the caterer offered to cut the cake into small pieces and deliver it round on deck shortly.

As they went outside once more, they were blinded by the glaring sunlight.

'About time we had a swim, old boy.' Art turned to Jordan.

'Can we stop somewhere up here? This is your territory, Art.'

A swim sounded like music to Bronte's ears. She was feeling hot and clammy.

'There's a delightful little creek up the Parramatta river. It shouldn't take us long to get there. I'll have a word with the skipper. Hold on.' Art went back down below.

Phoebe, who was always quick to pick up on and put to her advantage anything discussed by grown-ups, turned to her father and said: 'Swim, Daddy?'

'Give us a chance, sunshine. We'll find somewhere to stop. But you'll have be a very good girl and let me hold you, because I don't think we've got any life rings for you,' and to Bronte, 'she does love the water.'

'So I've learnt.' She was busy tying her hair into a knot on top of her head. It was just too hot to wear it down, the way Jordan liked.

The creek Art had mentioned was private and secluded and turned out to be the perfect place to anchor for a swim. Looking down, the water was crystal clear, although too deep to see right to the bottom. Bronte couldn't wait to feel the transparent waters envelop her boiling skin.

Most of the lunch party had gathered on deck, either to join the bathers or to watch the activities. By that time, the majority of them were clad either in Bermudas or bikinis, with the scent of coconut oil lingering in the air.

There were two ways of jumping ship – either by taking a dive from the platform jutting out from the back of the boat, or by going more sedately down the steps to the level of the water and sliding gently in. Most of the women (including Chelsea) took the latter option while the men, flexing their muscles and fiddling with the elastic round the top of their Bermudas, chose the more challenging route.

Bronte stood on deck watching Jordan who carried Phoebe in his arms. He picked his way carefully down the steps and into the water with the minimum of splashing. For some reason, once he was in, she felt far less self-conscious and stripped off to reveal a flattering costume with navy and white hoops up the body, a wide band of green around the bust and thick green straps over the shoulders. The costume drew tightly round her shapely figure and gave lifting support to her breasts. As she tidied away her clothing into a beach bag, unbeknown to her, one of the male crew members behind her took one look and sucked in his breath, letting out a quiet but meaningful whistle, as he admired the perfect female form before him.

Almost the last to go, Bronte stepped on to the diving platform, took a couple of bounces and then hurled herself into a perfectly symmetrical dive, entering the water at perpendicular angles which caused hardly more than a ripple on the surface. This went unnoticed by only a very few of the party already in the water.

Heaven! A little apart from the others, she glided like a mermaid, her hair once more detached from its moorings and floating round her like a veil. She dived down, down, feeling a delicious sense of cool after the fire, as she stretched every part of her body sensuously. Each time she rose to the surface, she put her hands to her face to smooth away the rivulets from her eyes and wipe the hair from her forehead. She had just emerged from one such under water exploration, when she found Jordan by her side, with an ever-excited Phoebe splashing about in his arms.

'Sorry, but she wanted to come over this way and see you,' he said, as if he felt the need to explain his presence.

'This is just wonderful!' She felt so relaxed in the leafy green surroundings and the ice blue water.

'It's a pretty neat place, isn't it? I must say, I needed to cool off.'

'Want to swim with Bwonte.' Phoebe had had enough of the adult chatter and wanted to get down to the serious business of swimming.

'I don't know if Bronte will appreciate your drowning tactics!' He laughed in Bronte's direction.

'Try me,' was all she could manage, once more feeling a strange tingling which she knew she should not be feeling.

'OK. You asked for it!'

He propelled himself closer to where she was treading water and made to pass the child to her, taking care not to let Phoebe go under the water. Physical contact was the inevitable outcome of the manoeuvre – it could not be avoided, and as their bodies touched in places which later that night, Bronte struggled to remember for sure, shock waves bolted through her, stronger than anything she had ever experienced before. To an observer (if indeed there were any) it was a perfectly innocent encounter, but to the two of them, it somehow symbolised the inevitable. It was now just a question of time.

Bronte recovered herself as quickly as she could, and concentrated firmly on playing with Phoebe, firstly on her back and then later on her front, until Chelsea came to take over.

'Here, I'll take a turn. You've been dunked long enough.' She seemed happier than she had been earlier.

'I don't mind, honestly. But I'm sure you'd like a swim with Mummy, wouldn't you, Phoebe?'

'Mommy, Mommy.' She thrust her little body longingly into her mother's arms. It was pathetic to see how gleefully she reacted to the least bit of affection shown by her mother.

One by one, the party climbed back aboard the boat, tired but refreshed after their dip. Bronte was one of the last to emerge. Jordan, who had been one of the first to return to the boat, sat sprawled in a director's chair on the upper deck, with one leg dangling over an arm of the chair and a cocktail in his hand. Behind the black lenses, his eyes were watching what was happening below. His heart nearly skipped a beat when he saw Bronte's svelte figure for the first time, with the clinging wet costume leaving little to the imagination. He knew she was well-proportioned, but he had never actually dared to imagine just what those never-ending legs, that tiny waist and those curving breasts would do to him. Her skin, dotted with droplets of sea water, glistened with a coppery sheen in the sun as he drank in the vision, silently grateful for the glasses without which his eyes would surely have betrayed the surge of emotion that he was feeling. Blissfully unaware of the effect she was having upstairs, and indeed she would have crumbled to a bag of nerves, had she had the remotest idea, Bronte reached for a white towel which she draped round her back and tucked carefully into her cleavage.

For the first time in his married life, Jordan felt as if his whole inner security was being seriously threatened. Indeed, searching back, he could not remember any woman having such a profound effect on his very being in such a short space of time. Although it left him feeling excited, he began to wonder if he should stop that runaway train at the next station and make a hasty exit. But then again, he was not entirely certain that he could.

234

CHAPTER SEVENTEEN

'Bronte? Bronte, are you upstairs?' called Chelsea from outside her bedroom door.

'Hang on a sec. Be with you in a mo . . .' Bronte covered the mouthpiece of the 'phone and yelled back from the study. 'Sorry, Mr Charmen, please continue. Which date was it you were thinking of having Jordan on the show?'

Wherever Jordan went, it was par for the course that he would be pestered by the local TV and radio stations to do live interviews on air. As a rule, the invitations were politely declined on his behalf by his press agents or personal assistants unless of course it was to help promote a new picture, in which case he felt more or less obliged. But if it was merely for a delve into his personal life – which, goodness knows, was becoming complicated enough – as most of them turned out to be, he wanted nothing to do with them. However, in good faith, Bronte felt it her duty to take down the details and at least consult him.

A few moments later, she trotted downstairs to find Chelsea and see what it was she had called up about. Charlene had been given a well-earned day off, because she had worked non-stop for the past seven days ever since the outing on the boat. It was Jordan who had suggested she looked a little peaky the night before (much to her acute embarrassment) and that as Chelsea had nothing particular planned that day, Charlene should take a little time to herself.

It was already mid-morning and Bronte, who found her days becoming busier and busier, had not even had time to look at her watch since the moment she had crawled out of bed that morning, which had been well before seven.

She found Chelsea in her bedroom, putting the final touches to an elaborate hairdo with which she had been experimenting. It looked fine for the cover of a magazine, but Bronte secretly thought it wouldn't last five minutes outside as, for once, there was a little breeze around.

'Sorry, Chelsea. I had a chap on the phone from the morning chat show, wanting Jordan to appear and trying to wheedle details of the movie out of me.'

'Bad luck. They're a pain in the ass, those people. Jordan'll be livid if too much leaks out at this stage. Did you tell him to go take a hike?' She held the can of hair spray a few inches from her head.

'Not in so many words. I was trying to be diplomatic. I did promise to at least discuss it with Jordan, although I know already what he'll say.' She felt awkward for some reason, standing on the threshold of the marital bedroom.

'So do I. Anyway, changing the subject, I've been introduced to a local publisher who may be interested in seeing what I've been writing over here.' Another squirt at her fringe.

'That's good news, isn't it?' It was rare that Chelsea bothered to go into details with Bronte – there had to be a reason.

'I don't know. It may just be a waste of time, but it would be worth knowing if he thinks there'd be people interested in reading it here. Anyway, I need you to be a darling and have Phoebe. I'm not sure how long I'll be out. You hadn't got any plans had you?' She turned to face Bronte for the first time since she had come into the room.

'Nothing I can't do later.' She jolly well did have masses to do and she knew for sure, that with Phoebe's distracting influence, she didn't have a cat in hell's chance of getting anything done at all. Still, she had no choice and she was, after all, employed for both business and domestic reasons – it was just that the business ones didn't allow much time for the domestic ones.

'The other thing is that I promised to take her to one of the Ken Done shops today to get her some new clothes. You know, T-shirts, skirts, swimming costumes and such like. Could you do that instead? You could go to the shop at Neutral Bay or what about the Rocks, and have lunch there?' She dabbed a little expensive perfume on her wrists and her neck, leaving Bronte wondering if she really was going to meet the unnamed publisher.

Blast, thought Bronte. That really did blow all chances of getting a few much-needed hours in on the computer.

'How much do you want me to get for her?' It was going to be quite a responsibility choosing clothes for Phoebe, particularly when her mother was so fashion conscious herself.

'Oh, just get her a few outfits. I'm tired of the clothes we brought over for her and the Ken Done collection for children is really inspiring this season.'

'Right. I'll go and find her and I think we'll head off sooner rather than later, before the 'phone has the chance to trap me again.'

'What?' Chelsea was distracted by a last personal mirror inspection. 'Oh, yeah. Sure.' She could have been agreeing to anything, for the interest she showed.

'Yes, but where are we going, Bwonte?' Phoebe sat beside Bronte on the bus, barely able to see out of the window.

'For the tenth time, Phoeb,' she smiled and stroked the little girl's head, 'Mummy has gone out and she thought it would be a good idea for us to go and buy you some new clothes and have lunch at the same time.'

'What clothes though?' Phoebe was showing signs of developing the same sort of interest in clothes as that expressed by her mother.

Good question, thought Bronte and out loud she replied: 'Let's just make that a surprise for when we get there, shall we? Wait and see what the shop has?'

But Phoebe was not satisfied and carried on the inquisition: 'Are we just going to one shop, Bwonte?'

'Yes, I think so.' Bronte had not found the time to visit any of the Ken Done shops since she had set foot in Australia, but she was familiar with the name, as a number of stores in London imported that label.

'But what if we don't like that shop? Will there be another one?'

'There might be. Look, there's the zoo we went to last week.' Desperate to change the subject, she pointed out the entrance to the zoo.

As the ferry bumped towards the wharf, the water gushed up over the wooden boarding planks and was sucked back down through the cracks. At each wharf, a couple of sturdy-looking ferry crew were employed to tie the boat steady, as she danced on the joy of her own wash, and to lend a helping hand to the passengers as they stepped on and off.

'Mind how you go. Hold Mummy's hand tight now,' smiled one, as he put his arm out to help Bronte and Phoebe board.

She really had begun to feel a bit like Phoebe's mother. They wandered to the front of the boat and sat on a wooden slatted bench with their backs to the cabin. That way, they would have a little shelter from the wind which would be bound to pick up as they crossed over towards the Opera House.

Phoebe insisted on climbing up onto the seat so that she could 'see the boats', as she put it. Bronte grasped her round the knees to prevent her toppling over if the boat were to lurch too far, and sat back to admire the view.

Bronte knew from the tourist map in the house that the Rocks area of shops and restaurants lay directly to the right of Circular Quay and from what she could see, it wouldn't take them too long to get there.

As the Opera House grew and grew in stature, she made a mental note to check into performance times when she had a moment. There was bound to be something good on with Christmas fast approaching and it would be a shame to come all the way to Sydney and not visit one of its most famous landmarks.

Quite a swell had built up at the docking area, probably due to the frequency of the incoming and outgoing ferries, as well as the hydrofoils and tourist boats, for it was the nerve centre of the harbour activities. Bronte managed to find her sea legs as the earth beneath her swayed, and she steered Phoebe off the ferry and towards the ticket office.

Feeling wildly windswept and praying they wouldn't meet anyone important or even anyone she recognised, she studied the map before leading a chattering Phoebe towards the shops.

'I don't want this.' Phoebe shed her pink cardigan and would probably have dropped it there and then on the pavement, if Bronte hadn't made a dive for it.

'Nor do I, Phoeb. But if you insist, I'd better carry it. We can't leave it there, can we?'

'Where's the shop, Bwonte? Does it have toys?'

'Just clothes, I think, but we'll find out. Hold on, we're about to cross the road.'

Fortunately, the shop which turned out to be two shops joined into one, was situated right on the front of the Rocks, overlooking the harbour.

'There we go.' Bronte held Phoebe's hand, as she took an exaggerated leap up the curb. 'This place looks like fun!'

The shop was designed to appear welcoming. The bright colours inspired the customer to venture in, if only to browse. However, once inside, the merchandise was so inviting and cleverly displayed that only the meanest of shoppers managed to escape without parting with at least a fraction of their worldly wealth.

There seemed to be an unlimited choice of items that she could have bought for Phoebe. The fabrics were delightful and there was no shortage of dresses, swimwear, trousers, skirts, sweat shirts and T-shirts for children. Her biggest problem was trying to prevent Phoebe from pulling all the clothes off their hangers.

Finally, after just managing to keep her temper, although sorely tempted on a couple of occasions to sweep the child off the floor and storm right out of the shop with her, she selected a bundle of garments which she hoped would be suitable, and with the help of a sympathetic sales girl, she frog-marched Phoebe into the changing room to see which would actually fit.

'Too tight,' wailed Phoebe, as she was squeezed into a charming swimming costume with electric blue and green fishes gliding round her middle.

'Do you have that one in the next size up, please?' Bronte was beginning to see why Chelsea had delegated that particular shopping trip to her.

'I'll go and check. Now, you don't want these do you, because I'll take them back at the same time?' The assistant seemed used to chaotic customers, but was probably also eyeing up the pile that Bronte had already agreed to buy.

'Hold on a minute. You'll rip those!' Bronte shot forward and prevented Phoebe from pulling the straps of the costume so far out in front of her, that they were about to come away from the body piece.

'Don't like this one.'

'I know. I'm getting you a bigger one – just don't tear that one or we'll end up paying for both.' Not that Phoebe would worry about that in the slightest.

Exactly one hour and ten minutes after they had first walked in, Bronte was relieved to be standing by the cash desk, watching the garments she had chosen being carefully wrapped in tissue paper and stowed in brown paper holdall bags. She had not had a moment to look for anything for herself. That could wait until she was able to return on her own and take the whole thing at a more leisurely pace.

When the girl gave her the total bill, she was glad that Jordan was paying and not her and hoped that he was used to his wife's extravagances and would not think she had anything to do with it. At least Chelsea would be pleased with the eight items which were now packed into four different bags, one of which Phoebe insisted on carrying because it contained her favourite dress with pink and blue koalas on a white background. The only trouble was that as they wandered out of the shop and down the street, the bag, which was at least half the height of Phoebe herself, trailed along the ground after her. Oh well, if the dress got dirty, there was always the washing machine, which had probably never seen such active service as it had since the Innes family moved in!

As they trooped off in search of a pavement café which would serve something outdoors for lunch, Bronte found her mind wandering back to Jordan. She had not seen him at all that morning. Despite the fact that she found herself getting up earlier and earlier, there were some days when he had breakfast meetings and he would get up, dress and slip out of the house virtually unnoticed. On those occasions, he would usually leave her some cryptic message, scribbled with one hand while he was shaving with the other, which let her know where to reach him and gave her various instructions for the day.

Although the pace of life had permitted very little time alone with him over the past week, she had become aware of knowing looks and smiles, either over the meal table, or just when they bumped into each other in the corridor. She was immediately thrown into confusion each time it happened and, although her heart (which felt as if it was on a kind of dangerous roller-coaster ride at an amusement park) told her to return the looks and let him know how she was feeling, her head got the better of her and forced her to examine the toes of her shoes momentarily or embark on some inane topic of conversation.

The truth was, she was beginning not to trust herself too well. She would have been even more wary, had she known that ever since Phoebe's birthday, Jordan had been unable to wipe the vision of her coming out of the water from his mind, and he was seriously beginning to doubt how much longer he would be able to restrain himself.

Reflecting afterwards on the chance meeting in the street that day, Bronte came to the conclusion that it was uncanny how just by thinking of something or someone, it was almost as if you could draw that event or that person into actually being. There she was, lost in thought over Jordan, at the same time trying to find somewhere to stop and feed Phoebe, when they turned a corner and bumped literally, headlong into the subject of her thoughts! If that wasn't fate . . .

Jordan was being taken to lunch by a couple of people whom Art had employed to oversee some of the production of the movie, and as it was reaching a point where shooting seemed imminent, they wanted to have the chance to finalise a few delicate matters with Jordan, away from telephones and other distractions.

'Daddy!' Phoebe leapt into his arms, much to the amuse-ment of Jordan's companions and to the horror of Bronte, because brown carrier bag, dress and matching cardigan parted company in three different directions.

'Whoa! Wait a minute, darling! What are you up to then?' He was as pleased, if a little surprised to see them, as Phoebe obviously was at finding her Daddy so unexpectedly.

However, seeing Bronte scurrying after Phoebe's trailing purchases, he put his daughter back on her feet and bent down to see if he could help.

'Didn't expect to find you two out this way today? Been shopping?' He was still crouched, looking as compelling as ever.

'Phoebe needed some new things, which I'm glad to say we've now managed to find.' She grabbed the cardigan and stuffed it back into the bag, looking round his legs at the same time to check on Phoebe, who was busy charming the co-producers with her cheeky smile.

'What! All these for her?' He laughed in surprise.

'Yup. Every last one.' She stood upright and risked a look at his face for a second.

He whistled silently and said: 'But I thought Chelsea was taking care of her today. Didn't she come shopping?'

Bronte worried that he might think she was neglecting her duties in the office and replied: 'She's had to go and meet some publisher and asked me if I could do the honours with the shopping. I got through a fair bit before we left and thought the rest could wait until I get back.'

She found it hard to tell exactly what he was thinking but he had certainly turned more serious. His face straightened and the smile had faded.

'I only suggested Charlene take the day off because I figured Chelsea would be around today. I'm sorry. I didn't mean you to have to do this, you know.'

'Jordan, it's OK, really. I don't mind.' She suddenly felt as if she had been telling tales and from the tone of his voice, she could sense he was displeased that his wife had relinquished her responsibility for whatever reason.

'Daddy, look what I got!' Phoebe felt she had won over the co-producers and wanted her Daddy's attention back.

'Not now, my little cherub,' as she began to pull the garments from the bags which Bronte was still holding. 'I've got to go and eat. Show me later? When I get home?'

'OK.' Luckily, she didn't make a fuss.

'You eaten yet?' He looked at Bronte again, who silently wished she had taken a little more care over her choice of clothes and at least attempted to tame her hair in Ken Done.

'No, we're about to. Actually, we were just looking for somewhere, when we met you.'

The fair-haired of the two co-producers, who had over-heard Bronte's reply, piped up: 'There's a great little place just up there.' He pointed towards a tiny alleyway. 'They serve truly amazing sandwiches and there's a wide choice of food for kids. I take mine there as a treat sometimes.'

Bronte, who seriously doubted whether any sandwich could ever be 'truly amazing', thanked him politely and gathered up Phoebe's hand. 'We'll see you later then, Jordan.'

'Sure. Have a good lunch. Goodbye sweetheart.' He gave his daughter a loving kiss on the cheek.

'Thanks. You too.' Bronte turned around.

They parted in opposite directions and, for one awful moment, Bronte thought Phoebe was about to dash back to her father, but in fact she merely stumbled on a loose bit of paving stone. However, as she steadied Phoebe, she glanced backwards to Jordan who walked half a pace behind the others, lost in thought.

Lunch had been a success and Bronte even had to admit that her prawn and crab sandwich had come up to all expectations.

She wasn't quite sure where the time had gone to, because it was nearly four when they eventually wandered back into the house, complete with the brown bags which looked a crumpled shadow of their former selves. Fortunately, the clothes inside were still intact, even though a couple would probably require washing prior to wearing.

'You been busy then?' greeted Beccy, as she spied the bags.

'This was only an hour in one shop!' replied Bronte, glad to be home because her feet were beginning to feel as if they'd been shoved through a mangle.

'I know what it's like once you get into Ken Done. Everything's so well laid out that it makes you want to buy.'

'This is madam here's collection.' Bronte laid a hand on Phoebe's head. Phoebe must have been feeling weary herself, because she had stopped chattering and stood angelically by Bronte's side. 'I'm going to go back when I have a moment.'

'Good idea. Now, how about tea?' . . . and to Phoebe: 'Would you like to come and see what we can find in the kitchen?' Beccy could see that Bronte needed relieving.

Phoebe nodded and put her hand into Beccy's outstretched one.

'Is Chelsea back?' asked Bronte, as she picked up the bags for the last time. 'I'd better go and show her what we bought.'

'She got back about half an hour ago, I guess.' Beccy consulted her watch. 'She was in the conservatory when I last looked.'

'Thanks. I'll be up in a moment.'

Bronte went down to the conservatory, only to find Chelsea lying neatly on the sofa, fast asleep. Her thin frame did its best to cover the cushions but the result was pitiful. As she rested peacefully, she appeared almost like a child herself, with her legs curled up in the foetal position and her arms tucked around her.

Her lunch must have exhausted her. However, pondered Bronte, it didn't take much to exhaust her. She ate so few nutrients that any energy she derived from her food was quickly expelled. It was best not to wake her, she could look through the purchases later, if she wanted to. Bronte turned to go back upstairs and join the others for tea. It would have to be a quick one because the study still beckoned and she really should put pen to paper and get something off to her father. She had been putting that off for far too long.

CHAPTER EIGHTEEN

It was much later that night before Bronte found herself with a little time on her hands to hibernate in her room and get down to personal letter writing. Shortly after she had arrived in Australia, she had sent off some hurried postcards, just to let her father, a few friends and of course Alex and the gang at the office know that she was alive and well and had at least survived the job as far as Sydney.

Since then, she had found so little time to repeat the exercise, that she had begun to think that when she did return to England, they would all have forgotten about her completely. It was time to set that right.

The atmosphere over dinner had been positively uncomfortable and Bronte couldn't help getting the feeling that something was brewing and, if it was, she didn't want to be around to find out what. Jordan had remained serious throughout the meal, hardly talking to his wife, or indeed, Bronte. Perhaps lunch had not gone that well after all? Chelsea had picked at her food, far worse than usual, saying she had eaten a big lunch and wasn't hungry for more. Bronte could see that Jordan, who was usually visibly patient and understanding with Chelsea over meals, was not far from boiling point and Bronte was determined not to witness that. As soon as she could, Bronte had made a fuss of clearing the table and excused herself with the explanation of the letter writing which waited for her downstairs.

It must have been around ten thirty when she heard the door of the master bedroom slam shut and the exchange that ensued come flooding across the corridor towards her room. It was not that she was eavesdropping. Far from it. She thought the whole neighbourhood would be alerted. There was nothing she could do except sit there and try to concentrate her mind on her letters and not on what was going on in Jordan and Chelsea's room.

'Darling, we've got to talk.' That was Jordan's voice.

'I'm too tired. Try me in the morning.' Chelsea hated confrontations and she could tell Jordan was in the mood for one.

'This can't wait, so you're just going to have to listen.' He was adamant.

'What are you getting so heated about all of a sudden?'

'Don't come the innocent. You know what I'm going to say, Chelsea, and you also know it's not the first time.'

'What are you going on about?' She remained calm, but refused to look in his direction.

'Chelsea, it's you. It's you and our daughter. Look at you, you're skin and bone. You're not even trying.' He sat down heavily on the bed.

'Don't bring all that up again. I don't need to hear it.' She picked up her brush and began taking down her hair.

'Well, I think you do. That child needs a father and a mother. Not some nanny or assistant as a substitute. Chelsea, I really wonder sometimes if she knows who her mother really is.'

'Of course she does. Don't be so ridiculous. You know I'm busy too. You've got your damned films and friends and fans and I have to have a life as well, you know.' She was also angry.

'I know that, so calm down and let's get this sorted once and for all.'

'No, I won't calm down. You're the one who started this. And while we're on the subject, why don't you stay home and take care of your precious daughter?'

That hit a sore point.

'Chelsea, she is our daughter, although you wouldn't have known sometimes by the lack of interest you show.' He punched a fist into the bedclothes.

'If you remember, you're the one who wanted children. I was happy with my life. You know I'm not particularly maternal but I do my best with her.' She softened a little, trying a different approach.

246

Jordan thought Chelsea might be heading for something he didn't want to hear and veered to another subject.

'Can't you make some more effort to get this anorexia thing under control?'

That time, it was Chelsea who felt a raw nerve being struck.

'Jordan, don't you dare mention that again! You know I don't have a problem with that now. I eat a perfectly normal diet and that has nothing whatsoever to do with Phoebe.'

'Whether or not you admit it, you're sick. You know what the doctors have said. You'll never be fully cured until you can accept your condition and consciously do something about it. Not just for a day, or a week but all the time.' He kept himself under control.

'I AM NOT SICK!' she screamed, before the floodgates opened.

Jordan realised he was not getting anywhere and that he had to back off if he was ever going to get the message home.

'Come here and listen to me. This is important.'

'I'm perfectly fine where I am, thank you, and I've had enough of listening to you.' She swiped at a tissue on the dressing table.

Jordan ignored her and carried on anyway: 'I deliberately gave Charlene the day off today because you told me you would be around, and I figured you might want to spend a little time with Phoeb. She loves you, Chelsea, can't you see that? She wants to spend time doing things with her Mom. But it's like you push her away.' Chelsea appeared to be listening. At least she had stopped shouting. 'Today would have been the perfect chance for you to take her some place or go with her to shop. She needs her Mommy.'

'I know I planned to be here. But something came up and I had to see a publisher. It couldn't be helped.' She sniffed.

'But it's your attitude. You don't get it, do you? You just don't seem to care. It doesn't worry you that you've let her down, or me down if it really comes to it.'

'Don't go on to me about 'caring' or 'letting you down'! How am I supposed to feel when you're out day after day and sometimes night after night, on 'business'?'

'You could come with me. You know I prefer to have you along than leave you behind. It's just that you always say you can't handle the crowds and media attention. Well, unfortunately that goes with the job. I can't back out now. It's a part of our lives and we're stuck with it.'

'That doesn't make it any easier, I can assure you. Anyway, Bronte was around to take Phoebe out today. She seems to like being with Bronte. So where's the harm in that?'

'The harm is in the fact that it should have been her mother I saw out shopping today with Phoebe and not my assistant!'

Chelsea looked surprised. 'You saw them? What were you doing?'

'Never mind that. What I saw was my daughter, not with her mother as I thought she would be, but with Bronte, because as I later gathered, her mother preferred to go to lunch with some unknown publisher rather than take her daughter shopping. Who is this publisher, who is more important than Phoebe, anyway?'

'Don't give me the jealous husband crap.' The tears were now dried in streaks down her cheeks and the venom had crept back into her voice. 'While we're on that subject, do you really think I haven't noticed who you prefer to spend your time with around this house these days?'

Bronte's hand froze around her pen and her heart skipped what felt like several beats.

'. . . and just what are you inferring by that?' Jordan was icy.

'You know exactly what I am inferring. She's young and attractive and don't think I haven't noticed the way you look at her sometimes. So don't come on to me about my meeting with a publisher.'

'Maybe I do enjoy Bronte's company . . . but I can assure you right here and now that I have never been unfaithful to you since we were married.'

He was bubbling over, but at the same time trying to use all the powers within him, not to say anything he might regret. It wasn't easy, she had touched on an area which was still very cloudy for him.

248

'At least Bronte is stable and we can carry on a normal conversation. There are times, since Phoebe was born, when I think that I don't really know you any more and I can't think what to say to you . . .' He finished softly and then looked away, pain clearly etched in his eyes.

That softening was the straw which broke the camel's back. Chelsea left her seat by the dressing table and crossed over to where he was sitting, tears once more cascading down her face. She knelt quickly down by the side of the bed and buried her woes in the covers. He sat silently staring at a tiny speck on the wall, with two lonely droplets bulging, one from each eye. He had no idea where they could go from there. He didn't know what was to become of their relationship or their marriage. He was weary from the effort of constantly keeping up appearances that everything was fine, when inside he was crying out. He knew he must make up and carry on somehow, for Phoebe's sake, if nothing else, but he wasn't even sure if that would work for very long. How many more times would they have scenes like that? They never really solved anything in the long term anyway. How much longer could he keep up the charade?

He reached out a hand and laid it on her trembling shoulder, at the same time looking down and travelling over the quivering frame of the woman he had married.

'What's happening to us? We're drifting apart, Chelsea. I know I'm wrapped up in the movie at the moment and I probably don't give you enough attention back home.' It wasn't the first time he'd had to back down and take the blame for something he really didn't believe was his fault. But for Phoebe, it was important. 'Come here. I'm sorry.' He pulled her gently over so that her head lay in his lap. She didn't resist. 'It's just so hard sometimes. We both lead lonely lives, you know. But we've got to face the fact we have a little girl who needs us both.'

Chelsea raised herself on to her elbows and rested her chin on the palms of her hands, looking up at him with bleary, sad eyes.

'I know,' she whispered.

'That's my girl.' He took her into his arms. 'We've got to promise here and now to try harder . . . and really mean it.'

He put his hands round her face and drew her towards him.

She nodded, as fresh tears fell over his fingers.

'You need to spend more time with her and I'll make sure I'm around more. Christmas is coming up. Let's make this one really special. Something to remember . . .'

Bronte didn't hear any more from the room after that and she was glad. It was only right that whatever transpired within those four walls from then on remained private to those concerned.

Christmas. That was one of the last words Bronte had heard. What would Christmas hold for her that year? Certainly no cosy stocking and breakfast in bed with Dominic. The previous year it had snowed for the first time in years! They had had a wonderful time, playing in the snow like children, rolling over and over, dodging missiles and then retaliating with full force before collapsing in front of the fire and Christmas dinner. Things would be very different and, particularly after what she had just heard, Bronte hoped she could escape to Avalon and spend time with her cousins. She would have to check first with Jordan. She prayed he would have no objection.

Bronte had a basin in her bedroom and did not need to set foot into the corridor to clean her teeth. Once in bed, she knew that sleep was bound to be difficult that night. Her mind was churning with a mixture of guilt and passion. She seriously wondered how on earth she was going to face Chelsea, or even Jordan for that matter, the next day and pretend everything was normal and that she had not overheard any of the argument which now seemed to echo inside her head. She knew that by any change of attitude towards them, she would instantly betray herself but it would be hard, particularly when her own feelings and emotions had become so fragile of late.

Had she needed to step outside her bedroom to clean her teeth, she would have found Jordan wandering in the conservatory, struggling under the weight of his troubles, unable to settle – having left his wife sleeping soundly at last.

CHAPTER NINETEEN

The atmosphere in the house continued to be strained over the next few days, despite the promises Jordan and Chelsea had made to try harder. Bronte was torn between feeling sorry for Jordan and then for Chelsea, and of course for Phoebe who was stuck in the middle of her parents' problems. In some ways, she was glad she had overheard the row that night because at least she knew how the land lay. Otherwise, she might have begun to wonder if they were displeased with her work. From what she had gathered from Jordan, it had all happened before and she hoped it was just a passing phase and that the two of them would be able to sort their lives out. It would then make her own way forward a little more obvious.

At times, she even considered whether she should offer her resignation. Perhaps that would help matters, at least for Chelsea. But she seriously doubted whether Jordan would accept it and being totally selfish about the whole issue, she was thoroughly enjoying all that she was learning and didn't want to give it up one bit. She did vow, however, to keep her feelings in check and to give Jordan no further idea of her inner turmoil. That had actually become a little easier of late because Jordan seemed to be consciously paying her less attention, presumably now wary of Chelsea's watchful eye. She didn't mind in the least. In fact, it was probably the best thing possible. On the other hand, he didn't ignore her, nor was he in any way rude – just more business-like than usual where she was concerned.

Bronte, whose own mind was far from clear on the subject of Jordan, felt she ought to contribute what she could to save his relationship with his wife and, at the same time, spread her own wings a little. She made a conscious decision to use what free time she could muster more constructively. She was, after all, only twenty five years old and although tragedy had forced her to grow up far beyond that at times, she could still go out and have some fun. It wasn't banned from the curriculum for the rest of her life. She had her own sadness to cope with and, although she had come on in leaps and bounds since she had left England and the day-to-day memories behind her, she was still desperately lonely at times. It was therefore important for her to meet new faces and regain her flagging self-confidence.

On that particular morning, Bronte once again found herself the unintentional witness to another heated exchange between her employers. She had been up especially early that Saturday morning because there were some letters to complete for Jordan and she did so want to squeeze in some time to herself in the afternoon, if she could. So, by making a head start, she thought she could set herself up for the day. While she was working in the study, she realised that Jordan and Chelsea were having breakfast together in the dining room. With both doors wide open, it was easy to hear what was being said. Once the conversation had got underway, Bronte felt trapped – unable to make an exit for fear of alerting them to her presence and possible suspicion that she had been deliberately listening. She had no choice but to sit there and take a deep breath.

It was not so much of an argument that time, not like the night the previous week. More the hopeless discussion of two people, who instead of trying to come together towards a mutual understanding, seemed to be pulling further and further apart. Phoebe had already been whisked down to the beach by Charlene, who on seeing the diagonals of sunlight bursting through the windows and dancing on the polished wooden floors, had decided to take her charge off for her daily swim and subsequent wallow in the 'sandpit'.

Bronte, who found her concentration seriously wandering from the correspondence in front of her, allowed herself to reflect that it was a good thing Phoebe was not able to hear her Mummy and Daddy, because even though she was too young to appreciate the implications, she was quick on atmospheres and would have inevitably picked up the gist of the conversation.

'Jordan, I have decided that I would like us to go back to New York or even Los Angeles for Christmas.' Chelsea dropped her bombshell.

There was a crackling of newspaper as Jordan put down what he was reading and addressed his wife's last remark: 'I thought we had agreed on an Australian one? Didn't we say we'd make a real effort for Phoebe this year?'

'Yes, of course we did and I didn't mean we should play it down any, just go home rather than staying here.'

'Darling, you know things are hotting up on the movie now and there won't be time to go back.'

'And you know I don't much like it here. Couldn't we just go back for a few days?' She was almost pleading.

'We went back just recently and besides, why are you so against being here?' His heart was sinking as if weighed down by lead.

'Several reasons. My work for one thing. I've gone about as far as I'm going to be able to from here and I want to get back so I can develop some new ideas I've been having.' The excuses came tumbling forth. 'For another thing, I miss our friends. My girlfriends if you like. I need to see people I know, not be trapped here like some caged animal, putting on the show every so often for your film associates.'

He chose to ignore the dig and not rise to her: 'Is that how you see your life here? Trapped? Chelsea, we've gone through all this. I want a marriage with a wife by my side. Not just for the press and the cameras but for me, for my own sake. That's why I suggested we all came to Australia, you and Phoebe too so we could be together as a family. Have a kind of holiday if you like . . .'

She interrupted him: 'But this isn't a holiday, Jordan! Seeing you in between meetings, if we're lucky. If you're going to be so preoccupied, I am damn well going to be too! Left to you, how much longer are we supposed to stay here, anyway? It's been weeks already.'

'We're so nearly there on the final details. The script's done and it looks as though shooting will start right after

253

Christmas.' He had another thought. 'Why don't we see Christmas through here as planned and then do a compromise? You go back for a bit if it makes you happier, although I'll probably have to stay because once we're rolling, it'll be impossible to commute from the States.'

'I'd really rather go back before. Phoebe could stay or come back. Can't you work it out?' It was as if all he had just said had floated out on the shafts of sun, still flooding the room.

'You're not listening to me! I'm just not getting through, am I? The whole point is to provide some sort of family Christmas for our daughter. God knows, we need something to spice up this family. If you go gallivanting back to the States, with or without Phoebe, what kind of family Christmas is that going to give her?'

'That's my point. You come too.'

'We're going round in circles here. I know you're homesick, you've told me often enough. But could you not just make the effort this time and save the trip back until after Christmas? Hell, if you throw yourself into getting things fixed up, you know, a tree, lights, cake and such, you might even find it's not so bad here after all. We've never been here at this time of year before.'

'. . . and never for so long, either,' she muttered. But she did soften a little. Perhaps she knew she wasn't getting far and after all, Christmas was only a couple of weeks away. 'OK, OK.' She stood up. 'We'll stay for now, but I really can't stand it for too much longer.' Her statement was ambiguous.

He lightened up. 'Come on, let's go to town. We've got presents and decorations to get. Let's put some life into this house!'

He sounded far happier than he felt. Inside, he just couldn't see where it was all going to end.

CHAPTER TWENTY

Christmas week had crept up on them all, even before they knew it. The general atmosphere in Sydney was one of celebration and merriment. The shops were laden with festive goodies, ranging from tinsel decorations to chocolate Santa Claus and tempting present ideas, all decked in the most colourful Christmas wrapping paper and ribbon. The malls were full of people dashing about doing their last-minute shopping, or simply wandering aimlessly in search of inspiration. Carols rang out from most establishments and choruses of Oh Come All Ye Faithful and We Wish You A Merry Christmas filled the streets with harmonious seasonal good will.

Amongst the working population, office parties were in full swing! Most days, from lunch time onwards the chink of glasses and the sound of laughter could be heard as bosses whooped it up with secretaries and directors risked cheeky suggestions to receptionists. As the days turned towards evenings, lines of city suits weaved their way unsteadily towards the public transport system or even onto the next drinking venue, all determined to enjoy life to the full. The next day, the dark glasses and stomach settlers took a hammering, as they returned to face the embarrassment of their behaviour the night before.

The restaurants were overcrowded and often overbooked. Despite the recession, the Sydney revellers were ready to party and if that meant all night, then so be it. It was Christmas time after all.

The shopping trip the previous week had been abruptly cut short as Chelsea had developed a migraine in the middle of David Jones department store and had spent the next half hour in the ladies with her head down the loo while Jordan hovered outside, not sure whether to go in and help her and risk being seen in a ladies' lavatory, or remain outside and wait for her to come out. He had opted for the latter.

The result of that was a sharp downward trend in the quantity of packages they brought home with them and meant that a further expedition or expeditions would have to take place in order to furnish the house with the required Christmas decorations.

Jordan had fully intended to do much of it himself and to involve his wife and daughter as far as possible, but right at the beginning of the week the movie schedule suffered a setback when the leading actress went down with chickenpox – of all things! That sent Art, Jordan, the co producers and various other people into hurried meetings behind closed doors to try and reorganise the film crew around the now unavoidable delay. Jordan was left with no choice but to delegate some of what he had mapped out for himself to Bronte, who was also rushed off her own feet by the increased workload resulting from the unfortunate timing of the chickenpox.

Jordan marched purposefully into the study where Bronte had just put the 'phone down to his press agent in New York.

'I need a favour. Hold on, let me start again ...' He looked up to the ceiling before his eyes shot back down to meet hers. 'I need yet *another* favour ... better?'

'Depends on the favour. Go on.' Even though she was tired, she couldn't deny that his very presence in a room could fill her with energy and life.

'I know you are going to need this like a hole in the head right now, what with the movie getting screwed up and all, but any chance of you fixing up a real 'English' style Christmas around here?'

There he went with his fixing up again.

'What exactly did you have in mind?' She really wanted to be up at Avalon for Christmas and not there, but she still hadn't plucked up the courage to ask him.

'You know, a tree with coloured balls and candy and such? Streamers and lines of cards. Fake snow, if you can get it that is. Oh, and a cake. We must have a Christmas cake.'

She was touched by his sentimentality and laughed: 'Is that not an American Christmas too?'

'In some ways. But we take Thanksgiving more seriously and then Christmas just kind of tends to follow on. It'd be great for Phoeb. You could get her to help you, if you could stand it.'

How could she possibly refuse him?

'I'll have a go. I hope I can live up to your expectations of an English Christmas. We've never been ones to go overboard on the celebrations. I may have to call home for some inspiration.'

She leant back in her chair.

'Call who you like. Sounds good to me. Anyhow, you really don't mind me dumping this on you?' He was more serious.

'No, of course I don't. Actually, it could be quite fun. I've never had to prepare for Christmas with a child around. Somehow, it gives the whole thing more meaning. You want me to start right away?'

'ASAP. We're getting close now.'

Although it was unlikely that Phoebe would have been able to remember her previous three Christmases, and who knows where and under what circumstances they had been spent, she was fully aware that something exciting was brewing and she was intent on not missing a single thing. So much so, that everyone who left the house was questioned as to where they were going and for what. On returning, it was a challenge to slip back into the house undetected, to hide whatever had been bought that day. Even Chelsea was a little more cheery, or perhaps she was pulling out the stops and at last making the effort that Jordan so desperately wanted her to.

It was as Bronte was preparing to go to the local shops the next morning that she was subjected to one such cross-examination by little Phoebe. There was no escape!

'Bwonte. Are you going to the shop?' Phoebe pattered down the corridor, trailing her koala bear by the leg.

'Which shop, my love?'

'The Chwistmas shop? With all the toys.' She had toys on the brain, perhaps because she had been given so many in her life to compensate for other things lacking.

Bronte couldn't hide her smile. To Phoebe, all the shops were the 'Christmas shop' because every one she had seen was prettier and more elaborate than the last. So much so that eventually they must have all seemed as if they were rolled into one to such a small child.

'I'm going to the local shops to find a Christmas tree that we can decorate. Want to come?' She felt obliged and after all, she didn't intend to be very long.

'Yippeee! I want a big, big tree!' Phoebe was ecstatic.

'Let's go and see what we can find, shall we?'

Charlene had recommended an excellent florist just up the hill in Mosman, which she knew sold evergreens around that time of year. Of course, it wouldn't be quite the same as the traditional pine, but at least it would be green and leafy and once the baubles and tinsel were in place, it would create the right effect.

Phoebe could hardly contain herself as they drove the short distance to the shop.

'Can I help you put the pretty things on the tree, Bwonte?'

'Sure you can, sweetheart. Perhaps Mummy and Daddy will help us too. If we can find an angel to go on the top, we'll need Daddy to stretch up for us, won't we?'

Damn, the car in front of her had just taken the very parking space she had earmarked for herself.

'I don't think Mommy likes Chwistmas very much.'

Bronte gulped. 'She does, she's just been working very hard and you know she was poorly last week.'

Phoebe was more sensitive than she realised.

'But she doesn't like it in the way you and Daddy like it.'

There were no flies on her.

'What do you mean, Phoebe?' Quick! Another space.

'Daddy talks to me every night about Mr Chwistmas and tells me that he will come and see me if I'm a good girl. And you talk about baby Jesus and the sheep . . .' Bronte had tried to explain the Nativity in the form of a bedtime story . . . 'but Mommy doesn't say anything . . .'

'Mummy's probably got some big surprises for you that she's saving. You just wait and see . . .' Bronte thought that highly unlikely and she could have cried for Phoebe at that moment. But at least she didn't look as sad as she had a moment before.

'Don't touch that, Phoebe!'

They were in the florist's shop, surrounded by magnificent floral displays, both fresh as well as dried, which had been ordered specially to decorate homes for Christmas. Bronte feared that Phoebe was coming close to re-arranging a number of them and stepped forward just in time.

She had selected a good-sized evergreen with full skirts tailoring up to a neat crest which would make the perfect perch for an angel, if she could find one. The shop also sold a varied selection of tree decorations, much to Bronte's relief, as that would mean she need trail no further to get what was required.

'Come here. Let's choose some of these.' Phoebe was at the dried flowers again.

'What are those, Bwonte? Look ... a dolly ...!' It worked.

'These are what we will hang on to the branches of the tree. Look, each one has a little red loop.'

There was a delightful selection of replica Victoriana, presumably made from papier-mâché or a very light wood. There were large round baubles painted with a variety of Christmas scenes and finished in a shiny clear varnish. There were wooden dolls on sledges, on ice skates and some bearing gifts. There were Santas and snowmen, none of which seemed appropriate for the scorching beachy Christmas that was promised for Sydney. But, nonetheless, they made very attractive decorations.

'I want this one. And this one. And some of this.' Phoebe was in seventh Heaven!

'One at a time. You can have all those if you like, but give them to the lady so we can pay for them.' Bronte could see that the shop assistant was hovering anxiously nearby, as Phoebe grabbed happily, dropping some on the floor as she did so.

'Not so fast. Which colour tinsel do you want?'

'Excuse me,' Bronte turned to the assistant, 'but do you have any angels we could use for the top of the tree?'

'Certainly, madam. This way please.'

A choice of five different ones was duly produced and naturally, Phoebe chose the biggest.

'I hope that won't make the tree bend over.' Bronte giggled.

'Daddy can do it,' and to the assistant, 'my Daddy can do anything.'

'I'm sure he can.' She remained stony-faced. 'Now, will there be anything else?'

Miserable old bag, thought Bronte to herself. 'Just a few chocolate ones now and then I think that'll be all, or the tree'll never stand up under the weight.'

It was lucky that they had managed to park nearby, because it took two journeys to ferry the tree and all the decorations as it was.

When they got home, all hell seemed to have broken loose on the 'phone and Bronte scarcely had time to unpack the car before she had to rush inside to take charge of the situation. It turned out not to be anything too disastrous, but her time was taken care of for the rest of the day. She had no choice but to offload a disappointed Phoebe onto Charlene, with the promise that they would decorate the tree later that evening, when Daddy would be back to lend a hand.

Jordan wandered into the study around six thirty, looking at a letter that had arrived that day and said casually: 'We've got that big cocktail reception tonight. You coming?'

Blast! She had forgotten all about it. It was being organised by one of the public relations companies who were contributing their services to the movie and all representatives from the press would be present, anxious for details to brief their waiting public. However, not only did she have nothing suitable to wear, but she didn't really have time to shower and wash her hair.

'Jordan, I've promised Phoebe I'll do the tree with her tonight. I haven't had time today.'

'You don't have to, you know. That can wait.' His heart was disappointed, but his head was relieved at her decision, because Chelsea would be there with him, and it would only create potential friction between them if Bronte went along too.

Bronte thought that at just about the same time he did and was even more sure she wouldn't go.

'No, thanks. Besides, it won't feel like Christmas around here until we get the tree up. By the way, I think I've roped you into helping a bit on that one.'

'Great! Let's make a start, but I'll need to go and change after seven. The car's booked for seven thirty, right?'

Fortunately, she had booked that last week.

'Right.'

There followed at least half an hour of hilarity! She had never dreamed that decorating a Christmas tree could be quite so much fun, but then she had never dreamed of doing it with Jordan Innes.

Very quickly they were knee deep in baubles, tinsel, coloured paper, ribbon, tree foliage – where they'd had to lop a few branches off to fit it in the corner of the hall, and general debris from packets of this and that, which had been collected over the previous week. Jordan had insisted they all wear silly paper hats with tiny threads of white elastic under their chins to keep them on and he tied garlands of tinsel around his neck. He had also acquired – he said from a joke shop in town – a false nose, moustache and glasses set, which he proceeded to wear as well!

'Daddy, you do look funny!' Phoebe chuckled with delight. 'Mommy, come and see what Daddy's doing,' she called downstairs to where her mother was going through her beauty routine, ready to face the party. It helped give her confidence.

'In a minute, darling. You carry on and I'll be up to see what you've done.' The clock was ticking away. The car would be there soon.

'Concentrate, Phoebe. That's fallen clean off!' Bronte pointed to a little wooden doll which Phoebe had tried to attach to the end of a branch so fast that she had missed it altogether.

'Help! What was that?' Bronte put her hand up as a loud noise went off in her ear and something buried into her hair.

Phoebe danced round them in circles as Jordan blew on the whistle again, which sent a colourful tail of paper shooting out, before it recoiled, ready to do battle again.

'Have some of this!' Bronte picked up a can of pink spray string and aimed it straight at Jordan.

What a sight! Pink, soft goo covered his face, his hair, his shoulders and dripped off his ears, the false nose and the end of his glasses, until he was barely recognisable! They all fell about laughing as he tried to peel off the face set so he could at least see out. Stumbling over to the mirror beside the front door, he took one look and said: 'Jeez! What if I turned up like this tonight?' He stood to attention: 'LADIES AND GENTLEMEN ... MR JORDAN INNES, AS YOU'VE NEVER SEEN HIM BEFORE ...'

Bronte was doubled up on the floor with tears pouring down her face: 'You can't!'

'I jolly well could! But actually, I don't think I will. I don't want to get fired as actor and director of this movie. Not yet at least.'

Phoebe had got hold of the can and begun firing it all around the hall. Jordan made a dive for her.

'Oh no you don't!' He tickled her at the same time, so that she squirmed about in his arms. 'Only on the tree, if you don't mind. Bronte was a very naughty girl for spraying that at Daddy.' He winked over his shoulder at Bronte, who was trying to regain her self-control.

'I think Daddy asked for it, don't you?' she said to Phoebe.

'Asking for it or not, Daddy's going to have to run if he's going to be in any shape at all to go to this party.' Jordan had just seen the time. 'Here, new game for you, sunshine. It's called clearing up.' He put his daughter back on the floor.

He had only been gone a few moments when Bronte heard the clacking of heels on the stairs and Chelsea appeared in all her finery. Bronte had to admit that she looked stunning and every bit the film star's wife.

'Mommeeee ...' Phoebe was ready to receive her next playmate and she made as if to run into her mother's arms.

'Now listen here, young lady, I don't want that stuff all over my dress, thank you.' She was referring to the pink string which Phoebe was busy collecting up in handfuls, so that her mother wasn't left out of the fun.

'But Daddy's got it all over his face!' She stared with huge rounded eyes.

'So I have just seen. But Daddy's gone to change. I'm already done and there's no time for me to wash up again. Besides, I thought I would come up and find the tree looking all pretty. Instead, there's mess everywhere and it looks as if someone's had a fight.'

That wasn't far from the truth, but not the sort of fight she meant.

'Sorry, Chelsea. That's partly my fault.' Bronte felt she ought to apologise. 'Come on, Phoebe, let's get this cleared up and the rest of the bits on the tree before bedtime.'

'But I don't want to go to bed . . .' wailed Phoebe.

'Darling, you finish the tree and then do what Bronte says. It's much too late for you already.' Chelsea stood back to avoid spoiling her cream sequinned dress. She glanced in the mirror while Bronte bent down to sort the remaining tree decorations from the rubbish. Chelsea liked the image which reflected back at her. The hairdresser had found a new and interesting style for her and the strapless dress flattered the outline of her collarbone, whilst emphasising her suntan. In her ears she wore the diamond drop earrings which Jordan had given her when Phoebe was born. She wore a pair of high-heeled strappy shoes to add a few inches and that extra height somehow made her feel better about herself. She was determined to get it right that night, but she wasn't sure if it was for her sake or for Jordan's.

The car was early and Jordan was, inevitably, late. The driver, however, didn't mind at all. He was being paid regardless of what time they got there and it wasn't every day that his clientele was as important or as famous.

When he did finally come charging up the stairs, Jordan was still fighting with his cufflinks and his bow tie hung loosely around his neck, waiting to be tied. That would have to wait until they were in the car. Hopefully, his hair would dry too before they got there.

'Darling, you look wonderful!' He glided across the polished floor and gave his wife an encouraging kiss on the cheek.

You don't look so bad yourself, thought Bronte as she glanced at his designer dinner suit. His starched dress shirt had a winged collar which she always found most attractive on a man.

'See you guys later then.' He opened the door for Chelsea and looked round at Bronte and Phoebe, who were standing by the tree which was gradually taking on a more respectable appearance.

'Sorry I couldn't stay and help you ...' and inside, he really meant it.

Bronte hadn't noticed that the time was nearly midnight, as she sat picking at the odd bobbles of fabric on the living room sofa. The television was playing to itself in the corner. She had seen the movie several times before anyway. Her mind was tormented for some reason and she had found it hard to focus on reality since having eventually finished the tree, put a wilting Phoebe to bed and grabbed some cold soup from the fridge.

Perhaps she was over-tired, or maybe it was just the first Christmas on her own – or perhaps even, it was the fact that she had been so busy since she left England that the natural course of grieving after a loss such as hers had been put somewhat on hold. Whatever the reason, that night she felt lonely. There was no other way of describing it. She felt downright miserable and had allowed a few tears of self-pity to roll down her cheeks. She craved Dominic's embrace and reassuring words, but try as she might, she found it hard even to conjure up his face.

There would be no special little present under the tree for her that year, wherever she ended up spending Christmas Day. Dominic had always taken tremendous care over her presents. He used to shroud himself in secrecy for days beforehand, dropping little hints here and there, which drove her nearly mad with curiosity, but there was never anything concrete enough to guess what he had actually bought. On the day, whether it be birthday or Christmas, he would usually pretend to have forgotten her main present and give her something tiny, just so she had 'something to open'. But there would always be an elaborately-wrapped present waiting in the wings somewhere, which he would proudly produce just as she was beginning to wonder whether, for the first time ever, he had actually forgotten!

There had always been streams of ribbons and brightly-coloured bows all over the outside that almost hid the wrapping paper altogether. He used to spend hours choosing her cards. Or so he told her. But they were always well worth the time he spent, because his choice would capture her heart every time. She would find some loving little message inscribed within, which said everything and more about the way he felt about her. She had kept every one – until he died.

She sat there hugging her legs to her chest and resting her chin on her knees, trying to picture the card Dominic had given her for her birthday that year, when Jordan strolled into the room to turn off the lights. He hadn't realised she was still up. Chelsea had already gone downstairs ahead of him.

'Hey, sorry. I didn't realise you were still around,' he called from the other side of the room.

'I didn't feel tired.' She made up an excuse, because inside she knew she was in fact exhausted.

'Good movie?' He stood before the television.

'What?' She was only half concentrating. 'Oh, that. Yes, I guess. But I've seen it at least three times before.'

'You all right over there? You sound a bit down.' He glanced towards the sofa.

She took a deep breath: 'I'm fine, really.' She didn't think it was the time or the place to burden him with her misery, particularly because she would surely be as right as rain in the morning.

But he sensed all was not well and knew that he would not sleep a wink until he had made sure she was all right. He flopped into an armchair and began to undo his bow tie . . .

'That's better. This thing's been strangling me all night.'

'How was the party?' She tried to show some enthusiasm.

'Usual sort of thing. Lots of people. Plenty of questions – some of which were about the movie. Actually, it felt more like a press conference. Thank goodness Art got us out of there and into a restaurant, so we didn't have to take too much of it. I think Chelsea had certainly had enough. She doesn't really like those parties.'

'Mmm.' She found it hard to respond.

'Look, you sure you're OK? You're awfully quiet.' He was concerned.

'Yup.' She put a hand through her hair and pulled it slowly out to the ends, which as usual, were tangled together.

'It isn't me, is it? I know I've loaded the pressure on lately. I've never really thought to ask you if you're happy here? I guess I've just assumed you would let me know if not. You're not about to run out on us are you?' He tried to make light of it.

But she was deadly serious: 'No, Jordan. Nothing like that.' A stray and unwelcome tear crept beyond its boundaries and she wiped it away quickly, hoping he hadn't noticed. But he had been studying her closely, and seeing her cry tore him to the very core. He went quickly to her side on the sofa. Very softly, he put out his hand and rested it under her chin, gently raising it off her knees towards him. She was powerless to resist. But her stubborn eyes were the last thing to face him. He knew from her tear-streaked face and watery red eyes that something was definitely amiss and he was going to find out what it was.

'Hey! Come on, you can't go around like this,' he whispered. 'You hurting in there?' He meant in her heart.

She nodded very slightly, unable to speak.

'Is it Dominic? Are you missing home?'

'Kind of . . .' was all she managed to say.

He let go of her chin but left his hand lingering on her leg. He turned to face the room and pushed his hair back off his face, holding it on top of his head for a moment, before releasing it to fall back into the perfect layers she found so appealing.

'Hell! What a fool I've been! I've been so goddamned wrapped up in myself, the movie and I suppose my own marriage, that I haven't given a moment's thought to you. After all, it was me that suggested you come out here to help get over it all. I'm so sorry, Bronte.' He looked back with feeling and sympathy flooding from his eyes.

'It's not your fault. Heaven knows, you've all been good enough to me.'

'There's no excuse. What's the phrase – life's supposed to be give and take? Well, I sure seem to have been doing a lot of taking where you're concerned.'

She smiled, feeling a little awkward and trying desperately to stem the flow of fresh tears which threatened:

'You've got your own problems. You don't need mine too.'
She wasn't going to mention Chelsea unless he did, which in fact he didn't. He was more worried about her at that moment.

'Do you want to go back or something? Will that make you less sad?'

She resisted the urge to throw her arms around him. He looked so like the little boy lost and she realised then that he probably needed her around as much as she needed him, even in the platonic way it had to be. They were a comfort to each other.

'Go back to what? There's nothing waiting for me there. I should be sitting here being grateful to you for giving me such an opportunity when I needed it most, not moping around in self-pity.'

'I would hardly call three months widowed, self-pity. I never really thought, but I guess you must be lonely?'

For some reason, that word choked her. It wasn't as if there weren't people around, but she knew she was lonely for the emotional security that Dominic had given her.

'A little ...' she sniffed, needing a hanky which he instantly produced from his trouser pocket and dabbed at her face, before giving it to her to attend to her nose. 'Thanks.'

He didn't say anything for a moment, instead kept on looking at her as if he was waiting for her to continue ...

'. . . a bit short on cuddles, I guess.' She laughed through her tears.

He squeezed her hand but again, said nothing. However, inside he couldn't help thinking how much her comment hit home to him and how he could have said the very same thing to her, had the circumstances been different.

'Can I let you have this back when it's been through the wash?' She lifted the hanky and he smiled.

'Sure. That's the least of the problems.'

'Jordan, can I ask you something else?'

He wasn't sure what she was going to say: 'Go on . . .'

'I've been invited to spend Christmas Day with my cousins at Avalon. Would you have any objections if I went?'

None that he could tell her there and then. She thought it would be better for them to spend the day apart.

'I think that's probably just what you need right now. A day with your family. That's how Christmas should be spent anyhow.'

She was grateful for his understanding, but she couldn't help detecting a note of sadness in his voice.

CHAPTER TWENTY ONE

Christmas Eve day was born amidst another glorious dawn. The leaves on the trees shone in the flickering light of a lazy sun, just about to get up and spread her wings. The flowers pricked up their ears and stretched out to receive the warmth of the sun's thermal blanket, safe in the knowledge that they would receive refreshment once the gardener came round to see to them. They were the lucky ones. Out in the bush the trees had been reduced to explosive tinder, just waiting to be ignited after one of the driest starts to the summer on record.

All suggestions of meetings or appointments had been shelved for at least three days. Indeed, a number of the American film crew had made the dash back to L.A. or New York, to snatch a couple of days with their families before the onslaught of the hectic shooting schedule that was planned for January.

In the Innes household, there was a buzz of activity as each person prepared for Christmas in their own way. The sound of sellotape could be heard now and then, together with the crinkling of paper. A couple of last-minute missions to the shops and deliberate attempts to sneak back into the house, followed by time spent behind closed doors, all added to the intrigue.

The house had been decorated during the week and Jordan was satisfied that they had created a traditional English Christmas atmosphere. The cake he had specifically requested stood proud on a silver platter in the dining room, displaying its wintry scene, complete with snowmen, ice skaters and other ingeniously crafted figures, all made from white icing. When she lifted her skirts, the tree revealed a bulge of presents, some of which had arrived from friends and relatives overseas. It had proved quite a task, preventing

Phoebe from just 'having a little peep, please' all week. However, the threat that Mr Christmas might not visit her if she did seemed to do the trick.

Bronte wanted to get a move on. She still had a couple of presents to wrap and the afternoon was already slipping away. She had promised Angela she would be at Avalon by early evening because apparently there was a drinks party to which they had all been invited. At last she tied the final bow and attached a label, before staggering up the stairs with her load.

Choosing presents had not been easy. She felt that it was not really her place to be too extravagant, but she wasn't sure to what lengths the others would go on her presents, if, indeed, they would buy her any at all. Hoping against hope she had made the right decision, she had opted for practical and cheerful, rather than expensive. After all, it was the thought that counted. There were so many gifts stacked around the tree that hers seemed to pale into insignificance, which probably wasn't such a bad thing.

Jordan had told her to drive the station wagon to Avalon in order to save either Chris or Angela the trouble of collecting her. He would be able to use the sports car for their purposes.

Finally, she was ready to go. She had her overnight bag and the presents for her family stowed safely in the boot of the car. As she stepped back inside to say goodbye and to wish everyone a happy Christmas, she couldn't help feeling a little strange that she was actually leaving them for a couple of days. It was the first break she had had in nearly two months. Still, it would do her good. Give her the chance to meet a few new faces.

'Where you going, Bwonte?' Phoebe asked her again.

Bronte bent her knees so her face was on a level with Phoebe's: 'I'm going to spend Christmas with my cousins. I'll be back the day after tomorrow and you won't even know I'm gone. You'll be so busy with all those lovely pressies over there.' She pointed to the tree.

But Phoebe, who never liked being left out of anything, replied: 'Can I come with you?'

'And what would Mummy and Daddy do without you tomorrow? Who would open all those presents then?'

Jordan, who had been doing a little wrapping of his own in the study, overheard the conversation and came out to prevent a scene.

'. . . and who would Mr Christmas come and visit if you weren't here?' She had forgotten temporarily about Mr Christmas.

'Maybe I should come after Mr Christmas has been . . .?' Her loyalties were divided.

'Perhaps . . .' Bronte let the subject drop. 'Chelsea around? I was going to say happy Christmas,' she added.

'She's downstairs.'

He didn't say any more and Bronte thought it best to leave her undisturbed.

'Tell her that from me, will you? Have a really great day tomorrow and see you on Boxing Day.' She made as if to turn to the car, but like lightning, Jordan was by her side giving her a warm kiss on both cheeks and taking her very much by surprise.

'Enjoy yourself. You earned it. See you soon,' and then to dilute the confusion, 'won't we Phoeb?'

Bronte wasn't sure what to say and decided the safest thing was to go as soon as possible. As she waved through the car window at father and daughter standing on the steps, she found herself saying under her breath: 'I'll miss you.' She wouldn't have been able to admit truthfully what portion of that sentiment was aimed at Phoebe.

The traffic pouring out of town was predictably heavy, as people scuttled away to reach their Christmas destinations. Consequently the journey took far longer than usual and she eventually tore up Angela and Murray's drive much later than she had intended. But like most Australians she had met, time came second place to most other things and both Angela and Murray were about as laid-back as any.

Murray greeted her in the drive where he had a tool box out and was trying to mend a crack in one of his precious surfboards.

'Hi there! Great to see you again,' he enthused.

'Sorry I'm so awfully late. The traffic's murder on the highway,' she apologised.

'Bound to be, being Christmas Eve. But there's no problem, just take it easy.' He took off his traditional bushman's cork hat (until that moment, Bronte had thought those hats were only ever used in films) to wipe the perspiration from his face. Even though the sun had called it a day, the temperature was still uncomfortably high.

'Ange is in the house. Go up and have yourself a nice cold beer and a shower if you like. I just need to finish this and I'll be in.'

A nice cold beer was a good and often resorted to answer to the heat problems in Australia.

Angela was bustling in the kitchen and hadn't heard the car.

'Sorry, Bronte. I didn't hear you arrive. You look shattered!'

'Thanks. Hot, certainly,' she laughed.

'Come, let me show you where you're sleeping and you can freshen up.'

'OK. Can I leave these down here somewhere?' She was referring to her bag of presents.

'Wow! Sure you can, but you shouldn't have brought all those!'

Angela led the way to the sitting room which was bedecked with strings of cards. There was also a little tree on the window sill where a number of interesting-shaped packages were all waiting to be opened.

'That delicious boss of yours give you anything for Christmas?' Angela was dying to know.

'As a matter of fact he did thrust something into my hand this morning, but I'm sure it's just a seasonal token.'

She had become more and more guarded about showing her feelings for Jordan and worried constantly that someone might be able to read them in her face.

'I bet you'll treasure whatever it is. I know I would.' Angela was still totally starstruck by the idea of her cousin working for such a famous person.

Bronte, anxious to change the subject, said: 'Would you mind if I gave Dad a ring? I'll leave you some money of course, but I haven't spoken to him in two months and I really ought to make contact.'

'No, you must, I agree. Why don't you try now? The lines'll probably be better tonight than tomorrow.'

'I suppose so.' She checked her watch. 'It'll be early morning there now. Might be a good time to catch him.'

'Use the 'phone in the hall, while I go and get changed.' Angela turned to leave the room and then threw over her shoulder: 'Do you want a drink or something?'

'Not right now, thanks. I'll just have a quick shower, if that's OK. By the way, what's the dress for tonight?'

'Oh, strictly casual. From what I gather, there's going to be quite a few English marines there. There's a ship in at the moment and Richard's brother, who's currently attached to it, seems to have asked a load of mates.'

'Sounds lively. Are we in a rush?' It was already seven thirty.

'No-one rushes much around here. You've probably gathered. No, seriously, Ann said to come anytime. I think they're hoping everyone doesn't turn up at once because the flat's very small. Won't be long.' She bounded up the stairs. 'Help yourself to the 'phone. You know the code, right?'

'Yes, thanks.'

The phone at the other end rang and rang and Bronte was just about to hang up when Clare snatched at the receiver and somewhat out of breath, gasped a quick 'hello'.

'Clare? It's Bronte. Have I dragged you away from something?'

'Bronte! Actually, I was at the other end of the house.'

'Sorry about that. I was only ringing to wish you and Dad a happy Christmas.'

'We were just talking about you the other day and wondering if we'd hear. Your father couldn't find your number or he was going to call you. Are you well?'

'Yes, thanks. Having a great time here.'

'That's good. Weather nice?' Clare really couldn't hang around on the 'phone for long. There was so much to do that day.

'Wonderful. It's so hot! I don't think we've had any rain since I got here.'

'Would you like to talk to your father?' Where was the time going?

Bronte could sense Clare was in a rush: 'Is he there?'

'He's just about to walk the dog, but I'll get him if you like.'

'Thanks, Clare. Have a good Christmas.'

'You too. Goodbye.'

The line went quiet and, with it, any ideas Bronte might have had of homesickness withered to nothing. The fact that Clare was so busy and didn't seem particularly interested in Bronte's life came as little surprise. She had always been like that. Still, it was important to keep in touch. Her father and Clare were the only family she really had left and she might need them one day.

'Bronte? Bronte is that you?' Her father at least, sounded more pleased to hear from her.

'Dad! I gather you're just off out. I don't want to keep you. I only rang to tell you I'm still around and to say I hope you have a nice Christmas.'

'Are you working hard out there? I got your letter the other day. Sorry there hasn't been time to write . . .' She hadn't expected him to. After all, she could almost count on the fingers of one hand, how many letters she had received from her father in her entire life.

'Don't worry. I know how busy you are. Everything's fine here. They start filming next month.'

'Are you mixing with the rich and famous these days, then?'

'Not exactly.' She laughed at her father's interpretation of her job. He really didn't have any idea of what she was doing. 'It's pretty hard work.'

'Good for you, I suppose. Coming back this way at all?'

She thought she detected a hint of feeling. That he wanted perhaps to see her again? Or even that he was missing her, just a bit? She was touched. Maybe after all those years, there was a chance they could develop some sort of father/daughter relationship one day.

'Not just now, Dad. Things are getting busier by the day. But when I get the chance, I will be back. I don't know how long this'll last but I may well come home and get into something else one day.'

'Oh, well. We'll be here when you do . . .'

Bronte could hear her step-mother in the background, anxiously reminding her father of the time. They had their own lives and she had no right to resent Clare. She wasn't really part of those lives, nor had she been for a very long time.

'Won't delay you, Dad.'

'I'm glad you rang. I hope they're looking after you out there. It's funny, you seem so far away . . .' his voice drifted off.

Hadn't she always been? Ever since her mother had died.

'Bye, Dad. Be in touch soon.'

Never having been one for sentiments, her father simply wished her well and put down the receiver. Neither of them had mentioned Dominic. She, because she found it hard to uncork that which she was trying to store away inside, and he, because he had simply forgotten that it was her first Christmas alone. It wasn't that he had deliberately neglected to enquire where she was spending the holiday period, or with whom, and whether or not she was happy. It was just that it hadn't occurred to him to ask. She no longer held it against him, the fact that he had rather failed to fill the role normally expected of a father whose child has lost its mother at an early age. She had never known anything different and besides, she knew that in his own way, he did love his only child. It was just that he wasn't very good at showing it.

Bronte was determined to make the most of her night out. It had been longer than she cared to remember since she had been to a party, and at least no-one there would have the slightest idea that she was recently widowed, nor that she worked for Jordan Innes. If she primed Angela and Murray not to mention those two things to anyone, she would be able to spend the evening without the sympathetic looks and hushed whispers which she had been forced to endure since September. Chris and Mark were also going to be there, so that was four people she would know and seeing as how all the Australians she had met in Sydney had been so friendly and hospitable, she was sure to have a good time.

Murray took the wheel of the car. Apparently he and Angela took the driving in turns and neither would hear of

Bronte using the station wagon, despite her offering several times.

'No way! You're having the night off. Anyway, you haven't been to any Aussie parties yet have you? And Richard mixes a firewater punch!' Murray was insistent.

'Your Dad well?' Angela turned round to face her from the front seat.

'I caught him at a bad time, just as he was going out. Still, I've done my bit and it was good to hear him again.'

'I can hardly remember your Dad.' Angela and Chris hadn't really kept in touch, seeing as they were related down Bronte's mother's side and not her father's. 'I think I only met him once or twice.'

'He's fine in small doses.' Bronte smiled. She shuffled her bottom and crossed her legs to the side. Murray's car didn't allow for tall, long-legged people.

'Have you got enough room there? I can go forward a bit.' Angela was directly in front of her.

'Don't worry, I'm fine. It's one of the penalties of long legs.'

'Your penalties look great from where I'm sitting!' joked Murray.

'Oh . . . you . . .!' Angela pretended to swipe him over the head.

'Steady now, I'm driving and we're nearly there.' He winked at Bronte in the mirror.

They pulled up outside a house littered with balloons and paper streamers, right down the path and into the road. There was obviously a party on in full swing. In sharp contrast, high above them, the moon drifted peacefully in a twinkling sky, gently surveying the earth from its lofty tower, content to remain aloof and not be punctured and battered by the alien sound of music thundering far below. Bronte was probably the only one who noticed the stars, as she unfolded her legs and stepped out of the car, but then she had always been vulnerable to romance.

She wore a brilliant white shirt over her short black leather skirt. As usual, her appearance was striking and again, as usual, she was unaware of the attention it caused when she followed Murray and Angela into the party.

People spilled out of the flat and down the steps. There just wasn't room for everyone inside. The main living room was packed with steamy bodies and overflowing cleavages, which in turn, resulted in bulging trousers, particularly in the case of the lads from the Marines who had been without it for far longer than was good for them!

The space between the heads and the ceiling was a murky smog of cigarette smoke and it took a few moments of peering to focus the eyes into any sort of recognition. Chatter and laughter drowned every so often by the thud of music from the ancient stereo system, reverberated off the walls and the ceiling . . .

'What would you like to drink?' Murray turned and yelled down her ear. She immediately covered it in an attempt at recovery.

'Sorry, but it's terribly noisy in here.'

She nodded: 'Whatever's on offer's fine.'

'You want to try the punch?' He winked again.

How could she refuse, when he had recommended it so highly?

'Might as well.' She returned the grin.

'Wait there and I'll grab you some.' He disappeared in the direction of the kitchen.

Momentarily, she was left on her own, as Angela had been pulled into a group of old school chums, who were busy swapping gossip about a fellow member who had just decided to leave her husband. Fortunately, Chris who had spied her sister's arrival across a very crowded room, excused herself from the leering Marine who had feasted his eyes on her breasts for the last ten minutes, and came to Bronte's rescue.

'So you made it then? Everything going well back at the ranch?'

'As far as I know. At least the house is still standing!' returned Bronte with a laugh. 'Don't look so horrified, Beccy runs rings around us. You'd hardly know we're there most of the time. I say, there's a lot of people here. Do you know them all?'

'About half of them have come off the ship. Did Ange tell you about them?' Chris was having to shout by that point.

'What, the Marines you mean?' she asked, refusing a plate of garlic bread that had been roughly shoved between them.

'Yes.' She cupped her mouth as if to deliver a secret. 'You can tell them by the short hair cuts and wandering hand trouble. Watch your bum – mine's black and blue already!'

Just then, they were interrupted by a couple of stout lads, one of whom turned out to be Richard's brother, Johnny, who was responsible for spreading the word about the party to his mates on the ship.

'And who is this amazing-looking creature you've been hiding then, Chris?'

Chris had known Ann from school days and since Ann had married Richard a couple of years earlier, she and Richard had become close friends of Chris and Mark. Chris had met Johnny a few times when he had been staying with his brother on leave.

'This is my English cousin, Bronte. You leave her alone! She hasn't been over here very long.' Chris looked into his stubbly face.

To Bronte's horror, he proceeded to go down on to his knees in the midst of the throng of people. 'I knew we'd get along! We've already got our nationalities in common. Let me kiss your hand.' He offered her no choice, as he took her long slim fingers in his chubby warm ones, and planted a smacker on her wrist.

'As long as that's all you kiss. Now, get up, Johnny. You're going to be trampled to death down there.' Chris hoped Bronte was up to it all.

'Ma chérie! You look so serious. Such a pretty face should not look serious.' He tried a different tack but Bronte stood her ground, not certain whether she was enjoying the attention or not.

'Take no notice. No manners, hasn't Johnny. I'm Sean. How do you do?' Johnny's mate spoke for the first time. 'Have you got a drink?'

'It's on its way, thanks.'

'What brings you all the way over from England then?'

'Work. I've got a job here in public relations.' It was only a white lie.

'You like it here, then?'

'I haven't had much time to get around. It's been very hectic since I arrived.'

'So, no boyfriends on the scene yet then?' His question came as a surprise, particularly when she noticed it was meant seriously.

Johnny, who had downed the best part of a can of beer while chatting up Chris in the last few moments, overheard that one and butted in: 'Hey! Hold on there. I spotted her first.'

They really were desperate, thought Bronte. They practically had their hands on their zippers and asked the questions afterwards. She found herself rising above them. She was not used to mixing with such unsophisticated types who betrayed their age and intentions with every word they spoke. In her mind, she shut out their banter for a moment or two and allowed herself the luxury of Jordan. The fine cheek bones, the perfect skin, those dreamy eyes, the worldliness, the maturity – everything that was missing from those she had just met. She found herself longing to be taken in those strong brown arms and to be kept safe for a while.

'Bronte . . .?' Murray was back with her drink.

'Sorry, I was miles away. Thanks, Murray.' She accepted the drink and took a gulp of the dark red liquid, which she could then feel seeping into every nook and cranny on its way to her stomach. All at once, she realised exactly why they called it firewater. A couple of those and she'd have been anybody's!

Chris, who had begun to sense that the lecherous Marines weren't such a good idea for Bronte at that moment, thought she ought to introduce her to some other people. Otherwise, she might have been put off Australian parties for life.

'Come over here and meet a couple of my girlfriends, Bronte.'

Bronte was definitely ready to move on and tried to walk in front of Johnny and Sean.

'Where are you taking the new love of my life then, Chris?' Johnny took another swig of lager and wiped the dribbles from his mouth with the back of his hand.

'To meet some civilised Australians!' She knew she could get away with a comment like that.

'Don't we qualify then?' he persisted.

'Not in that state, you don't. Perhaps five or six beers back, you might have done.'

'Can't we at least get her 'phone number . . .?' He was becoming a crashing bore.

'She lives with her boss.' Bronte replied in the third person. It wasn't a lie and he could interpret it how he liked.

'I knew she was too good to be true. Those types are never single for long,' predicted Johnny, as he and Sean turned to seek out other prospects, on whom they might be able to practise their manhood.

'Sorry about that,' apologised Chris.

'Don't be. I can take care of myself. I just hope they manage to score somewhere else. They seem extremely frustrated.'

'That, and drunk. But it's Christmas after all . . . goodwill to all men . . .'

'At least they're having a good time.' Bronte wasn't upset, she just felt alien to such uninhibited sexual flirtation.

'Come and meet Penny and Julie. You'll be safe with them.'

They had to squeeze past different groups of people, most of whom seemed to be yelling to each other in an effort to be heard above the din.

'Ah, Pen, meet my cousin.' Chris introduced her to two long blonde-haired, freckle-faced girls who looked remarkably like each other, and who had been carrying on an in-depth conversation, totally oblivious to the merriment around them.

'Crumbs, it's crowded in here!' panted Chris.

'We arrived early on and grabbed this corner,' said Julie.

'Very wise. We've just been accosted by Johnny and one of his mates. Boy, are they arseholed or what!'

'Johnny obviously hasn't met you before, Bronte,' answered Penny. 'Anything leggy and attractive and he's straight in there.'

'Must be because of all the time they spend cooped up on that ship,' remarked Julie. 'It's a wonder they don't turn on each other.'

'I think some of them probably do,' grinned Chris. 'But maybe not this lot. They seem too hot-blooded for that.'

'So, how long are you here for, Bronte?' Penny began

with one of the questions which seemed to come up time and time again whenever she met anyone new. The problem was, she had no straight answer and determined as she was to keep quiet about her job and about Jordan, it meant it was a difficult one to comment on.

She was saved by their hostess, Ann, who arrived on the scene with plates of nibbles which she was trying desperately to distribute.

'Here, you guys, have some of these. I'm really trying to get this lot to eat . . .' She nodded her head in the direction of two particularly inebriated Marines. 'Might sober them up a bit with any luck.'

'I think it's a lost cause,' replied Chris. 'Most of them seem to be beyond the point of no return.'

'Still, they're enjoying themselves. That's the main thing.' Ann was truly in the party mood. 'I want to try and get everyone dancing. Excuse me while I grab Rich, he can get the music going.'

Bronte secretly thought that if the music got going any more, there would be a serious danger of windows cracking or some of them going completely deaf.

Bronte wasn't in the least bit sorry when, about an hour later, Murray came to find them saying he was famished and wouldn't it be a good idea to go and tackle a pizza? Although she wasn't hungry and could have easily gone without, she was more than ready for a change of scene and enthused wildly about the idea.

It wasn't that she was a party pooper. In England, she had usually been the one who didn't want to go home and Dominic had even been known to leave her to roll back in the early hours by herself. It was just that she found it hard to crawl beyond the walls of her cosy, self-protective shell just at that moment and certainly was not ready to let anyone inside there. Anyone that was, except perhaps for Jordan. But that was an unrealistic dream.

To her relief, the pizza party turned out to be just family and the local pizza restaurant not only produced delicious food but the service was speedy, which meant that they were in and out by midnight.

In the street outside, they heard a church bell chime, indicating that it had turned twelve and therefore Christmas day had well and truly arrived! There ensued much hugging, kissing and well-wishing, before they left in two cars to go home.

'Glory! My ears are still pounding after that party.' Murray was once more in the driving seat.

'I hope you didn't think tonight was too awful?' Angela was worried that they had taken Bronte to the wrong sort of party.

'It wasn't awful at all. It was a real eye-opener for me. A couple of months ago, I wouldn't have been able to face something like that. But I'm really glad I went.'

And she *was* glad, not because she now knew that she was up to that sort of social activity again, but because it had shown her how much her recent experiences had made her grow up. She was no longer at home with the fast, wild life she had known before her marriage. Instead, she was ready to mix with people who had a more mature outlook, who didn't find it funny to lark around and get drunk at every opportunity. Jordan crept into her thoughts. But then he was never very far away from them anyway.

'You sure you don't want a drink of anything before you go to bed?' Angela had just put the kettle on in the kitchen.

'No, really I won't, thanks. I'm actually quite tired and that would probably keep me awake. By the way, thanks for tonight. It's very sweet of you and Murray to have me to stay.'

'Hey, don't mention it. Come up more often. We love having you around. Besides, we'll probably come over to England one of the days and we'll need a place to hang out then.'

'Make sure you look me up, if I'm there then.'

'Do you think you might go somewhere else after here?'

'Who knows? I'm fast becoming one of life's wandering spirits. Home isn't really anywhere right now.' Bronte wasn't looking for sympathy.

'Do you mind that?' Angela couldn't imagine what she'd do if Murray died, the way Dominic had.

'I'm getting used to it. It's a strange thing when your world gets turned upside down with you still on it, and with no notice at all. It would have been so easy to fall apart . . .'

'I'm sure I wouldn't be nearly as brave as you.' Angela admired her cousin's inner strength.

'It hasn't been a question of being brave. I've had moments when I've felt like jumping under the nearest bus. But the secret for me has been to recognise an opportunity and put all my eggs into one basket, even if it has appeared to some like a reckless gamble.' It wasn't easy to explain.

'You mean your job with Jordan Innes?'

'That's right. It's been a series of . . . 'if I hadn't's . . .' – like, if I hadn't gone to Cannes . . . if I hadn't gone to the Western TV dinner . . . if I hadn't gone for some fresh air . . . and so it goes on. On the other hand, I am also a fatalist and part of me is inclined to think that all of what has happened over the past few months, was mapped out for me and I'm just following the road signs . . . but who really knows?'

'Will you stay with Jordan Innes, once this film is finished?'

She hardly dare think about it. She was partly afraid of the answer and for the moment, preferred not to worry about it.

'I suppose it will depend on his next project. If he takes time off and he's based in the States, he might not need me.'

'Then what would you do?'

'Take it as it comes, I guess. See how I felt at the time.'

'I do admire your courage, Bronte. Anyway, you get some sleep because tomorrow's Christmas and it's going to be another lovely hot day!'

As she lay in her bed under the window, she reached up and opened the curtains just enough so that she could look up at the sky. A cool, refreshing breeze drifted in through the slatted panes and it seemed as if it were bearing messages, none that were decipherable, but messages all the same. Beyond the road and away across the beach, the surf pounded the shoreline, sucking the sand back and forth as the water rose and fell once more. Her emotions were again stirred by the romance of the stars, the gentle wind and the rolling waves and she found herself whispering 'Merry Christmas, Jordan'. Her words were carried away by the sound of the sea.

CHAPTER TWENTY TWO

Every family has its own special routine for Christmas Day, and as a rule, they tend to stick to the order in which they do things such as opening presents, eating meals and often, attending Church too. Bronte had no strong feelings either way about when things ought to be done and she was very happy to go along with Angela and Murray's schedule for the day, which seemed to be all but written down in the form of a timetable. That surprised her, because she felt it was most out of character for them.

Breakfast, which consisted of some of the most tantalizing fresh tropical fruits Bronte had ever eaten, followed by warm croissants and home-produced honey, which tasted of fresh flowers and sunshine, took place at nine on the dot. Once that was cleared away, Murray carefully carried each present from the living room and arranged them on a table in the garden so they could begin the grand unwrapping.

Chris and Mark were also invited to join them and, according to Murray, they had let the side down badly by arriving fifteen minutes after the agreed time of ten o'clock.

'Sorry we're late everyone,' Mark apologised, even before he stepped out of the car. 'That punch did me in last night. I couldn't wake up at all today.'

'Come and find a seat, you two, and let's get stuck in.' Murray wasn't to be restrained for much longer.

Bronte's pile was inevitably smaller than the others. But she didn't mind at all. She hadn't been expecting anything and was therefore a little surprised to find five or six parcels with her name on.

'One ... two ... three ... GO!' Murray couldn't wait another second!

Bronte deliberately left the present from Jordan and Chelsea to last. Part of her didn't want to open it at all. She had no idea what would be inside the silver striped paper, tied tightly with glittery ribbon. The card only said: To Bronte, Happy Holidays and best wishes, Jordan and Chelsea. It was Chelsea's handwriting.

She took several minutes to untie the ribbon and peel back the sellotape which bound the paper together. For some reason, she didn't want to tear anything. She didn't know which one of them had chosen her present or indeed wrapped it . . . that was, until she opened it up and then, she had a fairly good idea. Inside, there were sheets of white tissue paper loosely gathered around a folded leather jacket! She sat and stared, while the others around her concentrated on their own excitement. It was very soon after she had unfolded the tissue paper, that she noticed the bulge in one of the pockets. She put her hand inside and drew out a little white fluffy teddy bear, with a red ribbon round its neck and a 'B' in red felt, stuck to its chest. It was that which left her in little doubt as to who had done the choosing, and the wrapping . . .

'Gosh, Bronte, what have you got there?' Chris had spied the jacket.

'It's from Jordan and Chelsea.' She lifted the softest black leather jacket she had ever felt from the paper and held it aloft for all to see.

'That's amazing! You are lucky.' Angela was impressed.

'Turn it round so we can see the back,' said Chris.

By that time all five pairs of eyes were fixed on the jacket, which had a padded, rounded collar and batwing sleeves. It had undoubtedly cost a fortune and Bronte was highly embarrassed about the whole thing. She kept the teddy to herself, though. That was private.

'If you ever change your mind about your job, put my name forward, won't you?' Chris was green with envy.

'Must have cost a packet!' Mark was extremely careful with his money.

'Bit warm for this weather, but great for the winter.' Even Murray had stopped what he was doing to admire the present.

Bronte was keen to play it down as much as possible, at least until she had had the chance to digest the generosity herself. She was worried about the presents she had left behind, but it was too late to do anything about those.

'Drinks, everyone? Then we'll get the barbie lit. Mum and Dad'll be here soon.' Murray was firmly in charge of the day.

Once all the presents had been opened, examined, tried and tested where applicable, there was hardly a blade of yellowing grass to be seen for bits of paper strewn in all directions. While Murray went inside to fetch the champagne, the others did a rapid clear-up.

Not long after Murray's parents arrived, bringing with them his younger brother and girlfriend, the barbecue got underway. Bronte knew that Australians took their barbecues very seriously and so it came as no surprise to her that the traditional Christmas lunch, which she had only ever known around the dining room table in the depths of winter, here, was cooked on the grill outside, with everyone standing around in shorts and T-shirts. It was certainly a Christmas unlike any other she had experienced.

'G'day everyone and seasonal greetings!' Murray's brother, Joe, was an amusing fellow, with a ruddy complexion and an overweight body. 'You must be Bronte? We've heard a lot about you. Come and meet Sheila.'

Sheila turned out to be a human mouse! Tiny, timid and rather grey-skinned, but charming and very friendly with it.

'That sure smells good, Ange. What are you cooking?' Joe, who could always be counted on to eat for two, was ravenous.

'We've got turkey, steak and chops, Joe. We knew you were coming, mate.' Murray stood tending the meat, waving tongs and skewers around in an alarming fashion.

'Watch what you're doing with those, honey! You're going to whack someone in a minute.' Ange was nervous of Murray's enthusiasm.

'No danger there, love. Besides, it all adds to the flavour if you toss the meat around a bit.'

'You been to many barbecues here then, Bronte?' asked Joe.

'Not so far. I've been very busy since I arrived and there hasn't been much time to socialise yet.'

'You'd better put that one right. You can't come to Australia in the summer and not barbecue! It's a national institution!'

She instantly liked him, just as she had taken to Murray too. They were kind, honest, fun-loving people whom she could not imagine to be angry or unreasonable.

'How's the surf, Murray?' Like his brother, Joe was a keen sportsman.

'Got your swimmers with you? I thought we'd go down this afternoon.' Murray was never away from the beach for long.

'Never leave home without them, mate. Let's get this food down and give it a whirl.'

Murray's parents, who had been engaged in conversation with Chris and Mark since they arrived, were introduced to Bronte and it wasn't long before Bronte learnt that his father worked for the television distribution company in Surry Hills that Alex's company represented as sales agent in the Caribbean area!

Although he was not personally involved in the distribution side, he knew all about how it operated and of course, knew only too well the programmes that Bronte had been responsible for selling in that part of the world. It was like a blast from the past to sit down and discuss the business. Even though it was only the relatively recent past, it did feel like ages since she had worked for Alex. It made a refreshing change from dodging around her current work and trying to avoid any mention of Dominic or her reasons for throwing in the towel and jetting across the world.

Angela had taken a lot of time and trouble to create the right festive atmosphere for their lunch. She had hand-sewn a beautiful table cloth, in a fabric which was already printed with a Christmas theme. She had pinned tinsel to the edges of the table and arranged little bows at intervals down the sides. Crackers were piled high down the centre and red, green and white napkins stood tall and proud in each wine glass, like the points of a sail.

Goodness only knows where she had found the time, because she had not obviously been slaving in the kitchen, but Angela had also put together a number of decorative salads (partly because she knew that Bronte did not eat meat and partly because she enjoyed cooking for special occasions) incorporating unusual combinations of ingredients such as nuts, carrots, loganberries, dried fruits, bacon chips and palm hearts, as well as the more conventional items one would expect to find in salads. Jacket potatoes had been cooked through in the oven and then transferred to the barbecue to give them a smoky flavour.

'Who's ready, because this won't wait?' The chef was satisfied that his feast was fit for sampling.

'Girls?' Joe was anxious to get in there, but he did know his manners, especially when his parents were around.

Bronte took a plate and began helping herself to the salads.

'No meat for you?' Joe found the vegetarian way of thinking utterly peculiar.

'No, thanks. You have my share, Joe.' She found a way out. It wasn't the time or the place to explain why she didn't eat meat.

'Put like that, how can a man refuse?' he grinned.

'You hear that, mate?' he said to Murray.

'Joe, have you ever gone hungry when you've eaten with us?'

'Point taken. Haven't you girls finished here yet?'

They all tucked into the meal and the conversation lulled for a bit, as they savoured Angela and Murray's combined effort and toasted each other's health. By the end of the meal, the perfectly-laid table was littered with the innards of crackers and screwed-up balls of napkin. Each person had attempted to put on their paper hat, some with more success than others and some, like Joe, with no success at all. His hat had split right down the middle at the very thought of trying to fit round the circumference of that great big head!

The barbecue was still smouldering happily and Bronte could see thin trickles of wispy smoke, weaving up towards the spotless blue sky. The air around them was heavy and the cooling wind from the previous night felt more like a sirocco in the full heat of the day. As she took a moment to look around her, her gaze was drawn to the sky behind the house. Up there she could see what looked like thick, grey clouds, all merging together with an orange glow menacing round the edges. She decided to draw Mark's attention to it as he was seated beside her, and because it seemed odd to her that the rest of the sky should be so clear and yet there was a dark mass gathering ominously in the distance.

'Mark, why is the sky so changeable over there? Is there a storm brewing?' She pointed towards the clouds.

He followed the direction of her finger and jumped to his feet!

'Hey guys, look over there! It's a huge bush fire.'

The rest of the party wasted no time in having a look.

'Wow, yes!' Chris was just as concerned.

'That's a big one and no mistake.' Murray's father had seen a few bush fires in his time. They had lived out in the country when the boys were small.

'Where is it coming from?' asked Chris.

'At least, it's not Sydney way, that's something. But it's hard to tell exactly what's over there,' replied Murray.

'It looks like it's almost over the house.' Bronte was alarmed, having never seen anything like it in her life.

'One thing you can be certain of is that it's a lot further off than it looks,' Murray's father reassured her.

'It's all this hot weather we've been having. The bush out there's like a fire just waiting to be lit,' added Angela.

'I'm surprised there haven't been more of them, myself. With all these nutters around. They reckon most of the fires are started deliberately, you know.' Murray's father sat down again.

'But what on earth for?' Bronte was horrified.

'You tell me. For kicks, I guess,' he replied.

'But how do they stop something like that from spreading? If everywhere is as dry, how can they ever be sure it won't just carry on burning?' She had never felt the fear of fire until then.

'There's several ways they do it. One way is to soak the earth a distance in front of the fire and hope it burns itself out. Another thing they do is light controlled fires, again ahead of the main blaze, so that when the fire reaches the already-burnt ground, there's nothing left to feed it and it dies down. But they always lose acres and acres of bush before they can get one that size under control. The real worry comes when it heads towards homes or the edge of town. Then it can do much more serious damage.'

'It'll be on the news, that one, you can guarantee. Then we'll find out just where it is,' Murray informed them.

They could hear the sound of sirens in the distance, which was even more eerie because the immediate area around them was silent. All the time, the patch of orange cloud was spreading before their eyes.

'They call up all the fire services from miles around when it's one that big. Even then, that's sometimes not enough. We've had no rain for weeks, even months, you see. That's the real problem. Fires are always the result of a drought like this one.'

Bronte couldn't believe how calm Murray's father was. But then it was obviously nothing new to him and, in some ways, it was a comfort that he was so relaxed and matter of fact about it. She shuddered, nevertheless.

'Well there's nothing we can do from here, so I reckon it's time for the beach. Any takers?' Joe was not to be deterred by bush fires, or anything else.

'Good idea. We'll never cool down just sitting under these umbrellas. What we need is a surf.' Murray was just as keen.

He stood up and let down one of the two sun umbrellas which had offered them a little shade while they ate. 'Coming, pops?'

'No, son. You young ones go on ahead. It's more like siesta time for your mother and me. Specially after all that good food. The meal was a tribute to you both.'

'Come on, then. Let's get down there.' Murray already had a surfboard tucked under his muscular arm.

Bronte had a few minor reservations about going back to the beach, which previously had been the scene of such anxiety. She had still not mentioned the incident to Jordan or Chelsea, or indeed even Charlene. Phoebe herself seemed to have forgotten all about it.

She pushed her doubts to the back of her mind. After all, it was hot and she did fancy another go on the surfboard. Since Phoebe was not with her that day, there would be no responsibilities for her to fret about.

The seven of them set off for the beach, towels, sunhats and surfboards at the ready. The three boys went a cracking pace, leaving the girls behind to catch up.

'Look at them! They can't wait.' It amused Chris to see the three differently-shaped bottoms, striding out ahead, each 'modelling' a different coloured set of Bermudas.

Sheila, who had hardly said a word all day (but then Joe did enough talking for the both of them) piped up:

'It's the addiction to the surf board. I'm glad that we live in town. If we were this close to the beach, I think Joe would sleep in a tent on the sand.'

'Murray's not far from doing that sometimes,' agreed Angela.

'Have you had a go yet, Bronte?' That was two comments from Sheila in less than a minute!

'Murray gave me a lesson recently. It was really good fun.'

'She's a natural. But then you've got the right build, being tall and strong,' added Angela.

'Frightens me to death,' said Sheila, who looked as if the least gust of wind would knock her sideways, let alone the might of the surf.

'How about a swim in the pool first, girls? We can lever ourselves in gently,' suggested Angela.

'Good idea, sis. I think I would sink after all that food, if I tried to surf right now.' Chris was all for it.

When they reached the beach, the boys had already decided on a spot to discard their clothes and towels. They were each struggling with shoes and T-shirts in their hurry to launch themselves into the water.

'At least they're happy now,' commented Chris, as the girls arrived beside the strewn clothing.

As they wandered towards the sea-water rock pool at the far end, Bronte was surprised to find how many people were on the beach – far more than the previous day she had been there. She presumed some people brought their Christmas lunch down with them. Either that, or they cooked in the evening instead. There were sprawling groups of families spread all over the sand and the designated bathing area, which was a no-go for the surfers, was littered with bodies splashing and shouting.

The relentless sun bore down on them, seeking out the sensitive areas and threatening any skin which was unprotected by creams or clothing. The wind, which blew warm and sticky, did nothing to cool the sun's violent rays. It merely served to scatter particles of sand over sandwiches, crisps and chocolates and also deposit them into drinks or ice creams in a most infuriating fashion. Of course it helped to fan the bush fire too, which continued to blaze out of control, some several miles behind them. The people on the beach seemed either not to have heeded the fire, or to be unconcerned. Bronte found that a little unnerving.

The pool was every bit as crowded as the sea, but this did not deter them as they piled in at one end. Being a natural pool, simply walled off on two sides, there was no shallow end. People really went in there for a serious swimming effort and Bronte thought she ought to follow her cousin's example, which was an immediate length. She was a strong swimmer and enjoyed the sensation of powering her way through the water, stretching every muscle from the tips of her fingers to her toes. Every so often, a wave would break over the wall and send the water flooding across the pool to the far corner, before it retreated and slipped back beyond the boundaries. Bronte caught up with Angela, who had paused at the other end to grab onto the side and wipe the salt water from her eyes.

'I'm not surprised you come here every day. It's a great place to work out.'

'I prefer sea water to the chlorine and germs you find in most of the other public pools.'

'I'm amazed how packed the beach is. Is it always like this at Christmas?'

'Usually, if it's a fine day. Aussies love the beach and the surf, as you might have gathered. This is one day in the year when no-one works, so hence, they all head down here.'

'Would you ever give up living at the beach?' Bronte ducked under a wave which came charging at her, sending her body crashing against the wall. She had, however, braced herself for it and was none the worse for the experience.

'Oooh, you all right there? That was a strong one!' Angela managed to her regain her grip on the wall. 'What did you say? Oh yes, ... I wouldn't mind being nearer to town. The travelling gets a bit much sometimes, but we honestly couldn't afford to move. Murray prefers it out here. I don't think he'd agree to go unless I was really unhappy about being here.'

'I can't imagine anyone being unhappy here. It's heavenly!'

'It's not a bad life. Specially at weekends.'

'Seems more like a holiday resort than part of a city.'

'It's very different from where you are in Mosman. That's one of the things I love about Australia. The fact that everything's on your doorstep, even snow skiing in the winter's not far from here. You should consider staying, you know, if you're really not in a hurry to get back to England.'

'I may just do that. But it's a little early to say yet.'

'Let's swim back down the other end. I want to check Sheila's OK. She's such a funny little thing, I feel we need to keep an eye on her.'

'I know what you mean. Race you ...'

They pounded back at top speed, Bronte just pipping Angela to the post, but not by much. One by one they heaved themselves out of the water and dried off by the side of the pool.

'I needed that,' said Angela, rubbing her towel vigorously from side to side across her back. 'I'd have gone clean out in a chair at home otherwise.'

'Come on. Let's go and see if the others have managed to drown themselves yet.' Chris picked up her T-shirt and draped it round her shoulders to protect them from burning.

The boys were deep into the surfing lane and waved wildly when they managed to focus on who it was, standing at the shoreline. Each was determined to show off his very best skills for the trip into the beach and one at a time, they waited to select the tallest and strongest wave which would carry them all the way to the sand. Murray came in strong and stylishly. Mark arrived a little more carefully, but with equal expertise, while Joe thundered towards them like a bat out of hell and landed – splat! – face down in the sand! Their concern only lasted a second as he bounced back up with his usual cheery smile, seemingly unhurt. When his eyes clocked Bronte in her wet swimsuit, the first thing he did, much to her acute embarrassment, was let out a loud and meaningful wolf whistle.

'Where did you say she'd been for the last twenty years, Ange?' he asked cheekily.

'Sorry, Joe, she's not available right now,' Ange returned, aware that Sheila was standing just beside her.

'Well, darling,' Joe seemed to notice his girlfriend for the first time, 'looks like you're stuck with me after all.'

Sheila, who was very used to his teasing and luckily for him, wasn't the jealous type, replied: 'That's a shame. I thought I was about to get a reprieve!'

'No chance. You and me baby . . . we were made for each other . . .' Then Joe ran up to Sheila and sweeping her tiny frame up into his arms, he began to dance about in the water with her, much to the amusement of the others and the relief of Bronte, who for a moment, had feared that he was serious.

'Put me down, you great big oaf!' Sheila was laughing too.

'Any of you girls like to have a go out there?' Mark offered his surfboard.

'Bronte will. She was really good the other day,' volunteered Angela.

'I don't want to deprive anyone of their board,' protested Bronte. 'I'm just as happy swimming.'

'Nonsense! Here, take mine. I'm ready to nurse my bruises, not to mention empty the sand from my shorts,' insisted Mark.

'Mark! Please, there's ladies present.' Chris acted shocked as Mark began to tug at his shorts and remove some of the sand which had forced its way into places it shouldn't have.

'Ladies? Where?' grinned Joe, who had tired of whirling Sheila round like a spinning top.

'It's one of the hazards of the sport,' Mark carried on.

'Bet he won't get far on that,' hissed Joe, much too loud for comfort, as an enormous mound of flesh wobbled past them, dragging a surfboard towards the water's edge. From the back he had about five spare tyres round his middle, one piled on top of another, and from the front his bosoms drooped down as far as his waist and there was not a hair in sight on his flabby chest.

'Yuk! How can people let themselves get like that?' Chris was repulsed.

'Tell you what, I could do with one of those tyres for the jeep! I had a flat the other day. I think I'll go and ask him.' Joe pretended to run after the sickly, white body.

'Joe! Come back here at once.' Murray was the only one who was capable of calling him back, the others had dissolved into uncontrollable laughter! 'Can't take you anywhere, can we?'

'I'm bored of all this,' said Joe. 'Come with me, Bronte, and I'll show you what life's really like on the ocean wave.' He picked up Mark's board and carried it to the water for her.

'You've got no choice,' remarked Chris. 'Just yell at him if he gets out of hand.'

'I don't know if I'm looking forward to this . . .' Bronte looked nervous.

'You'll be fine. Knee him in the balls if he tries to get you to do something you don't want to!' The others turned round and stared in total amazement, to hear such a statement from a tiny person like Sheila! None of them could imagine her even reaching his balls with her knee, let alone having the inclination to do so. Still, you could never tell.

Before long, Murray and Bronte, with Joe closely at her heels, were up riding the waves and thoroughly enjoying every minute. The beach party wandered back to where the boys had originally left their towels and clothing, and sat down to watch the activity in the water.

A helicopter flew overhead, presumably just as a precautionary beach patrol, but it did seem to linger and circle over Avalon for some reason. Most people ignored it – nothing out of the ordinary, and certainly none of Bronte's party paid it any attention.

Chris had remembered to bring her camera and wanted to get some good snaps of her cousin's attempts at surfing, so she would be able to show her friends back home how she had spent her first Christmas in Australia.

'I must get a picture of all of us together, when they come out of the water. Don't let me forget, sis. Wow, that was a dive and a half! Do you think he's OK?' Chris clasped her hand to her mouth, as she watched Joe doing a circus act that seemed to have gone rather wrong. He was under the water for a long time.

'Bound to be. He's got so much fat on there that he wouldn't have even felt it.' Sheila wasn't worried and she didn't have any need to be, because once he did surface, he was soon back trying the same stunt again.

'He just doesn't give up, does he?' Angela couldn't help remarking.

'He knows when there's an audience. Particularly one as pretty as Bronte.' Nothing seemed to ruffle Sheila.

'I don't know how you put up with him, Sheila,' said Angela.

'He has his moments. Few, granted, but they're worth it.'

Just then, a deafening siren resounded all round them, which seemed to echo from one end of the beach to the other. Shark alarm . . .!!

They leapt to their feet, as did the majority of other people. A loud-speaker could be heard above the screams and sounds of panic: 'PLEASE GET OUT OF THE WATER! THIS IS AN EMERGENCY! PLEASE GET OUT OF THE WATER!'

'No wonder the helicopter was buzzing over here. Look . . .' Mark pointed to where the massive silver bird hovered over the water, not at all far from where Bronte, Murray and Joe were frantically paddling to the shore and safety.

The three girls and Mark dashed down to the sea, waving madly at the swimmers and shouting words of encouragement as they did their best to propel themselves quickly through the water.

Everywhere they looked, parents anxiously hauled children away from the sea, while others strained their eyes to alight on their friend or relative who was yet to be declared out of danger. No-one knew whether there was an actual attack in progress or whether it was merely a sighting. Or possibly even a false alarm. But it was too serious to ignore. There was mass confusion on the beach and no sign of anyone obviously taking charge of the situation, other than the life guards with their loud hailers, who still boomed their deadly warning.

Chris and Mark waded out to help the others in with their boards, as they puffed and panted towards the sand.

'What's all the fuss about?' asked Joe, once he had got his breath back. 'It's only a little old fish, after all.'

'Joe, will you get real?' Murray wasn't joking. 'Someone might be injured out there . . .'

'Or eaten alive . . .' Joe made a horrible face.

'There's hasn't been a shark attack round here for twenty or thirty years.' Angela was glad to have them out of the water.

'I bet there isn't one now, either.' Joe was more serious. 'They love to stir it up on Christmas day.'

'Either way, I'm glad they're not taking chances.' Bronte's teeth were chattering. She suddenly felt chilly and she, for one, had certainly been frightened out there.

'Don't worry. I wouldn't have let it get you.' Joe slotted his arm around her shoulders. 'It'd have had quite enough of a meal on me.'

She laughed: 'I'm glad it didn't have a meal on any of us, thank you.'

'Let's get you a towel, Bronte. You need to dry off,' volunteered Chris.

By that time the water had been cleared with the exception of a few stragglers who were less than knee deep. On the beach confusion still reigned. People stood on tiptoes, peering out to sea trying to find out if there really was a shark or not. The helicopter continued to duck and dive over a certain spot, not more than a couple of hundred metres out but it had neither lowered a stretcher nor fired anything down into the water and it was impossible to tell what was going on.

'This is the first time I've heard a shark alarm,' said Sheila.

The noise still shrilled out behind them.

'I don't know if they've ever had to use one on this beach. Certainly not that I know of,' commented Murray.

'Must've known there was a Pommie around and laid it on for your benefit, Bronte! Sort of like a tourist guide to the real Australia.' That was, of course, Joe.

'I'll note it down for the record, thanks.' Bronte couldn't

help liking him and his down-to-earth, if a little coarse, sense of humour.

A further fifteen minutes passed. The loud-speakers had gone quiet, but the siren still blared out across the beach. They were none the wiser as to the full extent of the drama and seeing that it was obvious they would not be allowed back into the sea for quite some time, Angela suggested they go back home for tea and try her home-made fruit cake, which she had baked specially.

'Sounds good to me. Not had much to eat lately,' Joe teased.

'Joe! You are disgusting. You've just had the most delicious Christmas lunch,' Sheila reminded him.

'Yes, but that was ages ago. This is now and I'm offering, politely, to do justice to my dear sister-in-law's cooking. What's wrong with that?'

'Nothing at all.' Angela didn't mind. 'Besides, there's no point hanging around here any more. We'll no doubt see on the local news what it's all about.'

Bronte presumed the rest of the beach had had the same idea because most people were packing their bags and making their way towards the car park.

'What a day! Bush fires and shark alarms! Welcome to Australia, Bronte. I can only say that this doesn't happen every Christmas,' exclaimed Murray, as Bronte looked up and saw that the fire was still raging away in the distance.

CHAPTER TWENTY THREE

'No, thanks, I really must get back. I know there'll be things waiting for me to do. The Americans barely take Christmas Day off,' replied Bronte.

'Well, if you're really sure you can't stay for the afternoon – more surfing? Without shark alarms this time . . .' Murray tried to persuade Bronte to spend the rest of Boxing Day with them.

'Funny that, there being no mention on the television of the shark alarm,' pondered Angela, as she stood to clear away the brunch things.

'Can't have been a real shark or anything very serious, or they're bound to have had it as the lead story. Particularly being Christmas Day.' Murray had almost forgotten about it.

'Let me give you a hand, Ange.' Bronte offered her services.

'If we each grab something and carry it in, that's about all we need do.'

Angela had again done them proud with her culinary skills, producing a fine cooked breakfast which included smoked fish, specially for Bronte. Bronte was a little envious of her cousin's capabilities in the kitchen. She, herself, had little interest in cooking and therefore much admired the creations that other people came up with.

'You need a hand with your bag there?' Murray called up the stairs.

'No, thanks, Murray. I've only been here for a couple of nights, although from the size of it you'd think I'd packed for at least a week.'

'I should imagine that gorgeous jacket of yours must take up some space. What are you going to say to them about it when you get back?' Angela was jolly envious.

'I'm not really sure. I imagine 'thank you' will come into it somewhere.' It was a subject Bronte had been mulling over, ever since she opened the present.

Even though, of course she was thrilled with the jacket and couldn't wait for cooler weather so she could have the chance to show it off, somehow the teddy had been her favourite present that year. Maybe it appealed to her childish instincts – she had always had a soft spot for her dolls and bears when she was little. They had become surrogate mothers, brothers, sisters and friends to her in lonelier moments. Or maybe it symbolised part of what she was feeling for Jordan, and the fact that she was sure he had put it in there, almost certainly without Chelsea's knowledge, made it all the more special. It would be difficult to mention to him though, unless an appropriate opportunity presented itself.

As she put her bag into the car, she glanced again at the sky to see if there was any change to the latest bush fire. Ominously it appeared to be coming from Sydney, exactly where she was heading.

Angela noticed the concern on her face and said: 'You'll be OK getting through there. It looks as though it's nearer the coast road, rather than the highway. If you just go back the way you came, I think it will stay to the left of you.'

'Don't you find the fires scary?' Bronte still couldn't get over the way everyone merely accepted them as a part of life out there.

'We've seen too many to get really frightened,' replied Murray. 'Of course, you always worry for the people whose homes are in the path of the blaze and today it does look like some will be casualties. It's been a while since we've had one so close to residential areas.'

'This wind doesn't help either,' commented Angela. 'It pushes the whole progress along and makes the firefighting job much harder.'

'I'll feel happier once I'm on the other side of it.' Bronte was apprehensive.

'Would you like one of us to come with you?' offered Murray, realising that, as she had not seen one before, the bush fire must have seemed a daunting prospect.

'I'll manage. I'll just keep my foot down all the way.' Bronte sounded braver than she felt.

'Watch the police! Don't get had up for speeding,' warned Angela.

'I should think most of them'll be tied up with traffic diversions from that fire,' predicted Murray.

'Well, many thanks for everything. I've had a really good time and feel ready to face work again.'

'We've enjoyed having you. Come up for New Year if you can. Otherwise we'll be in touch to arrange something else.' Angela liked having her cousin around.

'Goodness knows what's been planned for New Year. I may be on duty.' It seemed longer than a week away.

'Send my best to your boss – and keep your hands off him. I know I wouldn't!' joked Angela.

Bronte thought it best not to pursue that and just smiled as she started her engine and pulled out of the drive, waving through the window as she went.

As she left the coast road and headed for the highway, which took her unavoidably through bushland, she fiddled with the radio to try and get some reports on the fire ahead of her. At least Murray's father had been right about one thing. The fire was always further ahead than it looked. Sometimes she felt certain she would drive right into it round the next bend, but when the bend came, it was always still a good distance away.

There was little traffic on the road, either because the fire now cut off several of the through roads from Sydney to the Northern beaches or because on Boxing Day most people were carrying on their festivities at home.

It was eerie, driving along the quiet, dusty highway, with mirages looming ever ahead and the radio crackling with faulty reception. All around her, meanwhile, were brittle branches and dry, menacing earth.

She came to a main junction with traffic lights controlling the flow of cars. The fire really was nearer then and it had become hard to tell whether it was straight ahead or to the left. No longer was it merely an orange tinted greying mass, high above her. There she could see thick black smoke rising from the ground and every so often, wicked flames danced high, as another tree fell victim to the fire's insatiable appetite.

There were a couple of patrol cars parked at the junction, but the policemen seemed to be lounging around, half in and half out of their cars, more interested in listening to radios and walkie-talkies, than sending the traffic in any particular direction. Certainly, no-one indicated to Bronte that she shouldn't go straight over and so she presumed all was well along that road. Most of the other cars seemed to be travelling across her path rather than the same way, but that did not deter her as the lights changed to green and she shoved the station wagon into gear.

The sirocco whirled around outside, stirring up the dust and blowing it in gusts across the road ahead of her. She was becoming alarmed, because it really did seem as if she was now quite alone and the fire was rapidly becoming more and more of a reality in front of her eyes. The orange glow was no longer an occasional feature but a permanent one, and the temperature, which forced its way in through her open windows, was more than just seasonal humidity. It was becoming intense.

There was little doubt that the fire had started to flare wildly on both sides of her and the road she was heading down was sandwiched in the middle like an oasis – except that there was no water to be seen. She wasn't sure whether she should turn back, but then glancing in her mirror, she saw that the fire was teasing the tarmac she had just covered and she began to fear that that route might well be closed to her already. The only way appeared to be forward.

'Oh why on earth did those police allow cars to come this way?' she demanded out loud, angry as well as frightened. 'Or rather me . . .?' There was no-one else in sight.

She very quickly had no choice but to slam on the brakes and try to turn the car around, because right in front of her a gnarled black tree had fallen dead across her path, forming a bridge which allowed the fire to cross the road from one side to the other. There would be no passing through there now.

She cursed the size of the station wagon and the lack of power steering as she rammed it first into forward and then reverse gears. She had no choice. It had to be back, and pray that there was still a way through there. Just as she was about to make the final reverse turn, she noticed what looked like a large red outline, a few metres beyond the now crumbling tree.

'God! It's a car.' She panicked.

It didn't appear to be moving and there was no sign of life anywhere around. But something inside her drove her to open the door and get out to take a closer look. What if there were people trapped inside? How could she drive away someone's only possible chance of surviving that nightmare? She had to check for sure that she hadn't condemned anyone to a ghastly, slow death.

The air was thick with smoke and she began to cough as it penetrated her lungs and clogged her wind pipe. She knew from first aid lessons she had taken at school that she wouldn't get far unless she could at least breathe. Remembering her beach towel which mercifully was still wet from the day before, she snatched it out of her bag, sending the rest of her belongings flying around the boot in the process. She wrapped it around her head and face. There wasn't a moment to lose as the fire licked across the road.

As she managed to scramble round the fallen tree, her bare legs below her shorts were scratched to bits on spiky branches of charcoaled bush, but she fought on relentlessly especially once she realised that the vehicle ahead of her was a red sports car, just like the one Chris had hired for Jordan!

'Oh my God!' As she got nearer, she recognised the registration plate but the smoke was still too thick for her to be able to see clearly how many people were inside, if indeed anyone at all. She struggled on, stumbling in her haste to reach the car before it was all too late. It was only a matter of a few metres between the two cars, but it felt like hundreds, as she spluttered to clear the choking smoke from her throat and swiped at her legs to part tangled, sizzling undergrowth.

She pressed her face to the window and peered inside the car for a second. Immediately, she realised that Chelsea was slumped awkwardly over the steering wheel, obviously unconscious, and Phoebe, scarlet in the face, was strapped into her car seat in the back, whining pathetically as she was trapped and unable to move.

Bronte wrenched open the passenger door and virtually pulled the seat release right out of its socket in her attempt to drag Phoebe from the back.

'Hang in there, sweetheart. I'll have you out in a sec. Try and grab hold of my shoulders.' She was leaning right into the car at that stage.

It was impossible to tell whether Phoebe recognised her or not. If she did, she didn't say so. She merely whimpered and coughed, as tears streamed down her face from sore, red eyes.

There was a smell of scalding rubber, as the tyres on the car had more or less disintegrated in the baking heat of the fire.

Bronte prayed that there was not much petrol in the car as she straightened her back, tore the towel from her own head and plastered it around Phoebe's to try and give her more chance of survival. She had no choice. She would first have to carry Phoebe to the station wagon and then venture back to see what she could do about Chelsea. Supporting the child's head with one arm and hugging her to her chest with the other, she clawed her way back past the tree corpse, ignoring the trickles of blood which ran down her legs from the cuts she had sustained. If she ever got out of that mess alive, she would worry about those then.

Phoebe was a dead weight and barely conscious, as she laid her gently on the back seat of the car, closing the windows and doors tight shut to try and keep the air in there as clean as possible under the circumstances.

'Sorry, sweetheart, but I need that if I'm going to be able to get Mummy out.' She lunged at the towel and charged back in the direction of the sports car. She cursed her hair as it blinded her vision and had to use one hand to hold the towel to her face, while she held her hair back with the other. It must have unbalanced her because just as she was about to reach the driver's door, she tripped on a branch and fell headlong, banging her head on the side of the car.

Momentarily stunned, she hauled herself up to her knees and mustered every remaining ounce of energy, to wrestle with the door. For once, Bronte was grateful that Chelsea was so light and that she herself was tall and relatively strong. She half-dragged and half-carried Chelsea out of the car and laid her on the ashes for a second, while she felt for her pulse. It was faint but it was still there. Then she tried to help her with her breathing, clasping her nose together while she blew what breath she was able to down into Chelsea's mouth. There was nothing more she could do but get her back to the car and try to reach help, before all three of them perished.

As Bronte could feel the earth still sweltering through her leather-soled shoes and there were far too many crackling branches for her to be able to drag Chelsea, it left her no alternative but to heave her over her shoulder and stagger back. The towel dropped to the ground but she neither had the time nor the strength to retrieve it. With stamina she never knew had, she managed to get to the car and drop Chelsea quickly on to the passenger seat.

Bronte collapsed into the driver's side. Her legs, which no longer felt they were even part of her own body, gave way beneath her finally and she put a hand up to wipe the sweat from her face. It was only then that she noticed the back of her hand stained with reddish brown blood, mixed with black and grey ashes. She had forgotten about her head, but reaching up with her fingers, she felt the large swelling which had developed on her temple. She looked in the mirror for a second and saw an open wound on her head which had oozed down her cheek. That too, would have to wait.

'Don't you dare let me down now,' she warned the car, looking round first at Phoebe, who was still and quiet on the back seat, with only the teeniest rhythm in her chest to indicate her breathing, and then at Chelsea who was strapped into her seat to keep her upright.

The car started first time and she flung it round, back towards the junction, foot jammed on the accelerator. As it responded, they tore down the road with the flames still roaring fiercely on either side as if resentful of losing easy prey. She did her best to steer round the glowing debris which was scattered on the road. Nothing was going to stop her. The scorched earth and the frazzled bush, already victims themselves, seemed to look kindly on the mission of mercy and part to allow her to drive through on her journey of life and death.

Hazard lights flashing and horn blaring, she didn't even notice the colour of the traffic lights as she careered ahead, skidding to a halt beside the two police cars which were still parked in the same spot as previously. She didn't see that the traffic was now being prevented from using the road she had taken some half an hour before.

'Quick! For God's sake, we need an ambulance,' was about all she remembered gasping, before she passed clean out at the black-booted feet of the startled officer who had stepped out of his car to see what all the fuss was about.

Bronte found herself able to remember very little about the ambulance which was summoned to the scene and the subsequent journey to hospital. She just felt so tired as she allowed the officials, into whose care she had had no choice but to entrust herself, Chelsea and Phoebe to go about their business as was deemed appropriate.

She felt as if she were watching her own medical examination through a long tunnel but she couldn't be bothered to wait for the verdict, as she drifted peacefully off to sleep.

When she finally opened her eyes after what felt like days, but was only a few hours, she took a moment or two to focus on the floral-pleated drapes pulled round her cubicle in which the only furniture was the solid bed on which she lay and a small cupboard by her side. She could vaguely make out the shape of her handbag on top of the cupboard. For several moments she stayed still, inhaling the clinical smell of disinfectant and wondering what on earth she was doing there. She reasoned pretty quickly, that it was a hospital and once she had that one figured out, she hardly dare move in case something hurt. But she couldn't remember what would hurt. That was until a faint odour of smoke filtered up from her hair and then the morning's drama came back to haunt her like a bad dream.

'Oh, so you're back with us then? Goodo.' A cheerful Irish-sounding nurse popped her head through the curtain. 'We didn't want to wake you for a little while, unless it became necessary. How are you feeling?'

'I think I'm OK. Now you mention it, a bit of a headache . . .' Bronte gingerly lifted her arm, winced and dabbed at her temple. It was covered with a soft, lint bandage.

'You did take a nasty knock out there. Do you remember how it happened?' The nurse took Bronte's wrist and felt for her pulse, while checking the rate on her little breast watch.

'I know about the fire now. I think I fell and hit my head . . .'

Her memory was piecing together gradually.

'You're lucky it wasn't anything more serious. You've just got a sore head and a few scratches on your legs to worry about. We think you must have fainted with exhaustion. Nothing a few days rest at home won't sort out. We don't need to keep you here, you'll probably be glad to know.'

'Exhaustion? I've never fainted before.'

'I'm not surprised you were exhausted. Quite the little heroine by all accounts, rescuing that mother and child . . .'

Bronte sat up with a start, forgetting about her head and all other possible aches and pains she might have triggered.

'Chelsea . . . Phoebe . . . where are they? How are they? Can I see them?'

'Wait a minute! We'll need to keep you after all if you carry on like that.' The nurse put a reassuring hand on her shoulder to restrain her. 'They're both going to be fine, thanks to you. They inhaled a good deal of smoke and they're going to need a couple of days rest in here. So you know them, do you?'

'Yes, it's a long story. Is there a 'phone? I must call Jordan.'

'Jordan Innes, is that?' News of the celebrity admissions had already begun to circulate the hospital.

'Yes. That's his wife and daughter.' Bronte tried to swing her legs off the bed and in doing so, she felt as if her skin was being trapped and pinched. Her legs were cut in places where she had been caught by branches.

'Don't worry, he's already here. He's upstairs with them now.'

'He is? How did they know where to get hold of him?' Jordan was there, in the hospital!

'The police did it. Wasn't easy from what I hear. They had to trace the registration plate on your car and try to get in touch with the rental company, which on Boxing Day wasn't that straightforward. Anyway, they managed to track him down somehow and he arrived about half an hour ago.'

'Can I go and see him?' She needed his reassurance.

'They've got security crawling all over up there, what with him being who he is and all.' Nothing that exciting had happened in the casualty department since she had arrived from Dublin earlier that year. 'But seeing as you know them anyway, I'll have a word. Now, are you sure you're feeling up to getting out of bed?'

'I'm fine and you did say there's no need for me to stay.'

'Well, that's what the doctor said and we're busy here today, what with that fire still spreading out there. Hang on and I'll be back in a jiffy.'

By the time she came back, Bronte had managed to pull her shorts over her torn legs and had turned her T-shirt back to front to hide a couple of tears. There was no sign of her shoes – she presumed they had not made it on the trip to hospital – so she stood in her bare feet, ready to go with the nurse. While she waited, she pulled the long pronged comb from her bag and stabbed at her hair. Her head throbbed on one side and after a moment, she gave up. She felt a mess, but at least they had washed her when she came in and had removed the black sooty smudges from her arms and face.

'Ah Jesus, you're all ready then?' The Irish accent still sounded strange to Bronte. 'Come on, I'll take you up. Mind you get some rest, though. You need to take care of that bump of yours.' She was much enjoying the importance of escorting Bronte upstairs. Meeting Jordan Innes ... that would certainly be worth a letter home.

She took Bronte down a series of identical-looking corridors, each marked with grey and white signs indicating hospital departments or wards.

'I'm not going too fast, am I?' The nurse turned to Bronte over her shoulder. 'It's a habit I have. Walking quickly, I mean.'

'No. I feel a lot better now I'm up,' and she really did.

'We gave you something for the headache. Must be working. This way.'

Bronte could see from the signs that they were heading for a private wing of the hospital and it wasn't long before they went up a set of stairs and encountered a couple of hospital security men, loitering outside a pale cream door which was half glass and half solid. Over the glass on the inside, a blind had been drawn to prevent anyone from looking in.

'Here we are! It's OK fellas, she's the one who rescued them.' The nurse nodded towards Bronte and managed to halt the advancing guard.

She went forward to knock on the door of the room in which Chelsea lay motionless, wired up to a couple of machines on either side of her. Jordan sat on a hard wooden chair, his forehead resting on his hands.

At the sound of the door which opened just wide enough to allow Bronte to enter, he looked up and on seeing who it was, obvious relief flooded into his face. He sprang towards her. Still hovering, the nurse was torn between wanting to meet the famous star and knowing that she should really leave the family alone, particularly when she saw the embrace in which Jordan enveloped Bronte, tears welling in his eyes. She used her better judgement.

They stood there for a moment, each clinging to the other with feelings of consolation flowing between them. They had both been through the mill emotionally in the past few weeks. Some things they had been able to talk about, others they had not. Not so far, at least. Both felt unable to speak, but words were superfluous. They found comfort in holding each other.

Jordan was the first to break away but he continued to hold each of her forearms. He wanted to look into her face.

'What the hell happened out there, Bronte?' He had no more idea than the little the police had managed to tell him on the 'phone.

'How's Chelsea? Where's Phoebe?' Bronte's mind was a whirl.

'Chelsea's going to pull through. They both are. Chelsea's very weak still and she hasn't spoken since they got her in here, but they say there's no complications to worry about and she'll be OK in a couple of days.'

'And Phoebe?'

'She's next door. Same with her . . . but what happened to you? You look like you came off worse than they did.'

'What, my head you mean? From what I remember, I tripped and banged it on the car. I think I must have blacked out for a second after that . . .'

They still stood in the middle of the room, Jordan's grip tight on her arms.

'Banged it on the station wagon?' he asked, trying to picture what had gone on.

'No, on the sports car.'

'The sports car?' He seemed surprised. 'Where is that now, then?'

'What's left of it must be still out in the fire, by the roadside.'

Jordan released one arm and led her to the chair he had recently vacated. He gently sat her down and then crouching on his haunches in front of her, a hand on each of her knees, he carried on: 'What a mess, Bronte. What was she doing there?' He honestly didn't know.

'I thought you could tell me that. I just came across the car parked there and thank God I did, because nothing else was coming down that road after me. Chelsea was already out cold when I got to the car.'

His huge dark eyes, filled with pain and confusion, stared back at her out of that exquisitely-moulded face, silently begging her to put some order into his life. His smile was but a distant memory.

'Let me see if I've got this straight. You were in the station wagon and found the sports car parked on the road? Chelsea was unconscious at this point?'

'Yes, but everywhere was filled with smoke, Jordan. There were flames all around them when I got there. In fact, I very nearly didn't see them at all. I had just turned my car round because the fire was all over the road, when I spotted something red.'

She recounted all that she could remember from that moment onwards.

'Oh Jeez,' he despaired. 'What has she done this time? If you hadn't been there they would probably both have died.'

'What happened at your end, Jordan? How come she was

out that way with Phoebe?' Bronte didn't want the heroics dumped on her.

'That's just it, I don't know. I was out with Art this morning – only for a couple of hours. When I left, Chelsea was by the pool with Phoebe and everything seemed fine. We'd had a good day yesterday, Chelsea even cooked the meal and made a big effort all day. Then I got back with Art and there was no sign of either of them or the car. The house was wide open so I assumed she'd just gone out for a short time.'

'So what happened then?'

'Obviously, I had no idea what time she'd left so I wasn't too worried for a bit. After an hour or so, I started checking my watch and then the 'phone rang. It was the police telling me to come to the hospital as fast as possible because my wife and daughter had just been admitted.'

'How scary ...' Bronte touched his fingers absentmindedly and equally unintentionally, he entwined a couple of hers in his own. Meanwhile, Chelsea's shrunken form which made so little impression on the bed, continued to rest peacefully – unaware of anything going on around it.

'I called Art who came round with a car for me because of course, I had no transport at that stage.' Then, as an afterthought: 'I didn't want to call a cab.'

'No, of course.' She knew he was always conscious of publicity.

'That's about all I know. By the way, you look awful! You sure you should be up?'

'Thanks.' She managed a thin smile.

'Sorry.' He gave her knee a squeeze at which she flinched. 'Oh hell! That wasn't the right thing to do, was it?' He noticed the cuts and bruises on her legs for the first time.

She shook her head.

'You get those rescuing the others?' His emotions were stirred.

'Yup. But they don't matter.' She played it down.

'Aren't you sore?' He was concerned.

'Only a bit.' She lied. Changing the subject: 'Jordan, what are you going to do about Chelsea? I mean about today, really?'

'Million dollar question. Ask me another.' He still wasn't smiling, tension written all over his face. 'I guess, I'll just have to hang in there until she wakes up and tells us where she was going. I hope it's a good one . . .'

'Do they know when she'll come round?'

'Apparently, it's hard to say. Could be any time.'

'Are you going to stay here tonight?' Bronte momentarily regretted firing such a direct question.

'If she comes round I won't.'

'What about Phoebe?'

'She knows I'm here. I've spoken to her but she's sleeping right now. They want to keep her in, just to check she's suffered no more serious damage.'

Just then, they were interrupted by a doctor and nurse who came in to check on Chelsea's condition.

'No change, Mr Innes?' asked the doctor. From his tone, Jordan could have been any person off the street.

'Not that I can see.' Jordan took a step towards the bed, as the doctor bent over his patient and shone a light into her eyes, while the nurse took note of her pulse.

'She is going to be OK, isn't she doc?' Jordan needed to know. But as he spoke, Chelsea stirred, gave a sickly little cough and half opened her eyes. Jordan was there in a flash.

'Chelsea?'

Bronte slipped towards the door: 'I'll wait outside.' She needed space and hospitals were never her favourite places.

The doctor and the nurse emerged soon afterwards, leaving Jordan once more alone in the room with his wife.

Jordan was satisfied that both his wife and daughter were out of danger and, as Chelsea slipped in and out of sleep, there was little more he could do for her that night. Partly persuaded by the doctor and partly by the thought that he really ought to get Bronte home, especially as it was already well into the evening, he escorted her down the stairs and towards the exit of the hospital.

News of bush fire casualties was a big story in Sydney and with the added bonus of a celebrity being involved, the area beyond the hospital steps was awash with paparazzi and cameras. That was just what Jordan didn't need and made

Bronte feel immediately wary. As they forced their way through the swarming throng, questions like: 'How is Chelsea, Jordan?' 'And your little girl?' 'Who found them?' 'Was the nanny with them?' 'Will this affect the film?' were fired from all directions.

But Jordan, who was not about to stop and answer any of them, simply put up his hand and made sure Bronte was able to find space to walk beside him towards the car Art had lent him.

It was a mercy that they were not followed all the way home. Bronte felt as if something in her head might explode at any moment as Jordan pulled into the drive and stopped the car outside the front door.

Instead of getting out straight away, he threw both his arms over the steering wheel and gripped it at the top, leaning forward as he did so.

'What a day!' He sounded tired and serious, a combination which Bronte had yet to come across with him and she wasn't quite sure how to handle it. She thought she ought to say something . . .

'Do you know what's going to happen to the station wagon?'

He was miles away and took a little time to answer. She didn't push it. If it hadn't been for the little teddy, tucked up in her bag, she really wouldn't have cared if she never saw that car again. The rest of her possessions were immaterial, even the leather jacket didn't seem to matter, but she needed the teddy. It had rapidly come to mean a lot to her, in a way which she was frightened to explore.

'The police said they'd get it dropped round. I guess that looks like tomorrow now. Of course, I'd forgotten, you must have your bags in there.' It was an added anxiety for him.

'Don't worry about that, Jordan. I honestly don't need any of it and besides, belongings seem really trivial after what's happened today.' It wasn't the time or the place to thank him for his generous present. She would do that later.

'Come on.' He struck the wheel with his fist. 'Let's get you inside. You probably should go to bed.'

He opened the car door and came round to the other side to help her out. He led her by the arm into the house, before relinquishing his grasp gently in the hall.

314

She didn't quite know how to cope with the situation. Past experience didn't help her either. She knew she was not ready to sleep, even though her body had begun to ache all over. He, too, seemed at a loss, as he stood by the Christmas tree, not venturing in any particular direction. Did he want to talk? Did she, for that matter? A shower. That was the answer, and besides, she did want to rinse away that sickly singed smell which had hung around her all day.

'I'm going to take a shower.' She broke the silence.

She knew he had heard her, but he neither spoke nor looked up and she realised all at once how badly he was suffering inside. She negotiated the stairs with great caution; every step pulled the skin on her legs and set off reverberating rhythms in her head. Perhaps she ought to be lying down after all, but something nagged her that she was needed upstairs.

It wasn't easy, washing her hair with the bandage still strapped to her forehead. They had told her to keep the wound covered for a day or so, just until it healed over. As the warm water soothed her skin, she felt she was back in the real world for the first time since she had left Avalon that morning. The soft drumming of the water on the tiles beneath her feet and the gentle misty steam which caressed her helped to ease away her troubles, as she allowed her thoughts to be momentarily engulfed.

When she eventually switched off the shower, fearing she would shrivel to a prune if she stayed under it much longer, she could hear the sound of muffled music floating down the stairs from the living room above. She would put something on and go and see if he wanted coffee or even just some company for a while.

With her hair rubbed dry, she went up towards the kitchen to make herself a strong cup of black coffee. Wary of how she would find him, she slipped quietly into the living room and curled herself neatly on the fleecy white rug in front of the sofa, setting her coffee down with exaggerated care beside her.

'Would you like some coffee? The kettle's just boiled.' She broke the ice.

For a moment he didn't answer her. He merely continued to lie on his stomach, not more than a couple of feet from her, on a giant cushion on the floor. His legs were stretched out behind him. The music he had chosen was a melancholy instrumental CD which suggested everything about the way he was feeling.

He transferred his gaze from eternity to the present and lifted a tumbler to reveal a generous helping of whisky.

'This'll do for now, thanks anyway.'

She knew he should talk, if only to lighten the load he was obviously carrying. She couldn't bear to see that hurt look clouding those beautiful eyes and she knew she was qualified to help where misery was concerned.

'You once said to me, 'a dollar for them'. Well, now I'm saying it back to you, Mr Innes!' she began softly.

'Wasn't that back when I used to call you Mrs Richardson?' She was relieved to hear a spark of the familiar Jordan after all.

'Yes, but let's leave that one out – I think we exhausted it at the time. Don't avoid the issue, tell me what's on your mind.' She had braved it.

'What's on my mind? Well, how about a wife that seems to be going mad before my eyes ... a wife and a daughter who nearly died in a fire ... a movie which now looks as though it's going to be delayed even further ... a hire car that's written off, God only knows where ... will that lot do for starters?' He was leaning on his elbows.

'Well now, let me see ... the car's covered under insurance ...' That was the easy one to solve.

'... and of course, there's you ...' He looked straight at her.

'Me?' She thought she was hearing things.

'Yes, you, who have come along and in a very short space of time, turned my entire world upside down, nearly died today saving my wife and child, suffered a great whack on the head in the process – about which, I might add, there's been no word of complaint – and I haven't even asked you if you had a good Christmas!'

Wow! A loaded statement. How to tackle that one? Best to avoid the delicate part and stick to the safer bit. So she set off spouting, as if from a script: 'Christmas was really good fun. I was thoroughly well looked after and entertained, and before I forget, I must thank you for that fabulous jacket. It's a great fit and I can't wait to wear it.' But she couldn't help adding quietly: 'I liked the bear too, Jordan . . .'

'So did I. That's why I put it in there.' He made no further comment on it. 'Tell me, what do you think about the idea of soulmates? Do you believe there could be any substance behind the feeling I've been getting lately, that you and I were 'supposed' to meet up at some point?' He was venturing on to new ground with her.

'Sort of like destiny, you mean?' She wanted to keep up with him, but it was important that he led the way.

'Something like that. You see, I have this theory which stems from way back around the time I lost my parents. When I was younger, I began to get the idea that we're only put on this earth with parents as preliminary guides. Kind of to start us off. But really, we come into life alone and we are always really alone, regardless of who we team up with on a friendship or even physical basis, until we meet that person or persons who, to use your word, is or are predestined to link up with our souls. Am I getting too heavy? Must be the whisky.' He stopped.

Bronte replied: 'It's an area of thinking I've only recently felt able to approach. But if I remember back to when my mother died, I guess she took much of my childish vulnerability with her.'

'That's my point. She took away your main guiding light and left you to a large extent on your own – which is how you really had been all along, only you didn't know it until then. Or, maybe until only recently, if you say that's when you started to explore life on this level.'

She saw what he was driving at : '. . . and because Dad didn't really bother, not on any emotional scale anyway, I became very self-protective from an early age.'

'That's something to do with your birth sign too, though.'

There was much more to him than she had realised.

'So, do you think that when you meet this person or persons who turn out to be your soulmate or mates, you are not really alone any more?'

'That's the part I haven't decided on yet. I'm somehow inclined to stick to my first theory, the one which says we are born and die alone. But that can get messed up, when you bring soulmates into the equation. Do you think Dominic was your soulmate?'

That was a very tricky one and she wanted to hedge round it.

'I honestly don't know, Jordan. There are times when I think he was. But those thoughts have become stronger since he died, which makes me wonder whether it's more me missing him now and being sentimental about everything. It's something I never really considered at length when he was alive. How about you and Chelsea?'

'That's more straightforward. Especially now. I love Chelsea in a way I may never love any other person. After all, we've had a child together, although I think that means more to me than it does to her these days,' again his voice was tinged with sadness, 'but it's a more physical love – and I don't mean sexual. It's not spiritual or abstract and there's no point in kidding myself any longer that it is or ever could be.'

'Do you believe that soulmates have to be husbands or wives? Or that you can have any number of them?'

The music helped to carry them along.

'To answer your first question, no, I don't think that any commitment is necessary to feel that about someone. As to how many, you'll have to ask me that one again when I'm fifty or sixty because . . . and I'm not sure how to say this exactly . . .' he smiled shyly at her, almost as if he was half afraid of what he was about to say. 'Until I met you, I hadn't ever been aware of coming across a potential candidate for a true soulmate.'

'Jordan, should we really allow ourselves to be thinking like this?' It was her first admission of mutual attraction.

'Probably not. In fact, definitely not.' She couldn't tell if he was serious. 'But the more I try and fight it, the stronger the feeling gets and it's sometimes so real that it scares me.'

She began to wonder if the looks, the smiles, the odd casual touches which she had treasured, even from the very early days of knowing him, could all be strung together to back up his theory about soulmates? It was just that she had not taken them as far as he had, probably due to lack of experience.

'Jordan, I don't know what to say. Do you think I should leave?'

That was the very last thing she wanted to do, but if she was in any way contributing to Chelsea's state of mind or the apparent breakdown of his marriage, which looked as though it was now crumbling from both sides, how could she stay?

'Don't do that.' His eyes pleaded with her for a second. 'I need you. Apart from all the back-up with the movie – and remind me to fill you in on that one ... I need your support, if you can stand to carry on giving it, after what I've blurted out tonight.'

'I'm not going anywhere unless you think I should, for whatever reason you choose to name,' she whispered.

He wriggled forward a little on the cushion until he was only a few inches from her. She began to tremble and was glad there was no weight on her lower body which felt like jelly. Nothing to do with her cuts and bruises. She looked away, unable to meet his powerful gaze.

'My poor baby ...' He saw all of the childhood vulnerability she had mentioned, still very much inside her and it reached deep into his heart.

She didn't move. She couldn't move. She felt a tingling, damp sensation between her legs and a hardening of her nipples, as something long-neglected was aroused within her.

'Come here ...' He stretched out his hand, at the same time bringing his legs up underneath him and settling on his knees as he drew her face tenderly towards his own. Very, very slowly he tilted her chin until he brushed the end of her nose with his mouth. She could feel his warm breath on her skin as she surrendered her face to him, incapable of resisting his touch.

The music filled the room with a romance, stronger than anything she had ever known, as very, very softly their lips met and locked, parting naturally to allow their tongues to explore all the feeling flowing between them.

CHAPTER TWENTY FOUR

Chelsea and Phoebe spent a few days in hospital recovering from their ordeal. It was generally felt by the hospital staff that Phoebe was ready to go home earlier, but the general consensus of opinion was that it would upset the child too much to leave without her mother. Since she had come round from the accident, she had asked frequently for her mother and there was very little mention of anyone else who had featured thus far in her short life.

Jordan had asked Bronte to arrange a limousine to collect them that morning. He had become unavoidably detained in meetings to try to sort out the latest problems which had arisen over the holiday period and would inevitably delay the film even further. The female lead had, with no warning at all, pulled out altogether and flown to Europe. It was rumoured that she was having 'family problems', whatever that might mean. Her part would therefore have to be recast and as her character was so central to the film, it would not be easy to find the right actress again for such a challenging role. It would certainly take a little time especially since most actresses would be holidaying at that time of year. Then there were all the legal implications of her dramatic decision to consider.

On top of that, it had just come to light that the owner of the harbour-side house which Jordan had planned to use had been declared bankrupt and all his assets were about to be frozen. It was therefore looking likely that a new location would also have to be sought. It never rained but it poured.

That was how Bronte and Becky came to be alone in the house when the long dark limo crawled into the drive. A very pale, drawn-looking Chelsea stepped out of the back with obvious difficulty, followed by Phoebe, who also looked a shadow of her former self. Gone was the usual childish sparkle. Her face looked grey and tired and she suddenly appeared far older than her three years. Chelsea was even more skin and bone than before and the coat dress which she had asked Jordan to bring in for her the day before, hung limply off her shoulders. She had hardly bothered with make-up and her hair drooped from the clips which had been put there to hold it up. At least half of her face was masked by a pair of large black glasses, which she kept on until she was well inside the house.

The chauffeur closed the car door behind them and handed Bronte the small black leather case which contained the few personal items that Jordan had taken to the hospital for them. He touched his cap with a look of sympathy in his eyes and eased himself back into the driving seat. He had gathered that all was far from well. Neither mother nor child had spoken on the journey home, merely sitting huddled together in the back seat as if seeking comfort from each other. He knew the gutter press would love to hear his story, but he also knew his place. Folks such as Jordan Innes had a right to privacy in times of trouble and he, Albert Lancaster, was not about to intrude on that right.

Bronte was left standing in the hall with the case in her hand, not knowing quite what to do next. Jordan had said he would do his utmost to try and get back for their return and she prayed that he'd hurry, because she didn't like the atmosphere one bit. The moment Chelsea stepped into the house, it was as if the blinds had been drawn on a sunny day and all around had become shrouded in darkness. The fountain of light had ceased to flow. Beccy seemed to notice it too because she came scuttling out of the kitchen, her feet making no sound on the polished floor, and her usual cheery smile and bubbly conversation were held well in check. Charlene was on standby, awaiting a call from Bronte, but as she watched mother and daughter walk slowly to the stairs, hand in hand, Bronte hesitated over whether to 'phone or not. It didn't look as if there would be much for Charlene to do for a while.

Having exchanged worried expressions with Becky, Bronte followed Chelsea downstairs, still clutching the case. She knocked quietly on the half-open door and receiving no answer, she stuck her head round to see if there was anyone there. There was. Chelsea was standing on tiptoes on a chair in her bare feet, struggling to reach a suitcase on top of the wardrobe and Phoebe was sitting quietly on the delicate cream chaise-longue in front of the window. She was sucking her fingers and staring at nothing in particular, with a faraway look in her eyes. Neither acknowledged Bronte's presence in the room.

'I brought your case for you, Chelsea.' She had to say something.

'Thanks. Just leave it on the bed, will you?' Chelsea remained on the chair, with her back to the room.

'Do you need any help?' Bronte was half-afraid that being so frail, she might crumple under the weight of the case which she was trying to get a grip on.

'I can manage.' Her response was delivered neither rudely nor abruptly, but rather sadly and softly. Bronte began to suspect there were tears in her eyes.

'Are you sure there's nothing I can bring you? Something to drink or to eat?' She tried again.

'No, nothing right now, thanks.' She still didn't turn round.

Something inside challenged Bronte to find out what exactly was going on. She was getting bad vibes.

'Do you think Phoebe should go down for a rest? She looks very pale.' She thought at least she could make herself useful doing that. It was unlikely after all that Chelsea would want her daughter in the way. She didn't usually.

'NO! Want Mommy . . .' Phoebe startled Bronte by the ferocity of her tone.

'Leave her for now. She's OK there,' . . . and then almost as an afterthought, though on reflection, it must have been foremost in Chelsea's mind, she asked: 'Can you get me a couple of reservations on the New York flight today? For Phoebe and me? First if you can, but business would do. Just get us on that 'plane, will you?' Chelsea sounded desperate. She sighed and lifted her arms again to pull the case down.

It was not the time nor the place for questions. Chelsea had made the request and it was her duty to act on that and not to comment. So act she would. She could sense that it was pointless offering any further help, so she withdrew, replying merely that she would see to it right away and closed the door behind her. She remained outside the room for a second, not with any intention of eaves-dropping, but to try to weigh up the situation. Oh, Jordan, please get yourself back here ... Suddenly, there were danger signs all over the house.

Once in the study, she began to make enquiries about the availability of seats to New York that day. Being holiday time the flight was almost full, but two First Class seats did not seem to be so much of a problem. Economy would have been out of the question. While she was on the 'phone to the airline, she heard the front door bang and heavy footsteps pound across the hall. Jordan was home at last.

'What the hell are you doing?' Jordan had just opened the bedroom door onto a scene of chaos. Clothes were strewn over the floor, the bed, the chaise-longue, and the wardrobe was wide open, revealing a selection of empty hangers.

'I'm going back to New York,' replied Chelsea, barely audible.

'What on earth for? You've only just gotten out of the goddamned hospital!'

He had really been through it already that day and he didn't need to come home to find this.

'Jordan, if I stay here, I'm going to lose my mind.' She looked nervously up into his face.

'Chelsea, you need to rest. Not travel half-way across the goddamned world! What is wrong with you?' he demanded, eyes blazing.

'But that's just it. Don't you see, there's something going on in my head that I can't control any more. I just feel sick and so tired . . .' her voice tailed off.

'You've had a bad accident. You've been in that hospital for several days. Of course you're sick.'

'No, really sick, Jordan,' she whispered, almost afraid of him. 'I need help . . .' He had been trying to impress that on her for some time.

'I know you've got problems,' he was a little calmer, 'but you can see someone over here, for God's sake. Let's work this thing out together. Here.' He didn't know what he wanted any more, but he was afraid of all that might happen if she went. He knew their lives would never be the same again. Oh hell, he was beginning to think he was losing his own mind!

'Jordan, I want to go home. I don't even know what I'm doing half the time. Please listen to me. You said yourself yesterday that things are getting screwed up on the movie and we'll have to be here for longer. But I just can't take it any more.' Jordan wasn't sure if that was meant ambiguously but he was so stunned by her decision to leave that he wasn't about to question it. Meanwhile, Phoebe sat motionless.

Chelsea continued: 'Something dreadful's going to happen soon, Jordan. I can't remember things . . . the only bits of the accident I know are what I've been told. Don't you understand, I can't remember where I was going or why. I must have just driven off in the car while you were with Art, goodness only knows where I was going because I've never been out that way before. Why did I go, Jordan? What was I doing? Why did I stop? Why did I pull over there? Why did I have Phoebe in the car? What is happening to me? Have you any concept of what it's like, having no idea why I nearly died and worse, nearly killed our daughter?' She was sobbing openly now.

'What were you planning to do in New York?' he asked icily, his life felt as if it had been torpedoed.

'I'm going to call my Mom. She'll come over and help with Phoeb . . .'

'She'll *what?*' he burst out.

But she carried on: '. . . and then I'm going to check myself into a clinic where I can try and pick up the pieces of my life.'

'You're not seriously thinking of taking our child back with you in that state, are you?' One more nail in the coffin.

'I want her with me. She wants to come. She should be with her mother, Jordan, not a father who's out all the time and a nanny she hardly knows . . .'

'At least this has made you sit up and show some sort of responsibility towards your daughter at last. Isn't it all a bit late, though?' he asked sarcastically.

She ignored his implications: 'I've asked Bronte to book us on the flight out today.' Her voice was steadier.

'You've done what?' He was dreaming one of the worst nightmares of his life. It had to be time to get up, but he was having so much difficulty shaking it off . . .

'We're going as soon as I've packed and found some way of getting to the airport.'

'And where exactly does this leave us, Chelsea?' He managed to control his anger. 'Didn't you stop to think that all this might have been something we should have discussed before you went ahead and decided to walk out on me?'

'Jordan, I'm not walking out on you. I wish you could just understand that it has to be for the best. I can't go on like this. We can't go on like this. It's not fair on you.'

Ironically, she was beginning to sound more rational than she had in months. She added: '. . . and as for 'us', I just don't know . . .' her voice quivered again and she turned to the window.

'Was this all planned then? To end it like this?' he demanded, as the hurt flashed around like daggers inside him.

'No, damn you!' She spun round to face him once more. 'None of this was 'planned' as you put it. It just feels like the only road left open right now, before something terrible happens. Don't you think we've come close enough this week already to that? Listen, will you? For once in my life, I'm trying to get it right. Lord knows, I haven't done too well in the past.'

'That's the understatement!' He laughed a cruel laugh, born out of his own pain.

'I know . . . I know . . . you've got a right to be angry. But what else is there left for me to do? Perhaps we do need some time apart.'

'What choice are you giving me, Chelsea?'

'I just can't take the risk any more. It's now or it's too late. All I can ask is for you to give it time . . .'

'Look, I know you need help. If you remember, I'm the one who's been saying that. But there's got to be another way. You running off and taking Phoebe is splitting us up, Chelsea. You're shutting me out. Closing the door.' He still didn't know what he really wanted, but his eyes remained dry.

'I don't have any alternative and if you choose to see it like that, then there's nothing more I can say.' She was adamant.

'So it's all cut and dried, is it? You're off today and that's it?' He took two steps towards her and grabbed her. Phoebe still sat staring and silent.

'You're hurting me. Let go!' she cried. His fingers almost met in the middle as they clutched her arms.

'And *you're* hurting me, more than you realise, but you're giving me damn all choice about it.' He let go of her.

'Jordan, we haven't got anything in common right now, and it's not going to get any better by my staying here. I'm not going to get any better.' She might as well say everything. Matters couldn't possibly get any worse.

'Except our daughter . . .' Neither had given a moment's thought to the effect that overhearing their row might have been having on Phoebe. 'Where did I lose you, Chelsea?' His voice was weak but his eyes were still dry.

'You didn't 'lose' me. We just drifted apart. You said so yourself.' Tears welled up in her eyes again.

'I still can't see why you need to take Phoebe,' he clung on, almost in desperation.

Phoebe, who knew that something serious was going on between her Mummy and Daddy, spoke up for the first time: 'Want Mommy.'

Chelsea rushed over to the chaise-longue and knelt beside her little girl: 'I know you do, sweetheart. You and me are going home in an aeroplane! We're going to see Granny.' She hugged Phoebe round the waist, and looking up at Jordan, said: 'Now do you see why?'

He turned away so she couldn't see that he, too, was crying. It broke his heart to see his daughter so miserable and he blamed himself for not handling the situation better from the start.

'I guess.' He opened the door. There was nothing more he could do. He was powerless to stop his marriage from coming apart at the seams and he sensed it was going to be a hell of a job to repair. He was emotionally drained. Pausing before he left the room, he added: 'Let me know what happens and where you are. Take good care of her and make sure she knows her Daddy's coming to see her as soon as he can.' He didn't turn round.

'Jordan ...' Chelsea's frame was racked with sobs. 'Jordan, where are you going?' But it was all far too late.

'Out,' was all he replied, before walking straight ahead, up the stairs and towards the front door. He didn't once look back. Nor did he see Bronte, who had come rushing out of the study, half of her hoping that he was going to tell her to cancel the flights and that everything would be alright after all. But only half of her hoped that. And of course he didn't. In fact he didn't see anything at all other than a tangled web of hopeless confusion as he slammed the front door behind him, conscious only of the need to be alone with his thoughts and to try to reason out the chaos that had become his life.

Bronte hadn't heard any of what had been said behind that closed door. She didn't need to. She knew without being told. She was afraid of going down there after Jordan had left. She didn't know what she could expect to find. She had no idea if he was coming back or how they were getting to the airport, or even that they were definitely going. But she did know that if they were to make the flight she had booked them on, they would have to get a move on because it left in less than two hours. She had no choice but to knock once more on that door.

Chelsea's determination was far stronger than her physique and, once she had made up her mind, there was no going back. If Jordan chose to take it like that, to walk out and not drive them to the airport, then she would find an alternative way of getting there. She knew she had taken him by surprise and, inevitably, hurt him in the process, but she had been hurting far longer and it was time to do something about it. She honestly didn't know what the future held for them, if, in fact there was any future, but the

327

most pressing thing was to get herself well. To fight off the pounding in her head and sort out the knots in her stomach, while she still had the inclination to do so. She feared she might lose that too, if she went on much longer.

When Bronte knocked at the door, a little of her thought – and hoped – it might be Jordan, coming to tell her that he agreed with her decision and would stand by her through it all. But she knew deep down that that time it was asking too much.

'Chelsea?' Bronte entered the room which had been centre stage to so much unhappiness. 'The 'plane goes in less than two hours.' Then she added: 'I just thought you should know.'

'Thanks, Bronte. I've nearly finished here.' She stood with her back to the door and wiped her face with both hands.

Bronte felt uncomfortable.

'Did Jordan go out?' She knew the answer before she asked the question.

'Yes, he did.' What else could she say?

'You wouldn't do me a massive favour and take us to the airport, would you? I don't think we've time for a cab.'

'If that's what you want, Chelsea.' Bronte knew it wasn't up to her to try to change Chelsea's mind. Besides, she was being overwhelmed inside by a tidal wave of emotion. She was beginning to lose her own grip on right and wrong.

'It's what I want,' sighed Chelsea.

While Chelsea finished cramming the cases with clothing enough for herself and Phoebe, Bronte went to give Beccy a brief outline of what was happening. She omitted all but the basic facts which Beccy had already managed to piece together for herself anyway. She asked nothing. She would be told everything that was necessary for her to know in good time. She couldn't help hoping however, that all this didn't mean that her job was coming to an end. It had been a miraculous find and she wasn't to relish the thought of looking elsewhere so soon. But there was no mention of that for the time being.

Chelsea didn't pause for any trivialities as she left the house that day. After all, there was very little for her to say goodbye to. She had no fond memories of the two months spent in Australia, apart from the article she had written which was looking as though it might be published. But that was far from her mind that morning. She did say a brief word of farewell to Beccy on the way out, clutching Phoebe's hand as she went, but that was it. She had neither the time nor the desire to elaborate.

Bronte drove them through the lunchtime traffic, not knowing what to say as Chelsea sat silently beside her and Phoebe nodded off in the back. As Chelsea didn't offer anything either, she concentrated on the road ahead. It was the longest journey of her life.

The way back, in contrast, was the shortest. Weighted down by a sinking heart, she would have preferred to stay forever behind the wheel, never arriving back at the house where she did not know what would confront her. But she had no choice. Whatever she felt and whatever he now felt, she had to face it. In some way he would need her, if only to sort out practical matters. Would he stay? Or would he go too? But how could he leave the movie that far down the road? On the other hand, stars of his standing could probably do anything they damn well pleased. But he might just need her shoulder to cry on and if he did, she wasn't about to let him down.

CHAPTER TWENTY FIVE

There was no point delaying her arrival home. She would have to put in an appearance at some stage. But would Jordan be there? Would anyone be there? She'd know soon enough.

It was almost four o'clock in the afternoon when she took a deep breath and indicated to turn into their drive off Raglan Street. Her hands felt clammy and her heart was pounding inside her ribs. Outside the car, Sydney was being treated to a temporary cease-fire from the blazing sun of recent days. The sky had become overcast with wispy cotton-wool clouds and a fresh sea breeze parted the leaves on the trees and sent the flowers on a merry dance.

The house was ghostly quiet as she closed the front door carefully behind her and stole across the hall, like some criminal fearing detection. Everywhere there were shadows, previously unnoticed as they had been dwarfed by the happy laughter of a child who had been so full of life, or by the clattering in the kitchen, indicating some tasty dish in the making. But that afternoon, there was nothing. It felt cold and empty, rather as if someone had died there. But she knew they hadn't.

Pull yourself together. She pinched her arm to check she wasn't dreaming. She called his name a couple of times: 'Jordan? Jordan?' and again downstairs, but her words just echoed through the silent rooms. He was clearly not there. She knew there was work to be done in the study, but for a little while at least, she wanted to sit in the conservatory with a cup of tea and try to rationalise her situation and inject whatever logic she could muster, into the hollow cavity of her mind.

She had to try and bridge that gaping gulf between what she *wanted* to do and what she *ought* to do, because at that moment the two were poles apart.

'Oh dear! Oh dear!' She jumped, as the sound pierced through her like a knife. Sydney had been quick to take in the atmosphere.

'Sydney, don't do that! You really startled me.'

But he simply repeated himself : 'Oh dear! Oh dear!'

'Can't you squawk anything else, you dumb bird?' She picked up a cushion and threatened to chuck it at his cage. But really, she was grateful for the distraction.

'No violence! No violence!' He was all but human.

She raised her hands in apology: 'OK, Sydney. I won't fling this at you, if you promise to shut up.'

He took one spiky claw off his perch and began to scratch his head, sending a few fluffy feathers floating to the floor of the cage. Blinking several times and thinking carefully about his reply, he blurted: 'Very quiet! No people! Very quiet! No people!' before tucking his head under his wing and pulling out another offending feather.

'That's just it, Sydney. You hit the nail on the head. It's far too quiet and there's certainly no people.' She sighed and slurped the remainder of her tea.

'No hitting! No violence! No hitting! No violence!' He was off again.

'You really are impossible!' She grabbed the cushion again.

'Who's impossible?'

'Jordan!' He had just walked into the room, unbeknown to her.

'Are you earwigging on my private conversation with Sydney?' She smiled at him but didn't move from her chair.

'Am I what?' Some English expressions had him confused.

But before she had a chance to explain, Sydney, who was well in gear by that point, piped up: 'Take off his wig! Take off his wig!'

It broke the ice. Despite the air of sadness which had fallen like mourning around the house, the look they exchanged captured much of their familiar rapport and she couldn't help but be optimistic that things had to work out, one way or another, for the best.

Jordan wandered across the room and lifted the dark blue cover which was sometimes used to put over the parrot's cage to simulate darkness.

331

'Good night, Sydney. Sweet dreams.' He laid it carefully on the cage before retreating to one of the other chairs.

'Do you think you should have done that?' She fiddled with her hair nervously, unsure of what he might say next.

'What? Cover him up, you mean? I wish someone would do that to me, right now.' He didn't appear to be joking.

She didn't know how to reply, so she waited for him to say something else, which he did before long. But there was no mention of where he had spent the last few hours, or with whom – if indeed, with anyone at all. He'd tell her if he wanted to.

'Could you use a drink?' he offered.

'I've just had tea, thanks.' She studied him carefully, trying to weigh up his mood.

'I forgot. That great British institution. Tea, I mean.' He didn't intend to sound sarcastic and she took no offence.

He helped himself to a large whisky on the rocks and thumbed through a few CDs which lay scattered on the coffee table, before selecting one he wanted to listen to.

'I think we need some noise down here. The quiet around this house is giving me the creeps.'

'Touché! That's exactly what I felt when I came in. I'm really missing her clattering about . . .' She felt unable to say Phoebe's name out loud, until he had.

For a moment she feared he would break down, as a great dark cloud of abject misery fell across his strained face. But he took a gulp of whisky instead and set the glass back down loudly on the table.

'It's going to be hard. Knowing she's not around any more. Of course, we've had long patches of separation when I've been working, but I really thought that this time I had it all figured out. We could be a family for a bit and I could do this picture.'

'You know what they say about the best laid plans.' As soon as she had said it, she realised what a stupid comment it had been. But it wasn't easy striking the right chord with him just at that moment.

'Did you drive them to the airport?'

She was worried he might be angry with her for that. She nodded. But he was far from angry with her about anything. She was all he had left right there and then.

'Sorry you had to do that. It should've been me . . .' He didn't finish his sentence.

'For goodness sake, don't apologise. It was no problem, honestly.' She played it down.

'I flipped for a bit. Just wandered around like a spoilt child who couldn't get his way. We didn't deserve you, you know. You have to believe that when I met you and offered you all this . . .' he waved his arm in front of him and laughed at the irony of it: 'I really thought we would help *you* get over your problems, not get you so involved in ours.'

'But Jordan, you've done just that. I had nothing going for me back in England, other than a job I'd done for the last five years and knew backwards. Anyway, it's sometimes good to find out you're not the only one whose life's in a mess.'

'You sure as hell aren't, baby.' Another drink. 'Take a look at mine.' He sighed. 'I really think this time, she's done it.'

'Chelsea, you mean?'

'Yeah. You know, this has been coming for a while. It was just a matter of time. But I never thought she'd take the kid like that. Didn't occur to me she'd want to.'

'Are you just going to accept it?' If he wanted to talk, then she should encourage him, she decided.

'What else can I do? I could run after her and cause a scene. In fact, that was high on my list this afternoon. But in the end, we'd still be facing the same brick wall. Chelsea's not exactly all there most of the time, as you've gathered and if I really kick some ass and face facts, our marriage has been over for a long time. Probably even before Phoebe was born.'

'It's such a shame. She's a lovely little girl.'

'Tell me about it. That's the bit which really sickens right here. She's a great kid and the thing that galls me the most is that she's going to turn out of all this, screwed about her parents and marriage and all that kind of stuff which goes with broken homes.'

'At least we both lost parents, rather than them splitting up.' She agreed with him to a point.

'Yeah, we didn't have to listen to the rows. That's about

all Phoebe's heard between us lately. Oh, why did she have to be in the damn room today?' He clenched his fist and banged it down on his leg. 'I've been reliving that little charade ever since and all I can see is her sad face and big round eyes.'

It tore at Bronte to hear him say that.

'Don't torture yourself about it. It happened and there's nothing you can do. It won't change the way she feels about you. Jordan, she adores you! You know she does and if you don't, then just hear me say it because I've been around you for two months now and I know.'

'You really think so?' The boy cried out from the man's body.

'You'd better believe it! So don't push her out because you feel guilty. She'll be dying to see you when you get back and she'll need you. Just you wait.' Bronte could hardly believe what she was hearing from her own mouth. There she was, lecturing the great Jordan Innes on how to treat his only child – what a nerve! But somehow she knew she was right.

'Realistically, I don't know when I can get back to see her. What with all the problems down here right now. That hurts too.'

Bronte didn't want him to go one bit, but she knew that his daughter was far more important than she was and she had no right to let him suspect what she was feeling.

'How about the weekend? If you think you should go after them right away, that is.' She crossed her fingers and hoped he hadn't already decided to go.

'I've got other plans for the weekend. It's New Year and something's cropped up to take care of that. The point is, I just don't know what to do for the best. I don't think that by flying after them, I'll change very much. I know that nothing bad'll happen to Phoeb. Chelsea's mother is great with her and it'll be neat for her to spend some time with her grandmother. As for Chelsea, she's got to get herself straightened out before there's anything more I can do. Even then, it's probably a lost cause.' He put on the pale yellow sweater that had been dangling round his neck. 'Come on, we're going round in circles here and you don't need to hear any more of this. I'm starved! What's for dinner?'

Beccy had left just before Bronte arrived home from the airport, thinking that there was little point in her staying to cook a meal, if there wasn't going to be anyone around to eat it. She had, however, stocked the fridge as usual and so there was no shortage of food they could rustle up if it was required.

He had taken Bronte by surprise. But then again, that was part of his charm. He had a way of snapping out of the blackest of depressions, with just a fresh idea which managed to put all that had been discussed firmly away in storage, while he concentrated on a new issue.

'I don't think Beccy did anything before she went. At least she hasn't left a note, but there's bound to be something in the kitchen.'

Before she had time to blink, he had sprung off his chair and was towering over her with his hand outstretched ready to help her up.

'How about an Innes surprise?' He grabbed her hand and led her up the stairs.

She giggled: 'A what?'

'Me cook you dinner.' He was perfectly serious.

'You, cook? You never said you could cook!' She was astounded.

'You never asked me. Now, let me see . . .' He swung open the fridge door. 'It can't have meat in it, right?'

She nodded and then protested: 'But you'll hate a vegetarian meal.'

'Nonsense! Leave it to me. You go and fix the table, or drinks or whatever else you think could do with fixing and I'm going to create something like you've never had before.' He tied an apron round his waist and she had to hide a grin. It didn't suit him at all!

'But can't I at least help you?' What an extraordinary day it was turning out to be! But it was far from over yet.

'Why? Don't you trust me? Besides, all this moping around has given me an appetite. I've got to do something or I'll go out of my mind with thinking. Just leave me be.'

'I know where I'm not wanted. Call me when it's ready.' She backed obediently out of the room.

* * *

Much to her amazement, it didn't take him long to produce one of the tastiest pasta dishes she had ever eaten. He had made a sauce using tuna, tomato, wine, herbs and a number of sauté vegetables and served it on long thin noodles, covered with thick bubbling cheese. He had thrown together a crunchy green salad, all of which he proudly displayed to her when he beckoned her back into the kitchen.

'Why did you keep this secret so well hidden?' she asked.

'It's not often I find the time, or someone who appreciates good food.'

She knew he was referring to Chelsea again.

They tucked in as if they hadn't eaten for days. During the meal, he gave her a rundown of the problems facing them with the female lead and the location house, and filled her in on the plan of action which had been mooted and agreed that morning. She let him speak. However, only half of her concentrated on what he was saying and the other half tried to control the jelly feeling she was experiencing more and more, whenever he was close to her.

'. . . so, is it OK if you take that on?' He had finished.

Oh help, she hadn't been listening! She didn't have the faintest idea what he was asking her to do. But how could she explain why her mind had been so preoccupied? She would have to bluff her way out of it for the time being.

'No problem,' she lied. 'But tell me again in the morning, when you haven't ploughed me with so much home cooking and wine.'

He'd only filled her glass twice but it was the best thing she could think of to say.

He got up from the table, thrusting it away from him as he did so.

'Come on, I've got to get out of this house. It's too depressing right now. Let's go into town and take in a movie or something.'

Not giving her the chance to even think about it let alone disagree with him, he went out into the hall and came back two seconds later, pulling on his black leather jacket which he'd thrown on to a chair when he had come in earlier.

She was as keen to get out of there as he was but she was also a little worried about being seen in such a public place with him, when most of Australia knew that his wife had just been in hospital after being trapped in one of Sydney's worst bush fires for years. On the other hand, he didn't seem concerned about it and he was the one with the reputation and adverse publicity at stake, not she.

'What about the washing up?' Again she felt it was a dumb remark, once she'd made it.

'Don't be so practical. Beccy's here tomorrow, isn't she?'

'You male chauvinist pig!' She took a friendly swipe at him but he caught her hand and held it.

'Now, now! You know what they say about getting too familiar with the boss?' He was laughing at her but the comment hit home like a thunderbolt. If familiarity was the road down which they were heading, would he still turn round and ridicule her? But had she known him better, she need not have feared.

Art, who had turned up in a different car every time Bronte had seen him, was in no hurry to reclaim the one he had lent to Jordan and as it was altogether faster and far more the film star image than the station wagon, it was in that that they set off in search of the night life of Kings Cross.

The streets of Sydney were alive with post-Christmas and pre-New Year revellers. The shops and bars were illuminated by neon and glitter and the beat of music thundered down the pavements, blending with the cries of street sellers and general merriment. Bronte had been to New York. She had seen Soho in London. She had visited the streets of some of the African capitals and the Caribbean islands by night. But this was more than just one of those experiences. This was all of them, rolled into one. She stared out of the window as they cruised round the roads looking for a place to park.

At one set of lights, attracted by the flashy sports car and the prospects of a rich punter, Jordan's side of the car was approached by a pair of patent leather, thigh-length boots, followed by a set of boobs which tumbled from the top of a sequin tube. One look at the hunky guy with the beauty in the passenger seat was enough to send the 'boots' in search of a more likely victim.

'Are they always that blatant?' Bronte had seen prostitutes, but that was the first time she had been with someone who had been propositioned.

'It happens. But the interesting thing is trying to figure out which sex they are. That one, for example, would give most guys quite a shock.' He loved Bronte's underlying innocence.

'Are you telling me that was a man?' She knew that sort of thing went on in Cannes because it often came up as good late-night drinking conversation at the Martinez, but she had honestly thought she would have been able to tell a female prostitute from one in drag.

'Yup! Didn't you clock the Adam's apple?'

'All I could see were black boots and a pair of boobs.'

'That's all you were meant to see. Hang on,' he put a hand out to stop her from jerking forwards as he pulled up suddenly beside an empty space. 'This'll do.'

As they wandered in the direction of the cinema, Bronte seriously wondered whether Art's car would still be there when they returned. There were a number of seedy-looking characters loitering against railings, cars, tree trunks and just about anything else that was upright, nurturing either alcohol or drug habits, not entirely sure whether it was Monday or Tuesday week!

But Jordan didn't seem unduly worried. In fact, he strode purposefully on with her doing her very best to keep up. As usual, she seemed far more aware than he of the admiring looks he drew from women he passed, most of whom found their eyes pulled towards the handsome figure dressed in a black leather jacket, faded jeans and dark glasses. Shame he had such a pretty model in tow. But then those types always did.

The pavements and roads alike were crowded. It was a question of dodging oncoming bodies and weaving round groups of people chatting. Some browsed amongst the wares that could be bought, ranging from jewellery to sex aids. Bouncers tried to entice customers into their murky dens of sin and passers-by blocked the street, eyeing up the local talent. Whatever the reason, the world and his wife seemed to have flocked to the Cross that night.

The cinema didn't offer a wide selection of movies and Bronte was happy to go along with Jordan's choice. He ended up buying two tickets for a picture that he had already seen in Los Angeles, but assured her it was good escapist stuff which was probably what they both needed.

They sat side by side in their seats, Jordan slumped in his for most of the time, with one foot resting on top of his other leg, while Bronte shuffled every so often trying to get comfortable. That was a job in itself because the cinema failed to cater for anyone over five foot five. Although science fiction would not have been her first choice, the movie was entertaining enough and only a couple of times did her mind wander back to all that had happened that day. Her eyes, on the other hand, strayed frequently to Jordan. But each time they did, they returned unsure of whether he was engrossed in the film or in his own thoughts. Either way, he made no move in her direction – be it physical or verbal.

'I need a drink. Let's go find a bar.' It was the first time he had spoken since the film ended.

She had thought he might have looked for somewhere quiet and discreet. But she was wrong. He chose one of the noisiest places they passed and without consulting her, swung the door and went inside. She was left with little choice but to do likewise. Once in there, she immediately felt intimidated by the leering looks and groping hands which followed her all the way to the bar. At one end, a three-piece band churned out the kind of music which sent one scurrying to the bathroom for Aspirin. Looking around at the dubious-coloured cocktails being drunk on most of the tables, she thought the drinks looked as though they would send one just as quickly to the same cupboard in search of stomach settlers.

'Here, try this,' yelled Jordan, thrusting a bulb-shaped glass filled with a frothy, cream-coloured liquid into her hand.

'What is it?' She should try and enter into the spirit.

'You'll love it!' He hadn't even heard her.

The place was heaving and their only chance of a seat came when a couple of tarty teenage girls left their companions at the table nearest to the bar and Jordan was swift enough to snatch the chairs. He was only just ahead of several other people, all hovering with the same intention.

'Sit down while you can,' he beckoned to her to join him, 'and I'll get us another drink. Same again?'

She shook her head. She was having enough difficulty persuading her stomach to accept the one she had. She certainly didn't need more of it. In contrast, his seemed to be going down as if it were a glass of cold milk.

The people at the table on whose company they had forced themselves were well into the holiday spirit. They were a mixed group of young Australians who soon got into conversation with Jordan, telling him in great detail from a local's point of view, which places were 'in' and which should definitely be avoided in the Cross. They seemed intrigued by the effervescent Yank who told them he worked for an American airline ... (at which point, Bronte's jaw dropped noticeably open) and his shy 'friend'. They were even more interested in having him around when he seemed only too happy to finance the endless rounds of drinks they all ordered. While Jordan was obviously revelling in his newly-found anonymity, Bronte felt more and more out of it the further she lagged behind on the drinking stakes. Apart from anything else, she could barely hear herself think above the din around her. She was sure that if she had been out on some date and he had dragged her into a place like that and proceeded to ignore her in favour of a rowdy group of locals, she would have slapped him in the face and stormed out. But this was different. This was Jordan Innes, who she reasoned more than likely longed for the odd night out like that, but could rarely contemplate it for fear of being mobbed.

This was Jordan Innes, whose wife had walked out on him that day, taking his child with her. This was Jordan Innes, her boss. She could no more slap him in the face than she could bite off her own fingers and besides, they weren't on a date. She was just keeping him company in his hour of need. There was nothing for it but to stick it out.

She began to lose track of the number of drinks Jordan consumed. All she knew for certain was that she had forced down two of the sickly cream cocktails and she would be lucky if she managed not to see them again in the near future. Jordan had either not noticed or didn't care that she was drinking so slowly, as he became heavily involved in a heated discussion comparing the latest American music scene to that in Australia.

Bronte tried to pass the time by drumming up ways of getting the two of them out of that dreadful place. And quickly. She was determined not to make a fuss and particularly in the state he had rapidly got into, it was vital that those around them remained in ignorance of who he was. Otherwise, the press would surely enjoy a field day. She was therefore careful not to mention his name when she picked her moment to lean forward and shout in his ear: 'Do you mind if we go? I really think I'm going to be ill.'

His glazed eyes, still reminding her so much of the special person behind them, rounded on her in surprise. She was terrified he would tell her to get lost or something, but he didn't.

'Sure, honey. Lead the way. It must be two or three by now?'

She was hugely relieved. It was two thirty-five.

'Look, it's been great knowing you guys! Look me up if you fly the ol' airline. I'll get some drinks fixed on the house!'

She giggled to herself. He was spouting absolute rubbish! But they must have been equally drunk because not once during the evening had he mentioned which airline he was supposed to work for, nor had he told them his name – real or fictitious.

The level of intelligence of his conversation improved very little as she did her best to get him to the car in one piece. Fortunately, he was capable of walking but he didn't appear to be seeing too well. Or was he seeing double? She wasn't sure which. All she knew was that if she hadn't managed to pull him aside just as he was about to collide with street lights, signposts and the odd person in a similar state, he would have arrived home black and blue.

She was glad, on reflection, that she had paid so much attention to the area in which they had left the car. Otherwise she might never have found it again. As it was, she took a couple of wrong turns which made the walk back longer than it should have been. Jordan was little help when it came to navigation. He was more interested in dictating a menu for breakfast which included sausages, bacon, kidneys, black pudding and steak! It was enough to make her stomach heave without the help of the cocktails, which still threatened to reappear. She couldn't imagine who he thought was going to cook all that for him. But, then again, in the morning he would never remember ordering it.

When they finally reached the car, Jordan seemed to want to drive it home and it took all her powers of persuasion, starting off gently and then becoming a matter of hauling him round to the passenger side, to convince him otherwise.

'But it's Art's car!' As if that was reason for him to drive after a skinful.

'I don't care if it's the Pope's car! You are not driving it.' She buckled him into his seat.

'What's he got to do with it?'

'The Pope? Oh, never mind. Just hold on and we'll be home soon.'

'Musn't wake Phoebe when we get in.' He was confused and she wanted to cry for him. There was no point shattering his illusions in that state.

'No. I'll be quiet and you'll have to make a big effort.' There was no answer. He had already fallen asleep.

How on earth was she going to get him inside? There was no way she could carry him. If she couldn't wake him, he'd just have to spend the night in the car. Or at least until he came round. She had parked as near to the house as she possibly could, reducing the distance he would have to cover.

'Jordan?' She pulled his leather-clad arm. 'Jordan, please wake up. I don't want to leave you out here unless I have to.'

He rolled his face slowly towards her and raised his eyelids to half mast.

'Thank goodness for that! I'll give you a hand. Just sit there for a second.'

She rushed round to his side of the car lest he nod off again and half pulling, half shoving, managed to get him on his feet by the door.

Why were keys always so damned awkward in an emergency? She cursed as she tried to jam hers into the lock with one hand. He stood patiently, wholly reliant on her to lead him to his room. Had she abandoned him there and then, he wouldn't have known where to start looking.

Helping him down the stairs was not an exercise she looked forward to repeating in a hurry. It was a miracle they both made it to the bottom with no broken bones. She paused in the doorway of his room. For the first time since she had taken charge of him outside the bar, she was not sure what to do with him next. He was like a big, overgrown, sleepy puppy. No mind of his own and ready to obey her every command. She couldn't really leave him there, fully clothed. She would have to put him to bed.

He offered no resistance as she sat him down and stood over him to remove his jacket, which gave her an unwelcome reminder of the sweet smell of cocktails, mixed with cigarette smoke and steamy bodies. Yuk!

It took her a few minutes to reduce him to his boxer shorts. All the while he sat there, looking in her direction but not seeing further than the end of his nose. With difficulty, she laid him on the sheet, propping his head, which would unquestionably feel as if it had been used as a motor cycle grand-prix race track in the morning, on two soft pillows. She paused only for a fleeting second to admire his tanned body and allowed herself just the teeniest fantasy where, had he not been so hopelessly drunk, she took complete advantage of him. Then she pulled the duvet around his shoulders and tucked him in on both sides, lest he should wake up cold later on.

Her heart went out to him as he lay there, so vulnerable to the vagaries of life, with the sweet, innocent face of a child. Not one worry line marred that skin as he slept peacefully, unaware of the stirring he was causing within her. At first she feared it was her maternal instincts he was arousing. But then she knew that what she was feeling was far stronger and much more dangerous than that.

CHAPTER TWENTY SIX

Bronte overslept the next morning, which was hardly surprising, considering the time she eventually got to bed the previous night. When she did finally crawl out of bed and contemplated her wardrobe, she didn't wonder that Jordan's door was still tight shut and that there was no sign of him upstairs either.

She had managed to hold on to the contents of her stomach. Just. But she knew that strong black coffee and something light to eat would be necessary if she were going to be able to shake off the nausea which still lingered.

Another glorious summer day awaited her outside when she dragged back the curtains in the dining room. In the trees, the birds' choral practice was underway, while down on the sea there was a buzz of holiday activity, setting off early for a day on the water. After all, the next day would be New Year's Eve and local residents and tourists alike were making the most of the prospect of a hot day and time off work.

She was just about to go and pour the coffee she had brewed, when she heard a groan behind her and swung round to find a deliciously dishevelled Jordan, nursing one of the worst hangovers of his life!

'Hi . . .' he looked sheepishly at her, collapsing heavily into a chair and clutching his head in his hands.

She resisted the desire to throw her arms around him and give him an almighty hug. Besides, he didn't look up to it.

'Jordan, you look dreadful!' she greeted him.

'How come you look so damned good and I feel like this?' he grumbled.

'It could have something to do with the different volume of cocktails we both drank last night. Coffee?'

'Yes. Make it as strong as you can or something's going

344

to give way here. Cocktails . . .? What the hell were we doing drinking cocktails?' He looked puzzled.

She found another cup and poured the coffee.

'Here, get this down and you'll feel better. We went to some bar in Kings Cross after the cinema and you decided to introduce me to the delights of cream cocktails.'

'It'll take more than coffee to make me feel better today. That I can assure you. Do I have to apologise to you?' He took her by surprise.

'Apologise? For what?'

'For anything I did or said last night.' He honestly couldn't remember what happened after the movie.

'Not that I can recall. Except you were rather rowdy and you did tell some great stories about what you did for a living.'

'I did? Am I going to read about it in the papers today?' He drained the remainder of his coffee and pushed the cup over for a refill.

'I don't think so. At least I didn't see anyone with a notepad out. Or a camera for that matter. Do you want something to eat?'

'Give me a minute. First you'd better tell me the worst. Give me the rundown on last night . . .'

She proceeded to give him a detailed account of their movements from the cinema to the bar and then home again. He listened quietly, exclaiming 'Oh no' and 'Oh damn' every so often.

'Are you serious? Did I really drink that much?'

'Brownie's honour!' She stuck her fingers up and beamed at him.

'No wonder my head's throbbing like this! You're going to have to take my word for it that I don't usually hang out in places like that, nor am I in the habit of behaving so outrageously.'

'Jordan, you don't have to explain. I know what you went through yesterday. I was here, remember?' For some reason, his apology made her feel awkward.

'Nor am I in the habit of taking ladies out on the town and treating them like that.' He needed to get it off his chest. 'So you're wrong. I should be saying sorry. Heaven only knows where I would've ended up if you hadn't been there to nursemaid me home.'

'Sure you can't manage any toast?' She wasn't looking for gratitude.

But he ignored her question and carried on: '. . . and another thing, I need to thank you for tucking me up so snugly. No-one's done that for me since I can remember. It was about the only thing that made life worth waking up for this morning. I was touched. Dominic was a lucky man if he got that treatment on a regular basis.'

That time she blushed right up to the roots of her hair. He leant forward and covered her hand which still gripped the coffee cup, horrified that he had made her so embarrassed and worried he might have upset her further.

'Really, it was special of you . . .' He spoke softly and tried to look into her eyes, which were flitting all round the room, anywhere but his face. She was afraid he might just kiss her again and she wasn't prepared.

'I've got to make up for this somehow, haven't I?'

'There's really no need,' she protested, rapidly turning to jelly once more.

'I want to. Besides, I'm pissed off with hassles. Let's just get in the car and drive out to Palm Beach. I think I'm in serious danger of being very ill unless I spend most of the day in the fresh air, away from problems and, especially, from cocktails.'

'But what about the work that needs doing?' She couldn't think of anything she'd rather do than laze on a beach, but she did have a pile of things to attend to.

'Stuff that! Besides, I need to get my strength up for the dinner tonight. That reminds me, we'd better let them know Chelsea's not going to be there.' He was brightening up, like the sun rising on a cold November morning. 'I'm going to dress and we're getting out of here.'

The matter was decided. After all, it was her boss who had said stuff it and if that's what he thought, then she presumed it was OK for her to think it too.

She had no idea what the day had in store for her, it would be a matter of taking it as it came. One thing she needed to remember to do before they went anywhere was to call Charlene and break the news that she wouldn't be required any more. It was not a call Bronte relished the idea of making. Charlene had been a wonderful, reliable nanny and it seemed a terrible shame to make her redundant.

'You ready then?' Jordan popped his head round her bedroom door.

'Give me a chance! What am I going to need for this expedition, anyway?' Her mind had gone blank.

'Nothing other than your wonderful self and that sexy swimming costume you wore on the boat.' He smirked cheekily and dodged a towel which came flying in his direction. 'Oh, and you might need this!' He caught the towel and handed it back to her.

'My! We are recovering fast, aren't we?' she teased.

'Not that fast. I'm going to need more of the TLC you showed me last night. I'll wait upstairs.'

Tender Loving Care, as he put it, was something she had almost forgotten how to give. All men lapped it up but usually neglected to remember that it was required in return. Should she really be putting Jordan and TLC in the same breath? But then, hadn't he?

The wind whistled through the tangles in her hair as Jordan sped along the highway, roof down and stereo blaring. The route he took was the very same one she had used to go to Avalon and it ran right through the bushland, which just days earlier had been a death trap of fire. The devastation around them was shocking. The once-scenic bush had been reduced to a graveyard of death and destruction. Abandoned tree corpses and mutilated branches lay scattered on the battlefield. It would take years to repair the damage done by a carelessly-discarded cigarette or an empty bottle, thoughtlessly thrown from a passing car.

Bronte dreaded seeing the spot where she had found Chelsea and prayed that the car had been towed away. The last thing they both needed was to see the charred remains of a monument to so much pain and misery. Happily, there was no sign of it and once they reached the familiar set of traffic lights, she knew that the place was safely behind them. Jordan said very little on the journey to Palm Beach – perhaps because he, too, knew what had happened on that road, but also the combination of the wind and music made conversation virtually impossible.

The nearer they got to the resort, the slower the traffic became and it gave Bronte a chance to point out the Avalon suburb where she had spent Christmas Day. He was fascinated to hear the story of the shark alarm and seemed concerned when she mentioned that she had been in possible danger.

'That must have been frightening.' He looked at her, taking in the long scarred legs stretched in the footwell and going back up to her face, half shaded by sunglasses.

'I wouldn't do it again by choice, put it that way.'

'Is your head all right without the bandage? I haven't even asked you.' He had noticed her fingering the wound which was usually covered by hair, but when the wind brushed the hair aside he could see the bump had turned to radiant shades of red, brown and a bruised green.

'They told me to get the air to it, once it healed over.' She touched it again, that time self-consciously.

'You won't get more air than in this car,' he assured her.

'You can say that again! I've been pinned to the headrest for most of the way.'

'One of the pleasures of sports cars.' Cars were a passion of his.

'Of your driving, you mean,' she quipped.

'Any complaints from the passenger seat?' he warned.

'None so far. Except I don't think I'll ever be able to untangle this bird's nest.' She lifted a few strands of hair.

'Don't even try. It looks great just the way it is,' and he meant it. 'How about something to eat? I think my stomach would just about allow it now.'

They had recently passed the sign indicating that Palm Beach was only around the corner.

'It will? I'd better check with mine. Don't ever tell me that I'll 'love' a drink again. I can still taste that revolting mixture from last night.' She flirted harmlessly.

'I really thought you would, though. But I will admit that they make a much better version of it in Bermuda. You'll have to try it sometime.'

'Thanks, but no thanks. I'll stick to what I know. How about there to eat?' She pointed across his body to a beach front café, with tables laid out on a terracotta terrace under woven rush sun shades.

They both felt appreciably better after a little solid sustenance, although the liquid consumption had been kept strictly to mineral water. The beach firmly beckoned, with its clean white sand stretching as far as the eye could see and the clear blue ocean waiting to be explored, as the bubbly white surf tossed and teased the boards which were trying to master it.

They selected a spot to relax, a good distance away from as much of the rest of the population as they could find. The beach was large enough to be able to afford them some privacy, something that was rapidly becoming important to them both.

Neither had taken more than the essentials with them, such as bathing towels and sun cream. Jordan had thrown in a book at the last minute. There had been very little time for reading since he'd arrived in Australia but perhaps there was a chance he might snatch a few pages, so he'd brought it just in case.

Once they had spread their towels and assessed the direction of the sun, they began to strip off their outer layers. Bronte had obediently put on the costume requested by Jordan and he wore a pair of shorts which reached half way down his thighs. She was secretly relieved he hadn't turned out to be one of those macho men who found it necessary to squeeze themselves into the tightest trunks they could find and arrange their banana-shaped tackle in such a way, that it vastly exaggerated the extent of their manhood. Bronte had witnessed plenty of those on the Caribbean beaches and every time it had made her shudder. In her opinion it was vital to leave all of that to the imagination, particularly on a public beach.

Bronte was very conscious of the tears to the skin on her legs. Although she had been assured there would be no lasting scars, she felt almost ashamed to reveal them so openly to Jordan, and as the fronts were worse than the backs, she decided to lie on her tummy and keep the damage to herself as far as possible.

She was glad that her skin was sufficiently tanned as to not require layers of sun cream on her back, because that would have meant asking him to do the honours and again, she wasn't ready for his touch. Not just then, anyhow.

She stretched herself out, pointing her toes to the water and bringing her hands up into fists on which she rested her chin.

'Comfortable, are we?' He sat cross-legged beside her, his book lay on his towel.

She laughed and arched her back, drawing her buttocks together at the same time: 'Did I take that long?'

'Women always do. You all take sunbathing so seriously.' At least, Chelsea always did.

'Just a minute! In my case, it's because I get to lie out in the sun so seldom that when I do, I like to be prepared for a good session,' she defended herself.

'Well I can't sit still in this heat for long. I'm off for a swim. Coming?' He was up again.

'Men never can, sit still in the sun for long, that is.'

'Accepted. You got me back. Now, are you coming?'

The sun was in her eyes and she put up her hand to shield the glare. He towered over her, his dark hair shining and his white smile like bait, enticing her from her lair. But she felt pinned to the ground by nerves which prickled her skin. Now that they were really alone together, she wasn't entirely sure she could rely on her legs to get her down to the sea, just at that moment.

'You go on ahead, Jordan. I've got this serious sun-bathing to do, remember?' At least her voice did not let her down.

'OK, I'll see you later. Don't overdo the tanning while I'm gone. You might just catch up with me!'

He didn't stay around long enough for the handful of sand, which came hurtling his way to reach him. He had arrived at the sea and was diving head-long into a monster wave almost before he'd left her. She watched him until he disappeared from sight, powering his way out to sea. Taking a deep breath, she lay her head back down on her hands and closed her eyes. Bliss! Hot sun on her back. Dreamy cool air floating off the sea, ready to ward off any danger of over-heating. A finally settled stomach. Peace and quiet reigning

around her. Soft trickles of sand between her fingers. A light
. . . still, lighter head . . .

She had no notion of how long she had been asleep, nor of
when he had returned. She could clearly remember a lengthy
dream which took her back to her days of working for Alex,
but she knew that dreams were deceptive and minutes could
seem like hours. She became aware of a very gentle tickling
sensation on her back and gradually she opened her eyes,
thinking an insect must have taken the wrong turn.

But when she twisted her head to examine the offending
bug, she found that it was not a creepy crawly at all, but a
long green stem of whispering grass which Jordan was using
to draw patterns on her skin. He lay beside her with his
knees bent and his head propped on his hand above one
elbow which dug into the sand. He must have been out of
the sea for some time because the saltwater droplets had
either dried or disappeared.

He noticed her stir and offered her an affectionate smile
by way of explanation: 'Is that annoying you?' he asked her.

'No, actually it's great to wake up to.' She felt paralysed.

'You've been out for nearly an hour,' he informed her,
remaining exactly where he was.

'Have I really?' She could hardly believe it.

'. . . and I've read my book from cover to cover.'

'Liar!' She turned on her side to face him and he quickly
withdrew the strand of grass before it became crushed
beneath her.

'Well, the intention was there at least.' They were only a
few inches apart and he leant across with his free hand to
stroke back the strands of hair which threatened her face.

'Did I ever tell you how much I like your hair?'

She began to tingle: 'Not in so many words. You did once
tell me to wear it loose, though.'

'Quite right . . .' he murmured.

Before she had time to think of a reply, smart or
otherwise, he inclined her face towards his and covered her
lips with his own, moving his body slowly nearer to hers and
putting an arm out to support her head, which sank back
down under the weight of his passion. She kissed him back
with all the force of months of pent-up physical frustration,

as their tongues caressed. She closed her eyes, overcome by the power of his embrace while he continued to cushion her head and with his other hand, nurse the bruised side of her face.

He was the first to pull away, leaving his tongue lingering on the edge of her mouth for a second. She stared into his face, bewitched by the flame which burned strongly in his eyes. She was about to break the spell which had formed over them but he traced his finger from her hair, across her cheek and laid it softly on her lips.

'Hush. Don't say anything,' he whispered and offering her his hand to help her up, he led her silently into the waves, far beyond the sand.

He didn't pause to allow her to adjust to the sharp sting of the cold water, as it lapped around her warm body. She sucked in her already flat stomach to brace herself against the change in temperature, as he dragged her forward until they were at least waist deep. Only then did he let go of her hand to dive into the oncoming surf.

Putting off the final plunge, she stood searching round to see where he would reappear next and she was just beginning to fret that he might have banged his head or something, when she felt herself gripped tightly by the ankles and tipped upside down, all thoughts of remaining dry for one more second drowning as she over-balanced. She only just managed to hold her breath and pinch her nose before she was dunked beneath the swirling surface. However, she was not long under the water because no sooner had she opened her eyes down there, than she was lifted clean out again by one arm under her legs and the other around her middle.

'You looked awfully hot and dry, standing there.' His face sparkled.

'Just you wait!' She wriggled free of his grasp and propelled herself down to the seabed, forging ahead as fast as she could with her hair streaming out behind her. Not only was she a strong swimmer, but she was also very stylish. He followed in hot pursuit, as she had in fact intended for him to do, but each time he tried to snatch at one of her feet, she whipped round and changed direction. It was a game between them to see who could hold their breath the longest, before rising once more for air.

He eventually caught up with her when she darted the wrong way by mistake and ended up face to face with him. They both had to surface at that point because they were laughing too much to remain submerged. Putting his hands round her skimpy waist, he drew her towards him and once more crushed her lips with his, streams of seawater cascading from their foreheads and mingling with their saliva. She responded with equal yearning, entwining her arms around his neck and tilting her head slightly to prevent their noses from interfering with the full flow of their emotions. As they pressed their bodies together and each parted their legs a little to allow a foot in between, she could feel his hardness surging against her pelvis and his tongue bearing further and further into the depths of her throat. She was ready to surrender to him there and then, but the sea had other ideas and sent an enormous wave crashing over the pair of them, rendering their true union out of the question for the time being.

She knew that if she never experienced another day like it in the rest of her life, she wouldn't ever forget the one she spent with Jordan up at Palm Beach. In the years that she had been with Dominic, she had not known such a wealth of passion as had engulfed her that day. As she soaked the sun oil and salt from her pores in a bubble-filled bath later that night, she neither knew nor cared whether the fantasy would last. She massaged her hips and thighs and allowed herself to reason that whatever had happened between them, at least seemed to have been mutual. The fact that each embrace had been instigated by him rather than her, somehow detracted from the little pang of guilt she felt. Raising one leg luxuriously out of the water and watching the froth disappear back into the bath, she was glad their lust had not so far been completely fulfilled. Although in truth, that was more due to circumstance than any measure of control on their part. Certainly not on hers at least.

Regretfully, Jordan had had to cut their special day short in order to get back in time for the Australian Actors'

Benevolent Fund charity dinner, at which he had been asked to present the prize draw. Much as he would have liked to, it was not something he could back out of at that late stage. His attendance had been well-publicised and tickets for the party had been changing hands for exorbitant amounts.

Pledging that if she was still around when he got back, he would be happy to tuck her up, but at the same time not promising to be quite as professional as she had been, he had dropped a kiss on the top of her head before rushing out of the door to the limo. It had been waiting for him for half an hour already.

Bronte didn't mind him going out. In fact she was grateful of the time to bring herself back down to earth. After the previous night, she was quite happy to pamper herself and catch up on a little sleep. She was starting to be nagged by the thought of paperwork building up on her desk and she would need a clear head to tackle that in the morning, if her head would ever be clear again, that was!

Tiredness crept over her like an unwelcome spider, working its way up her body and pricking at her eyelids. Against her better judgement, she had decided to stay up and await Jordan's return after all, telling herself that he would want someone to discuss the evening with. But she had to give in shortly after midnight or he would have discovered her sound asleep on the sofa. Thinking it was probably for the best that she turn in, she padded down the stairs in her oversized slippers and intending to go straight to bed, was lured into Phoebe's room on the way.

The cot remained just as it had the day before, stuffed with every conceivable breed of furry animal. Chelsea had not had room to take any of those with her. Nor had she included the birthday koala, which sat in a lonely heap on the floor. Bronte bent down to pick it up and hugged it to her chest, as she sat down on the single bed.

The room reminded her of the happy days that Phoebe had enjoyed during her short stay in Australia. Days like the Captain Cook Cruise around the harbour, the birthday visit to the zoo, followed by the boat trip and the kangaroo cake. Even the shopping expedition to the Rocks flowed vividly into her mind. Through the open door of the wardrobe, Bronte could see little outfits that had been worn on different occasions, each one conveying its own special memory.

'I miss her too.' Jordan had slipped into the room and one look at her face had betrayed her thoughts.

She turned to him: 'What are we going to do with this lot?' She was referring to the toys and the clothes.

He sank down on the bed beside her, still wearing his dinner jacket and white silk evening scarf.

'I guess they'd better be packed up and sent back home. But there's no hurry. She's got a whole pile of playthings in the apartment in New York and besides, I'm not sure if I can really face doing it yet.' She could see the wound opening afresh.

'I'll do it next week, if you like?' she volunteered.

'Oh, I don't know. I'll probably get round to it. I've got to stop being such a sentimental Dad, because she hasn't died or anything. It just feels like it in here.'

'I know what you mean. I'm getting the same vibes. How was your dinner?'

'Average, I guess. But it was a good job I went. Art had made sure that promotions for the new movie – that's if there's ever going to be a movie at the rate things are falling apart – were on hand at every turn and even the printed menus had my name splashed on the front, right under the charity crest.'

She still clutched the koala, feeling distinctly under-dressed beside him.

'I don't know why I came in here. I was just off to bed.'

'You know, it's strange. Now that I've had a day and a half to get used to the quiet around here, I'm almost beginning to like it. Of course, I'm missing Phoeb' – no mention of Chelsea – 'but somehow it's a relief to know that I'm not going to come home and get annoyed over some domestic disagreement. In a kind of way, its like the calm after the storm.' He fingered the koala's squidgy paw.

Bronte didn't reply. She was trying not to think about Chelsea and the rows she had heard.

'I think I've heaped enough on to you about the state of my marriage to last a lifetime!' He put his arm around her shoulder, sending a pricking sensation running down her spine. 'You've earned yourself an agony aunt – isn't that what you call them? – for the rest of your life, by the way. Just come to me and I swear I'll drop everything.'

Her smile was quickly enveloped in his kiss, just as she was thinking up some troubles to take him up on his offer. With his mouth still pressed hard on hers, he stood up and clasping her to him, carried her down the corridor and into his room. He laid her carefully down on the bed, her dressing gown opening naturally as he did so, revealing just a pair of bikini briefs.

'I think it's about time someone made up for that lack of cuddles you were complaining of recently.'

With one knee on the bed and the other foot still on the floor, he tore off his jacket and struggled with his bow tie.

'Can I do that for you?' She was afraid he would tear the material.

He thrust his chin forwards, planting a kiss on the end of her nose as he did so.

'Hold on! I can't see what I'm doing.' She was laughing as she sat upright and crossed her legs in front of her, peering at the knot which refused, point blank, to co-operate.

The rest of his clothes proved to be far less of a problem as, one by one, they were shed and dumped on the floor. He climbed inside the duvet, throwing it over her at the same time. He flicked the dimmer switch beside the bed which immediately reduced the lighting to a warm, cosy minimum.

She tried to chase away the thought that until very recently, it had been the bed he had shared with his wife. But reading between the lines, she knew that sharing the bed was about all he and Chelsea had done for months. In all other respects, they might have been strangers.

He reached his hand inside her dressing gown and slipped it first over one shoulder and then over the other. She did not resist. He made sure that she was well wrapped in the duvet because he knew that sunburnt skin, however hot to the touch, had a tendency to feel cold at night. The sun and seawater had tightened the scars on her legs and instinctively, she felt for the sore bits. He realised immediately what she was doing and followed her hand down.

'Those stinging?' He stroked her forehead.

'Just a little. It's my own fault. I shouldn't have sat out for so long with no protection on them.'

His fingers entwined hers and brought them back up to where he could kiss each one individually.

'Anything I can do?' he offered with a wink.

'No more than you're already doing.' She felt as if her whole body was melting.

'That's OK then.' He rolled her over and with his mouth, he began to venture into the previously unexplored territory of her eyelids, her ears, her neck, her shoulders and her perfectly-shaped breasts, all the time continuing to hold her protectively to him. She ran the tips of her fingers across the smooth contours of his back, counting his ribs, feeling for the dimples above his buttocks, her breath quickening as he sought out her most secret zones with his tongue.

She knew she was ready for him. That at last she could shed the awkwardness she had feared would creep between her and any lover other than Dominic. But Jordan, who was prepared to comfort her and to keep her safe, was not about to jeopardise any trust she had placed in him until he was entirely certain she was ready to give herself to him as completely as any woman is able to give herself to a man. He realised again, just as he had really known all along, that Bronte was different. She was not some bimbo, starstruck by who he was or what he did. She was much, much more than that and he fully respected her. He would not delude that respect unless he was sure she would have absolutely no regrets. He knew already, that he would have none.

She fell asleep tucked closely in his arms, with her head on his chest and it was long after he heard the steady rhythm of her breathing, that he allowed himself to drift into a state of unconsciousness, with the reassuring warmth of her body conveying a sense of security. That was something which had been lacking from his life for far too long.

CHAPTER TWENTY SEVEN

They were woken on New Year's Eve morning by an unfamiliar sound. Rain! Heavy, pounding rain which teemed down like millions of little needles from a dirty white sky. Bronte had heard the monotonous drumming on the window panes and thought she was still dreaming. But when later she peered outside the front door, it was really true. Great big puddles had formed on the tarmac, as the drops continued to bob on the surface. She knew how delighted their gardener would be at not having to heave the hose pipe around the garden, as he had done every day since they moved into the house. She was also extremely glad that it had picked that day to rain and not the previous one. Things might have been very different had they not shared their precious day on the beach.

Jordan's attitude of 'stuff it' towards the heaps of work was forced to change dramatically after a 'phone call from Art, which interrupted the coffee and croissants that he had secretly rustled up in the kitchen and carried down on a tray to the bedroom.

When the telephone shrilled out loudly enough to rattle in its cradle, it gave Jordan and Bronte such a start that there was a fleeting danger of the white duvet cover playing host to two rivers of black coffee! However, both managed to recover sufficiently to prevent disaster from striking.

'Hello? Oh, it's you. Hi!' Jordan had snatched up the receiver to restore peace to the room. 'It was good, thanks . . .' Art enquired how the charity dinner had gone . . . 'but you didn't tell me you were going to plaster the place with so much hype about the movie.'

- silence -

'Yes, go on, I'm listening. What do you mean, am I sitting down? I'm still in bed, man! It's not even eight thirty, for God's sake!' Art's call was not a social one.

- silence -

'They've said what?! How the hell did they find out? I thought we'd all agreed the day before yesterday, to keep everything under wraps until we'd landed a replacement.'

- silence -

'But they can't do that! We've got a goddamned agreement, haven't we?'

- silence -

'What do you mean, it hasn't been signed yet? Why ever not?'

By that point, Jordan was sitting on the edge of the bed, all thoughts of breakfast driven from his mind. Although Bronte could only hear the one-way conversation, she was rapidly catching the gist of it and she knew all was not well.

'You bet! I'm going to get my ass over there this morning. We need those suckers off our back.'

- silence -

'Yeah, I have got plans for tonight, but we're going to get this straightened out today, right?'

- silence -

'Sure, I could handle it but it'd be better if we hit them together. What time can you be there?'

- silence -

'Not until then?'

- silence -

'OK, I realise that. I've got family too, remember.' He hadn't told Art about Chelsea's departure. He didn't really want to talk about it and he certainly didn't want anything in the press. 'You just get your butt round there and I'll catch up with you.'

- silence -

'I don't care if they say they can't see us. I'm not leaving until we get an extension on that deadline.'

- silence -

'Yes, but we're too far down the road on this one. We should've been shooting next week.'

- silence -

'OK, we'll talk about it later.'

- silence -

'Don't worry, my day isn't completely ruined,' he smiled at Bronte through his frustration and hung up.

As he stood up, he leant over and kissed her on the lips. It was such a natural thing to do. As if he'd done it every day of his life.

'Trouble?' she enquired.

'Nothing we can't handle.' He sounded far more confident than he had on the 'phone. 'I'm going to take a shower. Get dressed and I'll tell you about it.'

He stepped over the discarded pile of clothes, grabbed a towel that had been flung over the chaise-longue and went into the bathroom.

He was already waiting for Bronte in the study when she came in. Things must be serious, she decided, because he wore a formal dark suit that she had not seen before.

He was balanced over the arm of the sofa with a thick file of papers on his thighs. He seemed to be searching intently for something in particular.

'So, fill me in.' She sat down at the desk.

He didn't beat about the bush.

'The main finance company for the movie, the one here in Australia, has somehow got wind that Gianina isn't going to play her part any more and someone has leaked the news to them that we're looking for somewhere else to shoot the house scenes.' He jerked his hand to prevent the papers from sliding off his knee.

'But who told them?'

'That's just what I intend finding out today. I'm meeting Art at their office this morning so we can get to the bottom of it.'

'What have they said?'

'They've only threatened to pull out if we can't produce a replacement actress and location within a week!'

'But they can't do that, can they?' Bronte knew that Jordan had staked a lot on the picture. It was his big directing debut.

'The hell they can't! Apparently, the goddamned contract was never signed.' It was just one more thing he didn't need.

'And you thought it had been?'

360

'It certainly should've been, weeks ago. It's the old story, you can't leave anything to anyone else. It's the lawyers' fault.'

'So what'll you do?' She enjoyed learning from him.

'Get down there and re-convince them that we've got a hot project, that we'll have a lead actress and new location by the end of the month and demand they extend the deadline until then.'

'Will they agree to that, do you think?'

'They'd better,' he warned. Then changing his tune: 'Oh, I don't know.' He smoothed over the layers at the back of his head, still holding the papers in position. 'Sometimes I feel like jacking the whole thing in and wading through some of those other offers. Shedding all the responsibility.'

'There's certainly enough of them pouring in. Your agent told me the other day that he's turning scripts down by the hour.'

'Trouble is, so much effort has gone into this that I need to see it through. Even if it's only to prove to myself that I'm capable of directing my own picture. And another thing, I really think I should get my own life into some sort of shape before I start acting someone else's again. This movie aside, of course.'

That statement was not lost on Bronte.

'Look, I'd better go.' He snapped the papers together and stood up, feeling to make sure his tie was straight. 'Can you do something for me?'

She knew she would be having her work cut out just coping with the backlog in front of her, without any of his additional errands. But she wasn't about to refuse him.

'Yes, what is it?'

He rummaged in his inside jacket pocket and brought out some bits of paper, deliberately shielding them from her sight.

'Can you go into town and get yourself some sort of dress for tonight?' He proceeded to toss a wad of dollar bills on to the desk.

She was speechless! No-one had ever done anything like that to her before and it took a second or two for her to react, by which time he was headed out of the door.

'Jordan, wait!' She grabbed the money and sped after him. 'What do you mean, 'some dress'? I thought you had plans for tonight?' She had never dreamed she was included and was already starting to worry about the public scandal it might cause.

'I do have plans for tonight. It's just that you figure quite highly in them.' He was by the front door.

'Jordan, please wait! What kind of dress am I supposed to buy?'

'Oh, just something pretty.' He was deliberately winding her up, but in the most wonderful way.

'Where are we going?' He was about to start the car.

'Wait and see.' He leant out of the window with a knowing smile.

'I can't. I have no idea what to get,' she protested with her hands on her hips.

'You'll think of something. Oh ... and pack your case too.'

She pretended to boil even more, but in reality, it was with excitement mixed with burning curiosity.

'What on earth for?'

'Be ready by four ... Bye.' He blew her a kiss as he revved the car out of the drive, leaving her in a burst of exhaust and a wealth of cash in her hand. The rain still tipped down.

'Jordan ...' she shouted after him, but he was gone.

Try as she might after that, she was unable to concentrate on anything for more than a few minutes. She was dying to know what he had arranged and whether it would be just the two of them, which she would have far preferred, or whether he was taking her to some party, which was a daunting prospect given the circumstances. She had known for a couple of days that something was organised for New Year's Eve because he had mentioned it casually in passing conversation. But she had not stopped to think for one moment that it was anything more than one of his showbiz engagements and she'd had half a mind to take Angela and Murray up on their offer of staying at Avalon. Of course, now she was only too glad she hadn't called them after all.

In fact, she had not spoken to them since she had left on Boxing Day and it had quite slipped her mind that she had promised to call to let them know she had arrived back safely. It was probably because she had not arrived back safely that she had forgotten to ring and besides, she had had more pressing things on her mind since that day.

It was no good. By noon she was no further ahead with her work than she had been at ten and if she didn't put her best foot forward, she'd not have time to find a dress and be ready for Jordan by four. Why so early? She couldn't imagine. No dinner or party would start at that time. It was becoming more and more intriguing!

A combination of bus, ferry and another bus delivered her to the doors of the David Jones department store. She had made for there because she really didn't know where else to go. Certainly not for the kind of dress that Jordan expected her to buy. But that was just it, what was he expecting? She had enough money to choose the finest designer gown, probably about the amount that Chelsea spent on her outfits. Whoops, she was trying to lock Chelsea out of her mind. It was all too complicated to bring her into the equation now.

The windows of the store were as inviting as the atmosphere inside. No expense had been spared with the spangly silver and gold decorations which glittered and chimed in true festive spirit. Tiny little fairy lights flickered above the makeup and perfume counters which was the first department she ventured through. Christmas music still sang out from speakers raised high above the customers' heads, as if anyone needed reminding of the time of year.

The store, which had already begun its summer sale, was bustling with bargain hunters shoving themselves ahead of the competition and shopaholics, anxious to spend their Christmas money before it burnt a hole in their pockets. Bronte had no idea where the fashion area was and so began to seek out a floor guide. Clutching her bag tightly to her side for fear of unwelcome pickpockets – she almost felt like a criminal herself, carting all that cash around – she stumbled across the up escalator by chance and stepped aboard. It brought her, luckily, into the right department and so there was no need to look further.

Cleverly, most of the sale chaos had been deliberately confined to the ground floor and she might have entered another shop altogether, for the peace and quiet she encountered up there. There were a few stereotyped ladies, oozing wealth, and flashing enormous rocks on their fingers, ears and just about anywhere else they could show them off, clad in exactly the same sort of designer wear that they now looked through on the rails. That type of department the world over attracted such ladies like bees to a honeypot, which was partly why Bronte normally avoided them at all costs. But that day was different, she had no choice.

'Can ay be of help to you, modom?' That was certainly not an Australian accent. It was more like something out of Sloane Street!

'I'm just looking, thanks.' Bronte eyed the blue-rinse wig and the overdone orange lipstick suspiciously, but not nearly as suspiciously as the shop assistant eyed Bronte. She knew those types. Tourists, even if some of them were from the same country as she. They couldn't afford any of the garments in her exclusive department, even if they mortgaged their houses which most of them didn't own anyway.

'Was it something in particular that modom had in maind?' She didn't want this one handling more of her clothes than she could help.

'Actually, I'm after a dress.' Bronte knew she wouldn't be left alone.

'Ay see. And what sort of praice range was modom considering?' Might as well dispense with her that way.

Bronte thought that if she was called modom one more time, there was a serious danger of her slapping the woman across the face. Wig or no wig.

'It doesn't really matter. My husband has given me carte-blanche.' There, stick that in your pipe and smoke it! After all, she was still wearing her wedding ring.

The shop assistant was surprised. Perhaps this one might be worth pursuing after all. There was no doubt she was a very attractive girl – probably a model, in which case it was possible she had a rich husband who could afford to send her to the Ladies Designer floor of David Jones! Shame about the clothes she had come in wearing, though. Still, her commission percentage crept to mind.

'Would this be for a particular function?' She took a step back and turned her hands inside out.

'Yes. For tonight, as a matter of fact.' Bronte tried to look past her at some of the evening dresses hanging on the rails.

'What kaind of dress did modom feel would be appropriate for the occasion?'

Bronte gritted her teeth. That was a good question. If she knew what the occasion was, it might have been easier to give a straight answer.

'Can I see a selection?' That was a way out.

'Certainly. Please come this way.'

Bronte was shown a rail of garments, ranging from 'Ascot racing garb' to 'a night at the opera'.

'These are all about modom's saize. Perhaps I maight suggest trying one or two on? The fitting rooms are raight here.' She still wasn't keen on Bronte 'handling' too many of her garments but if she bought at least one, and preferably one of the most expensive of the collection, that would make up for it.

The majority of the outfits reminded Bronte of the type of thing women wore when they were trying to look twenty years younger than they actually were, all frills and fuss and far from the classical and more simple lines that went with chic and elegance. There was only one in the end that came anywhere near to what she would consider wearing and when she looked at the label inside, she was not surprised to see that it was made by one of the most famous French fashion houses.

'I think I'll try this one. I know the rest wouldn't suit me.'

Torn between delight that Bronte had selected just about the most expensive choice on the rail and horror that she could even think to say that the remainder of the garments, which she herself considered to be the most fabulous couture, would 'not suit me', the shop assistant pulled back the curtain of the changing room without another word. That was just as well, because Bronte had already had more than enough of her.

Praying that she would be left in peace long enough to make up her own mind as to whether she really liked the dress, she hurriedly stripped off her clothes and slipped into it, fighting at first with the zip at the back. But the infuriating voice, with a sizeable commission cheque now firmly imprinted on the mind, soon found its way through the curtain.

'Is everything alraight for modom?'

'Modom's fine, thank you.' She knew she shouldn't have imitated her but she just couldn't help herself.

'Is she happy with the outfit?' Perhaps she had taken the hint after all?

'I haven't quite got it on yet.' She lied.

'Well do let me know if there's anything ay can do.'

'Thank you. Won't be a minute.' Bronte thought she'd better try and behave herself.

The outfit consisted of a finely-cut, straight sleeveless dress in black velvet, with a scooped neckline and a contrasting jacket. Bronte liked it for the fact that it was flattering and elegant. The dress was complemented by the short bolero jacket made of emerald green taffeta. It might have been made for her. The size was perfect and the shade of green always went well with her own colouring.

'Are we ready now?' Modom had been wisely substituted by the royal 'we'.

Bronte had already made up her mind to buy it. After all, if it turned out not to be appropriate, it was hardly her fault. But at least it catered for most eventualities – black tie, warm weather, cooler weather, cocktails . . . Yuk, the very thought of cream cocktails!

'I think I'll take it, thank you,' she replied briskly to the assistant who couldn't wait any longer to feast her eyes on the vision in her fitting room.

'Oh, a very waise decision. We do look most attractive, maight I add,' and she really did have to admit to herself that Bronte looked absolutely stunning! 'Pass it out to me when you're ready and ay'll have it wrapped.'

She withdrew to find her calculator . . . let me see . . . three percent of . . . she would really have to find her spectacles before she could see those wretched buttons. But glasses were so unbecoming.

'Ay do hope your husband will laike the choice.' She was at least taking time and trouble over the tissue paper.

'So do I.' That was definitely true.

'A dinner party, would it be?' Her eyes nearly popped out of her head when she saw the stack of notes which Bronte handed over.

'Something like that.' She didn't feel like sharing her excitement with that woman.

'A surpraise, perhaps? Some men are so romantic, doesn't one agree?' Bronte thought it unlikely that anyone could possibly feel in the least bit romantic around that assistant. No-one who was of sound hearing and sight, that was.

'Yes.' In the end it was easier to agree, plus the fact that she certainly did find Jordan extremely romantic.

'Thank you, modom, and goodbaie . . .'

That was quite enough for Bronte. She was off without so much as a backward glance.

As she wandered out of the shop, a smart white bag with gold lettering and white cord handles under her arm, Bronte felt relieved that despite the sales assistant, the whole operation had gone so smoothly. It had not taken her nearly as long as she had thought it might and she still had plenty of time to get back home and pack a case. That, in itself, would be a task because she literally had no idea what she would need for wherever it was he had in mind to take her. Nonetheless, she was brimming over with anticipation . . . and nerves.

CHAPTER TWENTY EIGHT

'Well?' demanded Bronte, as Jordan stepped into the front hall just before four that afternoon.

'Well, what?' His expression gave nothing away.

'Well, what happened today? Did you get the extension or not?'

She was desperate to know whether the movie project was in imminent danger of collapse.

'Come here first ...' He pulled her into his arms and kissed her full on the lips.

'Jordan! Tell me. Or can I take it from your enthusiasm that you did?' She pretended to struggle free.

'You know what you should do is ...' he was deliberately spinning it out, 'have faith.'

'You did it?!' She was relieved and very impressed.

'Of course we did it! Went right in there and made those sonofabitches listen to everything we had to say without letting them get a word in edgeways. We made such a good case about how much money they would end up making out of the movie that even I was getting excited for them!'

'Well done!' She threw her arms about his neck in a natural expression of congratulations.

'Hey! You're strangling me.' He caught her arms, which immediately made her blush for being so forward. 'More importantly, did you get what you had to today?'

'Wait and see!' She tried to cover her embarrassment by playing him at his own game.

'I guess I asked for that, didn't I? Never mind, I'll find out soon enough. Are you all packed, because we'll have to go soon?'

'Considering I have absolutely no idea what I'm supposed to be packing for, nor for how long, I can't really tell you.

But if you mean have I got my toothbrush, then that's just about all I have got.'

'In other words, you are?'

'I suppose so. Are we taking Art's car?' There couldn't be any harm in telling her that much.

But predictably, he didn't stop to give her a straight answer, even to that question. Instead he rushed towards the stairs, saying over his shoulder in the most infuriatingly cryptic way: 'Where we're going, honey, we aren't going to need cars!'

She had no alternative but to gather her small overnight bag from her room, and the suit hanger, which now contained her new outfit, and wait for his direction.

The limo arrived to collect them, just two minutes after four. She was grateful that she didn't recognise the chauffeur from any previous occasion. She thought there would be less chance of his mind working overtime as to Bronte's role in the backseat beside Jordan, if he was a new face. She had already made up her mind that wherever it was they were going, she would conduct herself with the utmost discretion and avoid all public attention wherever possible. That was always assuming that they were going somewhere where they might meet the general public. It would certainly do Jordan no good at all for some gossip seeker to get a hint of anything that was going on between them, whatever that might be.

The window between the front and the back of the limo was firmly closed against all fraternisation and the darkened glass afforded them a good deal of privacy, as they sped through the afternoon traffic.

'Jordan, if I didn't know better, I'd say we were on the road to the airport?' Bronte turned to him after having studied the route carefully for a few moments.

He didn't reply. Just flexed his legs and stretched his arm along the back of the seat, but without actually touching her.

'Aren't you a little over-dressed for the airport?' she teased, trying to prise even the smallest clue from him.

'I didn't get the chance to change. Besides, I wanted to keep up with you.' He was referring to the linen shorts and jacket she had selected, hoping they would be suitable for wherever she was going.

'Yes, but I didn't know we were going to the airport and you did.'

'It looks great to me. Besides, I like to travel in style.'

Try as she might, she could get no further information from him and in the end she gave up, resigning herself to the idea that it would become clearer to her once they reached the airport. At that point, she would learn where it was they were flying to – assuming that they were flying. But then why else would they he going to the airport? On the other hand, anything was possible with Jordan.

Even on New Year's Eve, there was a rush hour traffic of sorts which had to be negotiated before they could reach the other side of town. It took them little short of an hour and ten minutes to get there, and although there was no sense of panic, Jordan did seem anxious not to hang around once they drew up outside the departure building. They were immediately approached by an elderly porter, who by degree of seniority had appointed himself in charge of escorting the wealthier customers to the check-in desks. Bronte couldn't help thinking it was just as well that their luggage was so small and light, otherwise the porter looked as if he'd never have managed it.

'That's us. This way.' Jordan heard a loud speaker announce the last call for passengers leaving on the five-thirty flight to Cairns.

'Cairns?' questioned Bronte, as Jordan presented the tickets to the stewardess on the desk.

But Jordan pretended not to hear. Noticing out of the corner of her eye that two girls, three desks down from them had undoubtedly recognised Jordan, Bronte hung back and didn't push the point. Not then at least.

But she definitely brought it up again once they were settled in the small First Class cabin of the 'plane, sipping a glass of champagne which had been thrust into their hands almost before they had been shown to their seats.

'What happens in Cairns that doesn't happen in Sydney?' Bronte couldn't imagine. She had heard of Cairns but she had no idea what happened there.

'We're not going to Cairns.' He was thoroughly enjoying stringing her along. In fact, he couldn't remember when he last derived so much pleasure from flirting.

She pretended to choke on her champagne.

'If we're not going to Cairns, then what are we doing on a 'plane that's taking us there?' She was enjoying it as much as he. She was almost getting to the stage where she didn't want to know where they were going for fear of disappointment.

She need not have worried.

'OK, that wasn't strictly true. I admit we are going to Cairns, but only to go on somewhere else after that.'

'Straight away?' she asked.

'Yes, straight away. Actually, we don't even have to leave the airport if the 'plane I've fixed is there.'

'What do you mean, 'plane you've fixed'?' Was there no end to his surprises?

'The one I've chartered to take us on from Cairns.'

The stewardess beamed a charming smile as she refilled their glasses. Jordan Innes' secret was safe with her. She wasn't about to spoil the good time he was having with that English girl. Besides, she didn't want anyone to know about her and the pilot, so why should she sneak on someone else?

She was also pleased for them that the other seats in First Class were only reserved on the journey out of Cairns and not the one from Sydney. That way, Jordan and his 'friend' would remain undetected, not to mention the fact that she could get to sit down for a little while to recover from her own activities in the airport hotel bedroom that afternoon!

'You've hired your own 'plane? Just for us?' She'd heard of rich stars doing things like that, but she'd never dreamed for one moment that she'd ever get to experience it too.

'Sure. The connections weren't great so it was the best way to get there. And I wanted to be certain we'd make it for dinner.'

'This is an awfully long way to go for dinner, isn't it?' she asked, praying her dress would be suitable after all.

'You haven't tasted the dinner yet.'

'Have you ordered that too?' Although she was trying not to look surprised, he wasn't ceasing to amaze, and thrill her.

'Certainly have! It's not every day I get to escape like this.' Looking at her genuine expressions of sheer innocent delight after each of his answers, made the whole trip more than worth while to him already. He wanted to savour every minute and lock them away tight, just in case he never experienced anything like it again. He knew it was all a little risky in terms of publicity, but he was so firmly trapped on that runaway train that he just couldn't get off – nor make it stop. Not for a while at least.

Yes, and it's not everyday someone organises such a wonderfully romantic trip for me, thought Bronte! In fact, she couldn't recall any unexpected occasions that Dominic had arranged without her knowing. She had always been the one to suggest, and indeed book, their holidays and even dinners together. So it was something totally new for her and she was treasuring every second as it unfolded before her eyes.

'So, let me go over the established facts.' She wasn't letting the subject drop. 'We're flying to Cairns, but we're not going to Cairns. We're picking up a private 'plane in Cairns to take us somewhere else. When we get to this 'somewhere else', we're having a dinner which you've already ordered. Right so far?'

'Yup!' He rolled up the sleeves of his white shirt and just looking at the tanned skin covered with dark smooth hairs made her feel sensual all over.

'Will there be anybody else at this dinner?' She prayed not and about that at least, he didn't want to disappoint her.

'No, just us. I hope it won't be too boring?' he teased and leaned round to kiss her, preventing her answer which he was convinced he could predict anyway.

When Jordan Innes personally booked something, it usually happened just so. At least that had been the case in recent years and so he had every reason to believe that the 'plane he had chartered would be waiting on the tarmac for them when they arrived in Cairns. He wasn't let down. There was a representative from the airline waiting at the door to deliver the only First Class passengers to the small, twin-engined 'plane which was fuelled and ready for take off.

They had to duck to prevent striking their heads as they climbed into the 'plane. Bronte, who was used to island hopping on her Caribbean jaunts, had travelled in similar 'planes several times before and her distinct recollections of those journeys were of the deafening roar of the engines and the unstable sensation of the flight, particularly when they encountered air pockets or clouds. Thank goodness the weather was behaving itself better in Cairns than it had been in Sydney that day.

Apart from the pilot and the co-pilot, whose cockpit with its maze of dials and buttons was clearly visible from the cabin, Jordan and Bronte were alone for the short flight.

As the propellers began to turn, the co-pilot shouted over his shoulder: 'A bit of engine noise, mate. Sit tight and we'll have this baby airborne in a moment.'

Jordan gave Bronte a reassuring hug, not entirely sure whether she was frightened or not. But he wasn't taking any chances and she was secretly grateful for the comfort of his protective arm around her shoulders.

'Been to Dunk before then, mate?' The co-pilot again.

'No. I've not had the time before.' Jordan had to yell.

The 'plane tilted suddenly as it was buffeted about like a snowflake by an unexpected surge of air pressure. Bronte gripped the arm rest, a gesture which wasn't lost on Jordan.

'Great weather they've been having over there. You've picked a good time to come ...' The co-pilot's words were drowned by the engine. Jordan didn't bother to fight out a reply.

'Isn't Dunk Island on the Barrier Reef?' Bronte didn't have to make quite so much effort to be heard, with Jordan just next to her.

'Yes, that's right,' he acknowledged.

'Is that where we're going, then?' she asked, as her eyes shone at the prospect of spending time with him on one of the Great Barrier Reef islands she had heard Chris rave about!

'Nope!' The mystery wasn't over yet.

'No? But why are we flying there if we're not going there, then?' She was confused because she had been convinced that there couldn't be any more surprises in store. But she was wrong.

'Because we're going on from there by boat!' He grinned at her knowingly.

'Honestly Jordan! Just tell me one thing. Are we going to be travelling all night? Is this dinner you talked about, today or tomorrow? The suspense is killing me!'

'Don't let it do that. It'd be pretty lonely without you at this place. Look, I'll come clean so you can stop fretting. We pick up a launch at Dunk which takes us on to another island called Bedarra. And that, oh worried face, is all you need to know.'

He fingered her hair, teasing it out of the tie she had bound it into behind her head.

'This launch . . . another private arrangement?' She really must have been dreaming that time.

But he nodded. He would not have organised anything less. After all the nightmares he had endured recently, he wanted at least to guarantee that the time they spent on Bedarra would be perfect. He had already shut his mind to the rights and wrongs of what he was doing and thought only of the good time he was about to have. He was also going to make damned sure she had a good time too. She had also been down a rocky road and now that he felt confident of their mutual attraction, he was going to pull out all the stops.

Everything fell exactly into place as if they were the only two souls existing on a solitary planet. The launch was hugging the dockside, ready to sweep them off to their paradise island and, apart from being offered a few light refreshments, they were left alone on deck to drink in the ambience of the balmy, still evening.

The light was gradually beginning to fade as they left Dunk Island, arm in arm, leaning on the rope railings of the polished wooden deck, gazing across a millpond of cobalt blue waters.

'This is stunning, Jordan!' Bronte couldn't remember any of the Caribbean scenery captivating her so entirely.

'It's pretty neat out there. I was worried when I saw the rain back in Sydney this morning, but I guess we couldn't ask for anything better now.' His suit jacket had been discarded on a seat behind them. He had no need of it.

374

'I just can't get over how quiet it is!' The boat seemed to provide the only hum in an oasis of tropical beauty.

'I decided to leave the rent-a-crowd team behind. But we could always call them up if you're missing the company!' There weren't too many times when he was serious, which made the ones when he was even more special to her.

'What are you going on about? This is heaven! I don't want to see one single other person for as long as I'm here.' She was adamant.

'Madam, your wish is my command.' How she'd longed for someone to say that to her. Just once in her life. 'But you might have to put up with the odd waiter bearing iced drinks or a maid here and there,' he added with a wink.

'I think I can just about stand that.'

As they drew towards their final destination on Bedarra Island, Bronte still found it hard to believe that she wasn't imagining everything. She had spent much of her time dreaming since Dominic had died, most of it leaving her feeling miserable, lonely or empty. So far, she'd never experienced anything which had made her feel so alive. So wanted. So loved.

It was as if she were floating on air, as they emerged from the lush virgin rainforest and arrived at the Polynesian-style resort, nestling amongst the swaying palms. She was barely aware of Jordan registering their arrival briefly at the reception, before they were ferried on a little mobile cart to an enchanting native-style cabin, with a natural vegetation roof and outer walls, situated in a secluded clearing well away from the main hotel facilities.

Inside the bedroom and the living areas were sumptuously furnished with the most uncompromising attention to detail and comfort. The adjustable lighting could be lowered to create a cosy effect against the varnished wooden walls. In the bedroom, a delicate lace covering was spread over the king-sized bed and soft ivory cushions were scattered to help create a homely atmosphere. The marble-effect bathroom led off the bedroom at the back of the cabin and in there, Bronte found an abundance of thick, cream bath towels neatly folded and draped over wooden rails.

She ran through the rooms like a child with a new toy, pointing out this and that to a bemused Jordan, almost as if she had never stayed away from home before. But this was like nothing she had ever seen before.

She stopped dead in her tracks when she spied the dinner table in one corner of the living area, with the crisp white cloth and matching napkins and the two candles flickering from little glass tulips. The silverware was laid expertly to cater for all six courses Jordan had requested! She had never seen so many pieces of cutlery on one table in her life.

'Is all this for the dinner you have been keeping such a secret?' She looked at him in awe, her eyes growing larger and rounder with every word.

'Yeah. Do you like it?' His former confidence slipped momentarily.

'Like it? I *love* it! How could I not? But what on earth are we going to eat with all those knives, forks and spoons? There's enough for ten people!'

'I can assure you that we're not about to entertain ten people.'

He was interrupted by the uniformed porter who had brought them over in the cart and who, while Bronte had been marvelling at all the luxuries, had been showing Jordan the well-stocked fridge and explaining the radio, the telephone system and the air conditioning, which Jordan immediately turned up to maximum.

'If that will be all, Sir?' He was never comfortable around young lovers.

'Yes, I'm sorry.' Jordan had almost forgotten he was still in the room. 'This is great, thanks.'

'Your dinner will arrive in approximately twenty minutes, Sir. We have arranged for a warming trolley to be delivered as you requested. Can I just check that you did not require any waiters for this evening, Sir?'

'No, thanks. We'll manage.'

'The waiter who brings your dinner will explain, but if you leave the trolley on your terrace, we need not disturb you to collect it later.' It wouldn't be the first time that staff had walked in on embarrassing scenes in those cabins. They seemed to attract all the honeymooners. Wonder if those two were on their honeymoon?

He withdrew silently, closing the door behind him and leaving a disbelieving Bronte staring after him.

'What was all that about waiters?'

'I thought we could do it ourselves. With six courses, we'd have them trooping in and out permanently otherwise.'

'Six courses! Jordan, where am I going to put that much food?'

'You only have to taste a bit of each. Besides, you mightn't like them all.' He was so sincere that she felt guilty for making light of it. Again her thoughts flitted fleetingly to Chelsea, for whom she was certain he would have never have thought of arranging a six-course meal.

'You should get that dress on that I've been waiting to see. Now you've had all my surprises, let's see what you've been hiding.'

'Twenty minutes doesn't give me long!' She looked at her watch in a panic and hurried into the bedroom to check whether she would need to order an iron. But there was one already in the wardrobe, had she required it, which fortunately she did not.

As it was the only part of the whole evening he had not been able to plan to the very last detail, she didn't want him to see her dressed until she had put all the finishing touches to her makeup and had made sure she had done everything she could to enhance her appearance. She therefore took her few possessions into the bathroom and closed the door, throwing him a playful look as she went.

'This is going to be worth waiting for, I can tell.' He was prickling with anticipation.

He wasn't about to be disappointed. She emerged about ten or fifteen minutes later, looking lovelier than he had ever thought possible. She glided out of the bathroom, the taffeta whooshing as she fiddled anxiously with the black velvet clasp she had used to sweep some of her hair on top of her head. She suddenly felt very nervous and terribly vulnerable, when she noticed that he, too, had changed, into black tie and dinner jacket.

He whistled as he took in the sleek black-stockinged legs,

the slim hips, the tiny waist, the merest hint of a cleavage between her uplifted breasts and her radiant face with its deliciously worried look, surrounded by the locks of cascading copper which he found so hypnotising.

'You look a million dollars!' He hadn't imagined she could produce such an effect on him.

'Are you sure you approve?' she asked quietly, relieved that she appeared to have passed the test – one she had been dreading when she knew how accustomed he must have been to Chelsea's expensive tastes.

'I have never seen you look so beautiful! May I?' He extended his hand to lead the way into the other room.

The meal had been delivered only moments before and Jordan had been instructed as to which cupboard he needed to open to serve each of the dishes. He was determined not to have Bronte work that night. She had earned a few hours off.

He had placed the crudités and the Kir Royales on the small table beside the swing seat on the terrace and it was to there that he took her first, thinking they should at least get some idea of how the land lay around them.

'Oh Jordan, this is amazing! How did you ever find out about this place?' she asked, as she sat carefully down on the seat which immediately began to sway gently beneath her.

'Art, who else?' But what he kept from her was the fact that when he had first made enquiries some time ago, he had originally planned to take Chelsea there as a last desperate attempt to save their floundering marriage. Now that he was there with Bronte, he admitted to himself that it had been more with her in mind that he had thought of his little escape over the recent weeks.

'Cheers!' She chinked his glass and took a sip from her own. 'Is that the sea I can hear?'

'I guess so. Each of these places is supposed to have its own private access to the beach, so ours must be that way.' He pointed to a little winding path leading through the scented tropical gardens.

He could easily have sat there for hours, her by his side, listening to the native sounds of the rainforest but he also did not want to spoil the food he had spent so much time choosing, and so once she had drained the last drop of her Kir, he suggested they retire inside.

She was touched by the way he produced each dish, course after course, from exactly the right place, almost as if it was a well-rehearsed play he was enacting. Little would she ever have suspected that deep down, he was almost as nervous as she and that by getting up and down to clear and bring out the next offering and refusing all her suggestions of assistance, he felt more in control of himself.

Each portion was minute, which was just as well because neither of them was terribly hungry. However, that did not detract from the romantic atmosphere which filled the room, created by the soft candlelight, the warm night air and two people who were obviously falling in love.

Finally, just as Bronte thought she would burst if she saw another single morsel of food, Jordan put a green glass bowl in front of her in which had been arranged three precisely peeled segments of fresh orange in a grand marnier syrup. She didn't even notice as those went down!

'I don't think I'll ever move again after all that.' She groaned as she folded her napkin onto the table.

'That's the whole idea. To keep you as my prisoner!' The truth was, she rather liked the idea of that.

'Then I surrender. If you ever get tired of the movie business, I think you might find a new vocation.'

'You do? And what might that be?' he enquired, looking into her eyes where the candlelight danced suggestively.

'As a waiter,' she teased him.

He laughed and threw his crumpled napkin on to his plate in protest.

'Come on, young lady, I need a walk to settle all that food into some place or other, and you're coming with me.'

'But what about all that 'prisoner' bit?' She pretended to argue, but really she couldn't think of a better idea. Had she known what she was expected to stuff into it, she might have had second thoughts about the 'fitted' dress. But on the other hand, she knew what a success it had been with Jordan and that was far more important than a little discomfort.

'Don't worry! I'm not about to let you out of my sight

under any circumstances, for a good number of hours.' It was getting better and better!

She quickly used the bathroom and checked her face in the mirror while he piled the plates back into the trolley and pushed it outside.

He held the door for her, letting it swing back shut afterwards. They didn't even think to lock it. It was as if they had found a little tiny corner of paradise all to themselves, undisturbed by dangers or other people.

As they wandered down the leafy path, arms entwined, each needing to be as near to the other as possible, they soon emerged on to the palm-fringed beach. Bronte stooped to remove her shoes so that she could feel the powdery sand between her toes.

'It isn't far to go if you need to cool off,' Jordan remarked on the ideal location of the sea, which at that time, lapped seductively at the shore with lace frills of froth bobbing here and there.

'Just right for an early morning dip,' agreed Bronte, looking forward to it already.

'Or a moonlight one?' It was a mere suggestion.

'I don't want to ruin my dress. It's the most expensive thing I've ever owned!' She didn't relish the thought of leaving it in a heap on the sand, even for him.

'I wouldn't let you. I need to see that again and again to remind me of tonight.' He squeezed her a little tighter to him.

'Jordan, if this is a dream and I do wake up from it, whenever that might be, I want you to know that nothing like this has ever happened to me before . . .'

He stopped her in her tracks and cradled her cheeks with his hands.

'This is not a dream.' He was very serious, as their lips parted and she swallowed his words in a single breath.

After a few minutes they strolled on further, still encountering no other signs of life. Neither would have changed a single word of the script – it was perfect just the way it was.

'That far enough?' They had been gone for quite some time and Jordan didn't want to tire her.

'I could probably just about sit down without splitting the

seams now.' But she wouldn't have minded if he'd suggested walking to the ends of the earth at that precise moment.

'There's a bottle of champagne which needs uncorking back there.'

'Are you trying to tell me something about my drinking, because I'm feeling pretty light-headed already?' She pulled away for a second.

'Never crossed my mind, I swear. But it'd be a pity to waste it.'

'If you give me much more to drink tonight, I won't make the afternoon dip tomorrow, let alone the morning one!' she threatened.

'Let tomorrow take care of itself,' he murmured into her ear, as he began to kiss her once more.

After some deliberation and a couple of wrong decisions, they managed to locate the right path back to their cabin. When they reached it, they discovered that the food trolley had been removed which was just as well, because neither felt like being disturbed as they mounted the steps to the door.

'Wait!' He said it with such suddenness that she started, fearing something was wrong. But instead, in one sweeping gesture he picked her up and carried her over the threshold, not pausing in the living room but taking her straight to the bedroom and laying her tenderly on the bed, which had also been turned down in their absence by a discreet maid.

That time, there was no struggle with their clothes, which seemed to fall away, all thoughts of champagne forgotten. He covered her naked silken body with the fresh-smelling white sheet as he slipped in beside her, just able to make out her form in the hazy light of the room.

She lay on her back reciprocating his flame and his passion with every ounce of energy in her body. His tongue ignited a burning fire of lust within her as it slid from her mouth, to her neck, across her chest to her breasts and settled around her nipples, sucking the ever-hardening rosebuds and making her squirm beneath his erotic embrace.

She put out her hand and engulfed his pulsating excitement, causing him to groan softly and venture still further with his tongue. But still he did not enter her.

She climbed higher and higher, forgetting who she was, where she was, what she was, but never whom she was with. That was something she would never forget. As if in a trance, she gave herself up to her Cupid – to his mouth, which sank to kiss the depths of her stomach and then her hips, before burying itself between her legs – and to his hands, which seemed to know instinctively just how to render her powerless to resist his spell. But still he did not enter her.

She began to pant rhythmically, certain that she would not manage to hold out much longer, when all of a sudden he looked to her face and slowly began to climb up her body until he was lying directly on top of her. His eyes became level with hers and his legs were outstretched between her parted ones.

She was frightened for a moment that she had done something wrong. That she was not satisfying him in the way he was satisfying her, like no lover before him. However, that could not have been further from the truth and he had to summon all the willpower he could find to stop caressing that adorable creature, even for a second.

But he had to know for certain that she was really ready for him.

'Are you sure you want this as much as I do?' he whispered, stroking the hair from her moistened cheek.

She nodded, incapable of instructing her lips to co-ordinate with her brain, and feeling faint beneath his melting gaze.

'Only I don't want to you to hurt inside afterwards.' He fingered the breast around her heart.

The only thing she knew for certain was that she couldn't bear for him to stop there – the rest she would worry about later, if it needed to be worried about. By way of response, she pulled his face down on to hers and lifted her knees to allow their love to be consummated at last.

He entered her finally, but so very gently that she was barely aware of the actual penetration. All the time he continued to reassure her with meaningful kisses which became more and more powerful as their bodies moved steadily together. Neither were able to control their desires for long, but he waited until he heard her soft moans become stronger and stronger, and until she arched her back and cried out in a crescendo of sheer ecstasy, ever increasing his rhythm to be sure of not robbing her of a single second of pleasure. In so doing, he was no longer able to hold back and allowed himself to come inside her with all the force of the love which now surged within him.

As they lay spent, breathless in each other's arms, an air of calm fell about them – the feeling that something wonderful and magical had just taken place between them. There was no need to capture it with words because what they felt for each other had been amply conveyed by their very beings, just moments earlier.

For Bronte it was as if a great weight had been lifted from her shoulders. She had never imagined that the first lover after Dominic could happen so soon, would put her so selflessly before himself and feel so right. In fact, she had not previously dared to imagine any lover after Dominic in case she became tormented by guilt. But just as she had laid his body to rest in that leafy grave, so now she knew she had laid his spirit to rest also. What had happened between Jordan and her was just the natural progression of their relationship.

As for Jordan, he too had had a weight removed, but his was of a far more confusing nature.

As he had suspected, he knew then that for him his marriage could never be the same again, if indeed he and Chelsea were to be reconciled. He also knew just how much he had craved the physical reciprocation of one as fiery as Bronte, to rekindle emotions that had been seeping away from him, driven by so much rejection and pain. He had no idea where it would go from there, if anywhere. All he knew for the moment was that she had made him feel happier than he could remember for a long time and that he wanted that sensation to go on and on. He didn't want to think any more or to allow reason or judgement to cloud that happiness and so he turned and began to make love to her all over again.

CHAPTER TWENTY NINE

They had made love through the night with all the urgency of two people making up for lost time and again, as the dewy light of a fresh morning flooded their bedroom, they fell upon each other once more.

Jordan eventually dragged himself out of bed to mix them a long tall glass of champagne and freshly squeezed orange juice which they shared together, whilst gazing out past the wooden shutters at the mystical beauty of the rain forest, beyond which lay the azure waters of the blue lagoon.

'Happy?' He cuddled her against his chest.

'Umm . . .'

'Reservations?' He could sense her mind was busy.

'Not for myself. Well, not really.'

'You want to talk about it?' He had an idea of what she might say.

'I'm not really sure how to.' She needed to air what she had been thinking, but then again, she was afraid it might tarnish the course of the love she had discovered.

'How about just coming out with it?' He didn't want to prompt her more than that.

She plucked up courage at least to make a start, which afterwards she felt she had bungled somewhat: 'It's just . . . well, it's . . . it wouldn't be so bad if I didn't know her . . .' She was stumbling.

'Chelsea? Is it Chelsea?' He spoke the name she had found so hard to say.

She nodded.

'As long as it's Chelsea and not Dominic, then we can deal with it.'

She looked puzzled: 'But she's still your . . .'

He interrupted her gently, but firmly: 'Shh, and listen. Chelsea is part of another world, far from here. This, here, is our world and someone somewhere has seen fit to introduce us to it. I know Chelsea is something I shall have to face before too long, there's no point in pretending she doesn't exist, but right now you, my darling, are all that counts. You and this heavenly place which is waiting out there for us.'

She wasn't entirely sure that he had allayed her fears but then, being one of life's realists, she knew that that was not possible. She also knew it was more than likely she would be a transient feature in his life and that it all had inevitably to end somewhere. However, for as long as it lasted she would cherish the dream, resorting to it for inspiration at times in the future when her life might sink to a low ebb.

'You're frowning!'

She hadn't even noticed: 'Am I?' She raised her eyelids to full mast and snuggled a little closer to him.

'Yes, you are, and I'll tell you something else, we have both forgotten that it's New Years Day!'

She sat up: 'You're absolutely right! Happy New Year.'

She straddled him playfully and planted a loving kiss on each cheek.

'If you carry on like that, we'll never see the outside of this room today.' He could feel himself stir once more. He began to tickle her.

'I'm starving!' She wriggled from his grasp.

'Didn't you eat much last night?' he teased her.

'That was hours ago and besides, I feel like I've run a marathon since then.' She trotted towards the bathroom.

'You're not far wrong. I'll order room service and get us some breakfast.' He lifted the receiver beside the bed.

'I hope they're still serving it. After all, it's nearly eleven,' she noticed as she splashed her face with cold water.

'That shouldn't pose a problem to a place like this.'

Bronte was suddenly reminded of the exorbitant amount that Jordan must have spent on their trip so far – First Class flights from Sydney – private 'plane – private launch – six course meal and of course, the hotel which she knew would be probably cost more per night than her flat in London had per month. That was not forgetting her outfit which she would need to rescue from the floor of their bedroom!

*   *   *

The resort prided itself on ensuring that its guests wanted for nothing and that it gave them no cause whatsoever for complaint. Therefore, in line with tradition, the breakfast Jordan ordered arrived at their door within minutes of him putting down the 'phone. They only just had time for a brief shower together before a knock at the door sent them scurrying for the bathing robes.

'Good morning, Mr Innes . . . Mrs Innes . . . your breakfast.'

For a moment, Bronte was taken aback by the greeting but she could tell from the waiter's face that the word Innes meant no more to him than the man on the moon. She also knew that Jordan had signed her in as Mrs Innes to simplify matters.

'Good morning. Just leave it out there on the terrace, will you?' Jordan stretched his arms and inhaled the heady sea air.

'Certainly, Sir. Another lovely morning.' And with that, he withdrew. It hadn't surprised him in the least that he had been asked to deliver breakfast at a time when the kitchens were already bustling with lunch. His job was to serve the food and ask no questions. There seemed to be no limit to the length of time those honeymooners spent confined in their cabins. From the looks those two exchanged, like the waiter who had brought their dinner, he assumed that they couldn't be anything else but honeymooners.

'Hey, where are you going?' Jordan called after Bronte who had just sprinted off the terrace and dived into a bush!

'Just doing a spot of gardening. Won't be a sec,' she answered mysteriously from the undergrowth.

'Gardening? But what about breakfast?' He couldn't imagine why she'd want to suddenly start gardening.

'I'll be right there.' And she was, bearing in each hand an oval-shaped green fruit, with a hint of rouge.

'What are those?' He peered suspiciously at them as she approached the table.

'Mangoes! What do they look like?' She remembered picking them once in a friend's back yard in Trinidad and had recognised the tree.

'I had no idea they looked like that. Mine've always been cut into segments before they reached my plate.'

'There's a special knack to peeling them. Watch this.'

She took a sharp fruit knife from the tray and cut a large section from the side of one of the mangoes, tracing the knife down the edge of the centre stone. Once she had done that, she cut a criss-cross pattern in the flesh of the fruit and bent the skin back so the cubes of mango could be scraped away with ease.

'That's pretty artistic. Is there no end to your talents?'

'Shut up and open wide!' She spooned a couple of cubes into his mouth before popping two more into her own.

'It's like eating sunshine,' he beamed, letting the sweet flavour slide down his throat. 'Do they all have such enormous stones?' He was referring to the bulky white blob which she was busy sucking.

'Yes, 'fraid so. It's a real waste. Good though, aren't they?'

'You know, you're probably not supposed to strip the local habitat of its mangoes.' But he couldn't really have cared less, if it made her happy.

'They only taste this good straight from the tree. The ones you get in the shops are never quite the same. Not in London anyhow.'

'I promise I won't tell.'

'You'd better not or I won't pick you any more!'

Having devoured the mangoes, they began to tuck ravenously into the official breakfast tray. Both had developed quite an appetite since they had last eaten.

'Boy, I really needed that.' Jordan wiped his mouth and lounged back in his chair.

'Me too.' She drew her knees up to her chest and munched on a piece of toast. 'What did you have planned for today?'

'Are you making fun of my arrangements?' He faked a hurt expression.

'Would I? Never! It's just that you had yesterday organised down to the very last detail and I was just innocently enquiring about today?' She was pulling his leg.

'Well ...' he thought about it. 'Why don't we put on something more suitable for the water and make use of those masks and flippers back there?'

'What, go snorkelling you mean? What a great idea! Can we do it from our own beach?'

'I don't see why not. And what's more, I bet I can get down there faster than you.'

'Bet you can't!'

Breakfast discarded, they both leapt to their feet and charged back inside to snatch bathers and snorkelling gear, like two excited children. As it was, they both made it at about the same time. If anything, she was a little ahead, but only until he grabbed her arm, pulled her down on top of him and covered her laughter with a multitude of kisses.

Around them the sand, which was made of powdered coral, glistened in the glowing sunshine and as a backdrop to such a romantic setting, the palm trees abounded. There were a few other lovers dotted about on the beach, but all were so engrossed in their individual magic that no spaces overlapped.

Jordan led Bronte to the edge of the sea where they put on their flippers and carried their masks into the water ready to discover the largest coral reef in the world.

They had to swim out quite a distance before they could fully appreciate the gardens of coral which towered amongst shoals of dazzling tropical fish. As they floated side by side, slowly flapping their feet to propel themselves forward, they marvelled at nature's hospitality which was being offered so willingly to them.

The crystal clear water made no attempt to screen the vivid marine life and delicate sea fans which glittered all the colours of the rainbow beneath the sparkling sea. It merely served to magnify the brilliance.

'I thought I'd snorkelled in my time, but you've not done it until you've been here,' declared Jordan as he lifted his mask from his face and trod water for a moment.

'I can't believe how unspoilt this all is. Those chaps down there seem completely at home being watched by us, almost as if they're putting on some performance, just for our benefit,' agreed Bronte.

'You want to take a look over there?' He pointed to a group of ragged rocks which climbed alluringly out of the sea.

'Lead the way.' She followed him.

It was only a short distance across which they continued to absorb the spectacular underwater world which carried on about its business, confident that the two shadows far above would soon tire of the splendour and move on to other pastures.

They slithered out of the water like seals, shaking their heads and allowing the drops to slide down their oiled skin. Walking was impossible with an expanse of black rubber wrapped round their ankles, so they shed the flippers and the masks and left them to collect on the way back.

The rocks were kind to them and the jagged edges, which hundreds of years before would have ripped their feet to shreds, had been weathered flat enabling them to step freely with no fear of cuts or bruises.

'Let's see what's back here. I'm sure I can hear water flowing.'

He took her by the hand and followed the sound which she too, could make out quite distinctly.

It didn't take them long to discover a waterfall which gushed forth between rocks high above them into a natural pool where it leapt on the surface before dispersing out to the sides.

Jordan sat down, propping himself against a stone and bent his knees slightly to allow her room to sit between his legs while his chest cushioned her back. He locked his arms around her waist and rested his chin on her shoulder.

'I wonder if anyone else knows about this pool?' pondered Bronte.

'Oh, I should think just about everyone! In fact, it's probably written up in the guide book, if we'd bothered to read it.'

'Will you be serious?' She nipped his hand harmlessly. 'If it's so well known, then why isn't it teeming with people?'

'I put my reserved sticker on it first thing this morning. Told them all to stay away.' He interlinked her fingers in his own and held them so she couldn't repeat the nip.

She tried a different tack, she was getting nowhere on that one.

'It must feel good, being away from the world for a while. How often do you manage this sort of thing?'

'What, eloping with a gorgeous red-head, you mean?' He nibbled her ear which sent shivers down her spine.

'No, of course I don't! I mean escaping from the press and fans and all the other people who seem to hound your daily life, to such a romantic place.'

She rubbed the forefinger of the one hand he'd freed, absentmindedly down the front of his leg.

'What do you think?'

Did she detect a twinge of bitterness? She suddenly felt guilty for asking because it dawned on her that had his marriage been happier, he would probably have taken Chelsea on holidays like the one they were having. But she doubted whether he had done that for quite some time, if ever. Chelsea just didn't seem the romantic type.

'Not recently?' She hazarded what turned out to be an accurate guess.

'Let's just say, not since I married my wife,' he replied sadly.

She regretted bringing up the subject of Chelsea and was determined to bury it again quickly.

'There's a place I visited in Jamaica once, called Ocho Rios which had the most stunning waterfall I've ever seen. It seemed to go on for miles and you could start at the bottom and walk all the way up it, as long as you didn't mind getting soaked in the process.'

'Oh yes, and who took you there?' He leaned forward so he could see her face.

Relief that he was back to teasing her. Anything but sadness.

'Jordan Innes, do I detect a note of jealousy? There have been other men in my life you know.' She managed an indignant voice.

'I wish you'd come into mine a lot sooner,' and he meant it sincerely. 'It'd have spared me a lot of heartache.'

She by-passed the flattery because she really wasn't sure how to deal with it.

'Actually, I went there with a woman from the TV station in Jamaica and there was nothing remotely romantic about it.'

'Your foreign trips, were they all as hard work as they sound?'

'It's not as exciting as you might think, spending a night here, a day there and several hours in between on an aeroplane.'

'Tell me about it. It's me you're talking to, remember? The eternal hotel dweller.'

'Yes, but I bet you don't have to stay in your room each evening to avoid the frustrated, leering business men who think all single women on their own are just there for the taking.'

'You've got a point, but I can assure you that being trapped in a hotel room is something I know all about. But for different reasons. Sometimes it can get really frightening being closed in on all sides by people trying to touch you or ram autograph books in your face.'

'I can imagine. All those glamorous women, just dying to rip off your clothes. I don't know how you cope!'

'Now, who's jealous? And if you're not going to take me seriously, I'm not hanging around here.'

He jumped up and dived straight off the rock into the centre of the pool.

'Look who's talking . . .' she called after him.

He emerged a few seconds later. She hadn't moved.

'Come in here, it's beautiful! The water's so warm.' He went under again and reappeared arms outstretched, just below where she was sitting.

All thoughts of jest fleeing from her mind, the only thing she could think of was tumbling into those open arms and being held against that exotic body once more.

Together they branched out and crossed the pool to where the waterfall flowed down on them, splashing their faces and swelling around their shoulders. It was far noisier than she had thought possible and after a moment or two, she ducked under the torrents, leaving her pointed feet out of the water behind her and plunged back to the other side. Jordan swooped after her and pounced before she reached the edge, spinning her round and halting any resistance with a passionate kiss.

That time, neither had any desire to escape the other as he peeled back the straps of her costume and followed its course until he was able to lift it from the water and throw it to

391

safety. His Bermudas suffered a similar fate within seconds.

As the water gurgled around them, and high above, their only witnesses were the tropical birdlife and the butterflies who circled the private little haven they had fallen upon, she clung to him as he carried her out onto the rock once more, where he began to make love to her. She was soon lost in the electrifying abandonment of all physical senses, save the heavenly effects of their mutually supreme bliss.

Long after that, they returned to their love nest, satiated and ready to explore new avenues of adventure that were available to guests of the hotel, or simply to roam through the tree-shaded forests, admiring the flowers and the native animals and being serenaded by the colourful birds.

One thing that could be relied upon was that they never strayed too far from their bower where they were free to express the yearning that each now felt for the other, as often as the urge arose. All other matters were of secondary importance during the days and nights they shared in their little hideaway.

CHAPTER THIRTY

All too soon the red velvet curtain came down on the stage setting of the Barrier Reef, followed by the safety curtain which indicated that this act was over. The next scene would take place at the house in Sydney.

For Bronte, the long weekend she had spent on Bedarra with Jordan was probably the most exhilarating experience of her entire life and if she never felt that boundless freedom and intense happiness nor shared such divine intimacy with anyone ever again, she had truly lived – just once.

Days had slipped into nights and nights into days, the change only distinguishable by light and darkness. She hadn't dared to enquire how long they would be able to spend there, and he put off telling her when they would have to leave until, on the day of departure, he was forced to mention it.

So they left the persistent sunshine and the warm winds behind them and flew back into a cooler front which had escorted clouded skies and short sharp showers of rain to New South Wales over the New Year period.

Jordan had been noticeably subdued since they had returned, his sparkle temporarily dulled by the worries which began to weigh on his shoulders once again. The most pressing of these was the movie – until he found a fax which had arrived overnight from New York.

Bronte had been aware for the couple of nights they had spent back in Sydney that Jordan had been unable to sleep soundly as he had on Bedarra. Instead, he had tossed and turned restlessly around the bed. She had neither commented nor offered to help, fearful he might just tell her she was contributing to his insomnia. The truth was that she was, but not in any way she need have been afraid of.

He had surrendered the fight early that morning and she had been vaguely aware of him getting out of bed and leaving the room before she drifted back to sleep which for once, she was finding easy to do.

When she eventually awoke she could tell that the day was already well underway because the light peeped through the curtains and the clock registered after nine. She was surprised to find Jordan sitting on the edge of the bed, his head resting on his hands as he stared at a piece of paper lying in his lap. She had no idea how long he had been there but very quickly she had the feeling that something was up. She rolled over and laid a hand on his back.

'Bad news?' She could tell that it wasn't good.

'I guess you could call it that.' He seemed distant.

'Can I do anything?' She wasn't sure how to handle him.

'Not this time. I don't think that even the Richardson magic will be enough to sort this lot out.'

She wasn't sure if he was being sarcastic, which in fact, couldn't have been further from his mind, but she let it pass.

'Are you going to tell me what's happened?' She pressed him gently.

'What's happened is that Ron ... (Jordan's chief press agent in New York) has sent me this fax of an article from the front page of one of those damned gossip papers. Here, read it for yourself ...' He passed the fax over his shoulder where she only just caught it before it fluttered on to the duvet.

The headline was enough for her. It said it all. She didn't need to read any further.

RUMOUR OF MARRIAGE SPLIT AS JORDAN INNES' ANOREXIC WIFE FLEES AUSTRALIA AND BOOKS INTO EXCLUSIVE NEW YORK CLINIC

'Where on earth has all this come from? Have you told anyone about Chelsea going back?' Bronte had dreaded something like that might break.

'Not until this morning when I called Art. It only happened last week for goodness sakes! But those bloody journalists are everywhere. They find out everything in the end and what they don't find out they make up, just to sell their rotten papers. The more the story destroys someone's life, the more in demand the paper is.'

Bronte couldn't deny that back home she had been the first to pore over the gossip, particularly in the Sunday papers, but she had never stopped to imagine the suffering that could be caused by the printing of such scandals – true or untrue.

'What are you going to do about it? Can you sue?' She knew with a heavy heart that it would put a whole new perspective on matters.

'Sue against what? The irony of the whole thing is that what they have written is pretty much the truth. It's just that I didn't need the rest of the world knowing about it.'

'But how could they have found out?' She thought it unlikely that Chelsea would have gone to the press.

'Oh, I don't know. Someone at the airport. Someone at the clinic. Could be anyone. Could be just the paper putting two and two together and making a story out of it. That's almost not important now. What is, however, is that I'm going to have to go back to the States for a while and face all this . . . and quickly.'

She knew it had to be something like that.

'Jordan, I do understand . . .' She spoke softly, touching his arm.

He turned to face her, worry etched across his bronzed brow.

'Well that's far more than I deserve. The only good thing that's emerged from this whole damn mess is you. And now I've blown that, too.'

'How soon will you go?'

She was going to be adult about it. There was no point in blaming him. In reality, their dream had all been almost hopeless from the start.

'It's got to be today. I know that this is going to be as rough on Chelsea as me, probably worse, and she's not exactly in any state to be able to take it. If she also gets proof of something going on between you and me, then anything could happen. Whoever knows this much might well know more and all we need is for them to follow up the first story with one about us . . .'

'You think someone might have followed us to Bedarra?' Bronte was horrified.

'I really hope not but it's possible. I can't afford to take any chances. I've got to be seen to play the dutiful husband and father. Right now, they'll need me and I can't bear to have Phoeb dragged through all this.'

'You mustn't let that happen!' Bronte shuddered at the thought of such a sweet, innocent child suffering at the hands of evil scandalmongers, out purely for their own gain.

She shoved all thoughts of her own life to the back of her mind where she would cry over them in due course. Just then she knew he needed her support, not the hysterics of some mistress about to be dumped. She had known all along that the timer was set on them and that it would inevitably go off at some stage, but she hadn't prepared herself quite so well for the suddenness of it. Still, whatever was known or was written about, no-one could ever erase the memories of the past week which would always be kept alive in her heart. Those were hers forever.

He was speaking again: 'I called Art right after I read this and he's getting flights booked for himself and for me today. As it turns out, he was going to call me to suggest we spend a few days in New York anyway, because he's got a couple of girls lined up for the movie and he wants me there to give him the green light.'

'Well that's something. At least there's a bit of progress.' She tried to lift his spirits, her own hopelessly sunken.

'Yeah. He also said they've managed to strike a deal with the receivers on the house we were going to use here, so that's all on again. It's a miracle that Greg's not backed out of this fiasco by now, but apparently because most of the filming is taking place here, he's happy to spend some time down on his ranch in Victoria, as long as we have all systems go by the end of the month.'

'What did you tell Art about the article?' She had to know if he was going to disclose their relationship.

'I just read him the headline and said I'd have to get my butt over there to set things straight, pretty damned quick.'

'And what did he say?'

He sighed a heartrendingly miserable sigh: 'Oh, he agreed and told me that if I was planning on shooting anyone at dawn, could he be in on the kill?' He half-smiled the smile she had grown to worship.

'I'm glad he'll be there by your side.'

'Come here,' he cuddled her close. 'You know what's eating me the most about all this?' He didn't give her the chance to reply. 'It's you. I don't know what to do about you.' He kissed the top of her head.

'You don't have to do anything about me, you know. I'm a survivor.' She said it with far more conviction than she felt.

'I know what I have to do but I'm not sure I can stand the realities of it. It's destroying me already. You've shown me a life in the last week that I never thought could exist for me and I don't know how I'll carry on without it now.'

'You'll do fine.' She knew that one of them had to be strong.

'But I'm torn inside about what I must've done to you, just when you didn't need it. You've got to know this wasn't planned.'

'Jordan, I did need it. Probably far more than you realise. It's helped me bury the ghosts of my past and I've begun to live again. That's got to count for something important. Besides, you didn't 'do' anything by yourself, you know. It's been a two-way thing all along.'

'It doesn't help with the guilt or the miserable way I'm feeling.'

'You'll get over it. Only we'll both probably hurt for a while.'

'But I know I've messed you about – offered you a job, screwed up my life and my marriage in front of you, taken you for a ride emotionally and now I've got to run out on you.'

'You said it yourself, it wasn't something you foresaw when we met in France. And we're both just as guilty about the 'emotional ride' bit, remember?' She wasn't sure how much longer she would be able to keep up the convincing act before she broke down into an uncontrollable state of self-pity. She could feel it bubbling up inside.

'How come you're so amazingly understanding? You've got every right to tell me what a bastard I've been.'

'And leave all this on an argument? Besides, I could never hate you, no matter what you'd done. I don't want to look back on any of our time together and see anger.'

'You know I'm going to have to stay over there, probably until we actually start shooting at the end of the month.' He hated having to mention such final-sounding arrangements.

'. . . and you want me to close up the house?' She knew what was coming.

He nodded. 'I can safely say the others won't be coming back here and when I do, I don't think I could stay in this house again. I'll check into a hotel or perhaps Art'll put me up for as long as it takes.'

Bronte had already resigned herself to the fact that her brief 'job', if that's what it could be called, was nearly over. She could no longer work for Jordan after all that had happened. It would tear her apart and probably him too and would be certain to lead to further anguish all round. Even if he'd suggested her staying on to work out of New York as his personal assistant, she could never have agreed to it. He sensed what she was thinking and realised there was no point in even talking about them carrying on as they had before New Year.

'I'll take care of it with Chris. I can't see there'll be a problem.'

'What'll you tell her?' But Jordan knew their secret would always remain safe with Bronte.

'I'll give her some plausible story.' She'd think of something.

'Pay up whatever they ask. I don't want to cause you any problems with your family.'

'I'll see what Chris thinks.' In the light of everything else, money seemed so trivial.

'And what about you? What'll you do now?' He hardly dared to ask. It really stung him to think of a future without her.

'Go back to England and pick up the threads, I guess. I know what you mean about living here, I don't think I can stay either, any more than is necessary to tidy up loose ends, that is. It'd be best to go back.'

'But what'll you do there? You gave up your job and your apartment for all this.' He was reminded once more of how much damage he must have done to her and felt the urge to kiss her again. To protect her for the few hours that was left to them.

'There's Dad and Clare. I should pay them a visit at some stage. And there's always Alex. I could go round grovelling

398

and offer to make tea for a bit! On the other hand, Jane and Donna could be so sick of shouldering my work that they might even welcome me back with open arms.'

'Is that what you really want?' He knew he shouldn't have asked.

'No, but it's the best I can come up with.' She dared not think about what she really wanted. 'I've got some money saved now so I may even launch myself as a property owner!'

'Look, if you're ever short . . .'

But she was proud. She would accept what she had earned, but anything more would cheapen all they had been through and he realised it too.

'I'll be fine. I've got far less to worry about than you.'

It was no good. Neither one could be strong for another second as they were overcome by the unfair hand that had been dealt to both of them by fate and they sought comfort in their love-making for one last time. Floodgates opened on both sides, as together they soared to heights neither could recall reaching previously and then descended back to wallow in their sorrow and their tears.

Bronte, who hadn't even bothered to dress since their shower, followed Jordan about the room, helping him pack what he thought he might need. He had wardrobes of clothes scattered around the various homes he owned and so there wasn't a great deal he would take with him that day. Besides, the winter weather in New York would have different requirements from the summer in Sydney. Bronte had already planned to send a trunk after Chelsea and Phoebe and it would take little extra effort to include whatever he chose to leave behind.

The thought of breakfast, so lovingly shared by them over the past week with fresh mangoes plucked daily from the tree outside their cabin, was too painful even to contemplate. Besides, hunger was not one of the pangs that plagued them that morning.

All too soon, the limo drew up outside the house and from it stepped Art, looking dapper in a beige linen suit. He rang the bell and Jordan crossed the hall to open the door.

'Hello, Art, I'm just coming. Give me a moment, will you?'

Jordan had never liked goodbyes and this one he was dreading more than any he could remember.

'Sure thing. We've got ninety minutes before the 'plane goes. I'll wait in the car as I've got a couple of calls to make.'

That was best all round.

Bronte hadn't moved from the study where she had been attempting to brief Jordan on a few issues he needed to know before he got to New York, and also stacking papers together to send with him. The door bell had gone through her like a bullet and, try as she might, she knew that fresh tears were just around the corner.

He came slowly back into the room. They both knew that was it. They had been left no choice but to do what was being individually asked of them, but it didn't make the parting any easier.

It all became a little hazy after that. One minute she was sitting at the desk and the next, she was lost in his arms, sobbing uncontrollably.

'I don't know how to say this . . .' he began.

'Don't!' She couldn't bear to hear it. 'Just leave it the way it is.'

'You know that . . .' but he felt the need to add something, anything that might help to relieve the agony of it all.

She stopped him again.

'Yes, I know,' she whispered.

He lifted her chin, biting back his own tears for all he was worth and kissed her quivering mouth, not letting her go for several minutes. When he finally drew breath, he quickly returned to kiss away each little trickle that tumbled down her cheeks.

She couldn't even remember if he said anything from then on, before he backed unsteadily out of the room. She vaguely recollected the door banging as he left the house, but she never knew exactly when the car pulled out of the drive. She remained rooted to the spot, staring out of the window at the white horses far below, which bucked and reared on the water, tossed by the wind. All she could think of was that she had never given him her address. But then what address would she have given him? She no longer had one. What did it really matter? All the best things in her life had never lasted and it was very probable that she would never see him again anyway.

The only path through the gloom was to get all the chores that awaited her done and out of the way as quickly as possible. The sooner they were completed, the sooner she could make her own plans and escape from that house, which everywhere she looked, made her feel as if the circus had left town, abandoning her in the process.

She wasn't looking forward to 'phoning Chris, with whom she had had no contact since Christmas Day. She realised that her call would come completely out of the blue and it wasn't going to be easy pretending that everything in the garden was roses, when in fact her garden had been stripped bare.

There was no sense in putting it off any longer and so that afternoon, she armed herself with a notepad, a pen and a good deal of courage and dialled up Chris at the office.

'Chris? Hi, this is Bronte. Happy New Year.' She swallowed hard.

'Bronte! Happy New Year too, I was going to 'phone you today. How's it all going? I hear you've been fighting Australian bush fires! You must tell me all about it.'

'I will, at some point.' She had almost forgotten that it was only ten days or so since that awful day. Both her head and her legs had healed even quicker than she could have wished for and so much had happened since then.

'We missed you on Friday night. What did you do in the end?'

Best to be non-specific. 'It's a long story, Chris, but we've had a few dramas round here.' That was the understatement! 'What with the fire and everything, Chelsea flew back to New York and took Phoebe with her.'

'When's she coming back?'

'That's just it, I'm not sure she is. She's been under the weather for a bit and I think she's decided to try and sort herself out over there. Getting them both off, and one thing after another, took up most of last week.'

'I bet it did. You should've called me and I'd have come over.'

That wouldn't exactly have helped matters, particularly as Bronte had been hundreds of miles from Sydney. But it had been said with the best of intentions.

'We managed. Anyway, that's not quite where the story ends. They've had problems with the movie and what with that and his family returning to New York, Jordan has gone back there today himself, probably until the end of the month.'

'Has the movie fallen through then?' She sounded disappointed.

'No. At least, hopefully not. They're having to re-cast the female lead and some of the financing has suffered a hiccup, but I think it'll definitely happen. Just a bit delayed, that's all.'

'You should've volunteered your services, for the female lead, I mean. You'd make a great team with that Jordan Innes.'

Her remark, thrown out innocently enough, cut deep with Bronte and it took her a second or two to reply.

'Bronte, are you still there?' Chris thought perhaps the silence on the other end of the 'phone meant they'd been cut off.

'Yes, sorry Chris. Just looking at a fax that's come in,' she lied. 'I don't think acting would be my strong point,' she braved. 'Anyway, what I'm leading up to saying is, that we're going to have to give the house up.'

'You are? Why, where are you going to stay?' Chris sounded surprised.

'Well, as Chelsea and Phoebe probably won't come back now and Jordan'll be away until the end of the month, there's no point in keeping such a big house on.'

'But what about you?'

She knew that one had to come sooner or later. Another deep breath: 'I'm going back to England in a couple of days.'

'What? He's not keeping you on either? The rotter!' Chris jumped to natural conclusions for which Bronte couldn't blame her.

'It's not that bad, really. When he comes back, which'll be for the shooting of the actual movie, he'll probably stay with the producer. He says he'd rather be on the spot with the producer for his first directing role anyway.'

'Sounds like a pretty raw deal to me. Drags you all the way over here and says goodbye after a couple of months! Aren't you livid?'

It was getting harder and harder.

'No, not really. Besides, I've decided that I prefer the TV business to the movie one and I'm thinking of trying to get my old job back.' She hoped that sounded credible.

'Well, I've gone right off that boss of yours. They're all the same, those film stars. They think the world revolves around them and their whims and fancies.'

'It's honestly not his fault that Chelsea's had to go, nor that the movie's been set back. If all had gone according to plan, they should've been shooting by now.' She couldn't bear to hear anything bad said about him. Her own wounds were still far too fresh for that.

'Do you really want to go back? You could easily stay here with us and look for another job if you'd rather.'

That was the second time she'd been asked what she 'really wanted to do' that day, and neither time had she been able to admit that what she would most like to do was run after that 'plane bound for New York and hear Jordan say that he loved her and that they would never be apart, not for a single second, despite everything that was happening around them.

Instead she replied: 'That's a very sweet thought, Chris, but I've had a great time here and I've seen what it's like to live on the other side of the world. But I'm missing London a bit now and I'm ready to face everything back there.'

'Well, you know best, but do remember the offer'll always be there if you change your mind. Don't worry about the house because Uncle Mack and Aunty Flo'll be back from Florida in a couple of months and it won't matter a bit to them when you leave.'

'Chris, could you ask the agency to let Beccy know that we won't be needing her any more? We gave her a few days off from last Friday because there haven't exactly been many meals in since then and she's due back tomorrow. Make sure they give her a bonus or something, she's been wonderful to have around.'

'I'll do it after I put the 'phone down. Is there anything else I can help with? Do you want me to come over? You sound rather low about all this.'

'I'm really all right. Just a bit tired, that's all. There's been quite a lot to do lately. All I've got left now is some packing and then I should be straight. I don't think there's any lasting damage around here. No breakages that I'm aware of, anyhow.'

She was ticking off the points one by one on her notepad, trying to keep her mind on the conversation and away from wondering just how Jordan was feeling and what he was thinking, and also whether he was as miserable as she.

'When did you say you were leaving?' asked Chris.

'I'm about to call the airline, but hopefully Saturday.'

It didn't sound nearly soon enough. Two whole nights ahead of her, alone in that house.

'That's a real shame because we've got to go out of town for a wedding tomorrow or I would have driven you to the airport on Saturday.'

'Don't worry, I'll get a taxi.' She would feel far more anonymous that way. 'Will the hire car firm collect the station wagon? I'm afraid it's not in quite as good condition as it was when we first had it. It didn't exactly get burnt in the fire like the other car, only a bit singed.'

'I'll arrange that too. Shall I get them to call round on Saturday for it?'

'Anytime really. I'm not planning on going far between now and then.' There wasn't really anywhere she could face going which wouldn't remind her of happy times spent with Jordan around.

'Well look, if there's really nothing else I can do and if you're sure I can't persuade you to stay for a while, then I guess this is goodbye for the time being.'

'Sadly, yes. I'm sorry, Chris, you've been so good to me, organising everything and I've been so busy that I've hardly seen you.'

'It's been fun just knowing you were around here for a while. Now you'll just have to come back so we can spend some more time together. Perhaps in the snow season, we can all go up to the mountains for a while?'

'I'd like that.' But Bronte knew she wouldn't be returning to Australia for a long time. 'Thanks for being such a brick. I couldn't have managed without you.'

'You never know, Mark might even spring some wonderful surprise trip on me and whisk me over to England for a romantic holiday.'

That, too, stabbed at a very recently injured nerve for Bronte, who was instantly reminded of Jordan's wonderful surprises less than a week before.

'He might just do that,' was all she could get out.

'And pigs might fly! Still, we can go on dreaming, can't we?'

But Bronte thought the time had come for her to stop dreaming.

'Take care of yourself, Bronte, and be sure to write once you get back home and let us know where you are and what you're doing. We mustn't lose touch.'

'I'll do that. I'll also give Angela a call to say goodbye to her and Murray. Thanks again for everything – lots of love to you both.'

That had been one of the hardest calls she'd ever had to make. She wouldn't be ready to talk about Jordan to anyone else for quite a while.

Looking back over all the gloomy days she had spent in her life, Bronte could not remember two passing quite so slowly as her last in Australia did. The clock seemed to be ticking backwards rather than forwards and each time she checked to make sure another hour had gone it was always less than half of that.

One bonus came when she rang the airline and discovered that there were a number of Economy seats available on the flight to Heathrow that Saturday. She couldn't even consider the idea of staying on for a third lonely night. Jordan had told her to use his card and fly back First Class if she liked, but the idea of that carried too many painful memories with it and she was far happier to travel with no luxurious reminders.

It took her less time than she had anticipated to put the remainder of Jordan's, Chelsea's and Phoebe's clothes and belongings into a trunk and to add the rest of Jordan's files and papers. Included was the precious koala which soaked up her tears as she cuddled it for nearly an hour, before lying it carefully on the top. She hoped the damp fur would have dried by the time the trunk was unpacked at the other end.

She located an international carrier firm and they promised to collect the trunk by Friday afternoon. That much, she wasn't going to ask Chris to do for her. She needed to do the packing and the seeing off herself because in some way, it symbolised what she knew she had to come to terms with sooner or later. The fact that a family which had become so much a part of her life so quickly, had just as rapidly ceased to be anything to do with it.

After the trunk left, she simply wandered through the various rooms recapturing memories which she knew would continue to haunt her mind. She could picture his joyful, laughing, beautiful face in every corner of every empty room as her footsteps echoed on the bare wooden floor. One place she dared not venture any more was his bedroom which was a shrine to their love. She settled finally in the conservatory where she figured that Sydney's company was one better than no company at all.

'Very quiet! No people! Very quiet! No people!' It was the first bit of light relief she had felt since Jordan left.

'Yes, dear boy, you're right. Will you miss us all then?'

'Sydney's friends! Sydney's friends!'

'Sydney's friends have nearly all gone now. Just you and me tonight and I go tomorrow.'

'Welcome from Sydney! Welcome from Sydney!' he chirped away, delighted that someone was paying him attention.

'No, you silly old fool. We're going away, not coming to Sydney.'

'Mack's a silly old fool! Mack's a silly old fool!' sang Sydney, wagging his head merrily from side to side.

'Don't, for goodness sake, say that when your master gets back! He'll think we taught you it.' Bronte listened, horrified.

But he carried on, as cheekily as ever: 'Mack's a silly old fool! Mack's a silly old fool!'

*   *   *

Her own case seemed to be packed in a flash once Saturday morning came around. She couldn't wait to shut all the windows and check the rooms (except for the master bedroom) one last time, before looking at her watch yet again, to see if the taxi was due.

Fortunately, it was a mid-morning flight which reduced the time she had to hang around the house. But seeing as she'd hardly managed to sleep a wink since Thursday morning, it still felt like an eternity before she heard that horn in the drive.

She didn't even glance back at the house, once she had locked the front door and posted the keys through the letterbox for Chris to find. However plush and however envied by the neighbours the house might have been, the only thing she wanted to do now was to get away from it as soon as possible. It had to be eyes forward all the way from then on.

The taxi driver asked merely where she was flying to as they rode up Raglan Street and then she was glad when he left her to her own thoughts and refrained from pestering her with unwanted questions.

Bronte hadn't felt inclined to make any effort at all with her appearance for the journey to London. She had thrown on the first things that came to hand. Under her arm, she clutched the black leather jacket which she knew would become a second skin to her, once she was back home. That, her precious little teddy which she had named simply 'J', and the velvet dress with the green taffeta jacket were now her most treasured possessions. Each signified momentoes of one of the most special people she was ever likely to meet and she would cherish them until the day she died.

Driving to the airport, she knew she was following Jordan's tracks of two days earlier. That felt good and she continued in them until she was seated on the 'plane, which after a short delay, took off. But that's where his tracks ended. She was making new ones of her own – in the opposite direction.

As Chris de Burgh, to whom she always resorted in a crisis, sang evocatively in her ears, she did allow herself one last look down on a city where so much had happened to her with so many memories stamped on her mind forever. It was where her life had become whole again – just for a while.

She permitted a few reminiscent flash-backs as she picked out the Opera House, the harbour, the high-rise apartments and the zoo before she closed the door tight shut.

'Ladies and Gentlemen, this is your Captain speaking. I would like to apologise for the delay in commencing our cabin service this morning, but air traffic control have alerted us to a cyclone ahead and for your comfort and safety, we will be resuming our normal service once we are through the bad weather. So, if you will all return to your seats and fasten your seatbelts, please sit back and enjoy the flight and I will talk with you all again a little later.'

THE EPILOGUE

'Pass the Yorkshire puddings will you, Bronte?' Her father touched her arm and Bronte stretched forward to lever a couple from the blue china dish.

'Scuse fingers, Dad.'

'All tastes the same to me. Nothing like a good old traditional English roast for setting a man up for Sunday afternoon, even if it is mid-summer.'

'But darling, all you ever do after Sunday lunch is sleep in the afternoon.' Clare corrected him.

'Exactly. Sets me up for a good sleep.'

Bronte's father had mellowed considerably in the six months she had spent under his roof. He had been asked to accept rather more than his stuffy, middle-class upbringing had conditioned him to expect from his only daughter since she returned from Australia, but he had adjusted impressively after a few initial outbursts and was even secretly looking forward to being a grandfather!

He had recognised, although only in private to himself, that he might fare rather better as a grandfather than he had as a father – at least one could hand the thing back if it cried too much. As a father you were more or less stuck, unless of course you had a wife who turned out to be a natural earth mother and removed the child at all awkward moments. Clare, on the other hand, was not looking forward to the prospects of being a step-grandmother. She found the term most ageing and being that bit younger than her husband, knew that she would be the first of her girlfriends to be labelled as such. Still, Bronte was almost seven months pregnant and there was nothing any of them could do to put off the imminent arrival.

'Are you all right there, Bronte?' Her father looked concerned as Bronte squirmed in her seat and frowned, rubbing her ever-increasing bump at the same time.

'Yes, I am. Just got a belter in the ribs.'

'He's going to be a big lad and no mistake!' He took another bite of succulent, underdone roast beef.

'Might be a girl, Dad!' But she secretly hoped it would be a boy who would have the same smile and the melting eyes of his father.

'Nonsense! Bound to be a boy, the size of that lump. Besides, I reckon that's what those butch surfers would produce out there.'

'Darling, Bronte only looks that size because the rest of her is so thin. Any sign of a baby would be bound to look big on her.' Clare was still very much in charge of their marriage.

'Are you still planning not to tell the father after it's born, then?' he continued.

'Dad, we've been through all that a hundred times. It was just something that happened in Australia, with my full consent, and he doesn't even know that I'm pregnant.'

'I still think it was pretty rotten of that actor fellow, whatshisname? – Innes or something – to throw you out when he found out you were . . . in that state, shall we say.' He took a gulp of red wine, indignantly puffing out his feathers and for once, protective of his daughter – although rather too late in the day.

'Look, this is the last time I will discuss the matter.' The subject was still painful for Bronte. 'It wasn't like that, OK? Neither he, nor the father of my baby knew that I was pregnant before I left Australia. In fact, nobody did. I just resigned, saying I had to return here for family reasons and left it at that.'

'He can't have been too impressed with you to let you go just like that, without any questions.' Her father wasn't quite able to fit it all together in his black and white mind.

'Dad, can we drop it now? It really is all in the past.'

'Darling, I agree with Bronte. I think we should.' Clare found it so embarrassing to discuss the subject of illegitimacy.

Within two weeks of arriving back in London in the January of that year, Bronte had discovered she was pregnant. On reflection, it was hardly surprising in the circumstances because, possibly irresponsibly, contraception had not even entered her head during the time that she and Jordan had been lovers.

When she had first returned she had spent a little time catching up with friends and trying desperately to keep herself occupied as best she could. She had done the home test the very day she had decided to go into the office to see Alex and the gang, with the idea of sounding-out the possibility of working there again. The result on the end of the white dipstick was undeniably pink, although she could have predicted that it would be, even before she looked. She had known for a few days by the tenderness of her breasts and the enlarging of her nipples that she was pregnant.

The visit to the office, therefore, turned into more of a social call than anything else. They were all delighted to see her and to hear first hand what it had been like working on such an important movie project. As a plausible reason for leaving Australia for good, she had been forced to tell them a similar story to the one she told Chris, although she omitted all but the most vital details.

Alex had been quick to beg her to rejoin them, claiming with a twinkle in his eye that Jane and Donna were doing a lousy job and would she please come back and save him from them! But when she told him she needed to spend some time with her long-neglected father and step-mother, he backed down just as fast, only because knowing her as well as he did, he suspected that that was not the real reason for her need to return to Yorkshire. There was more to it. However, he knew she would tell him when she was ready.

Shortly after that, she had travelled up to Yorkshire unannounced. She wanted to surprise her father and, boy, did she have something to surprise him about! She hadn't expected to be welcomed with open arms, but incredibly, that was just about what happened. Even Clare seemed genuinely pleased to see her back.

Their reception had given her the courage, a few days later, to break the news that she would be expecting a baby in September. She had firmly intended to make her stay in

Yorkshire only very temporary and then to return to London, using the money she had saved to start her off in rented accommodation. Temping work would have had to follow so she could support herself until the baby was born. Beyond that, she had no ideas.

However, after several heated exchanges, mostly it had to be said between Clare and her father, much to her amazement they united in their insistence that she remain with them, at least until after September. They would not hear of her flitting back to London in her condition where they knew she had no real security.

So at home, if you could call it that, she had been ever since. Really, it hadn't been too bad at all. Very early on she had had to make up the story about the surfer who remained nameless and with whom she was supposed to have had a brief affair, resulting in her pregnancy. The real truth remained firmly locked away in her heart. No-one would ever know about her and Jordan. They wouldn't even begin to understand all that had happened in such a short space of time and she was determined that no words of scorn or disapproval would be allowed to mar her precious memories of him. Far better that they blame some non-existent surfer for the damage, if that's how they chose to look at it.

She was equally determined never to contact Jordan himself again, especially not with news of a forthcoming child. Not surprisingly, there had been no word from him in the last six months, considering that even if he had wanted to find her, which she had successfully convinced herself he would not, he had no idea where she was, other than somewhere in England. She was not going to be responsible for burdening him with further scandal or shame.

Besides, her own wounds would take a long time to heal and although she knew all the telephone numbers and addresses of his homes by heart, speaking to him or even just knowing for sure that he was thinking of her, would simply open up fresh sores. It did not, however, stop her wondering to herself just what did happen after he returned to New York? Whether he was reconciled with Chelsea after all? How the movie had gone, once they started shooting? She scoured the press daily for information about it and even tuned into the film review programme on TV each week, but there had been no mention.

Bronte was thrilled about the baby, although naturally a little apprehensive about being a single parent and bringing up a child by herself. It was a responsibility she knew she could face but it would not be easy. That, however did not detract from her joy at knowing she had after all, captured a little part of Jordan. The kind that was more real than any material gifts or souvenirs. It would be something that would be theirs forever.

Predictably, there were those in the local village who quietly eyed her swelling middle with suspicion. Gradually word spread, as gossip did, that she had got herself into a mess while jaunting around the world with film stars and that she had been forced to run back home crying to Daddy ... and wasn't it good of Clare to take her under her wing? Everyone seemed to have heard about the 'no-goods' of the film world, exploiting young girls and then dropping them in times of trouble. But there was also a note of sympathy for Bronte, who had been so tragically widowed only last year. Such a shame, and a nice lad as they remembered him. Mind you, it hadn't been proper and decent for her to jet off round the world so soon after she'd buried him. Asking for trouble, they called it.

Bronte was aware of what was being said about her, just from the looks and stares and the odd snippets of conversation she managed to overhear when she walked her father's black Labrador through the village each morning. But it didn't spoil her happiness about the baby. She had never been all that bothered about what other people said or thought, although she was mildly concerned about the shadow she might have been casting over her father's house, as a result of her return. But when she brought the subject up one day, her fears were smartly dismissed.

'Rubbish!' her father had roared. 'Idle gossipers with nothing better to do than hang over their white wooden fences and create a rumpus. You leave them to me, my girl. I'll soon tell them what for, if I hear any of it!'

'I don't want to cause you and Clare any bad feeling round here, Dad.'

Clare had remained silent, secretly worried by it but her father, for once, had laid down the law in the house.

'Bad feeling? What bad feeling? If we can accept it then what business is it of theirs to comment?'

She had no idea what had contributed to her father's remarkably changed attitude towards her, but she wasn't about to question it. It was the first time in her life that she felt she could actually call the house under the roof of which her father lived, her home.

Bronte had still retained the idea of temping work, if only to pay her way and try to save a little for after the baby was born. Besides, she had a very active mind and it needed to be stretched to stop her thinking about Jordan.

She managed to get on to the books of the local secretarial agency and although the pay was laughable, it was better than nothing and it did mean that on the days when the side-effects of pregnancy caught up with her, she was able to ring in sick.

Alex had been on the 'phone several times, just to see what she was up to and to weigh up the chances of her returning to the television business. Early on, she spilled the beans about the baby, confirming his suspicions. He was naturally delighted for her and told her so several times, enthusing down the 'phone line. During the last of those conversations she had promised him that she would pay a visit to London the following week and take him up, at least on his offer of lunch. Besides, she had done nothing at all about looking for the baby equipment that would soon be required and what better place to start with than the vast range offered at the London department stores?

In the end, she had stayed just one night in town at Jane's flat, much enjoying catching up with the ever-intriguing goings-on between various television executives whom she remembered only too well. It appeared that nothing much had changed since she had left. Mike, the sports distributor, had been enquiring about her welfare, daily, on the stand at the annual MIP TV festival in Cannes that April, and simply wouldn't believe that Bronte could actually be enjoying her confinement in rural Yorkshire! He was convinced she was being held prisoner there and threatened to go right up and rescue her. No-one told him about the baby. In fact Alex, Jane and Donna had kept that very quiet out of respect for Bronte. Bronte, herself, wouldn't have minded anyone knowing, but she could appreciate that the circumstances of how she had arrived in that condition might have proved difficult for others to explain. After all, it had been hard enough for her.

Lunch had been a hoot! Just like old times. Alex had whisked her off in his car to some smart French restaurant and proceeded to wine – the very best the house could offer – and dine her, in true Alex style. Conversation flowed throughout the meal and the only slightly sticky point came when he pressed her gently on the subject of the father of her child. He almost regretted bringing it up because he immediately sensed her change of tone. A strained look crossed her face and just for a second, her eyes betrayed the heartache she still very much felt before she launched into the surfer story. Alex listened intently to as much as she wanted to tell him, all along knowing that there was far more to it than she was letting on. He was shrewd enough not to labour the issue but there was little doubt in his mind that something wonderful, but also something agonising, had happened to Bronte in Australia and that the memory of it was obviously still causing her considerable pain. That upset him but the only thing he could do was to offer an ear and his support, should she ever need to talk.

'OK, if that subject is banned, let's find another we can talk about,' continued Bronte's father, shoving his final mouthful of fresh garden carrot and roast potato in, before drawing his knife and fork together on his plate.

'Darling, I think it's about time we replaced that carpet in the drawing room.' Clare was off on more important matters. 'It is so frightfully marked where the fire has spat over the years. You must try and order proper wood which will burn without shooting sparks out all over the place.'

'Anything you say, dear. You choose the carpet and give me the bill.' He had always let Clare have exactly what

Clare wanted. He had learnt, very early on, that it made for a more peaceful life.

'But have you no idea of what you would like to replace it with in there?'

He couldn't win. Sometimes she was never satisfied.

'Why don't you arrange for someone to come here with samples which we can match up with the room? Or I'll do it, if you like?' Try that, it might please her.

There was a knock at the front door.

'I'll go,' volunteered Bronte, heaving herself up from the chair. Anything to get out of listening to Clare's wants.

'Not expecting anyone to call at this time on a Sunday are we, dear?'

They didn't normally use the front door of the house. Most people who visited regularly knew to call at the back door, which led through a porch to the kitchen. Consequently, it took her a moment to remove the chain, draw back the bolts and wrestle with the lock before she managed to open it.

'Did I use the wrong door or do you always lock people out so firmly?'

She wasn't sure what hit her first – the enormous smile, the adorable eyes, the slick dark hair, the familiar leather jacket over the faded jeans, the black sunglasses or the voice, which instantly sent her weak at the knees.

'Jordan!' She grabbed the door to steady herself.

'Hey, I never had that effect on you before!' If only he knew.

'But what ...? But how ...?' She was speechless, clinging on to the handle for support.

'It's a long story and from the look of you, you've got one to tell me too. Why don't we take this guy for a walk?' Sam, the Labrador had come bounding out of the kitchen to see what all the fuss was about.

He could have asked her to fly to the moon at that moment and she'd have agreed. She was so stunned to see him standing there on the doorstep.

She nodded: 'Wait there. I'll just tell them where I'm going.'

She knew enough to realise that it would have been far from tactful for Jordan to show his face in the dining room, at least not until they had had a chance to talk.

She put her head round the door and by way of explanation, said: 'An old friend has just turned up out of the blue and we're going to take Sam out for a bit,' praying they wouldn't think that odd.

'Whatever for? Bring your friend in first,' said her father.

That would be awkward.

'Dad, Sam's heard the word 'walk' now and you know what that means.' She forced herself to laugh. 'Leave the washing up for me when I get back.' That might help.

'Suit yourself.' He returned to listening to the various merits of green carpet over blue carpet to go with cream walls.

She had no need of a coat because the summer sun was smiling down on them and the early morning breeze, which had helped to dry the dew on the mossy green grass, had dropped as the temperature rose.

She led the way down the path to the gate, Sam leaping along beside her, delighted that he was getting a bonus walk. They passed a black, gleaming sports car on the road which she presumed was Jordan's because certainly no-one in the village drove a car like that. It would definitely set even more tongues wagging. But let them, she couldn't have cared less.

The house was set on the edge of picturesque Yorkshire moorland near Ilkley and by going straight ahead rather than right towards the village, they soon left all signs of habitation behind them and their only company became the knobbly-kneed hill sheep whom Sam was under strict instructions to ignore.

Bronte felt a little uncomfortable with Jordan to begin with. Although he was only doing what he'd known every day since he last saw her, that he'd have to do one day, now that she was within his grasp, he wasn't yet able to take her in his arms, the way he'd so longed to do for months.

'How did you find me?' She broke the silence.

'Through kind of devious means. I managed to track down that company you used to work for and after I flew in on Friday, I went to see your old boss.'

'Alex?' When he mentioned it, it made sense that Alex was just about the only person Jordan would have known to go to, who could have told him where she was.

'That's it. He's a great guy, by the way. I liked him.' He grinned that same special grin he had always reserved for the people he cared about most. In fact, very little about Jordan had changed since she had seen him last. He was very tanned and just looking at his body made her want to tear off all his clothes.

'Anyhow, he seemed to know who I was and what I would want from him and sure enough, he told me just how to find you. I think those secretaries got quite a shock when I walked through the door, though!'

'I bet they did! They probably haven't stopped talking about you since.' She could imagine the reaction of the girls in the office, when they had seen Jordan. She could also imagine just how much that would have set their minds wondering.

Alex, for his part had been only too pleased to give Jordan all the information he asked for, except for the baby of course. He wasn't going to mention that. But ever since his lunch with Bronte, it had worried him that things were not quite as they should have been, and the moment that Jordan was shown into his office everything seemed to fall into place. He knew exactly what she had held back from him over lunch, and if by helping to reunite the pair of them, he could be certain that next time he saw her that sad look was no more, wild horses wouldn't keep her address from Jordan. He would see to it.

'So here I am! And Bronte, I've really missed you . . .' He quickened his pace so he could step in front of her and say what he had waited so long to say.

His words filtered deep, but she found it easier than she had expected to meet his eyes.

'I've missed you, too. If only you knew how much,' she whispered.

He was unable to let her alone for another second. His arms drew her to him and he pressed her head against his chest, burying his lips into her hair.

'The baby . . .?' he asked, after a moment.

'It's ours, Jordan. Yours and mine.'

As soon as he'd seen her in the doorway of her father's house he'd known it couldn't be anyone else's. Bronte was not that type of girl, which was partly why he loved her so dearly. He held her at arm's length so he could see her face.

'Why didn't you tell me? Did you think I would turn you away? Do you really think I could ever have done that, to you of all people – the only person apart from Phoeb, who really means anything to me at all?'

Damn those tears. Why did they always erupt at the worst possible times? But there was nothing she could do to stop them.

'Your family . . . the scandal . . . Jordan, I just couldn't do that to you,' she sniffed.

'There's a lot you don't know about my family and as for the scandal, that can go to hell! Don't ever imagine again, that I care more about causing a scandal than I do about you. Come and sit down, there's a few things you should hear.' He beckoned her into his lap, as he settled himself on a flat-topped stone.

'When I got back to New York I found that Chelsea had wasted no time in consulting her lawyer and had already filed for divorce . . . and what's more, full custody of Phoebe! Anyhow, I went to see her at the clinic to have it out with her.'

Bronte could hardly believe her ears!

'She seemed unprepared for the confrontation. It appears that she'd not seen the article I had – Ron had been quick to get that to me the day the paper came out – and she told me she never thought I'd come after her so soon.'

Bronte sat wide-eyed, her cheeks drying rapidly, helped by the occasional stroke from Jordan.

'Actually, all that's not important right now. What is, however, is that we're currently waiting on the divorce.'

'And Phoebe? What about the custody?'

'I think I quickly made Chelsea see that I wasn't about to sit back and give up my daughter and so we thrashed out an agreement whereby we share her, with help from her grandmother.'

'Chelsea's mother, you mean?'

'Yeah. She's a great person and she adores Phoeb. I don't think she approves of her daughter's behaviour much either. Anyhow, the fact is that Phoeb will have her grandmother, her mother, and I'm of course going to be around her as much as I can.'

'So what happened with the movie?'

'That's the reason I've been so long in coming to find you. That, and the mess with Chelsea. We started shooting in February and got the Australia bit over with by April. Since then, we've been working our asses off in Los Angeles with the studio scenes and the final rushes are only just being assembled now. Believe me, I'd have come over much sooner if I'd have been able to.'

'I never thought I'd see you again.' For the first time in months, she was laughing through her tears.

'I couldn't have lived through the past few months of hell, if I'd thought that about you. Finding you, holding you, loving you again was all that kept me going.'

That time it was she who covered his mouth with her own.

'How could you have imagined that I would forget the most wonderful week of my life and ever really let you go after that?' he demanded between her kisses.

'I didn't dare allow myself to hope that you'd come. I knew I could never go to you. It wouldn't have been fair.'

'Even when you knew about the baby?'

'The baby was just as much my responsibility as yours, and what if you'd made a go of it with Chelsea again? What would've happened then if I'd landed myself on you?'

'Don't let that thought even enter your pretty little head. Right now I'm here, which is all that matters. That, and the something I came all this way to ask you . . .'

Her heart stopped . . .

'Bronte, I want to marry you! If you'll have me, that is?'

The baby leapt inside her. It was the first time Jordan had felt his child move in her stomach.

'Do I take it that someone in there approves of the idea?' His smile ignited that old familiar flame for Bronte.

'I guess so!' She threw her arms around his neck and hugged him very tightly. Her heart was about ready to burst.

'I love you, Bronte!'

Much later that afternoon, as the sun was well on its way to setting in the west, and Sam, tired of all the human canoodling, had opted for a spot of rabbit chasing and was ready for his supper, they threaded their way back to the house to begin the task of explaining a little of the truth to Clare and her father. They would try to impress upon them, why two people who were so hopelessly in love, would never again allow themselves to be parted.